Court of Nightmares
by K.A. Knight
Katie Knight
D.
The Bookish Box Exclusive Luxe Edition

COURT OF NIGHTMARES

COURT AND KINGS

COURT OF NIGHTMARES

COURT AND KINGS

K.A. KNIGHT

COURT OF NIGHTMARES

The Bookish Box Exclusive Luxe Edition

This is a work of fi ction. Names, characters, places, and incidents are either the product of the author's imagination or are used fictitiously. Any resemblance to actual events, locales, or persons, living or dead, is coincidental.

ISBN 978-1-960854-52-0 (The Bookish Box Edition)

Printed in China

Concept and Art Direction: Stephanie Brown
Reverse Dust Jacket and Hard Case: Moonpress Design
Endpapers, Front Dust Jacket, and Edges: Olha Hyshchak
Interior Design: Evenstar Books
Proofreader: Madison Roe

Please note, this is a dark romance and as such there may be scenes that you find triggering. For in depth TW please contact K.A Knight.

STEP INTO THE DARK

AND

FIND THE NIGHTMARES WITHIN...

PROLOGUE

ALTHEA

THERE'S ONE THING YOU need to know about heartbreak—it will make a monster out of you if you let it.

I did.

My fangs rip into the flesh of the innocent man below me as he screams for mercy.

His blood fills me, fuelling my body and making me crueller as his cries only grow.

You see, I'm not the hero of this story, I'm the villain, but maybe I should start at the beginning. That's where all good stories start after all. With a hopeful, young girl whose future is laid out before her with grand plans and hopes . . .

Before it is all taken away.

ONE
ALTHEA

"THEY NEVER GET VAMPYRS right," Simon, my closest friend, complains as he tosses popcorn into his mouth, groaning when one catches on his new fangs and sticks there like a hilarious Vlad the Impaler.

I turn away in jealousy, running my tongue along my teeth, wishing I already had mine.

Soon, I remind myself.

"Yeah, but Wesley Snipes sure is hot," I reply.

"That he is." Simon sighs, and we cheers to that.

You see, vampyrs are born, but we do not become true nightwalkers until the change. For sixteen years, we are neither human nor vampyr. We are stronger and faster than humans, but we have no fangs or thirst.

At sixteen, we either change or die.

Well, either way we die, but if we are strong enough, then we come back as a full-fledged vampyr or, as we call ourselves, sangui, which means blood in Latin. It's not very original, I know, but what can I say? Our race is a dramatic bunch.

My sixteenth birthday is only two days away.

Two days until I either die or am reborn and plunged into the night world, just like Simon.

They call us halfies until then, and we are not permitted to attend gatherings held by full-fledged sangui. We do not see that side of our society—well, he does now. He went to his first one last night, and I can already see the changes wrought by drinking blood.

He's now almost six feet tall, where before he was a measly five feet, and where he was once wiry, muscles are now growing. His blond hair is darkening and growing, becoming thicker and luscious, and his lips are plumped up.

Simon is becoming the perfect hunting machine, made to seduce and kill.

If he didn't like men, I'd jump him.

Foolish, I know, but I'd do anything for a taste of that life.

"Althea, you'll be fine," he murmurs, taking my hand like he knows my thoughts. "Two days of unimaginably agony, sure, but then life will be amazing, you'll see, and we'll spend our nights hunting and partying with the others."

"Until we turn eighteen, that is." I huff, and he rolls his eyes.

"You don't want a mate?" It's not the first time he's asked, and until now, I haven't really explained why. Maybe it's my impending death, but I finally do.

"No, I do. It's just . . . eighteen is so young to have to choose who to spend the rest of your life with," I mutter, not telling him my deepest fear, which is that I might not make it to eighteen, so why worry about who fate may or may not pair me with?

"Hardly anyone finds their mate that early, sausage." Simon grins, making me groan. "Some go hundreds of years and still never find their mate, so think of yourself as lucky if you find them that soon."

"I know, I know," I mutter, listening to the lecture I've heard a million times, but whereas Simon desperately wants to find his mate, I have reservations.

That's all.

Worries.

Fate is supposed to choose the perfect person for you, and when you meet them, the whole world will fade away. You'll only feed on each other and become stronger and more powerful . . . but I know firsthand how fate can be a bitch.

After all, on my mother's death bed, she predicted that I would die young.

Yay me.

"She was delirious, Thea," Simon says, no doubt reading my expression. He tugs me against him, and I curl into his side. I used to fit perfectly, and now he towers over me, squishing me.

I hate how he can always read my mind.

"I know, but what if she was right? What if I die at the changing ceremony?"

"Then I'll drag you back," he teases, resting his head on mine—no doubt his neck hurts from having to bend so much, but I don't complain because his warmth comforts me. "I'll be there the entire time, you and me until the end. Then we'll have an amazing two years of honing our powers and becoming badasses, and at eighteen, we will both find amazing guys to spend the rest of our long lives together with."

"And they will look like Wesley Snipes." I grin, making him throw his head back and laugh.

"*Nox*, we can hope." He winks, and as I cuddle with my best friend, I let my mind fill with hope.

Hope that I will survive the change and hope that one day I will find the person destined for me, and that I will finally be loved again.

Two

Althea

Two years and two months later...

Tugging nervously at my dress, I bite my lip, my fangs almost piercing my painted red mouth before I release it. I don't want to draw blood because the scent would draw attention to me, and I don't want that.

Not yet.

I can hear murmuring beyond the closed double doors from those waiting for us to be presented. Turning away, I begin to pace, my heels clacking against the marble floor outside of the Vermilion Court's ballroom. It's my first presentation. I have four more to go in the other courts, but this one is the most intimidating since it's the oldest standing court and led by the meanest, oldest ruling family of our people.

Even now, I feel unprepared and giddy at the same time.

I suppose that's how every new sangui feels.

I never thought I'd make it to this day, though, since I was sure I would die at my changing ceremony, but I didn't. I survived, even if the agony I felt while I died and was reborn was the worst I've ever felt . . . not to mention what I saw in the darkness.

It's something I have not told anyone and never will. Not even Simon knows.

I pretended to be shaken from becoming the undead, which I think anyone could believe, but luckily, the court my mother was born into, the Specter Court, was nothing but welcoming. Simon helped me massively, showing me the ropes, and the first time I fed, he was the one who helped me learn how to stop and control the hunger. He's been with me every step of the way.

I've had two years to prepare and learn, and I did as best as I could.

I learned to harness my strength, speed, and power, even if I never received a gift like others hoped since my mother had one—visions.

No, concentrate, Althea, I tell myself.

Simon watches me pace. Since he is only a few months older than me, he is being presented at the same time, as are the others from our court who changed in the same year.

There are ten of us, all eager to see the legendary court and be thrust into the spotlight of our race, and yes, also to hopefully find our mate, our destined, amongst the courts we are to be presented to.

"Okay, you need to stop or you are going to fall on your ass." He smirks.

I flip my fang at him, making him laugh as I continue to pace nervously. My long, black silk dress trails after me. Unlike the other girls here, who are in elaborate ball gowns, I went for a simplistic style. The slip dress is almost see-through, showing my red lace bra and thong underneath. Before the change, I was barely five feet without any tits to speak of, and my hair was at best considered thick.

Now, I barely recognise myself. I'm almost six feet, nearly as tall as most of the men in our court, which is surprising, even for vampyrs. My hair is a luscious black with dark blue and purple highlights that hangs in a sleek curtain to my perky ass. My tits are a nice double D that, yes, I almost wept over. My face is sharper, my lips are fuller, and my eyes are bigger. Every part of me is smoothed and honed to make me the perfect killing machine.

I learned to use my looks.

I learned the power I wield, and I love it.

My curves give others pause. We aren't all stick thin despite the legends, but even for my people, I am curvy, but I love the way my dress clings to my hips and ass as I walk, outlining them and my long, thick thighs.

I am pacing back to Simon when the doors are thrust open behind me, causing me to whirl and stumble on my heels. A representative of the court stands there, eyeing us all before she bows, her coiled red hair moving with her like snakes. "It is time for your presentation," she purrs, her fangs peeking over her painted lips as she straightens.

Her eyes are lined with kohl, and I feel her power like the first touch of wind before a storm.

She is weak, nowhere near as powerful as most of the members of this court, which means she is low on the totem pole. A stronger vampyr would feel like a full-fledged storm battering my senses, and the ancient ones? Well, I have heard stories that it is impossible to do anything but fall to your knees and lie prone before their greatness and power.

"You will be presented in age order and announced. Do not enter before then," she reminds us, even though we have been preparing for this very moment since we survived the change.

We are to walk into the ballroom with our heads held high, as we represent our court, and show our strength, beauty, and purpose.

We will meet eyes and bring honour to our people as we bow before the king of the court. We are to be silent and mysterious and, above all else, respectful. I have practiced curtsying a thousand times, but it does not stop my nerves as I fall into line at the very back since I am the youngest.

Simon is somewhere near the middle, and he gives me a supportive thumbs-up, which makes me grin. He's such a nerd.

The first is announced, making me shiver. "Alyriance, first of her name, Elemental Court." I watch a petite blonde sweep into the room with a cocky smirk, her power flowing from her like waves crashing against a rock.

It's loud but harmless.

I hear the chatter beyond, and a few moments later, another voice rings out, and this proceeds until it is Simon's turn.

"Simoneth, third of his name, son of the great and wise Specter Court." Simon looks back at me, and I smile. He sucks in a breath, turns forward, and brandishes his charming smile as he sweeps into the room beyond to find his future. I can only hope it's at my side.

I know, realistically, we will be torn apart at some point, our destinies elsewhere. I felt it after his change, and although I tried not to be bitter, it was hard since he is my closest friend, but I support him now and always, even though I'm saddened that, at some point, we may become strangers.

"Willeth, tenth of her name, daughter of the one who serves."

"Titlem, first of his name, son of the reborn, Vermillion Court."

"Helga, twentieth of her name, Principes Court."

Then it is my turn. I step up to the front and swallow my fear, knowing better than to show it in a room full of hungry predators with thousands of years of experience hunting prey and weakness. There's a sea of masked faces, in all shapes and sizes, as men and women turn eagerly to see the last presentation.

The youngest of our court.

They are eager for gossip, for the first glimpse, for anything they can use.

I will not feed the wolves.

It's something my mother used to say, and I harness it now, even as I feel my strength twist through me. I simply don't use all my power as instructed, keeping just enough hidden so I will be seen as powerful without displaying so much that they will fear me.

Showing one's full hand is to give them a dagger to kill you.

"Althea, first of her name, daughter of the all-seeing, all-knowing seer of Specter Court."

With my head held high like my mother before me, the greatest seer to ever live, I step into the ballroom and my fate beyond.

Three

Althea

My eyes sweep the crowd like I was taught, and I wear a lingering smile on my lips. My hair flows over my shoulder as I slowly glide down the middle aisle of the ballroom. I try not to stare at the grandeur of the gothic architecture and gaudy gold décor of the ballroom big enough to fit an entire city. Rows upon rows of thousands of our kind line the way to the throne, obscuring my view. I am alone amidst a nest of them, yet I show no fear. I let my power wash through them, and I hear the whispers.

She's the seer's daughter?

Does she have the sight?

She is more beautiful than her mother was.

Do you think her court will allow her to mate?

I ignore them all, bolstering my confidence. They do not, nor will they ever have to know, that I have no intention of following in my mother's footsteps. After all, how can I when I don't have the sight like she did?

It's yet another thing my court is angry about.

They expected great things from the daughter of their most powerful seer, but instead they got me. I am powerful but without sight, just another of the masses. Nothing special.

It will, however, allow me to have a normal life within court, which is what my mother always wanted.

I do not let them see my own disappointment. Instead, I allow my excitement to fill me, and my steps quicken slightly. I want to reach the end, meet the great king they serve, and do my duty for my court and find my place.

The pure joy at what awaits me makes my dead heart beat once, twice, before it stills again.

My fangs lengthen with my emotions, and my power rises slightly. I know they feel it because heads turn unnaturally to see me. Some bare their fangs, hungry for my power, and I realise then how truly vulnerable I am without a claim, a court, or a mate.

I am so unused to this world, but I try not to let it show.

I finally breach the masses and reach the end of my walk, and my mouth drops at the sight, even as I try not to show a reaction.

I know the rules, so I do not look directly at the king. He sits on a raised podium, with candelabras surrounding his golden throne, dripping with blood to show his power. His hands lazily stroke the arms of his chair as if in boredom, and my eyes dart higher for a moment, seeing a chiselled chin before I drop my head and curtsy.

I wait to be released, but when time continues to pass, a cold sweat breaks out and I begin to worry.

Did I do something wrong?

This isn't the ritual.

A ripple goes through the crowd, and I lift my head, seeing the king leaning forward in his throne. His hands hang between his parted thighs, thick with muscle and veins, leading up to a black doublet hugging his arms and chest. My gaze moves along his form to his strong chin and jaw, where huge fangs hang over bloodied lips that scream of silken nights and pleasure.

I dared not look higher before, but now my eyes roam across high cheekbones, pierced ears, wavy black hair, and arched brows to settle on his bright purple eyes.

Eyes that strike me to my core.

I stumble forward as my body jolts.

My power rises to meet the king's.

My mate.

I feel it to my very core. No one ever told us what it feels like, but I can only compare it to my death, when my heart stopped. It's just like that moment between death and wakefulness where I floated in pure bliss, mixed with a surge of power as I stagger closer to him.

The beautiful king sits back with shock covering his face.

The whispers of the court fade, as do my lessons in propriety and honour as I face the man destined to be mine. He's beautiful, stunning actually, and so powerful I feel it in every aching bone as it sweeps through me.

"My king," I whisper, my voice filled with the awe I feel. "My mate."

There are roars, and chaos erupts, but I continue to face him, unsure what to do.

I was never prepared to meet the one I am to spend my life with, never mind a king.

It is unheard of, and both of us are shocked into silence. We stare at one another, the years we have stretching between us. I smile. I can't help it. For so long, I have been alone, and now I have him, a king, to show me the way, to fight and serve alongside me, and to love and grow with.

All the possibilities fill me as I peer up at those purple eyes with all my hopes and dreams—only for them to be crushed when he sneers at me.

"I am no mate of yours."

Laughter echoes, and I jerk as if I've been struck, my face no doubt showing my confusion as it heats with shame. "My king, I felt the call . . . Did you not?"

I glance back to meet Simon's eyes, but he swings his gaze from the king to me.

I don't even know his name, the man destined to be my mate.

"I feel it." He nods, and I slump in relief, but then I notice a female at his feet in a see-through dress. She crawls up his legs, shooting me a venomous look, and clambers into his lap. He pets her side. "But I chose to ignore it." He strikes the female's throat, drinking from her.

She moans, her head falling back as his fangs mark her, claim her.

Blood pours from the wound as he drinks her down, his pleasure and power hitting me and breaking my heart.

Mates only drink from one another.

"My king?" I beg, falling to my knees from the agony of the bond tethering me to him, solidifying with every passing second. Pure pain washes through me as he feeds on another, even as my fangs lengthen at the sweet scent of the female's blood.

He lifts his head, letting the blood drip down his chin to his chest as he glares at me. "I will never tie myself to another, especially one as weak as you. I am a king!" he roars, leaning forward as the woman tumbles to the floor in a lax haze. "You are nothing. I reject you. I reject the bond. I reject the mating. Go! Get out of my sight. You disgust me!"

"Please," I whisper raggedly through the agony and utter humiliation consuming me. "To find a mate and be rejected—"

He has already looked away, dismissing me.

I refuse to beg, and I refuse to die, even though it feels like I am.

I crack apart, staggering to my numb feet.

The bond between us snaps, ricocheting back into us, even though it will never truly break.

Only death can sever it.

Yet he does not care that he has doomed me to a life of pain and hunger, where I will be alone and without power or reputation. The cruel king looks over me like I do not exist, as if fate itself did not select us to be together.

Do not feed the wolves, my mother's voice floats to me.

Since he rejects me, dismisses me, then I shall go.

I will never beg for something that is not mine.

Even if it kills me.

With all the dignity and grace left in my body, I turn and stride quickly from the room, keeping my head held high despite the bloody tears gathering in my eyes. I ignore the pity, laughter, jealousy, and the glee on the blurring mass of faces as I flee from the king—my mate who rejected me.

My reputation, my honour, and my future is tarnished.

I told you fate was a bitch.

Four

Althea

Struggling to breathe, I rip at my dress, tearing material away as I sob and drop to my knees in my room.

My heart shreds like paper, shattering into a million pieces.

My blood boils, trying to pull me back to him to fix the bond.

My fangs ache as thirst floods through me for the man I cannot have—a thirst that will never be satisfied.

My bloody tears drip to the floor as my back bows in pain. All I know for a while is agony until finally it submits to a constant, bone-deep ache, making my fangs clench. It's only then I realise someone is stroking my hair and humming a familiar tune.

"Simon?" I whisper without opening my eyes.

"It's me," he murmurs. "Oh Thea, I'm so sorry. I'm so very sorry. I'd kill him for you if I could."

"What will I do?" I whimper, turning into him to bury my face in his warmth and familiarity, grounding myself in it.

"You will survive this, just like you have survived everything else. You'll go out there and show your face proudly," he snaps.

"How can I?" I cry, gripping him tighter. "They all know I am dishonoured, rejected, and unwanted. I will be shunned. The court might even kick me out."

"Then fuck them. We'll go to a different one," he yells, and when I lift my head, I see matching tears tracking down his face. "Thea," he croaks.

Every vampyr knows the agony that comes with a rejected mate, or at least the tales of it.

Though it's not often.

"I'm all alone."

"Never, you have me," he protests, but it doesn't fill the coldness inside me nor keep the pain at bay or fix the thirst as much as both of us wish it did.

He's wrong. He'll leave too. He'll have to because to be associated with me would ruin his chances.

His life.

I know he'll stay, even if it does just that, and as he sings to me, holding me tightly, I make a split-second decision.

I cannot save me or my future, maybe I never could, but I can save him from suffering this fate with me, even if it's the last thing I do.

Sliding from the bed, I slowly lower his arm to the pillow. I was once so excited over my black bedding, but now it fills me with nothing but anger because I'll never share it with another.

My mother's apartments, which are adjoined to mine, still stand empty in the top of the mansion I know I won't be able to keep now. I don't think I could stand watching them rip that last part of her from me.

Sitting on the edge of the bed, I glance over my shoulder at the only family I have left.

Moonlight streams through the huge windows covering the entire right side between the decorative stone walls. Simon is lying on his side with his head turned towards me, his fangs bared as he snores.

Reaching down, I sweep the hair from his forehead. We've shared beds like this since we were kids. Every time one of us was sick, hurt, or upset, we were always there for one another.

The idea of losing him . . .

I gasp in pain, clutching my chest and my broken heart.

The bond rips into me, but over that is the agony of losing the only family I have left and seeing that love turn to hatred. I couldn't bear it.

No, he's better off without me.

Maybe it's cowardly to do this and I should face my court, but I've seen this far too often—not a rejected mate, which I saw only once as a child. He was our leader, our king of the court, and when his mate rejected him, he lost everything. Nobody believed in him anymore, and his power, his standing, his home, and his future were all gone in an instant, ripped away as he was tossed onto the streets like a pauper. But to be stripped? I see that every night for those who are being punished or who have broken social standing. It's common; our laws are absolute.

They will do that to me. I know it's inevitable. I will be forced to watch as I am snubbed and rejected once more, so I'll leave and reject them before they have the chance to do so to me.

I'll save Simon the only way I can. I'll give him, my brother, my best friend, my only family, a chance at a better life because if I stay, he'll stay right by my side with me, like he has since we were kids.

Tiptoeing around the room, I grab bits and bobs, knowing he won't wake up. He's always been a deep sleeper. Stepping to the walk-in wardrobe, I collect as much as I can without overpacking.

I know I'll never be back, but I have no idea where I am going, so there is no point in taking too much. I do take the photographs of Simon and me and my mother and me when I was born from my vanity, knowing I'll need them when I'm alone and scared. I leave the fancy dresses and masks, since I won't need them for court anymore.

With my duffle slung over my shoulder, I look back at the bed to see Simon in the same spot. Closing my eyes for a moment, I feel the love pouring from him before I turn away. The note I wrote is propped against the mirror where he will see it, stained with my blood-red tears that don't seem to stop.

S,

I'm so sorry. I can't stay, and you know that. They will ruin me, or what is left of me. Not only that, they will also do that to you as well. I will not take your future away from you, not even for my own selfish wants to be with the only person who has ever truly loved me.

You are my best friend, and you will always be my brother, my family. That's why I'm doing this. You'll be angry, and that's okay, you can hate me if you need to, but know this, brother—I'm doing this for you. Find your happiness, your future, and your mate and hold on tight.

Maybe one day, we'll see each other again, but if not, remember that I will always be your sister, and in the darkness, you will find me.

Yours always,

A x

I close my eyes when I reach the door, my heart thrumming with constant pain. I know I need to get somewhere safe before I crack and break. I feel it, like a shroud of darkness clinging to me, and as soon as I give in, it will swallow me whole.

But not yet.

Forcing my eyes open, I slip out of the suite door and shut it behind me before hesitating in the hallway. I hadn't planned to, but I find myself standing in front of the door opposite mine.

My mother's.

Opening the door, I crinkle my nose at the stale air as I slip into the dark suite. It's covered in a layer of dust, but everything is where it belongs, as is the rule. This cannot be touched unless it is so decreed, and our king had a soft spot for my mother, so he ordered it to be left as it was for me, so I could know her.

But I could never bring myself to step foot inside, not until this night.

The sitting room is through the open archway to the right—the same layout as mine. A huge fireplace stands empty with a mantel full of pictures of her life and successes, which I stop in front of, dragging my finger across one of her smiling face, cutting through the dust.

I look so much like her, but I couldn't be more different.

Turning away, I stop before the huge four-poster bed.

I close my eyes once more, searching for any signs of her, needing that motherly comfort now more than ever.

"I wonder if you were scared, if you saw what was coming for you. Did you regret having me, knowing it would kill you? Did . . . Did you see this coming for me? Did you know I would be cursed from birth to kill my mother and then to survive the change, only to be stolen away once more?" Shaking my head, I open my eyes and see nothing but emptiness.

She isn't here.

"I need you," I croak, breaking slightly. "I need you so badly. I'm so lost and alone. I'm scared, Mother, so fucking scared."

You are never alone in the dark, my child. They wait for you. Go and find them.

Find your destiny.

It's a whisper through the air, and I gasp, unsure if it's my breaking psyche or a promise from those who watch over us.

"Please, if you hear me, show me a sign," I beg, spinning wildly. When nothing happens, I lift my wrist and rip it open. "I offer a blood sacrifice, please."

Still, nothing happens, and I hear nothing aside from my blood dripping onto the stone floor.

Turning away once more, I step forward to leave when something pulls me through the room to her wardrobe. Her dresses remain forgotten inside, along with her suits, her armour, and her medals, yet it's a small box tucked away on the top shelf that draws my attention. It shines brightly despite being forgotten.

I pull it down and slowly open it. Inside is a mask, one unlike anything I've ever seen before.

It isn't like the small, delicate masks the females wear.

No, this one is pure silver, with gold tears falling from the open eye sockets. The mouth is parted in a sinister grin to allow fangs to pop through, and it has horns at the top. It would cover my entire face. For a moment, I stroke the metal, feeling a connection to it.

Or is that my connection to the woman who stored it here?

I don't know, but something will not allow me to put it back, so I gently set it inside the box and put it in my duffle bag.

I sweep the room once more but find nothing except emptiness, the same thing that will eventually fill me, so without wasting any more time, I shut the door.

Standing in the hallway, I hold onto this life for a moment—the life of my childhood filled with dreams and hopes—before stepping towards the stairs and letting it all go.

Now, nothing but anger, pain, and regrets fill me.

I make it all the way downstairs and to the front door of the mansion where our court is housed before I see anyone. He slips from the darkness like a wraith, his eyes hard and red. His red hair is swept back, and his beard is neatly trimmed.

He's Druig, the king's second-in-command.

"You're leaving?" he asks.

I hold my bag tighter and give him a firm nod.

He scans me from head to toe and finds me lacking. He's always intimidated me, and there's something cruel in his eyes, or maybe it's just because his job is to punish bad little vampyrs of our court.

"Good."

I startle at that, and the smile he gives me is almost . . . kind.

"What?" I murmur. "Aren't you supposed to stop me?"

"Probably." He shrugs, shoving his hands in his pockets. "But I owed your mother one last favour." He grins at my swallow. "I was her friend right up until the end, even if you don't believe that. I promised I would always watch out for you. I guess I failed."

"You couldn't have done anything," I reply.

"Not true. I could have killed him, but one simply doesn't kill kings."

"No, I suppose they don't." This is surreal, and we just stare at each other.

"Go far away, little vampyr, where they can't find you. If you stay, they will make your life a living hell. You would be their punching bag for all eternity, and someone of her blood, the daughter of the greatest woman I've ever met, deserves more. You deserve more," he states. "So find it."

"There's nothing left," I tell him. "I am rejected—"

"So what?" he snaps. "Do not let one foolish man you do not even know decide your future. Your mother was a fighter, a warrior until the very end, and I see her in you. Be that person. Find your own path, your own destiny, and live the way she never could. You owe her that." With that, he steps back into the darkness, releasing me from his power.

When I step outside, I know he's wrong because I'm not my mother.

I am not a warrior, and I'm not a fighter.

I've already given up, and each step I take towards the gates only proves that.

I know I will never be anything more than this agony-filled creature until the end finally comes for me.

The one I foretold.

FIVE

ALTHEA

GRIPPING THE CHEAP, STAINED motel sheets, I release a curse as another wave of pure agony rocks through me.

It feels as if every nerve is being burned and every part of me is being broken and reformed.

I drove for as long as I could, heading out of the city and into the next where the court couldn't reach me, before I finally had to give in. After checking into a cheap motel, I fell into a painful, fitful sleep, only to wake up in so much pain it bowed my back with a scream before I choked it down.

The last thing I need is the police. The humans are not to know about us after all.

Sliding from the hard mattress, I fall to my knees on the coral carpet. My head is thrown back, and a silent roar leaves my lips as everything inside me breaks.

The bond is killing me, yet there's nothing I can do about it.

I writhe as I slump forward, living in pure agony as it rolls through me, leaving me sweating and cold. It's trying to pull me back to him, but I would rather die than crawl back and beg to feed just to stop the pain.

I cannot see, and I cannot hear.

My limbs do not even want to work.

I don't even realise I'm screaming until my voice stops working.

Groaning, I open my eyes for a moment to see the ceiling.

Everything hurts.

A pounding knock on the door has me rolling to my side to look at the shaking wood. The curtains before the window are drawn, so I cannot see out.

"Hello? Is everything okay?"

My hearing is fuzzy now, but I can make out enough to understand the concerned voice. I groan, my hand flopping to the floor as my life drains from me.

"I heard screaming. Are you okay?" the distinctive male voice calls out, and the scent of a human reaches me from under the door—unwashed and male.

"Are you okay?" the voice demands once more, sounding urgent this time. "I'm coming in."

The door is kicked in, and a pudgy, half-naked man stands in the doorway, his eyes locked on me where I'm lying in a tangle of sweaty limbs and sheets, jerking from the pain.

For a moment, I think he might help me, but then his eyes fill with malicious intent, and his tongue darts out to lick his lips. He kicks the door shut behind him. "Well, that's one way to get a man's attention. How about we see what I can do to help?"

I can read his mind, and what he plans to do to me is obvious.

When he stops before me, I use my last bit of energy to lift my head. He crouches and reaches out to squeeze my breast, and his other slips between my thighs. I'm so weak I cannot even stop this human male. "Oh, but you're young and pretty, so we are going to have some fun."

Something inside of me just snaps.

The last shred of dignity and humanity I possessed leaves me, and I strike.

I force him to his back as I sink my fangs into his neck. I know I can't drink from humans, since they offer no sustenance, and if we drink from them often enough, their blood drives us mad, but there's something about the man's bellow of agony that matches my own, and the stench of fear makes me primal, so I sink my fangs in deeper.

I crave his pain as it washes away my own.

His blood floods my mouth as I drink, lighting me up, and for a moment, it drives back the pain, fear, and anger.

His thoughts flash through my head, and the possibilities—not the things he would have done to me—make me stab my nails into his chest. My sharpened claws rip into his skin as he bucks and writhes to dislodge me, but even in my half-dead state, I am stronger.

I pin him as I drain him, his blood infecting my own and changing me forever.

When I slump back, full and half crazed with it, his unseeing eyes are locked on me.

His body is still warm, and he's covered in blood.

A grim sense of satisfaction fills me as the monster we all keep inside takes over, and I let it.

I retreat into the welcoming darkness as I become the thing of legends.

Of nightmares.

A YEAR LATER . . .

Madness covers me like a second skin, as does the never-ending starvation I feel, leaving me half dead and weak for a vampyr.

I drop the dead human to the pile at my feet where six others like him rest, their faces contorted in terror.

Blood coats my mouth and neck, and I wipe it on my black leather trench coat. I guess *Blade* had the right idea there. For a moment, pain pierces the madness. I use it like a protective shroud before I push away the memories and plunge back into the darkness where nothing touches me.

Where I can survive.

You see, I told you I'm not the hero of this story.

I'm the villain.

I let my pain consume me until I was nothing but a nightmare, a monster stalking the night.

I cannot feed from other vampyrs due to the bond, even if they would let me, which they wouldn't, so I drain humans dry, uncaring about littering the streets with their bodies.

I am always moving, always running from my past, and death follows me in a trail of corpses.

Not drinking from vampyrs leaves me half dead and weak, while humans . . . well, their blood warps my mind until I am nothing but a feeding machine looking for her next kill.

I'm nothing but the predator their human stories depict us as.

I will never be anything more, and one day, either the blood virus will kill me or another vampyr will.

I cannot wait for that day.

Six

Althea

When I was younger, I heard rumours about places like this—places where those who are *other*, those who are not quite right, ventured. It's where those who are not pure blood enough to be in a court nor feral enough to be put down congregate.

Halfies, mixed breeds, and loners fill the club.

Wearing my low-rise leather trousers, bustier top, and leather duster jacket, I don't stand out here. Even the silky paleness of my skin and the bright red of my eyes doesn't draw extra attention.

Here, I am just another in the masses.

My senses are long since dulled, but I still pick up harpies, vampyrs, wolves, and even a hint of something other deep inside the crowd of writhing bodies. A halfie wolf is rutting what looks to be a pixie by the back wall, and a vampyr is feeding from a troll in a booth.

Blood is served at the bar, as is fresh human meat and bones.

It's not a place for a good little vampyr like I once was, but now, I fit right in.

I push my way through the crowd, baring my teeth at any who protest my rough treatment. Maybe they sense my brimming need for death and violence because everyone backs down, and when I make my way to the bar, I slam my fist on the sticky wooden stop.

"Blood," I demand.

The unknown bartender rolls his eyes, his whisper catching my attention. "Fucking vamps."

Smirking, I turn my back, feeling the music's bass pumping through the speakers, into the floor, up my vinyl, five-inch boots, and into my body. I almost find it hypnotising, and for a moment, I imagine being normal, sane, and loved as I dance here with a boyfriend or mate.

A sharp stab cuts that off, however, and I drain the glass unceremoniously dumped before me.

It's a halfie's blood, no doubt—half human, half vamp—and just enough to pull me back from the brink of madness a little. The old taste of power makes me close my eyes hungrily . . . wistfully.

I remember the days when I would be coated in it in the middle of orgies and filled with power from feeding. I felt so strong and invincible.

That was before I fell from grace, before I knew the truth.

Nothing in this world lasts forever, not even immortals like us.

My eyes continually scan the room. I know I should leave. I can't prey on humans here, and even the vamps in this place wouldn't let me feed, even if I could.

For a moment, though, I feel like I belong, and I don't want to go.

Instead, I blend into the background and watch others. As I observe the interactions between lovers, friends, or even new acquaintances, I realise I miss it viscerally.

I crave to connect with someone and just have somebody there for me to share laughter, hope, and happiness with.

But there is no room in my darkness for that.

The smell of something other hits me again, and I turn my head to see a beautiful, icy blonde woman slide onto a stool a few places down. She's short, though everyone is compared to me, and more muscular than willowy. She has high breasts spilling from a nearly sheer, sparkling sheath dress covered in sequins that catch the light. Her pale, toned legs are on display as she crosses them, waiting to be served.

She's beautiful, but when she turns to me, there's something in her gaze that's almost unsettling . . . powerful, but other.

Her irises are almost the same stark white as her hair before they bleed to a stunning cerulean blue, and then she glances away, freeing me from her thrall, and I snap right back to my darkness.

I've never been into women, but there's a power about her that's addictive, and when I recognise it, I realise she's probably half siren or something.

She's trouble for sure.

"Amara," someone calls, stepping up to her side, and I turn away.

I am the only one here who is alone.

Feeling more disgusting than when I walked in, I head to the back where the toilets are. Needing an escape, I slip inside and lock the door behind me as I hang my head over the sink.

Hunger takes hold once more, and I groan as I clutch the porcelain.

I hate this hunger and that I'm forced to kill and feed.

There's just never enough blood to heal the wounds in my soul.

I lift my head and see myself for the first time in a year, and it shocks me to my core.

Gone is the bright glow of life. My hair looks lifeless and dull, my skin is pale and almost translucent, my fangs are huge, and my face is bony. I look like a shell, and I quickly slam my hand into the mirror, cracking the glass.

In those fissures, I briefly see the reflection of another, who has pale skin and bright eyes, before it fades too.

The scent of my blood makes me hiss as I lift my fist and lap at the wound.

It won't do anything for me, but the taste is comforting.

I wonder if I will just die one day.

Nox, I hope so.

Turning away in horror, I slip out of the toilet and head down the corridor before breaking out into the night, where I suck in a deep breath of putrid air, tainted by garbage. After all, it's all I deserve. Leaning against the wall, I let weakness flow through my body as the hunger demands to be satisfied.

Hatred fills me for myself, who I've become, and for what I am, but mostly for the man who made me this way, the one who rejected and ruined me.

If Mother could see me now, she would be horrified, as would Simon.

Even thinking his name hurts, so I decide to distract myself, and when a human steps out of the door to the restaurant opposite and tosses a black bag in the bin, I strike. I need the release his death will bring, and I need the life that runs through him to push past the turbulent emotions and pain consuming me.

When I pin him to the wall and sink my fangs deep, however, it's his memories that crowd my head. I don't know if other vamps see them, I never did before, but now, I do. With each human I feed from, I see their lives, including their past, present, and future.

I don't know if it's a mutation or something else, but I hate it.

I want the life in their blood, not their actual lives, especially when I see some of the acts some have committed—it leaves me sick, and I scrub my body for hours after.

His life crowds my mind now, showing me flashes I try to ignore, otherwise I will never forget.

Who am I kidding? I never do anyway. They are inside me forever. His lifeless body falls to the ground, but the hunger isn't satisfied. I turn and gag, throwing up his blood. The blood poisoning is in its final stages now, and I hope for everyone's sake that I die soon. Stumbling away, I lean against the cool wall, letting the dampness there coat my forehead as I heave and try to push the memories away.

I'm so focused on my task, I don't hear or see anything.

I am so weak, I don't even sense anything amiss until something sharp sinks into my throat, and I'm out cold before I even hit the concrete.

Maybe this will be when I die.

I can only hope so.

Seven
Althea

Unfortunately, I wake up.

My body is weak, and whatever power I had left or stole from the blood is long gone, leaving me cold and barely able to move. I'm used to it, though, so I force my eyes open and lick my mouth, finding it dry and coated in vomit and blood.

Sitting up, I scan the room I am in. A cold wind blows through the space, freezing me to my core and proving just how weak I really am. My hands are chained together, the black iron shackles shaped like snake mouths with their fangs piercing my wrists, causing my blood to drip onto the floor. The sight of it looks wrong against the white and black tile.

There's a moan, and my head snaps up. I force my eyes to focus to truly see my surroundings for the first time. There are more people next to me—no, not people, vampyrs. Their hands are shackled just like mine, and the scent of their blood lingers in the air, making hunger slam through me. I barely manage to stop myself from going feral, using both my restraint and weakness to aid me.

Some are still passed out, tossed carelessly in a line next to me, while some are sitting. Two have their heads bent together, their eyes sharp as they look for an escape, and one is sobbing, her blood-red tears falling down her face.

I guess I should be more bothered about this, but I truly don't care. I can feel death in the air, and I want it.

Something in the darkness here calls to me, beckoning me home.

Beyond the group of shackled vampyrs is a huge, open cavern similar to that of the throne rooms in the courts, but it's equally as different. Unlike ours, which is filled with orbs, ghosts, and prophecies, this one is occupied with shadows and darkness.

Ornate black decorations hang from the ceiling and walls, with snakes slithering about.

It's like every vampyr's nightmares have come to life and were captured and placed inside.

In the middle of the room are two triangles drawn in blood, with black candles surrounding them and a circle in the middle. There are symbols and drawings I don't understand, also drawn in blood, and a black bowl glittering before it, but everything else fades when I see the thrones.

Multiple thrones.

Not one king sits in this court, but seven.

Seven thrones, all set in a semi-circle on a raised dais, face the blood circle in the middle. Each one is slightly different than the last, but with my eyes and hearing starting to fail as I die, it's hard to make out the details. What I can make out, though, are the seven large forms sitting on the thrones with matching masks on their faces.

They are silver and black, with gaping holes of darkness for their eyes and mouths and inlaid with delicate designs. Some have horns and some don't, but they all have the same kind of black robes obscuring their bodies.

Even though I can't see their gazes, I feel their attention on us as they judge us, and for a moment, I swear I hear a whisper in the night.

Welcome home, fellow nightmare.

I say nothing, and instead, I wait.

Slowly, as one, they stand, and when the voice comes, it's a combination of many, booming with agony and death, and those near me flinch and recoil. Then, the robed figures' power flows from them and reaches us, stealing my breath.

"You have been brought to the Court of Nightmares for judgement."

The Court of Nightmares?

There are only four courts. I've never heard of another, but as I look around, it seems forgotten, so maybe that's why.

"Your crimes against your own kind and that of others have been noticed. You will be judged."

They sit as one, resting their leather-covered hands on the arms of their thrones. We see nothing of them, yet I feel them brushing against me.

"Judged? Who the hell are you to judge us?" one man yells. Looking at his long hair, I would say he's a noble, and the entitled attitude he sports only proves it.

"We are the blood kings, chosen by those who made us to be the seven judges of fate. You will be judged." One leans forward, his voice deep and dark. "And you will pay for your crimes, no matter who you are or where you came from. Nobody is exempt here."

"You have no authority over me!" the vampyr roars, yanking on his chains. "Release me now or you will feel the wrath of my court."

One of the seven kings stands slowly, effortlessly, like water. His head tilts, and suddenly, shadows thicken in the room, and the struggling vampyr is wrapped in shadows, dragged into the circle, and deposited there as easily as one would move a child.

He sat once more, and the judges blended together, but I upped my estimation of their power and age. I have never seen someone control shadows like that.

Not ever.

"It is time for your judgement," one calls.

The vampyr continues to yell, but then a deep gash appears across his throat, making him gurgle on his words. His blood hits the air, making us all sit up, and we watch as he falls forward, his blood spilling across the drawings and into the bowl where it begins to sizzle.

"You are guilty. Your crimes are numerous, and you have been sentenced."

I watch on as one of the nameless masked persons leaps down from the throne, stops before the kneeling vampyr without breaking the blood circle, and snaps off his fangs before tossing them away.

The resounding agonised scream echoes the one that's always trapped in my throat, but hope fills me—hope that they will do the same to me, stop this infernal hunger, and stop me from hurting people.

A vampire's fangs never grow back, and without them, they slowly die.

They do not leave him to expire however. The one who snapped off his fangs slams his fist into his chest, rips out his heart, and holds it up.

"You pay the judgement. I, Nathair, King of the Serpents, declares your debt paid." His fist clenches around the heart, crumbling it to dust as the vampyr collapses and disintegrates until he's nothing but a skeleton.

That tells me he was an old vampire, truly old, so no wonder he had such a sense of entitlement.

His body is wrapped in shadows, and then it's discarded to the side, while Nathair sits down on his throne.

"Next to be judged," another voice calls.

I watch as those gagged and bound like me are brought into the symbols in the middle of the room. They all cry, scream, and beg, trying to make deals or pleading for their lives, and yet each one's blood is spilled and then a voice rings out true and strong, proclaiming, "Guilty," before their fangs are torn out and their bodies are dragged to the side to be burned in the fire to the left.

Another is pulled into the blood circle, sobbing, and after her blood is spilled, she also has her heart ripped out and is added to the pile of corpses. One after another, each person is judged and found guilty, until I am the only one left to be judged, found guilty, and killed.

I suppose I should be scared, but I'm not, and instead, something akin to peace fills me.

"The last will now be judged," a voice calls.

Not waiting for the shadows to grab me, I stumble to my feet and walk to the circle and pass through it, and then I willingly drop to my knees. I tilt my head back, facing my fate. I know I have been living on borrowed time, and I am prepared to meet my makers with a warm smile and gratitude.

This seems to shock them, and they all lean forward, but I refuse to face death while screaming or crying. I have been dead for a very long time, and I am done running.

I go willingly with open arms.

"You do not need to bleed me, though you can if you wish, for I am guilty of all my crimes. Kill me."

"You are . . . asking for death?" Nathair asks.

"It is what I deserve. Free me," I reply pleadingly. "Free me from this rot and evil that fills me, so I can never hurt or kill another."

"You are guilty of your crimes?" another asks.

"Yes, I have killed many," I admit without shame, humbling myself before them.

I feel their power, their destiny, and their responsibility, and I accept it.

"We still must see," one says softly.

A gentle cut is made on my neck, unlike the others whose throats were practically torn out. I lean forward and let what is left of my rotting blood hit the bowl.

There's a ripple of gasps as I fade into my memories with them. I feel them searching through my life, and nothing is left untouched as every part of me is exposed, from my mother dying to my traumatic turning, to my rejection and my fall from grace.

My life is sorted through like a file.

They dig deeper than I dare, yet I do not run away, and when they release me, I sit back, finding bloody tears sliding down my cheeks.

"Oh, my queen," one murmurs. "The world has failed you."

"No, I failed it," I reply, bowing my head. "I am no queen."

"But you could have been," a king counters. "I see the path you could have taken and the greatness you are capable of. Life is cruel, future queen."

"But you must be judged, and you must pay. We cannot alter that, not even if they were deserving."

"I'm sorry?" I frown, confused. "Who was deserving?"

"The humans you killed, you . . . you do not know, do you?"

"I don't think she does." The voices mix together until a robed figure sits forward.

"Little queen, the humans you chose seemingly at random were not so random. Deep down, beyond the blood poisoning and madness, you felt their evil. It's your mother's gift, no doubt, and you remember it now."

I nod as my mind clears for the first time in months, almost making me sob.

"You saw what they had done, or what they were planning to do—great acts of evil. They were not innocent. You were judging and sentencing them in your own way."

"But you exposed us to humans and put our whole race at risk, so you must be judged and pay." It's said wistfully. "I am sorry, truly."

"Do not be, I gladly welcome death like a lover. I ask only one thing."

"Ask."

"May I die on my feet?" I do not move, not wanting to risk their wrath. A simple incline of a head is my only answer, and I stand and bow my head. "Thank you. Burn my body to ashes so the rot may never spread."

"We have killed many, and we have never asked for names, but I ask for yours," the one in the middle demands.

"Althea." I go to offer my titles, but then I realise they do not count anymore. "The last of my line, rejected mate to a king I never knew," I admit sadly. "There will be no one to mourn me, so do not worry."

"That is where you are wrong," one murmurs before Nathair steps forward.

When he stops before me, he reaches into my chest, almost like the slide of a lover's caress, and grips my beating heart. I feel it and gasp, my wide eyes focused on the bottomless black holes where his eyes should be, and for a moment, I swear I see a flare of red there before it fades and my heart is extracted from my chest.

"May you find peace in death that you were never given in life," he whispers as he steps back.

I know he's passing his judgement as I fall to my knees and then to my side, crumpling as the life leaves my body, but I cannot hear it.

I am finally free, and I welcome death with a relieved smile.

EIGHT

ALTHEA

DEATH IS SURPRISINGLY BORING.

Serene but boring.

Or maybe I am not fully dead yet and I linger between.

Fog crowds around me, obscuring the landscape, and my feet are glued to the spot, but the best part? I feel no pain, hunger, or madness. I am as I once was, strong and peaceful.

It's a miracle.

I don't know how much time passes before my mother steps through a shroud of light. At first, I don't believe it, but it's her. Her soft smile is just as I've seen it a thousand times in pictures and dreams. Her hair is the exact same as mine, and her eyes, so filled with love, crinkle at each corner.

It's her, and she is beautiful.

"Mum?" I whisper. *I truly am dead.*

"It's me, my love," she assures me, taking my hands. "Look how beautiful you grew up to be."

A sob catches in my throat as I throw myself at her, and she rubs my back, soothing me in a way only a mother can.

"Shush now, my girl, everything is okay."

"I missed you so much," I whisper.

"I missed you too." She pulls away. "But now isn't your time." She glances over her shoulder and frowns before she looks back at me. "Or so I saw, but it is your choice, Althea. It always has been."

"My choice for what, Mum? I don't understand. We are together again, and I'm free."

She smiles sadly at me as she grips my hands. "I will always be here, waiting for you, but you have such incredible things to do back down there. Stop reaching for death when you were destined to live."

"But, Mum—"

"I know it hurts, and I know you have suffered so much already, and you will suffer much worse if you go back—"

"Mum, I'm dead! I can't go back!" I argue. This is not how I was expecting this to go.

"You are in between, my love. Not quite dead and not quite alive. They haven't burned your heart or body yet, so there is still time, but not much. I cannot give you the answers you wish to know, but know this, Althea—I knew you were destined for a great many things, and none of them included running into death's arms to escape pain. You are stronger than that, stronger than anyone even knows. You are the very best of us."

"I'm the worst," I hiss.

"No, my love. Nightmares and darkness are not evil, but they are as necessary as the light. So much sin has been committed in the name of righteousness, and it must be undone. Do you understand me? I bore my death with pride, knowing it left you to complete your destiny. The world needs you, Althea, and I do as well, but I can wait. I'm not going anywhere, but know this—if you go back, it will hurt worse than anything you've ever experienced because what you must face will leave even the most hardened warrior scarred, so I understand if you want to stay. I will fade with you, and we will be together again."

"I-I'm so very tired of being alone and scared," I tell her.

"I know, my girl, but in the end, everyone is alone. All that waits for us is our loved ones and our deeds. Can you truly tell me if this is the end, and that if this is your last day, you are happy with how you left it? Althea, you have such a big heart, someone . . . or several someones should feel that. You should love brilliantly and greatly, you should fight until you cannot fight anymore, and above all, you should be who you were always supposed to be. Embrace it, love it, and wield it. You, Althea, were always destined to be the death of others and be one in the dark protecting innocents. It is your destiny, just as being your mum was mine."

"You told me I would die."

"I did, and you have." She grins. "And I said no more. I kept those prophecies to myself to allow you to grow up without that pressure so you could choose. I will love you either way."

"If I go back, will I still be . . . that way? Corrupted from the rejected mating?"

A flash of anger crosses her face before it clears. "No. When you died, the soul bond to him died too, so you will be free once more." Squeezing my hand, she looks back again. "We must hurry, Althea. I promise that whatever you choose, I love you and I'm proud of you. All I ever wanted was to see you one last time, and now I have."

"But you think I should go back."

"I think you should live, Althea. I think you should live, and I think you should become the nightmare . . . the saviour."

"And if I'm not good enough?" I query, voicing my fears. After all, I wasn't good enough for my own mate.

"That could never happen. How could you not be good enough when you are fighting for hope and love? Now choose, my girl. Choose to live and survive, even unimaginable agony, or let yourself die and come away with me and know no more."

Licking my lips, I glance around. "If I choose to go back, you'll wait for me?"

"Forever and a day, my love. I cannot tell you anymore. This is your choice; it has to be."

I search her gaze, and I see her love and acceptance. If I choose to fade, she will fade with me, and we can be together again.

I would never be in pain.

But she's right. I barely lived.

I'd just turned when I was rejected, and I never knew the bliss of love or experienced everything the world had to offer. Instead, I sank into darkness and let it ruin me. I became something I didn't recognise, and I have to atone for that. Dying is too easy.

I must go back and make my wrongs right.

"I'll go back. I want to make up for what I have done. I want to be great like you said. I want more."

Smiling, she squeezes my hand and leans in, laying a gentle kiss on my head as my eyes close.

"Then go make your destiny and show them all who you truly are."

I burst back into life with a gasp and a cry, the way everyone comes into this world.

I feel my heart start once more and my body heal, leaking all the toxins and rot from my veins until I am . . . at peace.

My eyes are locked on the ceiling of the court I died in, but I can clearly see the epic paintings of monsters and nightmares shrouded by darkness now.

The room is lit by fire, giving it an almost cosy ambiance as my heart beats once more.

I wait for the pain, but it never comes.

There's thirst for sure, and twinges from my heart being ripped out, but other than that, I feel good, and I can smell again. Above the stench of death and burning bodies, musky male scents call to me. I roll to my knees and hang my head for a moment before tossing my hair back and sitting up.

In the corner are the burning bodies of the others, and the masked judges stand there, watching the flames consume the corpses.

"Hello, judges," I call with a grin, unable to help it.

They spin fast, but I can track the movement, and I meet them on my feet as they surround me.

"How?" one demands.

"How are you alive?" another exclaims.

Licking my fangs, I look down to see my shirt is ripped, but the skin there is whole once more, leaving only a mark where my heart was ripped out. It's a seal of fate, a promise. I've seen it before in history books. It looks similar to a death rune, with three short, jagged lines and one crossing through it that's tilted up the edges. I stroke it before looking back up.

"I paid for my sins, and now it seems I have a job to do."

At once, they all point to the mark between my breasts, and the silence is loud before a robe parts, exposing a pale, almost ghostly chest built with incredible muscles. It's not that, though, that makes my mouth drop open.

The same mark is on his chest right where mine is.

"You were chosen, just like us," he murmurs. "Another hasn't been chosen in many years, but here you are."

"I suppose we have some things to discuss," a cultured voice responds from behind another mask.

"I suppose we do, but I don't presume you have anything to eat, do you?" I lick my fangs again. "I'm so very thirsty." A shiver goes through the pale one, and I feel his blood calling to me.

"We must explain that too," the pale-chested man responds, his voice hoarse.

"Then explain what this mark means and who you truly are."

"We will, but first, Althea, the risen blood queen, welcome to the Court of Nightmares."

NINE

OSIS

I FELT A STIRRING at the gate between the living and the dead, but I had not been expecting this. I expected another of Azul's ghosts or ghouls, but never this.

A judge is chosen very carefully, and there has not been another in years. The last was Lycus, and that was a hundred years ago.

Shall we escort her from the temple to the formal siting room? Nathair murmurs through our bond. We are all locked down tight, not wanting to sense each other's feelings, but I still feel the shock, desire, and hope from the others, even as they try to restrain themselves.

I nod and step towards her, unable to stop myself. "Come with us, we will explain."

She eyes my chest, making my dead heart skip a beat as I shiver from her perusal and turn away with a dramatic flair of my cape to stop myself from striking. I trust her and the others to follow as I head through the temple to the curtained off hallway beyond, and then to the closed double doors.

Opening them, I stride into the formal sitting room. The fire is burning, like they always do here, the flames licking at the stone around it. I always find it cold in here, with the moon shining through the huge bay windows leading to the grounds beyond.

There are many sofas and chairs to seat guests, not that we have any anymore. No one has been here since the court was destroyed and the judges were born.

I feel the others filter into the room, our bond of brotherhood letting me feel it and . . . *her*. I feel her, and although it's not like I feel them, there's a calling between us. To cement our bond as judges, we are to be united as one, and she is going to realise that soon.

Realise she has come back from the dead only to tie herself to the nightmares of our world.

The bond does not have to be sexual, but I cannot stop those thoughts from filtering through as I turn to see her wandering curiously around the room.

It's our duty to wear our masks when serving judgement, so technically we don't have to now, but no one has removed theirs, since we all know where this is going.

After all, nightmares . . . judges feed from one another to survive, since we are all technically dead, which means she will feed from us.

That is why our robes and masks stay on, to stop us from offering ourselves too eagerly. Earlier, when she licked that wicked fang, I almost spilled in my pants, imagining it sinking into my neck with her lithe body pinning me down as she fed.

Gone is the half dead, corrupted vampyr, and in its place is a true queen, one she was always supposed to be.

She is magnificent.

Her black, blue, and purple hair flows down past her incredible round ass, which is encased by her tight jeans that hug her round hips, thick thighs, and long, perfect legs. Her top is ripped, and she tied it under her huge breasts, her nipples pebbling the material.

My cock thickens behind my robe, which I quickly close so she doesn't see, as my mouth goes dry and my fangs lengthen with my need to taste her.

When she turns her head and looks directly at me, I swear she can sense my need. Her glossy, full lips curve up in a grin.

When she was chained, she was skin and bones, with blue veins under her skin. She was already dying. I felt it the moment Azul dragged her in for sentencing when each of us brought our sinners for the weekly judgement, but even then, she called to that dead part of me, the one that exists between the underworld and this world. I was intrigued, but I knew my duty, and I did it alongside the others.

Now, here she stands as one of us.

"So I caught the name Nathair," she begins when none of us speak. There is no norm for this, as there's never been a female judge. Luckily, Nathair, the oldest, steps forward to handle the introduction like he did for all of us.

As the first of the judges, the first blood king, he has the most experience.

"I am Nathair," he responds. "I am the oldest blood king here."

"I see, and you all have to wear robes and masks continually?" She grins wider. "Don't get me wrong, it's a hot look, but I am curious."

Nathair chuckles silkily, making my cock jerk as I recall the way that feels when he feeds. With a dramatic flourish, he removes his mask, holding it at his side as he allows her to see his beauty.

He is the most beautiful man to ever walk this earth, and it is both his curse and part of his monstrous nature.

Her eyebrow arches as she scans his face, taking in his long black hair streaked with hints of blue, his slightly upturned, almond-shaped eyes, and his bright blue irises surrounded by long lashes. His high cheekbones almost look too sharp, as does his jaw, but his plump lips offer a softer contrast. Nathair's eyebrows arch perfectly above his eyes and taper straight across his brow, and his skin is pale—not as pale as mine, but still pale.

When I first saw him, I thought he was an angel or demon coming to claim my soul.

"Is that better, Althea?" he asks.

I see her startle, and then her eyes simmer with lust as she looks him over. "So, Nathair, are you two the only ones who speak?" She looks at me then. "And your name is?"

For a moment, I cannot speak with all that power and beauty aimed at me. "Osis," I reply, my voice still hoarse. I lean back into the wall to stop myself from going to her, knowing we must discuss this first and make her understand her duty now. "At your service, Althea."

"The others speak," Nathair says huskily, giving me a reprieve from her attention, and when her gaze moves to him, I sag like she has taken my power with her. "They are simply as shocked as we."

"Shocked?" she asks. "The mark . . ."

"Did the person who offered you the choice explain what it meant?" he asks, gesturing at the sofas before he sits delicately on an armchair. She sinks gracefully onto the sofa, seemingly unconcerned about being surrounded by the beings who killed her.

"No. She said I could come back and that I could help, but it wouldn't be easy."

"And why did you choose to come back?" he inquires, asking the question he gave all of us.

No doubt feeling its importance, she mulls it over, so I step forward and tell her, "I chose to come back because I wasn't ready to die. I wanted so much more."

She looks up at me before smiling softly. "I chose to come back because most of my vampyr life has been spent in pain, rotting from a rejected mate bond, and I wanted to feel life without it. I wanted to make up for my sins and help if I could. Death will always be there, waiting."

"Very astute," Nathair remarks, sounding pleased, and she sits up straighter.

"Well, Althea, when you made that choice, it sealed your future. You are now a judge, like us. We are not selected often, usually hundreds of years apart, and the gods pick us. They are fickle creatures, so it usually takes them awhile to agree."

"A judge . . . I'm a judge as in I kill sinners now like you killed me?" she asks.

He nods. "Let me start at the beginning. This was once the Court of Night, or Nox, if you wish. The vampyrs here were great, and their powers were over the creatures of night, which some people called nightmares. They let it corrupt them, and the power went to their heads, so the ruling kings had no choice. They killed them all and destroyed the court, leaving it to be forgotten. I know because I was once the king of this court."

Her eyebrow rises, but she lets him carry on.

"I was young then, and my father had gone mad, so I took the throne by force to try to save my people, but it did not work. I was also corrupt, and when I died, I was judged. The gods offered me a choice to make up for it, and they brought me back to mete out justice on our kind who are tainted and cruel. I was to protect those who couldn't protect themselves and to make up for my past sins. I, a creature of night, of nightmares, was reborn, and so was this court. The others came after, each with their own talents and powers that are their own to discuss or disclose with you. And now, we have you, the first female, the first queen. They chose you for a reason, Althea, and we will find out why. It will take time, but you will find your duty and your place. For now, however, I am sure you are hungry."

"Starving," she purrs.

"How long has it been since you fed on another vamp?" he asks.

She swallows but refuses to look away. "A long time. After the rejection . . ."

"You couldn't." He nods as he begins to unbuckle his robe. "You should know that we are technically dead, and like the mate bond, we cannot feed from other vamyprs, only the other judges. It is our curse and our salvation. You will only be able to feed from us now, and only from those who are willing. As you know, feeding can be sexual, but between us, it does not have to be. That is your choice. Today, you will feed from me. As the oldest, my blood is the strongest and will heal you quicker." He parts his robe, and I move around to watch. The others step closer to do the same, their own hunger on the air.

She grips the edge of the sofa to hold herself back, even as her fangs ache.

He tilts his head, exposing his long, pale, muscular neck, his hair lying across his chest like a silken curtain.

"Are you sure?" she asks. "My hunger is strong, and it has been too long, so I will not be gentle."

"I can take your fangs, Althea, do not worry. Feed." He holds his arms open.

We all wait with bated breath. One second, she is gripping onto the sofa, and the next, she springs through the air before climbing gracefully onto his lap. My blood sings, and my fangs ache with the wish to drink from her while she drinks from him, but I know she needs to feed.

She may need more than one of us. Who is willing? Nathair asks through our bond.

Me, we all answer, making him grin as she whines.

Good, then be ready. Our queen is ravenous.

We will provide, we reply instantly.

Gripping his hair, she turns his head and sinks her fangs into his neck.

He groans and closes his eyes as his hand comes up to her head and holds her against him. "That's it. Feed, my queen. Take it all, it's yours now. Your blood is ours, and our blood is yours."

He lets us feel his pleasure through the bond as she draws his blood into her. We feel her fangs in his neck and the slide of her skin against his. He overloads us with sensations until we are all desperate to feed her, pushing forward as she drinks and drinks.

She takes more of his ancient blood than any of us have ever been able to consume, drinking until his head lolls back.

I free my arm and step closer to her, ripping my fangs into my skin none too gently to entice her. She sniffs and turns her head, staying on Nathair's lap as she sinks her fangs into my skin. I fall to my knees, my back bowing as pleasure explodes through me. She pulls me closer, and the pain and pleasure of her fangs become too much as I roar out my release, falling to the side as she drinks deeply from me as well.

Sitting back, she licks her blood-covered lips as Azul silently slides closer, slipping around her like the ghost he is. He holds her up as he offers his thick, tanned forearm, and I almost jerk in shock. He must be feeling the need to bond with her after all, because he never offers himself willingly after what happened to him. She hesitates as if sensing this, and his voice comes, deep and from beyond the grave.

"Feed, little one."

Sinking her fangs into his flesh, she groans and rolls her hips against Nathair, who watches her with hooded, desire-filled eyes, but what he said is true. None of us will touch her this time, not even if she begs. She doesn't understand what that would mean.

She manages to make our silent ghost grunt, and then he glides away, and she sits back.

"Are you full?" Nathair murmurs as she curls up into him. He strokes her hair as I slide in, pulling her feet over my shoulder and touching every part of her I can.

"Mmm," she hums happily.

"Good, then rest for now," he murmurs, and we all watch as her eyes slide closed.

Just like we did when it was our time, she falls into deep slumber while her body changes.

"We will need to prepare her to drink from the rest of you," Nathair whispers. He's right. The others' blood is potent but different, especially Lycus's. "But only if you wish to feed her."

We feel their affirmation through the bond, and he grins like he knew their answers.

"Then let us finish our duty for the night. I will carry her to an empty chamber and allow her to slumber, and when she awakens, we will explain everything else." The others take one last look at her, and he chuckles. "She will still be here. Go deal with the aftermath of the judgement."

Nodding, they depart, and he turns his head to me. "Osis," he warns.

I lift my mask and lean closer, breathing her in before getting to my feet and heading off to help the dead cross, even if my mind is on Althea.

NATHAIR

She looks far too beautiful curled up in my lap. I wish to keep her here forever, but I know my duty, and I cannot force the others to do it without helping them, so I gather her and stand. She sighs and snuggles closer, her floral scent wrapping around me.

She is the most beautiful treasure I have ever seen in my long life, and after a lifetime of only being around the other kings, I find myself desperate for her softness.

As I remember the way her fangs sank into me, I almost stumble. None has ever hungered for my blood quite as much as she did. The old king that I was, the cruel mad bastard, would not have offered to let anyone feed on him, but now it is my duty to allow all of them to, and I do it gladly, knowing the blood exchange is important.

She had drunk so sweetly, so deeply, it shocked me, but I would have happily offered up every single drop I had to her.

A queen.

She's such a rarity, an anomaly, but I see why they chose her. Even close to death, she had poise, composure, and an inner strength that impressed me so much, I had been kind to her when I never had been before. Her deeds were no less heinous than any of ours, but she paid for them, and at least hers were for good, if misguided.

So yes, I see why the gods chose her, but I do wonder how this will change us.

Maybe change is good.

"Nathair?" she whispers, half asleep and adorable as I move through our court.

"Shh, sleep, Althea, we will keep you safe," I promise as I head into the welcoming darkness, my feet knowing where to take me without thinking. After all, this place was once my home, filled with such power, death, and monstrous beauty.

The hallways used to dance with people and life, but now they remain empty, filled only with ghosts of the dead as a constant reminder of how I failed.

"Thank you." She sighs. "Thank you for killing me."

I look down once more as her eyes slide closed. When I killed her, she said I freed her, and the look of relief on her face was so strong that I felt it in my soul. After all, hadn't I felt that way once, freed from torment and madness by death?

"You are welcome, Althea, but I am glad you are back. I am glad you are one of us. Now sleep," I order, pushing some power into the command, and she slides back into slumber. She will need it for what is to come.

I could head to many of the chambers that remain empty, but instead I head to the one I could never bear to reopen, although the others kept it clean—my mother's chamber.

She was queen before my father killed her.

The rooms were sealed up on my order after her death, after I took the crown from him to protect our people, but it is the only place I can imagine that is suitable for one like her—a true queen. Her soul reminds me of my mother's.

I head past the thrones and up the stairs to the room that overlooks them. The door unlocks at my approach, and a fire roars to life, warming the giant stone room. The white fur rug of the wolf my mother killed in battle still lies on the floor, and the deer leather chairs before the fire remind me of a time when I used to sit there before bed as a child, escaping my father and his declining mental stability.

The huge four-poster bed stands to the left near where I entered, and the balcony shutters are locked and long since sealed. The rooms behind hold her gowns, jewels, and bathing chambers.

The room is decorated in all black, with accents of yellow and royal purple, and although no one has stayed here in hundreds of years, it's clean. I lay her gently under the sheets, removing her boots before I tuck her in and brush her hair back as I press a gentle kiss to her brow.

"Sleep, my queen, and when you awaken, you will meet those you are destined for."

With that, I close the room and resume my duties, joining my brothers, my fellow kings.

TEN
ALTHEA

I WAKE, FEELING COMFORTABLE and restored, and for the first time in a long time, I am full and filled with power and strength. Stretching under the luscious silk sheets, I let out a soft sigh and sit up, pushing my hair from my face.

There, standing before a fire, a masked man watches me. His mask is in place but other than that, the only thing he wears are black cargo pants. His midnight skin is on display, stretched over huge muscles and streaked with highlights. His nipples are pierced and chained together, and tattoos dance across his skin of lightning, sun, moons, and wind.

He's huge, bigger than even Nathair, and I know he isn't one I've tasted.

"Who are you?" I ask without an ounce of fear, knowing I don't have to be afraid of them.

Whatever or whoever he is, he's one of them, and now someone I am bound to it seems, which is made apparent by the mark over his heart.

"Conall," he responds, his voice deep like thunder. I remember it from my judgement.

"You controlled the shadows, the darkness," I murmur as I slide from the bed and stretch before padding over to him and curling up in a chair, watching him curiously.

"I did, but that is not all I can do," he murmurs.

"No?" I ask.

"Ah, but that would be revealing all my secrets." I almost feel him winking at me. "I came to check on you. You slept a long time, but then again, I remember I did also after . . ."

"After dying?" I murmur.

"Yes," he says without shame. "After Nathair killed me and I made the choice to come back and face what I had done."

"It seems we all have a similar story," I reply carefully.

"We were all sinners reborn, nightmares," he says. "Now come, Althea, the others are waiting. Reve has selected some clothes for you to change into if you wish. They wait in the bathroom."

He stands and goes to leave, so I stand also. "Conall?"

He stills, waiting for me to continue.

"Do you regret coming back?"

"Not once," he answers. "I have found friendship, family, loyalty, and more importantly, I am able to pay for my past and help those who people like us hurt. I am proud of being a judge, and you will understand why soon."

He leaves, and I watch him go before looking at the fire and blowing out a breath. A lot has happened.

I died, I saw my mother, and I chose to come back to life to become a judge. I still don't fully know what that means, but I guess I will find out. First, I need to shower off the stench of dried blood and death, and then I'll go find the others and figure out what comes next.

Whatever it is, though, I know it is a chance for a better future, and if they don't regret coming back, how could I?

The whole world lies before me once more. It just so happens to come with a tie to seven masked men.

Deciding just to get moving, I find the clothes waiting in the bathroom like Conall said. I raise my eyebrows at the pinned leather shorts, fishnets, boots, ripped crop top, and my leather jacket. Shrugging out of my ruined shirt, I step into the shower, sighing at the heat as it washes away the blood and death, my hands sliding over the mark on my chest.

Knowing I'm wasting time, I get dressed and leave my hair to dry naturally, and then I leave the room I'm in, finding myself above the throne room. As I walk across it, I see no sign of the deaths that took place here yesterday, and for a moment, I wander closer to the thrones.

One has skulls across it, another gates, and the third has the sun and moon. Another has a snake, the next a spider, one has fire, and the next has a palace. Do the markings represent each person?

"Ah, there you are," Nathair calls, and I turn to find him in silk sleep pants and nothing else—not that I'm complaining because he truly is the most beautiful man I've ever seen. I lick my lips, remembering the way he tasted. He looks me over and nods in approval before holding out his hand. "Come, the others are waiting."

I move closer to him, and he grabs my hand, pressing it to his arm and holding it there as he escorts me to another room. The gesture indicates just how old he truly is, but I know it's rude to ask.

He chuckles. "It is, but I will answer. I am over two centuries," he says. I stop, and he grins. "I will answer all your questions, Althea, now come." He tugs me into moving. "First, how are you feeling?"

"Better than I have in a long time," I admit.

"Very good. I hope my mother's rooms were acceptable?" His voice holds no inflection, but a shadow of pain slides through my head.

"Your mother's rooms?"

He simply nods as he leads me through a maze of corridors.

"They were lovely." Unsure what else to say, I fall into silence as I look around. A thousand questions crowd my mind, but I am uncertain where to start.

He lets me debate them as he leads me into a surprisingly modern kitchen. The dark stone continues here, and it's all state-of-the-art.

Huge chandeliers hang from the high ceilings, and sliding, bifold doors open to the darkness beyond. It still holds the same gothic feel, and I fall in love with it right there and then. The kitchen is mainly to the left, with black cabinets with golden decorative handles, a huge stove, and plants draped across surfaces. Before it is a giant island with red and black stools with golden buttons, and pans hang above it all in copper and gold.

To the right is a giant black table with matching red-velvet wingback chairs, and that's where the others are gathered. A pot of tea is poured, though some are on something stronger if my quick inhale tells me anything. There is no seat at the head, with all the chairs spread around the sides, and Nathair leads me to the seat on the very left. He slides it out, and I sit as he pushes it under. I thank him as he rounds the table to sit opposite me.

Everyone but Nathair wears his mask, I begin to wonder what they truly look like underneath.

"Do I get a mask?" I ask instead, and someone barks out a sharp laugh.

"I hope so," the one who laughed responds, his voice laced with amusement. "Reve," he says, answering my unasked question, and with a flourish, he pulls the mask off. "They can be stuffy though." He winks as I take him in.

He is not what I was expecting. Where Nathair looks like a creature of night, old and traditional, Reve is clearly completely different. He's no less striking and handsome in an almost feral way. His black hair is streaked with pure, shocking white and slicked back past his tattooed and pierced ears. His neck is covered in ink, telling a story I don't understand, and his face is softer than Nathair's but still sharp. Reve's eyebrows are almost too stern, giving him a menacing mien, and his smile is on the edge of insanity. His nose is wide with a spike through the bridge, and his eyes are completely black. More tattoos continue on his face and forehead, as well as one striking across his cheek to his lips, which tilt up farther.

"Look away, Althea," he purrs. "I may not have been one you fed from last night, but I am offering now and in the future."

"Reve," Nathair snaps. "She must understand first."

"Of course," he agrees, but there's a wicked lilt to his brogue—Irish maybe?

More tattoos continue down his arms as he throws his leather duster back to reveal a skintight black shirt underneath. Tattoos also cover his hands, fingers, and arms. Some have colour, and some are black and white, but all are striking and give him a modern yet untouchable feel.

Like a rockstar.

I have to drag my eyes away from his beauty and glance at the others. Conall sits in darkness, shadows dancing around him. Osis is close, almost leaning forward to see me, yet I still haven't seen either of their faces.

I try to remember the others' names and come up blank.

Nathair must hear my unsaid plea because he takes my hand and plays with my fingers as he answers. "You have now met Reve and me, obviously. You fed from Osis and Azul last night." He indicates a man sitting opposite me, his skin just as perfect as I remember. He's bulky though not the size of Conall, but definitely still big. "We also have Lycus." He gestures to a man sitting far away from me.

He's massive, and I wonder how I did not see him before. Power rolls off him, as does an enticing spicy scent. Nearly all his skin is covered, and his mask is firmly in place.

"Zale," Nathair tells me.

The man sits next to Lycus. His long, wavy brown hair is streaked with lighter brown highlights, and it tumbles over his shoulder. His face is concealed by the mask, but some tanned skin is on display under his silk robe.

"The seven judges. Each was chosen for a reason, and each will decide when they wish to show you their face. It is and always will remain their choice. But now I must explain things."

"Please," I murmur.

"First, would you like something to drink?" Nathair's words are innocent, but flashes of blood and fangs fill my mind, and my eyes dart to the delectable Reve who smirks. Everyone shifts, and the air tightens with hunger, as if they sense the direction of my thoughts.

Reve leans forward, winking at me. "As I said, any time," he purrs.

"Reve," Nathair warns, but there's a familiar teasing note in his tone. "I meant tea? Wine?"

Reve slides from his chair with a wicked grin, and I watch the sway of his peachy ass in his tight trousers as he moves around the kitchen with ease. The sensual way he moves makes my fangs descend, and hunger ignites within me, but when Nathair starts to speak, I drag my gaze away.

"As I explained, you are a judge now, and there are rules. You will learn our stories, our history, and our secrets, and there is never anything but truth between us. There must be. The bond will pull us closer than ever, but you and they will decide in what manner—friends or lovers. Nothing is decided, but there are certain . . . members that if you choose to feed from, we will need to discuss first, but that can wait until later. We know much of you from your blood, but we will not ask if you do not want us to. Think of us as family, since that is what we will be now. You cannot feed from others outside of the seven of us, that is true, and I, Osis, Azul, and Reve have already volunteered to allow you to feed from us—"

"She can feed from me," Lycus volunteers, his voice spinning a web of darkness and silken sheets.

For a moment, shock reverberates around the room. I eye him and then Nathair.

"Are you sure, brother?" Nathair asks carefully.

"I will require help, but yes," he concludes. I want to ask, but I don't think now is the time.

"So be it, as I said no one will be forced to feed you."

"You never asked the rest of us," Conall interjects and then turns to me, his masked face locking on me. "You are free to feed from me."

"And me," Zale offers.

Sighing, Nathair shakes his head. "As I was saying, you can feed from all of us, it seems. You will never go hungry again, and the more you feed, the more power you will obtain. When we died, we all had certain . . . abilities. Since our deaths and rebirths, they have only been heightened. There is a reason they call us blood kings and nightmares, but you will learn that in time as we explore what your power is."

I almost shrink, knowing I have no special abilities—not like my mother or them, it seems. Great, I'm just another outcast, even now.

"You are not an outcast, Althea," Nathair says angrily, tilting my head with a finger and forcing me to meet his gaze. "Not here, trust me on that. We are the things in the dark others fear, but you will never have to. We're all outcasts."

"How did—" I start.

"When we shared blood, it cemented the bond. I can read some of your thoughts, but only those you are projecting loudly. I will teach you how to conceal them if you wish so you can communicate better," he murmurs.

"So you can read my thoughts? Can I read yours?"

Instantly, the silence in my head is replaced by clear, succulent thoughts about how he wishes to feed from me, how he thinks I am the most beautiful creature he has ever seen, and how he wishes the others will come to me so I can bring them from the darkness. He allows me to see and feel it all before pulling back.

"I have years of practice at silencing my thoughts and blocking others. It can be quite loud inside our heads if not, but all you have to do is ask, and I will always show you." He takes my hand and kisses the back of it.

Reve places a teacup filled with black liquid before me, as well as an ornate gold and black wine glass filled with amber liquid.

"The tea is a concoction Conall makes, and the wine is Zale's doing. Both are excellent." He leans down, his lips brushing my ear. "They are almost as delicious as you." With that, he moves back to his chair, leaving me weak-kneed and licking my lips.

Not wanting to hurt anyone's feelings, I pick up both, tasting the wine first since it's cool. The flavours of amber, jasmine, and sandalwood dance across my tongue. It reminds me of fire and warmth as it slides through me, making me moan out loud. The resulting hiss from the others causes me to silence it and lick my lips before tasting the tea.

The comforting warmth of shadows, darkness, and cosy nights fills my mind, and I moan again.

"She's going to kill us all," Reve teases, holding a goblet of wine delicately in one hand, his other arm slung over the back of his chair as he watches me with a hungry expression.

"Indeed," Nathair replies.

"They are both incredible," I say, thanking Conall and Zale for each before turning back to Nathair, who seems to be in charge. "So we can communicate telepathically after feeding, I can choose whom to feed from, and we are bonded now. Oh, and I am to be a judge."

"Yes," he replies, wearing a smile filled with happiness. "For now, we will have no judgements for a month or so to allow you time to hone your skills and heal. Your life has taken its toll, and we want you to be healthy and happy. This court is now yours. You are welcome anywhere here, and I will gladly tell you of its history if you wish. You should spend time with all of us and get to know us to deepen the bonds between us. It is important when it comes to judging that we are as one. For now, I will not overload you with information, but there are a few important things you must know."

I nod my head, and he leans forward.

"We do not kill unless we must. It is our duty to judge those who put our people and those of the other species in harm's way. We never kill for pleasure or revenge. We do not feed from the unwilling, and only from judges. Our existence remains a mystery, and that is the way we like it. You will never ascend to a throne other than the one in our court, and you will never take place in society. You will be apart from it. We do not leave this place unless needed."

"Why?" I ask curiously.

"It is easier," is all he says. "There are some who know of our presence and find it . . . repulsive. You will never mate another—"

"Been there, done that, no thanks," I mutter, making Reve and a few others laugh.

"And finally, we will always do our duty, now and forever. This is not a choice."

I nod in understanding.

"Good," he purrs. "Now, onto the fun stuff, as Reve declares it. Being a judge isn't all bad. Yes, we kill and have a serious duty, but the rewards are plentiful. We are more powerful than we would have ever been in life, and we have freedom not afforded to those when assigned to a court for life. We can go anywhere if we please and explore anything we wish. There will never be any judgement between us, ever, and your darkness is ours now," Nathair promises as I sip the tea. Before I know it, the cup is empty, so I switch to the wine, feeling the burn sliding down my throat and warming me from within.

"That's a lot to take in," I murmur, relaxing into my chair. "So what now?"

"Now, whatever you wish. Explore, rest, or eat. This court is yours, as are we," Nathair says, a wicked lilt to his voice.

"Are you hungry?" Osis murmurs, watching me carefully.

"Starving," I tease, and he jerks before hurrying to his feet and moving to the kitchen.

A moment later, Nathair's voice floats into my head. *Be careful with him, draya. He is desperate to please and love, and he has focused his intentions on you.*

I nod, telling him I understand, and since I don't know how to speak into his mind, I show him the truth—that I have no intention of hurting anyone the way I was.

We know, draya.

Before I know it, my wine is finished, and I reluctantly put the goblet down before turning to Zale. "The wine is incredible. I have never tasted anything like it."

"I make it myself," he says, his voice like embers on a dark night. "It is a hobby I learned."

"It's brilliant. The courts would go wild for it." Leaning in like I have a secret to share, I wink. "Good job it's just ours."

A delectable laugh floats from behind his mask, wrapping around me like a lover's caress. I tighten my thighs to suppress the flood of warmth and need between them. It seems like I'll be walking around needy all the time.

Not necessarily, draya. I'm sure my brothers are more than happy to oblige. I know I am.

Unsure what to say to that, I clear my throat and smile at Zale's mask. I don't ask why they hide, it isn't my place, so instead I study it. The front is the same ornate silver and black as the others, but the design tells a story. Flames lick at the edges, as do reaching hands, and at the very top is a baying black dog.

They will choose when to reveal themselves, draya. Some are known, while others have been used and abused and prefer the anonymity.

I'm glad Nathair is guiding me, so I nod in understanding.

"Here," Osis offers softly and places a plate before me. It holds the biggest pizza I have ever seen.

"Did . . . Did you just make this?" I ask, peering up at his mask. I don't know how, but I can tell he's smiling behind it.

"Of course."

He makes pizza.

I think I'm in love.

His head drops as I feel a blast of happiness from him, and I realise I may have projected that thought too loudly. Unwilling to take it back, I thank him and take a bite, moaning as the cheese melts in my mouth.

"Either this is fucking incredible or food has never tasted this good," I murmur after I swallow.

"Death has a way of enhancing things." Nathair winks. "But also, Osis is one of the best chefs I have ever met."

"Nathair is a flatterer," Osis says, embarrassment colouring his voice.

"Nope, I've had plenty of pizza, trust me. Simon and I—" I swallow thickly at the reminder of my best friend. "Well, let's just say I've had my fair share of pizza." Now my stomach feels like lead, but I eat anyway because it would be rude not to.

Simon thinks I'm dead or worse.

He'll never know I'm better. I was a fool to run. He would have stayed and loved me forever, but then he would have never had his own life. It doesn't mean I don't miss him. Nathair mentioned that we don't play the other courts' games, and no doubt Simon is at court now in his own place, maybe with a mate.

"Simon? I sense a great love there," Nathair queries carefully, his voice tight.

"My best friend," I reply.

For a moment, jealousy slams into me before it quickly dissipates, and I realise it wasn't mine. I'm unable to stop the smile curving my lips. "He has excellent taste in films. We pretty much lived together since we were kids and shared everything," I tease. "Oh, and he's very, very gay," I finish as I take the last bite of pizza.

I notice a lot of shoulders slumping in relief, and I'm unable to stop the giggle from escaping my lips.

"Oh, Nox, he would have loved seeing you all jealous because of him. In fact, no, he would have been flirting with every single one of you," I tease.

"You miss him," Nathair concludes.

"A great deal. He was the only family I had left," I tell him.

There's a deep silence filled with pain as I debate every single choice I made that led me here.

"I like movies," Osis says. "We even have a cinema. It was a nightmare to upgrade the wiring, but we did it."

The innocent, friendly way he says it as he tries to help me almost brings tears to my eyes. I see what Nathair meant about being careful with him. There's almost a fragile innocence to him that I didn't expect.

"Then you'll have to show me one day," I reply, offering him a grateful smile.

"We do not wish to overwhelm you. We all know how taxing the change is, so feel free to go back to your chamber if you wish, and if you need anything in there changed, let any one of us know and we'll do it."

"I've slept enough," I murmur. "I'd like to look around, if that's okay?"

"I'll show her!" many voices reply, startling me with the volume.

Nathair laughs. "I think only one needs to be her guide so it isn't too much. Reve, why don't you?"

Reve looks shocked to have been picked, but he smiles silkily at me. "Gladly." His response tells me he's thinking more about what he could personally show me than the court, but I smile back and stand.

"Oh, and Althea?" Nathair catches my hand once more. "Welcome to the Court of Nightmares."

Eleven

Althea

Reve leads me away from the kitchen. I find myself watching him more than our surroundings before he catches me and winks. Looking away, I take in the huge court. Done in mostly ornate black, grey, and gold with gothic features, it's more beautiful than I expected. He guides me past the kitchen to a less formal sitting room decorated in leather with a pool table, huge TV, a bar, and much more before we sweep out. Next is a formal dining room with large black chairs, a table long enough for a banquet, and doors leading to the kitchen. Beyond that are two open doors that go outside. He stops there and gestures out.

"We have miles of grounds and courtyards, but beware in the dark because the nightmares like to play," he teases, licking one fang as he watches me.

"Nightmares never scared me," I reply as I step out without an ounce of fear, and I am transported into an entirely different world.

Beyond is an octagonal courtyard with a dragon statue in the middle, and flowing out in different directions is ornate concrete flooring. The courtyard has open archways made from the same stone as the inside, with flowers of all colours draping over everything. Beyond, I see more grounds, like Reve promised. There's a maze to the left, and to the right is a flower garden, greenhouse, lawn, pool, and so much more.

There is too much to see before he pulls me back inside. We go back through the throne room, which seems to be in the centre of the court, and out into another wing.

"Here are the living quarters. They used to be extensive and full, but now that there are less of us, only a few rooms are occupied." He stops before an open door and grins. "This is mine, just in case you ever need it."

"Sure." I chuckle as I look farther down the corridor to see closed doors and cobwebs. "This place is huge."

"It was once the biggest court in the entire world," Reve replies.

"What happened?" I ask.

"What happens to anything? It was destroyed by greed and pain, and now only forgotten relics and death inhabit it." He winks, leading me back through the throne room and to another corridor. "You might have noticed that the throne and judgement room is the centre, like a pentagram, with corridors leading off. We have the living quarters and the common rooms, and this corridor is filled with the hobby rooms, as we call it. There are rooms to read, explore herbology, magic, gems—whatever you wish, this court has it."

I peek into the rooms, but there are just so many that I barely get a glimpse, and then we are moving onto the next point in the pentagram. "Down here is the history of the court," Reve informs me.

I smirk when I spot Conall in the shadows, following us, but I say nothing, allowing Reve to show me around.

"Nathair can tell you more about this place. I only know what he has told me or I have gleaned from his memories, but it was once a thriving place filled with power, and their control over beasts of the night was legendary." He licks his lips as he turns and walks backwards, watching me. "Though I guess yours will also be now." He cocks his head for a moment. "Wait here, Nathair needs me." He disappears back where we came from, leaving me to my own devices on the tour.

"Are you going to stay in the shadows?" I call to Conall as I turn to see him.

He's more of a silhouette, a feeling that he's there, than a person. The darkness wraps around him, obscuring him, and when he doesn't reply or move, I smile. "Fine." I step into the darkness, and a gasp slips from my mouth at the sensation.

Power flows over me, judging me, before I am welcomed into the shadows, and then I find myself right before him, where he leans into the wall.

"Why are you hiding?" I murmur.

"I am not." He sniffs. "I am so used to moving in the darkness, it is a habit," he adds as an afterthought.

"So can anyone see us?" I ask, looking back, but the hallway beyond almost seems like a memory with the darkness shielding most of it.

"The others can, but only because I allow it. Anyone else would see nothing but shadows."

"So you allowed me to see you," I tease, stepping closer. "Why?"

"Because I am unable to resist when it comes to you," he replies, his voice hungry behind his mask.

I crave to know what he looks like, but just like his darkness and shadows, his mask is another thing to hide behind.

"You hunger," he snarls.

"I'm fine," I respond automatically.

"The more you are able to feed in the first days after the change, the more powerful you will be. You almost drained three of us last night and hunger still. Very powerful indeed," he murmurs, and his reminder causes a hunger I was so used to ignoring to roar to the forefront of my mind. "You seem oblivious to your own hunger, however, so I will make the others aware that they need to remind you to feed."

The sweetness of that notion is almost my undoing. "I guess I am so used to being hungry, I didn't notice," I admit with a wince. Now that he mentioned it and I focus on it, my body growls with hunger, and I lean into him, knowing he's a source of sustenance. The scent of his blood calls to me, even through his skin.

"I have already volunteered to feed you, Althea, so you do not have to ask." Hearing my name in his rocky tone makes me shiver.

"I do not want to take what is not offered," I admit shyly.

For a moment, he stares at me, then suddenly, his huge hand rips off his mask, and he lets it clatter to the floor as I gape at his face.

Beautiful is not a word that would do him justice.

I don't know how he could ever hide such a face, but I cannot seem to stop staring now. His face is the same colour as the rest of his body, and just as thick and square. He's powerful and masculine. His square jaw is covered by a dark brown beard that continues down his neck, and his moustache outlines his pouty pink lips and smiling white teeth with huge fangs.

He has a mole on the top left of his cheek, below the brownest eyes I have ever seen. His irises are so deep, with echoes of gold in them, and they are surrounded by long, thick lashes. He has heavy, brown eyebrows between a thick nose with golden chains looped through piercings that thread back and forth in four lines across the bridge. His hair is dreadlocked and the same colour as his beard.

He's absolutely stunning, and I am speechless.

"You are not the same creature you were before, Thea." The nickname nearly makes me swoon. "You do not ever have to ask with us, but if it will help, you can. The answer will always be yes. We are yours now, just as you are ours. Our blood pumps to feed you, to power you, our hands work to protect and provide for you, and our bodies are alive to pleasure you."

I jerk at that, and he grins.

"But for now, feed, little one." He tugs me closer, but I cannot reach his neck. He is simply too big. Chuckling, he reaches down and slides one arm under my ass, lifting with ease until my hands grip his shoulders and my mouth is directly against his neck. Turning his head, he exposes his thumping pulse, and the sweetness of his blood fills the shadows around us.

"Feed, Thea," he commands, sounding breathless as his hand tightens on my ass, tugging me closer until I'm pressed against the length of his huge, hard body.

My fangs ache, but I lean in and kiss his neck in gratitude before licking his vein. He shudders against me, leaning back into the wall. Gripping his shoulders, I sink my fangs into his neck.

The explosion of his blood has my eyes sliding closed as I wrap my legs around him. He grunts and holds me tighter as I drink. The protectiveness of shadows and the welcoming darkness slides through my body, and the rich flavour of his blood makes me rub against him.

Desire, a feeling I thought long since dead, surges through me as I rock against him without thought.

"Thea," he growls, dragging me up and down his hard length, which is pressed against his trousers. "Fuck." His head bangs back against the wall, and his whole body shakes as I feed harder, tasting as much of his blood as I can.

Turning with a roar, he slams my back into the wall as his hands stroke my body and his hips thrust.

I'm finally sated, his power almost making me high, so I pull back and meet his blown eyes with my own. His blood covers my lips and chin as it leaks from the holes in his neck.

Both of us are panting and rocking together, and it's only then I realise that the shadows have fallen away, and leaning against the wall opposite is Reve.

"Oh, don't let me stop you," he teases, wearing a cocky grin.

Conall groans, pressing his head into my neck as he shakes. With my eyes on Reve, I lean down and lick the puncture marks, watching as his eyes narrow and his fangs descend.

"Didn't they ever tell you not to play with monsters?" he purrs as he pushes from the wall and comes towards us, pressing to Conall's back before licking the blood on his skin.

Conall groans and shifts his hips against me. "Fuck, if you both don't stop, I'm going to come in my trousers, and I hate getting the stains out."

"What do you say, baby? Shall we play with him or help him out?"

"I do like games. Plus, a few stains never hurt anyone," I purr, and with a wicked grin, Reve and I sink our fangs into Conall's neck.

He roars and slams me harder against the wall as he pumps his hips. I taste his release, his pleasure, in his blood as we both pull out and lap at the puncture marks. Conall slumps, and Reve wraps an arm around him, keeping us up until he can stand.

Reve grins. "Best tour yet."

"I think I'll like it here." I giggle, blood drunk.

They both laugh as we stand there, wrapped in darkness and covered in blood and desire.

My blood flows with a power so strong, I didn't even know it was possible.

In the dark, a whisper comes.

I told you not to fear the dark, daughter. Now make them yours.

TWELVE
ZALE

EVERYTHING FEELS DIFFERENT NOW.

A queen.

There has never been a queen on the judges' thrones. It is a changing of the times, one I am grateful for. The breath of fresh air Althea has brought has awakened a lot of my brothers and saved them from their mundane lives.

When she moaned my name around the wine I made? Well, I nearly lost it. Hence why I am now in the brewing room, checking on my stills. I want them to be perfect for her, but I also have a new flavour idea, one just for her.

Our queen.

Just as I begin focusing on my task, her scent hits me. She must be close or her blood has been spilled because it fills the air like a siren's call. I fall to my knees as need slams through me, holding back a howl as I thrust my hips.

Her scent drives me wild, and my back bows as I fall to all fours. The other half of me battles to be let free, to hunt down that scent and claim it. I hold it back with years of practice, but never before has it been this strong. Finally, when I can breathe, I clamber to my feet and fall against the table.

Unable to help it, I shove my hand into my trousers and palm my cock, fucking my hand quick and rough, her scent in my nose. I need to sink my fangs into flesh and draw blood. My skin heats to an unnatural degree from my powers that are clamouring to be released on her.

I have never felt such a strong desire in all of my years on this earth. I hear the others crowding my brain—they are feeling it too.

With a roar, my head drops back as I spray my release everywhere, but my cock still remains hard. I have somewhat better control, however, enough to turn when Lycus hurries into the room, his eyes wild and fangs extended.

"Brother," I call worriedly. He looks half crazed, and I see his skin moving with his gift.

"Calling to me," he growls, gripping the wall to hold himself back. "If I don't feed, I'll hunt her down."

"Fuck." Holding out my hand, I offer him what he needs. "Feed, brother. She isn't ready for that yet, so let me help you."

Relief fills his eyes, showing me how close he was to losing his very hard-won, careful control. It's incredible how easily our queen has toppled centuries of honing skills.

I taste his desperation in the air as he slides in behind me. His back is to the door to protect me as he feeds, an old habit from his life as a warrior.

I lean back into him as one arm slides across my chest and the other moves much lower, almost touching my erect cock. His bearded face rubs against my neck as he slowly thrusts his hard cock against my ass. Neither of us are strangers to each other's pleasures. After all, we have spent years here with just us men, so we learned not to care, but this time, it isn't about wanting each other's bodies—it's about needing her.

"She smells so good, doesn't she, brother?" I murmur, and he grunts, slamming me forward into the table with the force of his thrust. "Imagine I'm her if you want, I can take it."

My brother was dealt a cruel hand. Snarling, he sinks his fangs into my neck as his hand wraps around my cock, holding it tight as he drinks from my neck and rolls his hips. I lean back, trusting him, as I thrust into his hand and my blood pumps into him, strengthening our connection further.

Then, I can hear his thoughts as desperate, growled words in my head.

Tastes so good.

Imagine them mixed together, feeding from him as I fuck her.

Fuck, I can still smell her.

So close.

Fuck, I forgot how good he felt in my arms.

I only catch snippets of his conversation, but it has me groaning. "Ly." I thrust into his grip, and with a cry, I come again as he bows me back, pumping me with his venom as he drinks. It only heightens my pleasure.

A gasp has us both whirling.

I am still locked in Lycus's grip, with his fangs in my neck, and when I see her standing there. Our queen's mouth is open, her eyes are wide, and she looks so sexy I can't resist groaning and shifting forward, but Lycus hauls me back.

"Oh," she whispers.

I brace for rejection, for judgement, but instead, I see desire simmering in her eyes, and then her fangs lengthen, and the scent of her arousal winds around us. Lycus snarls and pulls his fangs from my neck so he doesn't rip it out—it wouldn't be the first time, nor would I care, but she might. He holds me up when I would have collapsed, and both of us just stare at her, unsure what to say or do.

Bet she doesn't want me now . . .

I hear him think, his self-hatred blasting loudly, and I almost bend in fear, nearly vomiting at the idea of her rejecting not just me but my brother who deserves nothing but love after everything he has been through.

It's only then I realise we are both unmasked.

Her eyes trace over my face before dropping to my cock, and then her tongue darts out, wetting her fangs before looking at what she can see of Lycus behind me. "I didn't mean to disturb—okay, that's a lie. I heard moans and followed them, but I'm not sorry."

"I—" I swallow, searching for something to say. "I guess we should explain." I wince. "We smelled your blood, and it, um, well, it affected all of us."

She holds up her hand, stepping into the room. "You don't owe me an explanation at all." She grins, making me shudder in Lycus's arms. "Are you two together?" she asks without judgement in her tone.

"Not like that," Lycus rumbles. "We have fucked, yes, and we shared blood. Zale is the only one who does not fear my drinking from him."

"The others do?" She frowns.

"They do not wish to. They do not even mean to, but sometimes they do, and I hate the tinge of fear, so I feed from Zale, who doesn't mind."

I shake my head, swallowing as he glances at me.

"Zale and . . . Lycus?" she guesses.

I feel him nod.

"Did the gods pick the hottest men alive or what?"

A laugh barks out of my chest as Lycus unwinds from me. I stuff my cock away as casually as I can, but the moment she looks at it, it gets hard again, and I have to shift in my jeans.

"Do all of the others feed and fuck at the same time?" she asks curiously, leaning into the wall.

"Not all." I shrug. "But I like to fuck and feed at the same time, and since we can only feed on each other . . ."

She nods. "Makes sense. Also, don't let me stop you. That was hot as hell to witness." I feel Ly jerk, and then she glances at him. "So why do they fear feeding you?"

He stiffens, and I feel his unease, but like the warrior my brother is, he tells her, no doubt to give her an out before he gets too attached. "The gifts the gods blessed me with help our cause, and they make me powerful, but there are also downsides . . ." I glance over to see him swallowing. "My bite is venomous, like a spider's bite. It can paralyze, can even kill if I intend it to. My blood . . . it's poison, *vecha*."

I startle at the endearment, my eyes widening. No matter how much Ly tries to pull away in case she rejects him, he can't seem to, like all of us.

"The others fear the venom without meaning to."

"They are idiots," she replies with a grin, and I snort. "Okay, maybe don't tell them that, but if you are worried that I fear your bite, Lycus, don't be." She slides closer to him, proving just that as she grins up at the giant. "I trust you." It's evident she means it, and then she winks at me. "And so does he."

God fucking damn, who created this woman and gave her to us?

She's fucking perfect. I feel her healing words washing through my brother and know he's as taken with her as I am.

"Anyway . . ." She claps. "I got lost when Reve went to shower, which I'm guessing now means he went to wank. Can anyone direct me?"

"Me," we both blurt, making her laugh, and I can't help but laugh alongside her.

Thirteen

Althea

Seriously, what is in the water—err, blood around here?

I walk between Lycus and Zale, and my tongue is thick with nerves. I'm experienced, and I've had my fun, but all of them look like walking gods. They are so far above me, and the power radiating from them is enough to leave me breathless.

I saw their insecurities, their worries, though, and I hope I didn't make it worse, but when they smile, it's like everything is right with the world again.

I know I thought my intended mate was the most beautiful man I had ever seen, but I was very, very wrong because here, in a forgotten court, I'm seeing what true beauty is, and it's more than their incredible faces. It's in their friendship, their love.

Zale is to my left, and he's nothing like I expected. He's taller than me, but only by a few inches, and he's stocky, muscle on muscle, but still skinnier than Lycus. His hair is styled like a wolf cut, which I saw is trending, and the deep brown, amber, and red locks fall in waves past his shoulders. His face is angular, with a shadowed jaw and lips, high cheekbones, and slitted orange eyes. One of his thick eyebrows has a scar through it. There's another scar running across his cheek on the right, and when Zale glances at me, I swear I can almost see a shadow moving beneath his skin.

Turning away quickly, I nearly stumble before I glance up and up at Lycus. His hand clutches my arm, catching me as he grins widely. He's massive, built with muscles that cover every inch of his body. He reminds of a giant or a Viking, and his wild hair and beard only help with that effect. His thick, black as night hair is currently in a bun on top of his head, with beads and bones threaded throughout. His beard is long and unkempt, surrounding thick lips with visible fangs. Lycus's stern, square face only adds to his appearance, with slanting black eyebrows and lines around his eyes and mouth. His hands are scarred, and his arms and chest are covered in black hair. Wearing nothing but some low-slung leather trousers with a strap across his chest for a weapon, he looks like a warrior of old. The whole look is finished with black leather knee-high boots with spikes on the sides.

Clearing my throat, I force myself to stop ogling them. "So, how old are you both?"

"Now that is a telling question." Zale winks, making me chuckle.

Lycus is just about to say something when we step into the throne room and freeze. A man, who I'm guessing is Azul, is standing without his mask on and having an animated conversation with . . . a wall.

"Erm, is he okay?" I ask softly.

"Not since I've known him," Lycus responds in a deadpan voice, and I gape as he chuckles.

"Did you just make a joke?" Zale exclaims. "Lycus made a joke!"

Reve pops out of nowhere, his hand going to Lycus's forehead. "Are you well?"

Azul turns and tilts his head, and I swear I could hear a laugh behind him.

"Fuck off," Lycus snaps, pushing away Reve, who just laughs.

"It's the scent of pussy, right?" Reve asks with a wink at me.

"This pussy will bitch slap you." I huff, crossing my arms.

"I'd love it. Do it right here." Reve turns his cheek, making me shake my head, even as a smile curves my lips.

Zale groans. "Don't encourage him." He knocks my shoulder, making me giggle.

They all become motionless, and I freeze. "What?" I ask, confused by the slack-jawed looks they are aiming at me.

"Nothing." Reve recovers first, but his smile is softer, and there's something in his eyes that wasn't there before.

"It's been a long time since the sound of laughter filled these halls," Nathair calls as he enters with Conall and Osis.

I blush slightly under all their adoring gazes.

Nathair notices Lycus and Zale at my sides, and for a moment, his eyes narrow, and I swear I hear them whispering in their minds before he smiles at me. "I figured you would need some new items. Reve and I have selected a wardrobe to be sent here, but is there anything else? Any comforts you would like? Anything in the world, Althea."

"Erm, no?" I reply hesitantly.

Nathair almost appears pained. "Anything?" he pleads.

I see the look in his eyes. He clearly wants to give me something, so I rack my brain. "I, um, like baths with different bubbles and bombs . . ."

"You could have everything in the world, regardless of the price or designer, and you pick bubble baths?" Reve asks before a grin splits his lips. "I love this girl. Let's keep her."

Azul hesitates as he moves closer, and I realise no one mentions the talking to nothing thing, so I don't either.

Nathair's voice comes then. *Azul's powers are . . . different, but he is not crazy—well, not crazier than any of us.*

My lips quirk as I send him a mental, *Thank you.* They all move around me as if waiting for my direction. "Erm, so what do you usually do all the time?"

They share a look, and Nathair speaks for them. "Usually we work, but . . ."

"Well, you're more interesting," Reve teases, making me grin.

She will never smile at me like that.

The voice is sudden, sharp, and filled with so much pain, I almost stagger.

Nathair frowns as he reaches out. "Are you okay?"

Evidently, he didn't hear it, but I see Azul duck his head. Clearing my throat, I nod. "I'm fine, sorry. I guess dying leaves a bit of a side effect," I lie, and Azul's head snaps up. We both know I heard him, but I smile softly at him as Nathair accepts my answer.

"We will stop crowding you," Nathair declares, ignoring the others' groans. "We all have work to complete, so feel free to explore or even just rest, Althea, and tomorrow, we can start to show you the ropes, if you wish."

"Sounds good." I smile, and Nathair drags them all out.

I watch them go, and my shoulders drop. I'm used to being alone, used to the solitude, but now, the cold and loudness of my own thoughts seem wrong after waking up connected to them, so instead, I wander around the throne room once more.

"The chairs appear days after our induction. They simply materialise and tell the story of our lives." The deep voice startles me, and I whirl, but I see no one until Azul suddenly comes into view right before me.

"How?" I ask, wide-eyed. I have heard stories of vampyrs in the old times who could walk among people unseen, but that was thousands of years ago, a talent that died out when they did.

"I can walk unseen," is all he says as he tilts his masked head, watching me. I didn't get a good look at his face earlier, but it makes me sad that his mask is back on.

"Why don't you show your face like the others?" I find myself asking, feeling a kinship with him. We both need to be loved.

I can tell I've shocked him by the ripple in his appearance. "I am not beautiful like the others." His voice is sad. "I would not wish to see the look in your eyes change."

"It would not," I assure him, stepping closer. "Beauty is more than skin deep. Vampyrs are supposed to be the most beautiful creatures in this world, but that beauty is empty if the person is rotten to the core. It leaves a mark. I've been surrounded by those sorts all my life, beautiful but rotten to the core. You are not. I sense you, and you wouldn't be here if you were, so beauty isn't everything, Azul. One day, I hope you trust me enough to show me your face, but until then, if you are comfortable, then that is what matters." I place a kiss on the mask over his cheek. "I will still look at you like the others," I whisper as I slide past him.

"My abilities are ghosts."

I turn back when I hear his rough, hopeful voice. "I was close to death when they judged me because of my mistress. It did not scare me. Truth be told, I think I saw ghosts before I even died, but when I came back, I saw the souls of the dead. I can talk to them and help them, and in return, they help me. I can move and speak unseen to judge and see sins, and I saw you, Althea. I was the one who raised your name."

I can see he is waiting for an attack, for me to hate him.

"Good," I say, shocking him, and I laugh bitterly. "I was a broken monster, Azul. You did the right thing. No matter what the others say, even if I was killing those who were willing to harm their own, it doesn't lessen the blood on my hands—blood I have to live with. I'm glad you stopped me before I did something much worse."

"I sentenced you to death," he retorts.

"You did." I nod. "And here we are. I guess the gods have a plan for all of us, and who are we to take that burden on ourselves? You did your job, Azul, and I do not hate you for that. I'm actually grateful." I let him feel the truth of my words as I clumsily reach out and feel him read my emotions.

"My mistress was a cruel woman. She made me into her creature of darkness, but the things she did to me left scars—both physical and mental. I am not like the others and never will be."

"She hurt you," I murmur.

His laugh sends shivers across my soul with its hopelessness. "She tortured me. For hundreds of years, she starved me, brought me back to life, broke all my bones, ripped off my skin, and sewed it back on. Every part of me was destroyed and remade into her image. I was judged for killing another in her name, and I wept in happiness when they delivered my death so it would free me of the pain."

I sense intense longing and loneliness in his tone. He wants a connection to me, just like the others, but he doesn't know how. That's okay because I do.

"When I need to feed again, can I feed off you?" I let the question hang, giving him the power to choose. If he says no, I won't hold it against him, but he needs the sense of control as much as I do.

His blood sings to me.

He stills like a ghost but does not disappear. "Even knowing my crimes and what was done to me, you would willingly feed from me?"

"Without hesitation," I reply.

"If you wish to feed from me, I am yours, whenever and wherever," he says, pounding his fist to his chest and ducking his head slightly.

"Good." I grin widely.

"I must work," he suddenly rasps, and then he disappears, but I still sense him close by.

"Goodbye, Azul," I murmur as I turn away, and at the door, I hear his whisper.

"Goodbye, sweet Althea."

Exhausted, I climb the steps to my room and sprawl on the bed. So much has happened over the last twelve hours, and my head is full of not just the others' presence, like whispers on the wind, but also dying, being reborn, and the new job.

For a moment, I ache for Simon, wishing I could share this with him, but instead, I slide under the sheets, shivering from the cold, and imagine he's there with me, holding my hand. I must reach for him with my mind, but the distance is too great, and our bond is too hollow after all this time, and for a moment, I feel completely alone. Tears spring to my eyes, as if saying goodbye to my old life has finally cut all ties with him.

My best friend, my brother, and the only family I have.

"Not all," someone murmurs, and I jerk up and around to see Osis at the door.

"Your pain called to me." He steps inside and shuts the door. "It is a big thing to be selected as a judge, but the others forget the loneliness and emotions that come with it. You miss your friend, but you are not alone, Althea. We are here. We can't replace him, nor would we wish to, but I can be here for you now if you would like."

I watch him before nodding slowly, and he strides over and slides onto the bed. I turn on my side once more, look at him, and smile.

Reaching over, he brushes away my tears, sucking them from his fingers with a groan. "Sleep, Althea, I am here."

"Promise?" I whisper, searching his gaze.

"For as long as you want me, and for as long as you need me," he vows. "We will look over you, Althea. You will never feel alone again, and one day, I will bring Simon to you to see once more."

A smile curves my lips as my eyes flutter shut. "I would like that, even if it's just to say goodbye. I never did."

"Then I promise you that too. You will get your goodbye, Althea," he murmurs, curling his hand around mine. A jolt of warmth, friendship, happiness, and hope flows from him and into me, and I fall asleep smiling and warm.

The tears dry on my face as if they never were.

Daughter of my blood.

The whisper makes me whirl around in the grey, smoky place I'm in, except there is nothing but darkness around me. "Hello?"

I am here.

I see nothing. Closing my eyes, I search with my senses and feel something in the dark. Something ancient. Something old. Something powerful.

"Who are you?" I ask, refusing to cower or shake.

I am a god, of course, but you knew that, even if you did not wish to admit it. Time is running out, blood of mine. We must speak. You chose well, like I knew you would. This was always to be your destiny, but now you must embrace it.

"Embrace what?" I demand, unsure if I'm speaking out loud anymore.

Your destiny, they hiss. *I have given you my nightmares, blood of mine, the strongest and most powerful of our race, so take them, make them yours, and become the change. Rain unholy fire on our world and cleanse it. Make it right once more.*

"Yours?" I whisper, my heart freezing. "You . . . You are the vampyr king of lore. You are Modatheth, the first vampyr."

Of course. My blood runs through you. All are mine, but they have turned their back on me, on our lineage, and now they are weak versions of what we should be. Your mother knew that.

"My mother?" I gasp, seeing the shadows wrap around me.

She spoke to me since she was a child. She called into the darkness with her powers without realising it. She knew her duty and her destiny was to die for you, my descendent. You are the one who will save our race once more. I loved her like my own daughter, as I do you. They thought she was strong, little one, but they have not seen anything yet.

Suddenly, a man bathed in blood-red flames emerges, so I bow.

A burning fingertip tilts my head back, and my eyes well with tears as I take in his power.

Teach them. Show them. Save them.

"How?" I reply raggedly.

You know how. Cleanse the world of evil. We were never meant to be that. We survive in darkness, that is true, but the dark is not evil, not bad or good. We were created to protect the monsters within it, to be regal, strong, and, most importantly, protectors. That has been corrupted. You will not be.

"What if I am not strong enough?"

Oh, my darling, you are because I am going to make it so. He leans down, and I finally see his face. *This will hurt, but it is my gift to you, my daughter—one last chance to save our race before the gods wipe us out for our crimes. The judges are failing against such evil, but you will change the tide. Are you prepared?*

Swallowing, I stare into the most beautiful face I have ever seen yet would never be able to describe. "If I don't take the gift?"

You will fail, and you will lose all that you claim. You will lose them all.

The judges, my new family, Simon . . . all of them. I will lose everything.

"This gift . . . ," I trail off. "What will it make me?"

A true queen of monsters. A nightmare, he purrs as he kneels before me, a god engulfing me in his flames. *It is needed to combat the rot, but it must be accepted willingly.*

"Will it hurt?" I query like a child asking a god to protect her.

Everything comes with a price, he admits.

"I will take it," I say without hesitation. "I will pay it if it will save them."

Good. For a moment, I see a smile, and I know I have pleased him. *I couldn't have chosen better. Now prepare, daughter.*

His flames race across my arms and sink into my skin, and I throw my head back with a scream of agony. I have no idea how long it lasts. My body burns, my blood heats and boils, and my brain explodes with memories, with possibilities, until I am a shattered mess of a vampyr trying to absorb a god's powers.

It finally stops, and I open my eyes to find him releasing my arm.

"What's happening?" I beg as he staggers to his knees and then falls to his back, his flames extinguished.

"I am dying," he murmurs.

"No!" I exclaim, curling around him. "Let me save you."

No, this was how it was always supposed to be. His flameless hand reaches up to capture my tear. *A person crying for me . . . I never thought I would see that. I have lived too long, daughter. The life of a god is lonely and not easy. I held out in hopes of finding one like you. I put everything I have in you—my hopes, my fears, and my future. Save them, daughter. I will be with you always.*

"What if I cannot?"

Then we will fade together. His hand cups my cheek. *You will not face this alone. I have selected the best over the years to be your companions, so allow them to help. Love is the cure, but do not fear or hate death. Life and death must always work together because without both, the world is nothing. Now, go back to them, and do not miss me. I am inside your heart now, and I will guide you when you are lost. Just simply look into the dark, and you will see me and remember, daughter, that the nightmares the others fear have always been yours.*

I wake with a start, pressing my hand against my heart as tears pour down my cheeks.

Reve is before me, watching me with a heavy expression. "I see you have met our god."

"How—"

"I am a dream walker." He grins. "It was his gift to me. He called me to protect you while he took you under." He looks me over. "Whatever he did has changed you. A visit from a god is never good."

"No," I admit softly. "But needed."

He nods. "I did not see much. We should meet with the others."

I turn to see that my body is still in the bed, curled around Osis, and Reve chuckles. "It's so we can speak privately," he murmurs. "I will wake you. Are you okay?"

"I-I don't know, but I don't have a choice, none of us do. None of us ever have, I think."

"There's always a choice, Althea, and you chose it," he reminds me. "But you're right. Some things are born with destinies, and I think you were."

Fourteen

Althea

Reve is right, and I find myself perched in the informal sitting room—the one they brought me to when I first woke up. I hold a cup of warm tea in my hands, thanks to Conall, and my feet rest in Nathair's lap as the others sit patiently, curious as they watch me. Reve stands behind me, leaning casually against the wall.

"I had a dream."

"That is how all good stories start." Reve snorts.

I throw him a grin as Nathair sighs.

"This wasn't like any I've ever had before. I saw a god. The god. Our god," I tell them, and there's a moment of silence, so I rush ahead. "He told me he selected me himself, and that I've been chosen to work with you, to . . . to save our race."

Nathair just blinks, the only crack in his composure.

"I know how crazy that sounds—"

"Not as much as you would think. Gods are known for being dramatic, and they often meddle," Nathair murmurs.

"Yes, well, he gave me his power. He . . . He's dead." The room falls into silence once more. "He said we need to cleanse our race, that we are . . . changing and becoming evil. He said that was always the plan, and why you were brought back, so we could do that together. This feels bigger than judging. It's as if we are on a clock that's ticking down, and if we don't save them, we are all doomed."

"In what way?" Nathair asks, no doubt speaking for them all. I can feel their minds working against mine.

"I don't know, he wasn't specific, but it was a feeling I got." I cannot bring myself to tell them that he called me a queen of monsters.

"Could you show us?" Nathair requests. "It might be easier. Reve can help you."

I nod hesitantly, looking at Reve.

"I will not delve deeper than I have to. I will, however, have to put you to sleep to retrieve it." Reve's hand strokes my face.

I put the cup down and curl up. "Do it," I murmur with trust in my voice, and before I know it, I am back in my dream, but this time I feel the others watching like a movie. I can see myself and the god, but it's as if I am far away from it all, and suddenly, everything pops back into reality as I sit up, gasping.

Reve strokes my hair from my face and crouches before me as he searches my gaze. "Queen of nightmares." He grins. "It has a ring to it."

"I often wondered about our purpose. It couldn't have simply been to try and hold back the tide of evil, but we weren't enough. Now, though, I understand that we were waiting for you to complete us," Nathair whispers. "He has given you a great gift, Althea. We will need to help you control it. In the meantime, I will think on what I have seen, but one thing is clear—this is bigger than all of us." He meets everyone's gazes. "We must continue our work, faster and bigger than ever before. Thea is right. I feel the ticking clocks. I want us to fall back into our routine. Thea, we will work with you on your new powers because unfortunately, unlike the rest of us who have had years to hone them, you will not."

I nod in understanding, feeling a little overwhelmed. I mean, a god, our god, asked me to save our race and then gave me his power. I'm no one. I'm a dead girl surrounded by the most powerful, beautiful vampires, and I'm supposed to . . . save everyone?

It sounds like some cliché YA books I used to read, just with more death, but I guess beggars can't be choosers.

"Shh, I see your mind whirling, Althea. It is not as scary as it seems, and you have us. We will move one chess piece at a time, that is all," Nathair promises, squeezing my foot. "Everyone else, we know what we need to do."

The others give me small smiles and hurry away, leaving me with Nathair and Reve. "I'm going to research more into the god and see what powers we can expect." Nathair leans in. "Stay here and rest. Even if you don't think you do, your body needs it. Between being chosen and now receiving more gifts, it is probably overloaded right now."

"I feel—"

"It wasn't a request, Althea, I will always give you a choice, but in regard to your well-being? It's an order. Rest." He kisses my head softly as he rises and takes Reve with him, leaving me with warm tea, fire, and nothing else to do.

I'm supposed to be the hero or some bullshit, yet I feel useless. They have had years to accept this life and their job, but I've had a day, and now I'm supposed to help them stop our race from being destroyed by their own evil misdeeds?

Maybe Nathair is right. I need to rest, figure out what I feel, and let my body come to terms with everything. All I seem to be doing is lying around, but I felt his determination. He will chain me here if he must to force me to heal.

Now that I focus on it fully, I do feel my body still knitting itself together after the damage of dying and the poison in my blood. It's like a fresh scar, healed but still tender, so I will do as I'm told this once. I sip the tea and laze around, and before I know it, I'm drifting off to sleep once more, lost in memories and futures that are not my own.

When I wake, the fire is out, and I can feel the darkness setting in.

Did I sleep all day? I guess Nathair was right. I really did need to rest.

I stand and stretch, my mind reaching for them without realising. Forcing myself to the door, I peer out. "Hello?" The hallway is silent, and I feel the emptiness of this part of the court. Someone must be here, but I wouldn't know where to look.

It's the first time I've truly been alone since waking up, so I make the most of it and wander through the hallways, taking inventory of my body. I feel stronger than I ever did before, and after showering and dressing in some shorts and a long shirt for comfort, I find myself in one of the hobby rooms, as they described them.

It's a huge room, split down the middle, and on the other side is a gym built for immortals like us. Everything is bigger, stronger, and harder. This side of the room, however, is a simple circle with runes spread around it. As I walk, I realise they are to contain powers.

To trap people?

No, that feels wrong.

It's to help them contain their magic while it's unstable. I almost feel the answer in my bones. I have all these new powers, and it's about time I learned what they are and how to harness them if I'm to help. I'm tired of sitting around.

I'm to be a judge.

A queen.

It's time I acted like one.

Taking a deep breath, I step inside the ring, feeling a magical pull sweep across me and over to the other side. I spread my feet and close my eyes, focusing internally, but for what, I don't know. Something has to be there.

I did this before when I first changed, when they all wanted to feel my seer powers, and I found nothing. For a moment, old doubts creep up, and I sense nothing. I want to cry, tell them I'm useless and that they chose wrong, but then something sweeps past so quickly, like a breeze, stealing those thoughts.

Focusing harder, I push away everything I was before I died—all the doubts, worries, pain, and pressure to be enough. Instead, I just am.

A being.

Concentrating on one breath then the next, I dive deeper and deeper inside myself, searching for that spark of something.

Anything . . .

Then, like a blooming flower, it grows from the darkness, small and almost opaque, but the more I focus, the bigger it grows. Petals expand out, filling my limbs and curling around my heart. It's a rose, I realise, as the thorns bite into me, but the pain fills me with comfort, as does the bloodshed.

I feel it stealing my blood as the thorns wind tightly around me, gripping me, but in return, I feel a new power flowing through me. I almost see myself gasp and fall to my knees, but inwards, it's a battle.

The thorns want to overtake me and steal everything, but I push back the tide, and they finally settle. I breathe through the pain and this new power that almost chokes me, and then my eyes slam open at the same time my hands rise without thought.

Blood dots the circle around me, the physical evidence of the fight, and as my hands lift, the blood bubbles and then flows into the air, creating a giant circle. I feel it call to me, and I know I can use it to hurt or to heal.

Instead, I absorb it back into myself, watching the mass head straight to my chest and sink deep, the shock of it jolting me as my hands fall.

Okay, so blood . . .

What else?

Closing my eyes once more, I reach deep past the roses and into that power. It floods me, and suddenly, I'm not in my own mind anymore.

No, I'm in someone else's and looking through their eyes.

For a moment, there is resistance as the strength of their power holds me back in a mental battle before they brush across me, realising who I am, and open.

Nathair.

He's sitting in a library with one leg crossed over the other, and a fire blazes before him. A book lies forgotten in his hand, and for a moment, I am him, and he lets me feel his age, his strength, and even his memories if I wish to look, but I don't. I want him to tell me about his past, not snoop through it. Instead, a new idea comes to mind, and with an inaudible giggle, I slide into his skin with him and take control.

Dragging the distinctly male hand across his chest, I explore lower, and the body I'm in gasps in pleasure.

"Thea." My voice is a groan out of his throat.

I feel his strength, but he never once protests or fights me.

"Because I am yours," he says.

I wrap his hand around his hard, trouser-covered cock, and he tries to drop his head back, but I keep it upright so I can see. His pale hand lifts and grips his hair, the tug of pain making him hiss and lift his hips.

Suddenly, like a lead balloon, I feel myself being pulled away, so with my last thought, I lift him and begin walking him towards me. Snapping back into myself, I pant as the power retreats, but it remains inside me.

Not gone like before.

My eyes open and clash with Nathair's gaze as he stands in the doorway. "I could have fought you," he says, answering my unvoiced question. "But why would I when it led me right where I wanted to be?"

Swallowing, I drop my hands as he steps into the room, running his eyes hungrily across me. "It took us months, years, to reach our powers, yet it took you mere hours, Althea," he purrs. "I can taste your power across my skin, but I can also taste your hunger from the exertion of using it. Come to me, let me feed you."

Tilting my head, I run my eyes down his body and back up to his. "And what if I'm hungry for something more than your blood?" I grin, flashing fang, and he licks his lips. "What if I want your body too?"

"I told you that I am yours, and I meant it. Blood, mind, soul, and body."

"Is that right?" I step out of the circle and prowl towards him, starving for everything he has to offer. The desire I feel for the man who fed me and is willing to teach and protect me only triples as he leans there, watching me approach. Like a Greek god of old, his power sweeps off him in waves, his hair falling past his shoulders in a silken curtain.

He stands as still as a statue, letting me decide, but I feel his plea in the air. He wants me to use him, to take him, and make him mine.

FIFTEEN

ALTHEA

When I get close, I fist his black locks, just like I did when I was in his body, and tilt his head to expose his neck for me. He watches me the entire time, his eyes shining brightly with want as his body vibrates with his lust.

"Do you want me to feed from you while I fuck you, Nathair?" I ask, leaning into his warmth.

His gaze tracks me, and his pulse jumps in his throat. "From the moment I laid eyes on you."

I taste the honesty in his words as he reaches for me, pulling me closer. Leaning in, I trace his fangs with my tongue as he groans, his eyes sliding shut in ecstasy.

"Thea," he begs. "I need you, please. Please, my queen."

Hearing the title strikes something deep inside of me, something akin to power. I cup his hard bulge through his trousers. His hips roll, grinding into my grip as I lick and kiss across his face to his neck.

I bite his pulse softly, and he moans, the sound making me grin against his skin as I glide my lips up to his ear.

"Then fuck me," I hiss before I strike, sinking my fangs into his neck.

He lifts me and spins until my back meets the wall with a loud bang. My hand is still in his hair, tilting his neck for me as I feed. His fingers trail down my body to my shorts and he rips them away, leaving me naked from the waist down. One hand cups my pussy, while the other slides under my big shirt and cups my breast. The warmth from his touch makes me shiver and groan as I suck harder, his blood filling me with power.

His mind slams into mine, mixing his pleasure with my pleasure, until I'm rocking into his hand. I need to come so badly and want to feel him fill me as I feed.

Soon, he promises in my mind as he tweaks and rolls my nipple.

My head falls back, and blood gushes down my chin. He turns his head, his lips seeking mine, and we crash together. He tastes his blood on my lips as his expert fingers twist and pluck my nipples. I moan, holding him to me as I grind and rock into his hand until, with a scream, I come so hard I swear I see stars.

His chuckles vibrate through me as he slides down my body, biting at my shirt and ripping it away until his lips seal around my nipple. "I won't fuck you hard and fast like some newbie, my queen. No, I'm going to make you come at least five times before you get my cock, and once I'm deep inside of you, I'll sink my fangs in until every inch of you is taken."

"Nathair," I groan as I grip his hair, holding on as he flicks my nipple with his tongue before sucking it into his mouth. Pulling back, he blows over the tight bud, making me shiver, and then he turns and gives the other the same attention. The pull of his mouth and the threat of his fangs makes me cry out, the arc of pleasure going straight from my nipples to my throbbing clit.

"I wonder if I could make you come from this alone." His fangs press against my skin. "Shall we find out, my queen?"

I can do nothing but stare as he grins wickedly and pushes my breasts together, alternating between sucking and biting until, once again, I shatter.

Nathair is determined to destroy me, and I willingly let him as he holds me. Every sensation is heightened in a way I've never felt before.

The taste of him on my tongue.

The feel of air hitting my fangs.

The ache in my oversensitive nipples.

The silky slide of his skin against mine.

It's all too much and not enough at the same time.

"You taste like death and blood," he growls as he licks down my stomach. "The scent of your desire makes me desperate to taste your cunt." I hear the moment his knees hit the floor. "Look at you, my queen. You're so fucking beautiful, I should paint it for everyone to see. I'm on my knees for you, a place I swore I would never be, but I kneel willingly for a taste of you."

"Nathair," I beg, wide-eyed and panting.

Smirking, he seals his mouth to my pussy and attacks me with that same silken iron-clad control. His tongue traces every inch of me, all the way to my ass and back up. The scent of our need and his blood saturates the air, making my eyes close in bliss.

"Eyes on me at all times, Althea. You will watch as your king brings you more pleasure than you have ever felt. You will watch me as you come and stain my skin," he snarls against my pussy, gently nicking me with his fangs. A drop of my blood hits the air, and he snarls before lashing my clit, tasting my cream and blood in one fell swoop.

My head wants to fall back as pleasure races through my veins, but I don't let it. I keep my eyes on him as he tastes me, those black orbs locked on me, memorising every reaction.

His tongue flicks my clit before curling around it, then his fangs press in, and the mix of pressure, pleasure, and pain makes my eyes roll back and my leg shake. Never have I come so easily, but with this powerful man between my legs, I can't seem to stop, and when his hands reach up and twist my nipples, I come all over his tongue, jerking against the wall with the force.

Power explodes through me, but he doesn't relent, licking me through it. He thrusts his tongue inside of me, stroking my fluttering muscles. It feels longer and thicker as it reaches those nerves that have my scream reaching new heights. As I ride his tongue, the orgasm rolls into another, and then his tongue slides out and down, around my asshole.

"What—" I feel the difference in his tongue.

Smirking, he pulls his wet mouth away, his tongue darting out to lap at his fangs, and my eyes widen. It's forked, thick, and long. Leaning in slowly, he drags the textured muscle across me, and I shatter once more. He slams it into me as I come, squirting my release as I rock my hips.

It's too much. I can't—

You can and you will. I want this floor stained with your cum. His silky voice slides through my head. *I want everyone who steps foot in here to know just how well my queen was serviced and just how many times she came for her king. I want my tongue so deep in your cunt you won't know where you stop and I begin.*

Oh gods, his words, his touch. I can't.

I lose myself in the pleasure, and then his fingers slide into my ass, and I come once more in a never-ending orgasm that cuts my strings, leaving me limp and at his mercy. He laps at my pussy as his fingers slowly fuck my ass through my release and then pull out. Nathair slides up my body and kisses me, his forked tongue tangling with mine as he lets me taste my release.

It drives me wild, especially when he grips my neck. How quickly our roles have changed, but I don't care, especially when he pulls my legs up and I wrap them around his hips. His hand slides down, and a moment later, I feel his cock pressing to my pussy. I watch him as he drags his huge, hard length back and forth across my folds.

"I'm large, my queen, and I only want your screams of pleasure this time, so get my cock nice and wet so you can ride me," he demands.

Whimpering, I scratch at his back as he pins me in place, dragging his cock along my pussy before pressing it flat against me and rocking his hips. He slowly rolls his hips, sliding along my slit and hitting my clit. Our chests heave with our breaths, and when I'm on the verge of coming again, he pulls back and slams into me, impaling me on his massive length.

I don't stand a chance. I cream around him, screaming my release until my voice is ragged, and then his mouth is on mine, swallowing my cries of pleasure as my cum drips down my thighs and hits the floor.

Then he begins to move, slowly sliding out to the tip and hammering back, his balls slapping against me with the force. His hand grips my neck tighter as I struggle and fight like a wild animal, needing to lash out, to hurt him from the pleasure.

"Look at you, my queen, so wild for my cock. You drip around me like such a good girl. I knew the first moment I saw you that you had the power to destroy me, and I was right. After one taste of this pussy, I'm lost. After one thrust, I know I will never feel at home when I am not inside of you. I will spend eternity fucking this tight little cunt and pumping it with my cum, and I will spend years marking every inch of your flesh with my fangs and cum," he snarls, hammering into me with the strength only a true sangui can possess.

He hits so deeply and then drags me higher, tilting me so his cock drags along that spot inside that has my eyes turning black with pleasure.

I feel my nails turn to claws, and then I rip at his clothes and back until I taste blood. Despite his grip, I slam forward, and he roars as my fangs pierce his neck. I don't feed, I punish, unable to stop, and he continues to fuck me.

Blood sprays across us. "Yes, my queen, take what you need. Use me, take your blood, your release. Everything I have is yours. Fucking rip me to pieces, drain me, or claw me to death, and I would still fuck this little pussy."

Done feeding, I leave my fangs inside of him to connect us as he roars, pounding me into the wall with the force of his thrusts. So much power circulates between us, I feel my hair lifting as the room sparks with it.

Blood flows over us, each droplet filled with power and soaking into our skin, heightening our pleasure. I feel the wall crumble behind me, but he doesn't stop.

His voice rambles in my head, singing my praises.

So fucking good.

God damn, I would have gone to war for this pussy.

So grateful this is mine.

I'm going to make her crave me like I do her.

Thea, Thea, Thea, my Thea, fuck.

"Nathair," I whimper against his throat, pulling my fangs out, and his hand cuffs my neck once again, cutting off my breath. He can have it. He can have my air. I couldn't fight him even if I wanted to. It's too good, too much, as power spins between us until it has no choice but to explode, taking us with it.

Both of us howl as his hips stutter, his cock filling me twice more before he stops. His length jerks inside of me, filling me with his scalding cum as I shake and break.

He holds me in place, gripping my throat until I know it will bruise. I want the bruises. Nathair moves, sliding his cock in and out as he continues to come like he can't stop, and every drop of his release sets me off again until it finally bursts and releases us. I slump back, and he groans, burying his head in my shoulder as he slowly fucks me until he finishes. I feel his body trembling and his power wrapping around me.

I love it.

Thea. His voice is full of pleasure in my head. *Forget the gods, true power and heaven are between these thighs.*

I close my eyes as a grin curves my lips.

"My beautiful Thea," Nathair purrs, pulling away slightly before licking my lips. "You taste like me and sex."

I open my eyes and feel my expression soften as I wind my fingers through his hair and drag him closer for a drugging kiss that leaves us both panting and rubbing against each other. "Then we did something right," I murmur.

He laughs, and I see a brightness in his eyes that wasn't there before.

In my mind, I feel satisfaction.

I have claimed one of my nightmares, just like I was told to, like I wanted to.

Only five to go.

Sixteen

Azul

Hunting is what I'm good at, and it also keeps the memories at bay. Despite Althea's words, they still haunt me, and when I'm feeling useless and restless, I hunt. I find our next target, research them, and watch their sins, reminding myself why I do this. It takes a while for us to build a case. We don't just pluck someone from the streets. We look into their past, their future, and their reasonings. We have to be sure if we are to kill someone.

That is why I am one of the best. Usually, those who have committed great sins have ghosts haunting them, and their past kills are all too happy to spill the dirt. Yes, they are usually angry, but I can get the truth from them, even if they are slightly jaded.

I should have rested like Nathair ordered, but night is the worst because the past plagues me, so here I am, in the back corner of a seedy nightclub. I watch every other being live their life, their essence so strong I can almost taste it. Their laughter is loud, their lust is overwhelming, and their jealousy and anger are potent as they vie for attention.

There are so many emotions, it's too much for a ghost like me.

One who closed himself off until she came along.

I feel too much when Althea is around.

It scares me, but I can't pull back now for anything, not after she looked at me and saw me. She saw past the mask, past the scars I use like armour, and she wanted me. It woke something long since dead inside of me.

I remind myself to concentrate. The faster this is over, the faster I can get back to her and see if she needs to feed. The thought is terrifying but also exhilarating. I haven't ever voluntarily given myself to another, but I want to for her.

I want to taste her pleasure, and I want her fangs in my skin as she drinks me down. I want to feel my power flowing through her. I want her to touch me with need, not disgust and obsession like the other one who took without consent. That woman stole everything from me, including my future and my life.

For the first time ever, I almost want to thank her for leading me here, to my purpose and Althea.

A ghost flutters by, and when he realises I can see him, he starts to yell and scream about his problems, making me sigh.

I'm used to it, but sometimes it's overwhelming, especially when it draws all the others in the room towards me. I nod and listen, all the while searching for my target. I tracked him for a week or two before Althea arrived. The man has killed more than half a dozen of his own kind. He has control and power, yet he still kills. One of his victims told me he likes the taste of death in their blood.

I want him to be judged next, but just as I'm homing in on his power in the crowded room, I feel a familiar brush of power, and then I see her.

My breath freezes, and everything in me locks down.

I am a statue, screaming inside my mind as memories take over.

Agony, pain, and humiliation leave me broken, and I fall to my knees, weak and unprotected. I am certain she will notice me, notice her mistress's broken toy, and take me back to her.

I should have known better, however, because my fear calls to my brothers, and they fill my head.

I'm the closest, Osis tells the others who are crowding my mind. *I will get him.*

Stay strong, brother, Conall says, sending his shadows down the bond to cover me so she cannot see me. Even the ghosts sense my panic, and they turn to protect me.

Reve steers my mind away from the memories, and scalding heat replaces the cold, warming me. Lycus's venom fills my blood in case I'm attacked, and Nathair projects an image, one that forces me to the present.

I see Althea with her head thrown back and blood flowing down her neck from puncture wounds. Her lips are parted on a scream, and her breasts are pushed up and marked. My cock hardens, and my fangs ache to feed.

Something I have never felt fills me so strongly, I almost fall, but then arms wrap around me, pulling me into a chest.

It's Osis, and then we are gone, his powers transporting us home. The usual sickness of his method of travel doesn't breach my heightened emotions. Conall's shadows pull back, exposing me, and I find Osis crouched before me. Nathair hurries into the room with fang marks in his neck. His lips are swollen, his pants are undone, and behind him is Althea.

Crying out, I spin away from her, not wanting her to see me like this.

Nathair must sense it because he tries to block her from getting to me as I grip at the floor, fighting back the memories. One flash of her, and I'm back to that weak, chained dog who was half-starved and covered in so many scars, you couldn't see unblemished skin anymore.

I am an animal who is unworthy of the queen in our midst. Darkness closes in on me until, suddenly, a hand jerks my head up. It's soft and warm, and it pushes back the darkness, telling it that it can't have me.

I'm hers.

I suck in a breath.

She's crouched before me, and her power cradles me to her when I would have scattered. "Shh, you are okay," she promises softly, her hands sliding across me before pulling me into her arms.

Without thought, I wrap my arms around her and bury my face and my shame into her stomach as she holds me. My brothers gather around us, offering their support and protection while I break.

"Shh, Azul, we have you. You are safe." I don't know what she knows or senses, but she keeps repeating it. "You're safe. We have you. No one else ever can. You are ours. We are here, and you're safe."

I relax, trusting her, trusting them, to protect me while I am raw and exposed.

She continues to hold me on the cold stone floor, talking softly so her sweet voice keeps me grounded to the present. Althea's hands trace every inch of me, reclaiming my body until I feel myself start to drift.

I am not quite asleep nor totally awake, so when Nathair's voice comes, I almost startle.

"He saw someone from his past, someone who hurt him greatly," he says, no doubt responding to Althea's mental question.

I should stop him, but honestly, it's easier for him to tell her so I don't have to. Maybe that's a form of cowardice, but I don't care. She deserves to know, but I cannot bring myself to say the words.

"Who?" Althea's voice is like a whip, and her power rises until I whimper, but she immediately softens. "Where?"

"You cannot kill them." Nathair chuckles fondly. "Not yet anyway. We are bound to our creed, and we have tried to find ways around it to go after those who hurt him."

"Who?" she repeats. Her voice is laced with such power, no one could deny her.

"Someone from his court, from before he died. Azul . . . Azul wasn't like us.

He was low in their rankings, and as such, a powerful vampyr, a mistress of the court, stole him and made him her pet. The court knew of it and did nothing. It was common for the weaker to be used and hurt. He became nothing but her blood bag, and she did whatever she wanted to him and allowed others to as well."

She stiffens against me, and I fight not to cry at her rejection before she softens. "Fuck our creed. I'm going to kill them. Did they force him to feed others without consent? Did they touch them?"

"Althea," Nathair begins.

"Yes," Osis answers, knowing my truth better than the others. "And much worse. They tortured him for years. It was fun for her, for them. They used their powers on him often, and they forced him to break others or suffer greater pain. His blood and body became theirs. Nothing was his own, and even in sleep, they followed him. They are monsters, Althea, the worst of our kind, but they close ranks and protect each other, and no one can prove it. To others, they are the perfect court, but it holds nothing except death and fighting. It's all about power and rank."

"How do you know?"

"I was there. I was part of the court before him, and when he became one of us, I asked him. I knew what it was like there, but I had never seen someone so truly destroyed by them before. He cried in happiness when he died. I think the only reason he came back was for revenge."

Not true, not the only reason, but that is my own and not theirs to share, not that they know it.

"We are bound," Conall complains. "I hate it. We all do. Through the years, we have sensed his nightmares."

"I have seen them," Reve snarls, "and if I could, I would stride into their court and rip every single one of them apart."

"Why can't we?" she asks.

"Rules, the same rules we impose and kill others for breaking," Zale answers sadly. "If we were to break them, we would need to be judged. We are supposed to be above it."

"Yeah, well, fuck that. I'll find a way." Her hand strokes my hair. "You hear me, Azul? I will find a way. I'll make them all pay for what they did to you. What is all this power worth if we cannot protect our own family and avenge the wrongs done to him? If we want to save our race, then we need to start with that court. We will begin with the monsters who did this to him, and before the blood moon rises, I swear on my grave they will all be dead. Every single person who ever touched him or helped will be killed, either by my hand or his."

The dead hear her promise, and the universe acknowledges her statement.

She bound her fate, her future, to it, and she doesn't even know it.

Queen or not, a god's gifts or not, she has made an oath, and it must be kept.

When I reach for her, though, consumed by fear for what she has done for me, I feel nothing but her determination and her promise.

She will do it, and for the first time in years, I slip into a dreamless sleep with my queen holding me, protecting me.

Seventeen

Althea

I stare down at the sleeping man, my heart aching something fierce. I could almost feel his pain, his terror, flowing over him in waves. The others sit around us in a circle of protection as he sleeps. My legs go numb from the stone floor, but I ignore them, not willing to move. His hands fist my dress to keep me near him, and his face is turned into my stomach.

His face is unmasked. It fell to the floor next to him when they brought him back. I know he would hate me seeing him, worried about my thoughts, but I can't look away.

He's absolutely breathtaking in a rugged, scarred way that steals every bit of my soul.

Unlike the perfect beauty most vampyrs possess, Azul wears his scars. I ache to reach out and touch the scar on his face, but I don't move, and instead, I trace it with my gaze.

The scar intersects most of his features, reaching from the tip of his forehead, through his eyebrow, then stopping at his eye, as if it were closed when it happened, before carving through his cheek and down to his jaw. It's brown, raised, and jagged, and it was clearly a deadly blow, yet it only adds to the appeal of the man in my arms. Without the scar, he would be beautiful, but with it, I cannot bring myself to look away.

His eyes, which are squeezed shut, are a shocking bright blue—the same colour of the sky on a summer's day—surrounded by thick black lashes. They almost appear to be lined, but I can tell it's natural.

His eyebrows are thick and arched, leading to a strong forehead shadowed by his wispy hair. His locks are brown, the colour of fresh mud, and the tips are almost white. It falls in a mussed way to his ears, giving him a rugged look. His lips are pink and full, surrounded by stubble that's bordering on a beard. His neck showcases another wicked scar, as if someone tried to cut his throat. His ears are almost pointed at the tips, with a bone pierced through the left one and a hoop dangling across from the other.

He is wickedly beautiful, and his face is made for nights spent between the sheets.

I would worship it. How could he ever think himself ruined or ugly?

Not everyone sees beauty like you, Nathair says softly, no doubt hearing my thoughts. Let him, let them all. I won't hide how I feel about them. Every single one of them is gorgeous, and I almost feel inadequate in their presence.

Inadequate? I don't know who the laughing voice in my head belongs to, but pictures suddenly assault me.

Of me waking up after they killed me.

Of me sitting in the kitchen, laughing.

Of me sleeping curled around them.

Of me feeding from Nathair.

In every single image, one thing is clear—their emotions.

They feel awe, and they think of me as the bravest thing they have ever seen. It's not the images of myself that have me smiling, but their feelings.

"The floor is cold. You shouldn't stay here all night," Osis murmurs.

"I won't move him," I reply softly. "Not while he's sleeping. I'll be fine. I've had much worse."

"Not now, not ever again," Conall retorts, his shadows gathering.

With a soft sigh, Lycus gently picks us both up.

I look down in worry, but Azul doesn't move as Lycus brings us to my room before laying us down. Azul sighs, and Reve tucks us both in, his concern showing on his face as he looks at Azul.

Not one of them leaves. Instead, they all find places in the room to sit or lie to stay with us.

"Will he be okay?" I ask.

"I think he truly will," Nathair murmurs. "For the first time ever." It's clear he means because of me, but I don't respond, unsure what to say.

"Sleep if you need to. We will watch over you," Zale offers kindly.

"I'm good." I pull Azul close. "But maybe while we wait, you could tell me more about this place?" I request quietly, not wanting to disturb Azul. "I keep meaning to ask, but . . ."

Nathair stiffens, and although it's barely noticeable, I'm so tuned into them that I see it.

"You don't have to," I tell him, sensing his reluctance.

"No, you deserve to know. I mentioned some, but I wasn't a good man back then. None of us were, I guess, hence the death penalty." He laughs without amusement, staring into the fire. "I was greedy and lost in the need for power. My father was the same way, and it drove him mad. He was a cruel king. Many died, and our court was scared, so I killed my father and took the throne by force. I declared myself king, and people were relieved, thinking I would be better. I hoped I would be, but the power . . . it was too much for any one man." He smiles bitterly. "We were great once and named after the darkness itself, for we hosted the creatures of it. Shifters, animators . . . you name it, we had it. We were once the strongest court of all, but it warped me. I had become worse than my father. The bones of those who once trusted me were stacked at the base of my throne in my thirst for power, for dominion, over everyone and everything."

"Nathair," I whisper, tasting the agony in his voice. I can almost feel the bones brushing my fingers as he speaks.

"No, it is okay, Althea. I know what an evil man I was. I am ashamed, of course, and I have spent my new life making up for it, but truth be told, when the end came, I fought it, not wanting to die. I thought I deserved life more than any other I killed. When I was judged by the gods and given a choice, it was like a curse was lifted. The thirst for more was just gone. I could finally breathe again, but the full force of the things I had done threatened to drown me. For years after I came back, I wandered through this place, just remembering their screams and pleas."

He became silent for a moment. "Sometimes I still do." He looks at me. "Some left, choosing to exile themselves rather than stay with a mad king, while others blindly followed me, allowing me to kill thousands—humans, vampyrs, anyone who got in my way. I tortured, killed, ate, and stole power. I was the worst king I could have ever been, and now they call me king once more, and sometimes I hate the title, but other times it reminds me of my duty so another king like me never rises. Then the others started to come, turned into masters of the night and born with new powers. Hence the Court of Nightmares. I could not bear to call it Nox anymore. That place is long since dead, as are its people, and in its place are . . ."

"Nightmares," I murmur.

He nods, smiling sadly. "I wish you could have seen it before my father's madness, when I was just a boy. It was such a sight to see. Laughter filled the halls, and there were more children than you could count. People were happy and prospering. It was a good, strong court. Our powers were legendary, and our people were destined for great things."

"So what happened? Why did your father change so much?" I ask, confused.

"I do not know. Some said it might be a curse, while others thought he had simply gone mad and our blood was tainted. I do not believe I will ever find out. I cannot change what was done, Althea, but I can change the future. I can make the courts a better place, and I can make our future better. Now, together with you, we stand a chance to be better. Maybe your god was right, and we are destined for death. Maybe it calls to us from beyond the grave, I do not know, but we have to change it. We cannot have another Nox Court. Our race couldn't survive it."

"What about your mother?" I ask sometime later, debating what he said.

"My father killed her," he answers calmly. "He'd already broken her heart, and I think she was dying from that anyway, but then he ripped it out. Ironic, really, since it had always been his. That is what finally made me step up. I was angry, so angry, so I gave into the darkness inside. Maybe they are right about our bloodline, for after I challenged and killed him, I was never the same."

"But you are now, Nathair. I feel the goodness in you. Whatever happened, you have paid for it, and you clearly regret it."

"Regrets do not bring back the dead, Althea," he replies sadly. "But you are right. I am working towards forgiveness. That is all each of us can do. We were never bound to be the good guys; we were always meant to be the villains. Each of us is filled with the ability to be so evil, even the gods took notice, but now we can choose to be better, and we do every day we wake up." He nods at Azul. "Like your promise to him. It will be hard to keep."

"I meant every word," I reply.

"I know you did" —Nathair leans forward— "and that is why I know no matter what is to come, Althea, it will only bring more death, but maybe in death, our race can be reborn."

I hope he's right.

"I don't have any piercings," I randomly call out a few hours later. I'm still pinned under Azul, and we have been talking for the last few hours while he sleeps. No doubt they all have duties, but they stay and keep me company. "Apart from my ears," I add. "You all seem to have some."

"You have no idea, baby," Reve purrs, making me sit up to look at him. He just winks. "What do you want pierced?"

"I don't know, but the old me never would have pierced anything, wanting to fit in and be perfect. That's not me anymore. I feel like I need to change . . . something." I shrug. "That probably sounds silly."

"Not at all," Zale replies vehemently. "We have all reinvented ourselves in a way. Reve didn't have any tattoos when he came to us, and now look at him."

I arch my brow at that, and Reve grins at me. "I like the pain, baby."

Laughing, I shake my head. "I don't know. I've kind of always wanted my tongue done."

Reve sits up with a hungry look in his eyes.

Lycus cocks his head to the side. "I could do that."

I blink. "You pierce?"

He grins. "We have a lot of spare time, and Reve let me experiment on him first. Don't ask him about the first few." He winces as Reve groans. "But I've had a lot of years to hone it, so I can pierce you if you want. To make it stay without your body healing, though, we have to use a baptised blade of flames, which sounds dramatic, and it hurts like a son of a bitch. I would say ask Reve, but he almost came when I pierced his cock."

Conall snorts as Zale shakes his head. Osis moves closer, listening but watching me.

"Let's do it," I decide suddenly.

Lycus nods and hurries off. I managed to slip from the bed, and Azul moans. We all freeze, but he just rolls over and buries his face into the spot I was just in, inhaling and settling down. I head over to the others, and Lycus comes back, kicking Reve off the chair. He sprawls on the floor, laughing. I take a seat and hold onto the arms, unsure what to expect but unable to stop smiling. I never would before, but they are right.

This is the new me, and I can be whoever I want.

"Open your mouth, Thea," Lycus purrs, a dark look in his eyes.

Smirking, I lick my lips, watching him track the movements, and then I open my mouth wide. For a moment, he just stares at me before shaking himself out of it and grabbing what looks to be a very tiny sword. I arch my brow, and he almost blushes.

"A gift." He coughs. I hold back my laugh. "Trust me?" he asks.

I nod without thought and try to project my voice into his head. "Do whatever you wish," Nathair says for me, and Lycus grins.

"Good, now hold on. This will hurt, but if you're good, I'm sure someone will kiss it better. Zale, if you could." Wearing a smile, Zale reaches out, and flames dance in his palm. He releases them so they sink into the blade, making it glow brightly.

The tip of the sword is more of a needle, but as Lycus grabs my jaw and tilts my head back, I still worry about the side. But I said I trust him, and I do. "Tongue, beautiful," he purrs.

Sticking it out, I hold onto the arms as he places the tip of the needle on my tongue, and with a slow breath, he slides it in.

He's right. It hurts like a son of a bitch, and red-hot fire rips through it, causing my whole jaw to ache, but I've had worse. I lived in pain for so long when my blood was rotten, so now I relax slightly. The wide-eyed look he gives me makes me want to smile.

"I knew she was like me," Reve calls. "Oh, Thea, we are going to have such fun."

Lycus slowly removes the needle, and I focus on him as he delicately places something in the hole. Expecting him to be done, I relax as he lines the needle up again and sinks it in. He does it three times, and when he steps back, I taste my own blood and smell burnt flesh. Closing my mouth, I move my tongue around. There's a sharp stab of pain, but then a moment later, my powers soothe it, healing the damaged flesh around the new piercings.

"Done?" I ask.

He nods. "You feel okay?"

"Sure, can I see?" I grin, no doubt flashing fangs in my excitement.

Nodding nervously, Lycus holds up an ornate, black and gold hand mirror, aiming it at my face.

My hair is silky and sleek. I look like the old me. With a grin, I stick my tongue out, and my eyes widen.

"Holy shit," Reve mutters as he moves closer, but I inspect it myself.

Along my tongue, in a vertical line, are three black spikes, which are small with a slightly rounded tip. "They are incredible." I grin at Lycus.

"I wonder what they will feel like on a cock," Reve comments, and Nathair kicks him.

"Though I am curious how they would feel when you feed or kiss." Lycus cocks his head.

"Want to find out?" I wiggle my eyebrows.

He doesn't need to be asked twice. Grabbing my head, he slams his lips onto mine, sliding his tongue into my mouth. Groaning, I grab at his chest, holding on as he leans me back and strokes his tongue along mine with a groan.

We break apart, both of us panting as he clears his throat. "Oh yeah, they feel good." His eyes drop to my lips, but then a cry makes us jerk apart. All of us rush to the bed, but I leap onto it and stroke back Azul's hair.

"Shh, we are here," I murmur, and he settles instantly. I share a grim look with the others.

Lycus suddenly laughs, rubbing at his face. "Azul is a cockblocker."

I burst out laughing. I can't help it.

EIGHTEEN

ALTHEA

When Azul wakes up, I see the panic on his face when he realises he isn't wearing his mask. Knowing words won't work, I reach for him. "Can I feed from you?"

He blinks. "You do not have to just because—"

"I'm hungry." I cock my head. "I need to feed, and I want to feed from you."

He swallows as he sits up in the bed, his head ducked and eyes downcast. "I—you should feed from someone else."

"But I want to feed from you." I channel some bravery I don't feel. "Your queen is asking you to feed her. Are you going to turn me away because you think it's out of pity?"

"No, never." He lifts his head, shame crawling across his features for a moment. "I just . . . You are perfect, Althea, and I did not want you to feed from someone such as me."

"That's for me to decide. I will never force you, but I want to feed from you, if you want me to," I say softly.

"More than anything," he whispers, hope filling his eyes.

I feel the others filtering slowly out, giving us the privacy he needs.

"What would make it easier for you?" I ask. "Would you prefer for me to sit?" He shakes his head, his eyes darting around in fear. "Okay, how about I lie down and you lie on top of me? That way you'll be in control. You can easily pin me and stop me at any point." I reach out and take his hand, and he curls his around mine.

"Yes, yes, that might work," he replies hoarsely.

"We don't need to do this, Azul," I offer, but he shakes his head.

"I want to. I want you to feed from me, please, Thea."

I search his gaze, but he seems sure, so I squeeze his hand and let go. Sliding down next to him, I lean back on the pillows. "If you're sure," I say, holding my arms open.

He looks me over, and when he meets my gaze, he smiles softly. "You are the most beautiful person I've ever seen," he whispers. "The only one to ever touch me with kindness."

That makes me want to weep, but I hold back my tears and smile. "And one day, you will see yourself through my eyes," I reply, knowing he won't believe simple words.

He slides into my embrace, lying against me. I don't wrap my arms around him fully, knowing he probably won't want the feeling of being held down, so instead, I wrap them around him softly, loosely, and let him tilt his head for me.

Not wanting him to think he's with someone else, I hold his hand as I run my fangs across his neck. He shivers, and I freeze. "Good or bad?"

"Good," he croaks.

I do it again, feeling his cock harden against me, but I don't push my luck. I need him to know my touch will only ever bring pleasure, and I don't want him to feel nervous, so with a soft kiss over his pulse, I slide my fangs gently into his neck.

The first taste of his blood is strong and cold, almost like touching a grave. I taste darkness, pain, and so much more. I can't hold back my moan, and I feel it vibrate through him as he jerks and groans.

The connection clicks into place, and I pour everything down it.

I let him feel everything, all the emotions, pleasure, and need. We are unable to lie in our minds, so he has to believe it. I know it won't heal him instantly, but I don't want him to hide from me. I love his face. I would fucking paint it if I were talented enough.

It's a face I'm dying to sit on.

For a moment, there's a projection of him sinking into me, fucking me as I feed, before he pulls it back, ashamed. Grinning against his skin, I drink deeper as I wrap my legs around him, letting him feel the heat of my pussy as I grind against his hardness, showing him my own fantasies through our connection. I send him images of me riding him, of his blood covering him as I lick and drink from his body, and another as he feeds from me, fucking me from behind.

"Althea," he moans, grinding his hips painfully against me. "Please, please."

I never want him to beg, so I tighten my legs around him and rub against him, giving him the friction he needs as I visualise him fucking me, his hands sliding up my body to cup my breasts as his fangs sink deeply into my neck.

He comes with a roar. Pulling my fangs out so he doesn't hurt himself, I lick the marks and stroke his back as he shakes and groans, rolling his hips before he collapses on me. I hold his weight, loving the feeling.

"Are you okay?" I ask, needing to be sure.

"Better than okay." He lifts his head, his eyes soft as he watches me. "I never thought I'd be able to let a female feed from me again. Thea, you are a miracle."

"Nope, just dead." I grin, making him grin back. "Now, how about we go find the others?"

"In a minute. I . . . ah, need to clean up." He blushes, making me grin wider, and I'm unable to stop myself from teasing him. I roll my hips slowly to feel the wetness across his cock.

"Really? I think you should walk around with your cum staining your dick so everyone knows just what your queen did to you."

His blush deepens, but I feel his cock hardening once more, as he's clearly liking the possessiveness of my words. He blinks then. "What happened to your tongue?"

While Azul cleans up, I play with the bags that seem to have appeared in my room and bathroom, rifling through skincare, makeup, and hair accessories. Shrugging, I decide to do my makeup. Something about it always makes me feel stronger and more confident.

I don't add foundation like before, since my skin glows with power, but I do add some blush and highlighter. I'm just drawing on some smoky black eyeliner when Reve appears from nowhere and hops up on the counter. Arching a brow at him, I focus on drawing the lines and then smoking them out. It makes my eyes pop, and when I lean back, he whistles.

"Goddamn, do mine," he says.

"You sure?" I ask. I used to do Simon's sometimes, so when Reve parts his legs and pulls me closer, I lean in.

This, however, is not like doing my gay best friend's makeup, I realise all too quickly. His spicy scent goes straight to my aching, still wet pussy, and my nipples harden as I feel all that strength pressed against me along with his huge, hard length, which he does nothing to hide. I try to ignore it, focusing on adding some to his bottom and top lids and then smearing it out as he watches me hungrily.

Stepping back, I admire my work and nod. "Hot."

His eyes seem darker, sultrier, and he looks every inch the bad boy.

Turning, he grins at himself. "Yeah, would you sit on my face now?"

"I would have before." I wink. "But you definitely have that bad boy rocker thing going on now," I tell him as I pop some mascara on and look through the many lipsticks.

"Red," he shouts out and grins. "Sorry, but red would look fucking sexy."

I pick up a red lipstick and lean close to the mirror. I had to learn to put on lipstick with fangs, but I'm used to it at this point. When I lean back, I see that he was right. The deep red stands out against my skin, almost looking like spilled blood, and when I turn for his approval, his hand fists in my hair, and his tongue darts out and swipes across my lips. The scent of his desire wraps around me.

"You look good enough to eat," he purrs.

"Then why don't you?" I whisper against his lips.

Turning me with a growl, he hoists me onto the side and drops to his knees before me as his hands slide up my thighs. "Oh, I will, Althea, now be a good girl and cover my lips in your cum so I can wear my very own lipstick."

"Make me," I order, gripping his hair and tugging him closer. He comes willingly. He grips my thighs and parts them, lifting so he gets a good view of my wet pussy and thick thighs.

"Nox, look at that," he whispers reverently. "Poets would write sonnets about your cunt, and painters would dedicate masterpieces to it. Fucking hell, Althea, you are going to kill every single one of us, and all with a look at this pretty, juicy pussy, begging for its kings."

"And what about you?" I question as I lean back, spreading my legs indecently wide and lifting my hips with a roll, making a growl erupt from his throat. "What will you do, my king, to taste my pussy?"

"Everything, anything," he snarls, slashing his claws into my thighs. "I'll worship at your altar like you are my fucking goddess, and you are, Althea. I'm yours, so use me. Ride my face to find your pleasure and let me taste it. Fill me with it. Fucking suffocate me with it. I don't care. I want it all. You are as close to heaven as this sinner is ever going to get, baby, so let me see those pearly gates with your screams in my ears and your taste on my tongue."

How could a girl refuse a plea like that?

I place my foot on his shoulder as he groans, watching my pussy greedily.

"Then make me come, Reve. Make me yours."

He doesn't need any other encouragement. He descends on my pussy like a wild animal, lashing every inch of me with his tongue. My head falls back to the mirror with a groan as I use his hair to tug him closer so he's buried so deep in my cunt, he probably can't breathe, but if the way he's tonguing me is anything to go by, then he doesn't care. In fact, he grips my thighs to yank me closer until I'm riding his tongue as he dips it inside of me and then back up to circle my clit.

"Reve," I moan, arching as I roll my hips and reach for my pleasure.

With a growl, his fingers dance across my pussy before thrusting into me, filling me with two then curling, rubbing that spot inside me as I grind and wind my hips, using him for my pleasure like he wanted.

"More. Let go, Althea. Let me have it all. I can take it, baby. Fucking take what's yours," he snarls against my wet flesh, the vibrations making me gasp.

My legs begin to shake, and I tug him closer, riding him like he ordered me to. I grind into his lips, teeth, and tongue as his fingers fuck me in time with his tongue on my clit.

It's agony in the best way.

"You're so close, beautiful. I can feel it. Your little cunt is greedily sucking at my fingers, desperate to be filled with my cum. Spill for me, fucking squirt down my throat," he demands.

His filthy words, coupled with his tongue and fingers, send me over the edge, screaming my release as I squirt all over him like he wanted.

He drinks it up, licking every drop with a snarl. His claws dig into my thick thighs as I heave above him, trying to push him away.

It's a mistake he punishes me for.

Turning his head, he sinks his fangs into my inner thigh. I scream, and my pussy clenches on his fingers as I come again, gripping his hair as he drinks from me. My back arches, and the pleasure becomes so intense, I explode again, screaming my release.

Panting, I fall back as he pulls his fangs free and licks the bite marks. My blood is smeared on his chin and lips just like lipstick, and he makes no move to wipe it away. "Fuck, you're delicious." He licks my thighs and pussy, cleaning every inch of me as I whimper, unable to do anything but watch him.

He is still on his knees before me, yet he is in complete control, and he knows it. After laying one more gentle kiss over my clit, he begins to stand.

He grips my throat and kisses me deeply, letting me taste my blood and cum on his tongue. "Next time, I'll spend hours between your thighs, covering you in cum and blood," he purrs against my lips. "But the others are calling for us."

"Spoilsports." I huff, making him laugh as I push him away and hop up. My legs are shaky, so he has to catch me to make sure I don't fall. "Your lipstick's smeared."

He grins smugly. It's smudged all over his lips and face, but he leaves it there like a trophy, and I can't help but feel smug at that myself.

Here is a man who is so proud to have made me come, he's wearing it like a badge of fucking honour.

It's hot as hell.

It's also very consuming.

"How about you smear it across my cock too, pretty girl?" he purrs.

Huffing, I fix my makeup and fluff my hair before grabbing some new clothes. Sliding into a super soft skirt that falls to my ankles with a split up one side and a crop top, I leave my bra and knickers off, comfy and stylish.

He growls as he watches me, stalking my every move as I get ready. I clench my thighs together, smearing my need across them, and the scent only drives him mad.

He tries to grab me again, so I dance out of his reach and rush to find the others before I let him pull me to bed and do all the dirty things he wants to, the ones I could see in his eyes.

The ones I want as well.

NINETEEN

ALTHEA

THE OTHERS ARE GATHERED in the room where Nathair fucked me, all in various states of training. I step in with Reve, and he instantly moves over to a blank wall at the back.

"Time to see what we can do." Nathair grins as he holds out his hand to me. "You have to trust us as much as we do you. You have to know you can depend on us. We will work on your powers, but first, it might help to see ours in action, yeah?"

"Yes!" I shout in excitement, taking his hand. He leads me over to a floor pad for fighting, but instead of sparring, he sits me down on it.

"Then watch and see." He winks, his hand lingering against mine for a moment before he walks away. Nathair glances at the wall he fucked me against, and it makes me tighten my thighs together as I fight the desire that twists within me so I can focus on what they are doing—which is not something I wish they were doing, like fucking me.

That comes after, Reve promises in my head, his silky voice making me shudder. I'm used to them talking in my head, but their whispered, dirty promises affect me so much more than if they said them out loud. They inflict the words with their intention so I can almost taste what will happen.

Focus, I tell myself.

"You've already seen some of Conall's, so why don't you begin, brother?" Nathair calls to the big man who's leaning casually against a mirror.

Conall nods and waits for me to look at him. One moment, he's there, and the next, shadows obscure him so I have to focus to even feel his presence. They stretch out into the room, crawling along the floor like ghostly fingers, and when they slide up my legs, I gasp at the sensation.

They are warm and almost feel like hands touching me.

They slide under my skirt, the tendrils tickling along my thighs before rubbing my mound and sliding up my body. They grip my breasts and then my neck before suddenly disappearing, leaving me panting and wide-eyed.

Conall grins innocently at me from the same spot he was in before the shadows stole him. "I can control any darkness, but more than that, I can control the elements to some extent." He holds out his hand, and I watch as a small tornado starts to spin on his palm, and then rain falls across him and thunder roars in the distance. "The sun is harder, but I'm getting there." He drops his palm, watching me expectantly.

I just stare, unsure what to say.

"Oh, and there is one more perk." He's gone again, but there are no shadows this time. Black swirls before me, and he appears out of it, making me fall back as he pins me. "I can use them to conceal myself, almost like transporting—well, I can in the darkness."

"That's so cool," I whisper, staring up at his face in awe.

"My turn," Reve says, and Conall winks as he rolls to lie at my side, resting his hand on my thigh.

I turn my gaze to Reve, even though Conall's hand slides up my leg and under my skirt, teasing me like his shadows.

"You know I can dream walk, but that's not all."

The wall suddenly disappears, and in its place is a field, a meadow, that looks so real, I lean forward to touch it. The grass is bright green, birds sing, and trees arch up to the blazing sun. I can even smell the fresh air and flowers, but then the scene warps into a graveyard so suddenly, I jerk.

"I can manipulate what you see. I could trap you in a fictional place if I wanted to or give you good or bad dreams and guide you through visions," he murmurs as the whole room suddenly disappears, and instead, I am back in my bedroom, asleep with them all curled up around me.

It also disappears, and then I recoil when something crawls from the floor before me, its clawed hand reaching for me before it, too, disappears into a poof of air. Panting, I look up at Reve before a smile curls my lips. "You are incredible."

He jerks before a slow smile curves his wicked lips. "I knew you would see it that way."

"Enough showing off," Nathair says teasingly. "Zale?"

Zale hesitates, and Nathair frowns. "We will not let anything happen. You can do this, brother."

"Do not be scared," Zale says, and without flourish, his power slams through the room.

He seems to melt, and I hold my breath, my jaw dropping when a black dog stands in Zale's place. It's huge, with vicious teeth and fangs and a barbed tail with flames dancing around it. It's the same shaggy colour as his hair, and his eyes are still the same.

It's Zale, but it's not. His eyes are swirling like a vortex, as if he's fighting something else.

He prowls towards me, but I don't move away. I watch him come, knowing it's still Zale and he wouldn't hurt me. The others seem worried, though, and move closer. He snarls at them and lashes his tail as flames spring up between them and me. I sit still and wait, holding out my hand, and he sniffs it before his forked tongue darts out. He laps at my palm, making me giggle, and then he sits and places his head in my lap, letting me scratch him. When I lift my head, the others are staring at us in shock.

"What?" I ask, suddenly unsure. Did I break a rule?

Power sweeps across me, and suddenly Zale is before me on all fours. "They are simply surprised, *mima*."

"Why?" I ask.

"My other half doesn't like anyone, ever. Even the others have been attacked by him," he says, watching me with a bright grin. "I can transform into him whenever I need to. It allows me to cross souls and walk amongst the dead, though I do not do it often if I can help it."

"Oh, wow." I don't know what else to say.

"Osis," Nathair calls, picking up on my shock and filling the silence.

Osis silently pads before me as Zale turns to watch, keeping his head in my lap. I reach out once more and stroke his hair as Osis smiles at me. "All of our powers feature the ability to cause death or to understand it, a gift from the gods to help us. Zale can help the dead cross, Azul can see them, and me? I guard them. I guard the passage between life and death." His power wraps around him, and just like Zale, he transforms, but Osis isn't a dog, no. He's a pure white tiger.

He's huge, beautiful, and almost serene looking, and a sense of peace floats from him. He heads closer, and his tiger winds around me before he stands feet away and transforms back into Osis. Even as a man, the same sense of tranquil peace flows from him, so maybe some of their gifts mirror their internal emotions?

"I stop anyone who tries to escape from the other side, and I also prevent those who shouldn't die yet from slipping away."

I look between them. "Your powers—"

"Oh, we aren't done yet." Nathair grins.

"My turn?" Azul asks. Nathair nods, and Azul smiles softly at me. "I can talk to the dead, and I see the ghosts. They help us hunt, but they can also protect and hurt if I order them to—I don't like to, though, unless I have to. If I ask, I can channel them and their powers." He murmurs something I can't make out, and then we wait as cold air blows across me, almost chilling me to the bone.

It's the touch of death. I would know it anywhere.

Azul seems to fade, becoming transparent, and then I cannot see him anymore, but a cold hand drags down my arm and across my breasts, making me shiver. I feel the ghostly touch slide down my belly and over my pussy before disappearing, that cold sting leaving me breathless as he slowly reappears.

"I cannot hold it for too long because it uses a lot of energy." He shrugs.

Nathair looks at Lycus, but he shakes his head. "Not me."

"We will make sure she is safe, brother," Nathair says as he nods at Lycus. "Show her."

With one last unsure glance at me, Lycus unties his hair and tosses the band to me. "Hold onto it. The change shreds everything for me. I didn't get as lucky as these bastards." He huffs and then he starts to strip.

Sweet fucking Nox.

My mouth actually drops open, and I am thankful Nathair made Lycus show me his gifts because I'm practically squirming on the spot. I only catch a glimpse of his body, but it's enough to leave me a wet, hungry mess.

His solid, thick, hairy thighs frame a massive semi-erect cock, and I'm about to suggest a different type of fun when Lycus changes into a spider.

He's not a tiny little spider, though, because this spider is bigger than a car. Its eight spindly legs are bent so its black body is lowered to the floor in submission. Its black eyes are locked on me, and its fangs drip with venom. For a moment, everyone freezes, no doubt expecting me to be scared, but when I only tilt my head, he stands, almost brushing the ceiling with his height.

Monsters of the night, just like the god said.

He slowly wanders over, and the others move closer as if they are worried he will hurt me. I can see the venom dripping to the floor and dissolving everything, yet the spider just stops in front of me and watches me the way I'm watching it.

"Do not make any sudden movements," Nathair warns softly. The spider turns and spits venom at him. He easily dodges it, as if he's used to its antics, and then the spider turns back to me. It doesn't scare me. If anything, I'm intrigued, so I slowly get to my knees before him, not wanting to spook him.

"Althea," one of them hisses, but I ignore him and focus on the spider.

"You're beautiful," I tell the spider, hoping Lycus can hear me. It's obvious he's worried about this side of himself. Tilting my head once more, I sweep my eyes over his body, and when I look back at his eyes, I notice he's moving his legs behind him, and then suddenly, a web flies at me. I jerk as the silken feeling wraps around my wrists like a net, binding them together.

"Oh shit," Nathair grumbles, but he sounds more resigned than worried, so I relax.

I fall back as the spider rushes over me, and then I feel more silken web wrapping around my ankles and up my legs, binding them together. I peer up at the spider, and my heart pounds with desire. It's not necessarily for the creature on top of me, but the feel of the silken bonds.

"What's he doing?" I ask breathlessly.

Nathair laughs. "Well, it seems Lycus's spider, erm, likes you. Either he's going to try and eat you or he thinks you're his mate."

"Reassuring," I mutter, and there are some chuckles. "Hey, big guy, as hot as being bound in silk is, I'm not down to fuck a spider right this moment, so can I have Lycus back, please?"

The spider lowers over my body, the hair on its legs and body surprisingly soft and almost comforting. "Please? Your webs are beautiful. They really are," I purr softly, and for a moment, those black beady eyes just watch me, and then, one of its front legs reaches out and brushes my face gently. My eyes close, and when I open them again, Lycus is there with his hand on my face. His silken bindings are still wrapped around my body, and his own naked form is pressed against me.

Our breaths mingle as our eyes lock together, and I feel his hard cock slide along my stomach.

"Lycus," I whisper.

I don't know if it's hearing his name on my lips or the fact that I'm practically rubbing myself against him that breaks the spell.

"You accepted my spider," he growls, flashing his fangs. "By not fighting the webbing, you accepted him as your mate." He lowers his mouth and drags his fangs across my lips, making me arch up. "Do you know what that means?"

"No."

"That you're mine." He groans as he turns my head and sinks his fangs into me. I scream as red-hot venom rushes through my veins, setting me on fire. Everything fades, and I lose my vision and sense of smell. The last thing I see are the others fighting to get Lycus off me and him holding them off with one hand.

He pumps his venom into me as I'm pinned and bound for him until the lava in my veins slows and cools.

Finally, I can breathe again, and my heart restarts. I gasp in a breath as my vision comes back and find the others crouched around us with their fangs bared, keeping their distance.

"Do not stop him. She's dead if he doesn't counteract the venom," Nathair growls at the others.

Growling against my neck, Lycus grips me tighter, and I sluggishly lift my arms and wrap them around him. I test the web on my legs and find I can move slightly, so I part them and let him fall between my thighs. We both groan as I finally get him where I want him, even as I die once more.

Mine.

The word is hissed in my head, accompanied by a vision of me bound and hanging down from the ceiling as he fucks me with his fangs in my neck, deadly venom dripping over my body.

Fuck yes.

Sliding his hands possessively across my body, he moves his hips, and I'm about to cry out when two thick fingers slam into me, claiming me like his fangs are.

I scream his name as my blood starts to heat again, this time with pleasure so hot, I cry out and clench around his fingers as I gush. When he curls his fingers inside me, I come with a scream, milking them so tight, he snarls.

He slides his fangs from my neck and lifts his head. Blood coats his mouth and beard, and his black eyes watch me as he fucks me through my orgasm with his fingers. He rips open his wrist and presses it to my mouth, smearing his blood over my lips, and when I stick out my tongue to taste it, that burning venom within me begins to settle. I fall back, gasping, and then he twists his hand, grinding his palm into my clit.

"Again," he snarls, more monster than man.

"Can't," I whimper, desperately licking his blood to douse the fire.

I scream when he adds two more fingers, stretching me to the point of pain, adding to the agony of my own blood and the venom now in my veins. Snarling, he fucks me with his fingers, and pleasure surges through me again.

I arch up and slam my fangs into the only place I can reach—his chest, right over his heart.

He bellows, his back bowing as his release sprays over me, my own rolling through me to him. He just keeps coming, and so do I, until the heat eventually dissipates and we both collapse, covered in blood, cum, and silken webs with lazy smiles on our faces.

Lifting his head, Lycus cups my face gently. "I was so worried he would hurt you," he admits softly. "I never thought you could . . ." He shakes his head, so I kiss him.

"I will never be scared of you," I whisper against his lips. "And next time, we can try exactly what was in your head."

He jerks back, his eyes widening before he throws his head back and laughs.

"Damn, why didn't I get that for showing my gifts?" Reve mutters.

Lycus rolls from me then gathers me into his lap, petting me like he can't bear to let me go. Lazy with pleasure and blood, I lean into him, my legs partially splayed in the silk bindings.

"Well, that answers one thing," Nathair comments mysteriously.

I want to ask, but he probably won't tell me, so I lean more securely into Lycus and look around. I turn my eyes to Nathair. "And you?"

Stepping back, he rips open his shirt, making me lick my lips in hunger.

Despite how much I seem to know about Nathair, he is also the one I know the least about.

"We are all monsters in some way or another, Althea. Some can hide it better, but deep down?" He drops to the floor, and a snake rises from the clothing pile. "We are all creatures of the night," it hisses in Nathair's voice, the tone slightly more chaotic.

I stare, unable to help it.

I didn't expect that at all.

It stands tall with its tail curled around its black body, which glitters with a golden sheen on its glowing scales. Huge fangs spear a forked tongue as his hooded head weaves. Unlike Lycus, Nathair feels more present, as if they blended.

"I have had centuries to practice," he hisses, lowering his head as he slithers to me across the floor, "to become one with my animal. Lycus will get there eventually."

He is just as beautiful in snake form as he is in vampyr form.

"Some myths say vampyrs descended from snakes. Nathair's species hasn't existed for centuries, since before the first blood king," Osis offers as I stare. "It is a gift."

"And a curse," Nathair hisses. "Like Lycus, I can use venom if I wish . . . ," he trails off as he lowers to the edge of my feet. "Or cause great pleasure."

He slides up my legs, and Lycus binds my arms, keeping me locked in place as Nathair's forked tongue lashes the air. He slides between my parted thighs, and before I can stop him, his forked tongue flutters across my pussy. My head falls back. This is wrong, so wrong, but I see Nathair in the snake's eyes and hear his voice in my head.

I can taste you, even in this form. You are sweeter than any blood or poison.

Oh Nox.

"Does he feel good?" Lycus murmurs in my ear. "Does that forked tongue feel good against that pretty pussy?"

Shit, shit, shit.

I try to squeeze my eyes shut, but then they open when his forked tongue thrusts into me, and I can't help but moan as it reaches places inside me nothing else ever has—places that have me lifting my hips and grinding into his tongue as his fangs scrape along my pussy.

"Does it feel good inside of you, wiggling around? Look how beautiful you are, spread and bound in my silk with Nathair eating you." Lycus's dirty words have my eyes lifting to the others. All of them watch me with undisguised lust.

It's wrong, so wrong, yet I can't seem to care when they don't.

After all, this is the Court of Nightmares, and we can be whatever we want here.

Giving in to the pleasure, I let Lycus hold me and whisper dirty nothings as Nathair fucks my pussy. His tongue thrusts in and out of me before sliding to my clit, the forked edges flicking over the nub until I cry out and grind into his face.

I accept the pleasure, even as the snake slides lower and thrusts its tongue into my ass. The pleasure that was kept at bay explodes as I come with a scream.

Turning his head, he sinks his fangs into my thigh, making me yell.

Unlike Lycus's venom, something else floods my veins—euphoria. The bliss of falling into my release brings so much pleasure, I actually black out.

When I wake up, Nathair is curled on my chest, flicking his tail through my blood and release. His heavy coils pin my leg, warming me, as Lycus strokes my hair and holds me.

"You're all going to kill me," I rasp, my chest heavy with his weight.

"Don't you mean kill you again?" Zale chuckles, making me giggle.

"I'd like to see Althea's powers," Azul says, and all eyes swing to me.

"Then I'll show you . . . when I can move."

TWENTY

ALTHEA

THEY GIVE ME A couple of minutes to recover before letting me go. Standing in the middle of the room, I try to conjure my powers once more, wanting to impress them after the incredible show they put on. I look within and find the rose there, awake and waiting, so I give it some blood, and it writhes. I open my eyes and watch them react.

Without meaning to, I slide into Reve's mind and see myself through his eyes. My bright lavender eyes blaze with power, my hair floats around me, and my skin glows from inside.

I look strong.

Sliding back into my own mind, I search for what I want and find it on Lycus. My cuts on his neck are still open, so I focus on the puncture marks. I feel his blood calling to me as if it's mine, and without a moment of hesitation, I reach for it. His blood pours from his neck as he stumbles in shock and falls to his knees.

I cut off quickly, realising the harm I could do with that. I only meant to touch it like I had with my own the other day, but it almost harmed him.

"Holy shit," Osis whispers.

The blood pools before Lycus, so I focus on it, and once it's bubbling in the air, I push it towards him, watching it absorb into his skin, and within moments, he's healed.

"You can heal," Nathair says, sounding shocked. "That's a very, very rare power, Althea."

"Sorry, Lycus," I say.

"You could rip me open and feed on my organs, and I would thank you, little one," he replies.

"What else can you do?" Reve asks excitedly.

"I'm not sure," I admit. "Shall I try something?"

"I wonder . . ." Nathair watches me curiously. "Althea, could you focus on an image, one that makes you truly happy, and try to project it?"

I frown, close my eyes, and try to do just that. "Anything?" I ask without looking.

"No, focus on something with so much deep emotion that you cannot do anything but see it."

Blowing out my breath, I focus my mind.

I automatically think of Simon in one of the only places where I was ever happy. We are curled up in my bed with junk food spread everywhere. We were younger then, and it was before the change. We created shadows on the ceiling with our hands as we laughed. For a moment, so much happiness fills me that it's almost staggering, and when I open my eyes, I see the image projected from me like a memory.

"Now change it," Reve instructs calmly. "Focus on what you want to see."

Frowning, I do as he tells me, his directives sliding into my head.

That's it. See what you want, envision it.

The image changes to one of us as we would be now, and a cry escapes my lips before the image drops, along with my concentration.

"What was that?" I demand.

"That was my gift," Reve murmurs, watching me with a guarded expression.

"I think . . . when you feed from us, it not only creates a bond but also a bond between us, and if you concentrate and strengthen it, you might be able to channel our gifts," Nathair muses. "At least to a certain extent. We will need to explore this further one on one, trying out each gift with you to see if that's true."

Rolling my shoulders to release the tension there, I nod and say, "No time like the present."

Nathair hesitates but jerks his chin. "Osis, you first. Reve, we already know she can channel yours."

Lycus heads my way, lifting me so he can give me a lingering kiss. "I meant what I said," he murmurs, and then he puts me down gently and heads out of the room.

Huffing, Reve approaches, rolling back his sleeves dramatically. "I can do better than that." He dips me, making me laugh before he kisses me so deeply, I moan, and then he swings me back up with a cocky grin.

Zale kisses my cheek on the way past, and Azul simply looks at me with such longing that it hurts. Conall winks and follows after them, whistling.

Nathair watches them go with a smile, and when he glances back at me, his eyes darken. "When you are done, I will send one of the others in. Behave, Althea. We all know you live to tempt us." He sweeps from the room, leaving me with Osis, who seems unsure.

OSIS

I don't know if she will be able to channel my tiger, but if Nathair is right and she can access some of our powers, then we need to try. It would be useful, and it would also make us stronger. I guess everything has changed with our queen's arrival.

Sliding gracefully to my bum, I cross my legs. She slowly heads my way, sitting before me in the exact same manner with her knees pressed to mine. Even that small touch sends need hammering through me, but I try to push it back and focus on what Nathair wants us to do.

Watching first Lycus and then Nathair feed and taste her drove my tiger wild. He roared inside, wanting out, but she didn't seem ready for that yet. I can tell she's slightly overwhelmed and lost. She needs a steadying hand, not a demanding one.

"A lot of my powers are from my mind, and they are about focusing and finding peace. It took me a very long time. Despite my tiger being hot-blooded, he is also a protector, and for that, he needs focus." She nods in understanding. "I do not know if you can access my change. We will try that later, but for now, let's clear your mind and focus on the other part of my powers—guarding the realm between death and life."

"No biggie." She grins, and a smile curves my lips.

"Close your eyes," I murmur.

She does as she's told, and other ideas of what I could order her to do fill me before I push them away. One eye cracks open, and she grins at me, making me realise she can probably read my projected thoughts.

Licking my lips nervously, I gruffly order her to shut them again.

"Yes, sir," she purrs submissively. "Just so you know, I like your orders."

Fuck, she did hear. This is not helping me with my balance.

Focus, I demand, feeling my tiger slash me inside, demanding to play and take her up on her evident offer. "Okay, and clear your thoughts." I watch the expressions play over her face and smile. "It is easier said than done but keep trying. You'll get used to this part, and it will become easy one day."

"Sure," she mumbles.

"Stop focusing on your emotions and your worries. Just focus on your breathing, slowly in and out. Imagine everything flowing out with it. Good girl."

She tenses at that, and I file that away for later. When she's relaxed, I take her hands, smooth my fingers across her slow, steady pulse, and lower my voice so I don't disturb her.

"Good." I close my eyes and focus on that spot inside me, finding it in seconds. It's a connection deeper than anything else, and it takes me to another dimension. I feel it flow through me to her because I have nothing else to focus on.

She gasps. *It's beautiful.*

"Those are the gates of death. Every soul must pass through them after judgement," I whisper to her.

I focus on what she is seeing. The gates are surrounded by fog. They change all the time, a myriad of colours. I don't know what is beyond them, only the dead do, but I've seen them open. I'm no god of death. No, he is a far more powerful and terrifying being, but I can drag the living here or I can help those who are struggling to pass over. I also guide them after judgement. I explain this all to her, and when our eyes open in sync, I know time has passed, but I do not know how much. I never do.

"Wow," she whispers, blinking slowly. "Your powers . . ."

I hesitate. They are not as flashy or as great as some of the others', but when she looks at me like that, I feel like I truly am a god.

". . . are incredible, Osis," she says, squeezing my hand. "I've never felt such peace, and what you do is more important than anything we could ever do."

I sit up straighter, and my eyes drop to her lips when I remember her reaction to my orders, to my praise. Althea liked it, and just like all of us, she has been searching for love most of her life.

I wonder . . .

Dragging my hand up her arm and across her shoulder, I grip her throat to keep her attention. Her eyes widen, and her pulse speeds up under my hand, making my fangs lengthen. "Althea, be a good girl and kiss me."

Eyes simmering, she leans into me. I make no move to help her as she leans in and brushes her lips softly against mine.

"Properly," I order, tightening my hold.

Moaning, she presses her lips to mine and kisses me. I don't kiss her back, but when she leans away, looking sad, I can't resist.

I pin her to the floor and dominate her teasing little mouth, showing her what good girls who follow orders get.

Her hands come up and grip my shoulders, holding me to her as I kiss her. My mind spins and whirls with her sweet, drugging kiss, invading my usual calmness as I groan into her lips.

"Well, Nathair was right," Zale says with a laugh.

I didn't even hear him arrive, but I can't stop myself from placing one more kiss against her raw lips.

"He sent me in just in case you two got distracted."

Pulling away, I feel my cheeks flush as I turn to see him.

He just grins, leaning against the door as he watches us. "I don't blame you." He shrugs. "But Nathair wants you, and it's my turn with our Thea." He rubs his hands together wickedly, and for a moment, jealousy fills me before I sit up and pull her with me, sliding my hand over her face in a loving caress.

I am desperate to dive into the feelings between us, the ones that affect my usual calm persona. I want to know what a good girl she would be when she's filled to the brim with my cock and cum.

She kisses my palm softly, and my heart skips a beat. "Be good," I purr before standing, then I clap Zale on the shoulder on my way past.

My body is alight with her touch, her taste, and the life I felt on her lips, as well as the death that lingers on mine.

Twenty One

Zale

I watch her for a moment. Her lips are red and swollen from kissing Osis, and her eyes glitter with want. She's so beautiful, it leaves me speechless for a moment as I just stare at her.

She watches me back, and that's when I realise she's worried I'm upset about finding her kissing Osis.

Pushing from the wall, I head her way, not stopping until I sit before her just like Osis was. "Do not ever worry about us catching you with another. It is bound to happen, and we are all together anyway. We will never not want or need you, Althea. Plus, I'm realising I like to watch," I admit without shame. Her eyes widen, and I grin at the shock on her face. "I'll show you one day, but I've never had a problem sharing," I tell her, licking my lips as she watches me. All sorts of images come to mind, but I push them away, needing to focus. "But we better get to work before Nathair finds us and we get told off, or maybe even punished." I wink, making her laugh.

"You saw me transform. Nathair is curious if you can channel that," I say, not voicing my fear regarding transforming before her or her getting close to the beast that lives within me, but he seems tame at the moment. "Shall we try it?"

"Hell yes." She wiggles excitedly, and my mind supplies me with an image of her wiggling on top of me like that. She laughs, obviously seeing it, and smacks my thigh. "Behave."

"If you do." I wink. "Okay, unlike Osis, my power does not come from peace. It comes from emotion . . . from fire," I purr, running my eyes down her body. "Use strong emotions, such as anger, hate, love, and desire." I lick my fangs, and she watches the movement. "You let that fire flow through you and change you."

"Sounds easy," she replies breathlessly, the scent of her need making me growl.

"Then let's try it." I hold out my hand, and she takes it, knowing power is enhanced with a connection. "Focus on those or something that makes you feel it."

"What do you focus on?" she asks curiously.

"Usually desire," I reply, not willingly to admit that focusing on any other emotion makes it harder to control. I don't want her thinking I'm weak. "I think of feeding, of fangs sinking into flesh, and the first moment blood explodes in my mouth. I think about Lycus stroking my cock as he feeds from me, or my own hand pumping myself to release as I feed. Recently, my thoughts have been of you riding me as you feed from me, or one of the others taking your neck as you do, their cock in your pretty little ass, all while you drain and fuck me dry."

"Fuck," she murmurs. "That would be so hot. I'd keep using you even when you begged me to stop."

"I wouldn't. I'd beg you to drain every single drop of blood and cum from me as you let the others fuck and feed from you," I tell her. Her chest rises faster as she watches me, her eyes sparkling with desire. "Good, you're feeling it. Let it flow through you." With that image in my mind, I reach for my change, but this time, I push it down my arm and through my skin to hers, only hesitating for a moment before I remember what Nathair said.

She will be safe.

It ripples under her skin, trying to get out, but when she falls back with a scream, I pull it back, guilt and worry assaulting me. Panting, she lies there as I hover over her, not wanting to touch her in case I hurt her.

"Okay, maybe I can't take your change," she says. "That hurt."

"Maybe with more practice?" I say, feeling unsure. My guilt triples at my relief. I would hate for her to take the beast even I fear. "But let's not do that right now. How about flames instead? They come from the same place, but they do not hurt."

I had forgotten how bad the change can hurt, and if caught in her skin, my dog would rip her to shreds from the inside. Hurt would be an understatement, but our queen is strong.

It doesn't stop my guilt, though, but the determination in her eyes helps a little.

"Flames, yeah, let's do flames." She huffs as she sits up, but this time, she slides onto my lap with her back to my chest and pulls my arms around her. I swallow hard as her perfect ass sits right on top of my hard cock. When she wiggles, I groan, fighting my desire. "Show me."

I struggle to focus beyond her perky ass. Flames require almost no thought. Holding out my arms in case it burns her, I let fire dance across my skin. She gasps and leans forward, making me groan.

"Touch one," I offer, my voice hoarse from my need.

She reaches out and touches a flame, and when it doesn't burn her, she places her hand on my arm. We both watch as the flames transfer from my skin to hers, dancing across it until we are both engulfed. She turns her head and slams her lips onto mine.

Groaning, I kiss her back roughly as more flames lick and swallow our bodies as we tumble to the floor.

My hands slide down her back and grip her ass, pulling her more securely across me. She tugs her mouth away and runs it down my neck.

"Yes, feed, fuck, take every inch of me. I'm yours," I beg.

LYCUS

I should leave, I should turn away, but I can't.

Althea is mine, my other half made that very obvious, but she is also theirs. I expected jealousy, but all I feel is a bone-deep desire as I watch her kiss and nip Zale's throat. Flames dance across their skin without burning them as she pins him to the floor. He moans, begging her to use him, but there is something else he loves more than being used, and so I step into the room.

His eyes roll to me, and a groan leaves his lips as he holds his hand out, welcoming me. Moving closer, I fist her hair, ignoring the flames burning me, even as my skin blisters and blackens. It heals, only to do it again.

"Don't bite him right away, little one, he likes to hurt," I murmur.

She lifts her head and looks back at me. "He likes to suffer?" She smiles. "Want to help me?"

"Always." I grin wickedly as he groans below her.

"Good," she purrs, leaning down to drag her lips along Zale's, my hand still in her hair. "He's going to fuck me on top of you. He's going to feed from me so blood covers us both, and I'll only bite you and sink onto your cock when he comes."

Fuck.

I can almost see it, and from Zale's groan, I know he loves the idea as much as I. The dirty bastard always loved to wait, but me? I much prefer the idea of sinking into that sweet cunt and drinking her blood again.

"Do you like the sound of that?" she purrs, rubbing her hot body against us.

"Answer her," I order, tugging her hair so she arches up, and then I drag my fangs across her throat as he watches. She whimpers and rolls her hips faster against his cock.

"Fuck yes, please, Althea," he begs, gripping her hips to hold her to him.

"Good, then lie on him, little one," I order, my cock aching to be inside of her.

Doing as she's told, she lies flat on him, nipping and licking his neck and face to tease him. We should be working on her powers, but fuck that, we can do it later. I want her too badly for that, and Nathair is on an errand with Reve anyway.

Dragging her skirt off, I fling it away and rip her shirt from her body, leaving her naked and so fucking beautiful it makes me drop to my knees. She looked exquisite wrapped in my webs. *Another time,* I remind myself, trailing my hand down her tanned back. Her skin is as soft as silk, and her curves make me harder than I've ever been in my entire long life.

There is no doubt in my mind that she was handmade by the gods. She is too fucking perfect.

My hand slides over her plump ass as my cock jerks. She parts her thighs and lifts her ass, letting me see her glistening pink cunt.

It's pink with her desire, and her clit is engorged. Her hair cascades over her shoulder as she looks back at me with a cheeky grin.

For a moment, time freezes.

The gods gave me a choice once, and I thank every single one of them right now for giving me that choice and then giving her to me.

My need for her is so strong it almost doubles me over. The bond between us grows stronger with every interaction, and it's unlike anything I've ever felt before.

Almost like a mating, but much, much more powerful.

"Are you just going to stare at me?" She grins.

"I might," I reply. "I've never seen something as perfect or as beautiful in my long life. You are too fucking perfect. I've seen beauty in my lifetime, but never like this." Words cannot do her justice.

She is the type of woman men go to war over, who makes a warrior reckless in his attempt to capture her.

Her eyes simmer, her fangs lengthening. "Then fuck me and touch every inch of this beauty," she purrs, and a man doesn't need to be told twice, not when she looks at me like she can't wait to feel my huge cock fill her.

I slide my hand over her ass then hesitate, but it isn't the time for that now. I'm a big guy, so it would hurt like hell. *Later,* I tell myself as I drag my fingers over her pussy, smearing her need as I circle her clit. Her head drops to Zale's chest as she pushes back to meet my fingers. Her pretty cunt is on display for me, showing just how much she wants this.

The memory of how she felt coming on my fingers is enough to have me spearing them inside her, stretching her for my big cock. "You'll need to come at least twice to take my cock, little one."

"Then make me." She groans, pushing back to take my thick fingers deeper.

I work my digits deep before pulling them out, watching my thick, scarred fingers slide out covered in her cream. I hold them out for Zale, and he sucks them clean.

She pushes back with a moan, so I push them back into her pussy, and as she fucks herself on them, I flick her clit with my other hand, needing to feel her come apart for me. Her mouth works over Zale's throat again, biting but never breaking the skin as he groans beneath her.

She's close, her thick thighs shaking, and I crave her release.

When I pinch her clit, she screams her first release. I pull my fingers out and shove them into my own mouth, desperate to taste her cum. Groaning, I fight back the urge to come from her taste alone, and instead, I slide my hands under her and grip her thick thighs.

I yank her lower body up, sealing my mouth over her pussy like a starving man as she kisses Zale. My hand slides up her body, over her belly, to her heavy breasts as I tweak and flick her nipples, attacking her cunt for more of her taste.

I spear my tongue inside of her, feeling her tight channel clench around it. I can't fucking wait to feel it around my cock, to feel her come on it. Dragging my fangs up her slit, I gently pierce each side of her clit and then seal my mouth to her cunt as she comes with a gush, screaming her release into my brother's mouth.

I swallow every drop of her cum, then I let her collapse as I pull out my cock. I drag it along her dripping pussy and grip her hair before she bites Zale, holding her back from him. With my fangs bared, I slam into her pussy all the way to the hilt, impaling her on my huge length.

She screams and claws at Zale, who bows with a yell over the pain.

"Fuck," I howl. "You should feel her cunt. Gods, nothing better." I hammer into her, unable to help it. Pleasure claws at my back, and my balls tighten. Her cunt milks my cock, stretching around it so prettily. The sight of my huge length sliding it and out, coated in her cum, is so fucking sexy, I know I'll come later just from thinking about it.

I project it down the bond, making them all stumble and come from the sight.

I slam into her, watching her fat ass jiggle with the force. Smacking one cheek, I watch my handprint appear there as she cries out, writhing between us, then I wrap one arm around her as I tug her up, widening my stance as I fuck her.

I power into her, the wet sounds of bodies coming together loud. Zale snaps below her, biting at the air to get to her, his eyes wild and on fire. Knowing we are all close, I scratch my fangs along her neck and sink them into her.

She bows in my arms, clawing as I lift my mouth and let the blood flow down her and onto him, driving him wild as she clamps so tightly around my cock, I have to breathe through the need to come, not wanting this to be over yet.

Instead, I sink my fangs in once more, in another spot, and stay there as I hammer into her tight cunt until it's too much, and when she comes again, she takes me with her. I spill inside of her with a roar, her blood flowing down my chin.

Snarling, she rips herself from my fangs and cock. I fall back, watching my cum drip from her pretty pussy as she rips open Zale's pants and slams herself down on him. They both cry out, her head thrown back as blood continues to flow down her to him, coating them like a second skin. My cock twitches and hardens again, so I wrap my fist around it and tug myself as I watch our goddess, our queen, ride Zale.

Her claws slam into his chest to hold him still, and he roars in approval, fighting under her to get to her neck. She holds him off, finding her pleasure with a scream, and then lowers to slam her fangs into his neck, making his back arch as he roars his release.

When she releases his neck, he turns his head and bites her throat, making her scream again. From my angle, I can see her pretty pussy clenching in another orgasm as he drinks from her until they both collapse. Stepping over them, I pump my cock and splatter my release across them, making her whimper.

Spent, I stumble to my knees and then my back next to them, and she slides off him to lie between us, panting and covered in sweat, blood, and cum. Turning my head, I meet Zale's dazed eyes to see him smiling for once.

"I guess we should practice powers," she says, making me chuckle.

"Later," I reply.

When I can move.

Twenty Two

Conall

"I expected this from Zale, but you, Lycus?" I grin, and they all jerk around guiltily, but then she giggles, and I can't resist smiling. I have no doubt the little minx instigated this, and honestly, none of us would have been able to resist.

Fuck, the image Lycus projected was enough to have me coming in the shower like some teenager again.

"I couldn't help myself." She grins, covered in blood and the others' cum, yet she has never looked so fucking regal or beautiful. "I guess I should practice." She sighs.

"You can rest. I brought some food, since I figured you would all be hungry." I wheel the trolley in, and they perk up. "There's water, coke, coffee, pancakes, and French toast, and Azul sent pizza and pasta since he said you would want it."

"Are you feeding a nation?" she teases, but then the guys lunge at the food, and I bat them away.

"Her first," I bark.

Ashamed, they shuffle back as she stands, her naked form on full display as she prowls over. My tongue sticks to the roof of my mouth, and every single one of us tracks her as she moves. She reaches the trolley, her tongue darting out, before she grabs a slice of pizza and demolishes it in one bite.

There is something so fucking sexy about a woman who eats without shame, and it almost has me coming in my trousers once more. Shifting to make myself comfortable, I watch her put a plate together, and then she gestures to the rest.

"You can eat everything else." She winks at me and then carries her plate over to the mat we train on, where she sits down and starts working her way through her food.

Unable to stop myself, I head over to her, laying my legs on either side of hers. She leans back into me as she eats, and before the other two have started to stuff their faces, she's done.

"Still hungry?" I ask softly.

She nods, so I take her plate, steal whatever is left on the trolley, then hand it over. She picks at it, eating slowly, and I'm about ready to bend her over and fuck her in the crumbs because of how hot she looks while she eats. My hands wander to her curves, squeezing in appreciation.

"Next time you eat, I want to be inside of you," I murmur, and she chokes on a bite of pizza, swinging her gaze around to me.

"What? Why?" She gapes.

Lycus and Zale nod in agreement.

"Because, Thea, you look so fucking sexy, and knowing I provided it for you?" I groan, biting my bottom lip as I feel the darkness swirl around me.

She laughs and shakes her head at us before offering me the last bite of pizza. When I raise my eyebrow, she presses it to my mouth, feeding me.

I hesitate, but at her urging, I take it, my eyes wide. Does she know the significance of her gesture?

The others are frozen, the same question in their minds.

"Althea," I begin after swallowing. "Do you know what feeding a male means in our culture?"

She turns away, but I drag her back, needing to know if she feels the same as I do. "Of course I do, I'm not an idiot." She narrows her eyes.

Groaning, I drag my thumb across her lips, humbled and so happy I could laugh, but I have to be sure. "Althea, are you sure—"

"Fucking hell, Conall. Does a girl need a neon sign?" she snaps, crossing her arms adorably. "Yes, I know feeding a male means she holds him in high regard and wants to claim him as hers." She swings her eyes to me. "Do you have a problem with that?"

"Not even a shred," I reply gruffly as I grab the back of her neck and pull her closer. "Just had to be sure."

"Good." She turns and spots a slice on Lycus's plate and perks up. "Can I have that?" she asks sweetly.

I've seen him stab someone for asking, yet the big softie hands over his entire plate without hesitation, mooning over her as she eats his food.

We are all fucked.

After eating and lazing around for a bit, Zale and Lycus finally leave so I can get us back on track with testing her powers. As much as I want to act on my impulses just like they did, I know this is important. She needs to be able to protect herself and be in control of her powers because I know what we are facing is huge, and I refuse to let her die again.

She is tempting, though, and despite the clear intention I see in her eyes, I keep her at arm's length. Eventually, she gets the message, and I hate the hint of hurt and rejection that flashes across her face, so I grip her chin and lift it.

"Make no mistake, I want you more than anything, and if it was just me on the line, I would say fuck it and take what we both want, but it's your life, and I will not risk that. We will practice for now, but I am yours, Althea, all the way through."

Happier now, she grins and nods. "Okay, so shadows." She rubs her hands together, making me chuckle.

"Shadows." I nod. "My power is more instinctual. I use what we already have. I don't conjure it. I use the shades of grey and darkness others fail to notice and the nip in the air to add a chill to the wind. I urge it, bending it to my will, but it requires a price."

She nods, listening intently and not rushing into this. It took me many years to learn control over my powers. Shadows are not toys, and if you're not careful, you could lose yourself in their darkness, and I wouldn't want that to happen to her.

"I think if you watch and feel what I do, I can help you better." Holding her gaze, I let the shadows dance across my hands and reach for her.

She tilts her head. "I felt your power calling to them. Is that it?"

I grin, unable to help it. "Yes, I spread it out in search of them, and they come to me. Would you like to try?"

She nods and takes my hand like the others told me they did to help ground her and hopefully transfer powers. It might be easier when we are more connected, the exchange of blood carrying our gifts, so when her nose crinkles adorably and nothing happens, I sense her frustration but expected it.

"You are tired—well, your powers at least—and you have stretched a lot today, so it is to be expected, but we will keep trying. The more you feed, the easier it will be for you to master this."

She huffs. "I want to try again."

Not one to be outdone, she closes her eyes and focuses. I feel her power brush over me, then through me, so I seek out shadows for her, and when they dance across our joined hands, she yelps in happiness and opens her eyes.

"I did it!"

"You did." I grin widely, proud of my girl. "Soon, you will have better control than I. We will work on it together, but I don't want to push it much more today. We know now you can use and enhance some of our powers, so as you feed and grow stronger, we will expand it, like growing muscle."

She nods giddily and falls into me, kissing across my face to my lips, which she smiles against. "Thank you."

"You never have to thank me," I tell her, and it's true.

We might have been chosen for this position and given a second chance, but Althea is our hope for the future—not just our race, but us as a people.

Maybe one day, we can find happiness once more. With her guiding us, I have no doubt she will make it happen, and I cannot wait for the day when we are bound as one in a way only judges could be.

Twenty Three

Azul

I arrive with Nathair and put everything on her bed, looking around with my hands on my hips. "It's a lot."

"I know." He has no shame as he starts to arrange things.

"Should I go test my powers with her?"

He tilts his head, his gaze faraway. "Not today, she's tired. Help me put this away for her. I want her to be happy here, and I think this will help, don't you?"

Nathair is a provider, giving us what we need before we can even think of it, so it didn't surprise me that he roped me into helping him. I simply had to ask the ghosts, and they led the way, giving us the information we needed to pull this off. We hear laughter and share a look, and when Conall and Thea burst into the room, her smile widens.

"Hey, what have you two been up—" Her words cut off as she glances around in shock. "Oh my Nox."

I wince, knowing this is too much, but then she screams happily, and Nathair grins smugly at me.

My jaw drops as she hurries to the racks upon racks of clothes that line the room. There are ten, each with different designers and matching accessories, that hold everything from jeans to leather to formal gowns, as well as her own cloak. All of the offerings are done to the highest degree and in her size—the perks of knowing fey. Nathair watches with glee as she oohs and aahs over everything. When she picks up a tiny leather mini skirt, I almost choke on my own spit.

Thea spots the mountain of boxes filled with hats, shoes, and bags and freezes. "Is that . . . Is that a Birkin bag and a Louis Vuitton?" She spins to us.

I shrug and point at Nathair.

"Of course, only the best for you. There is also FeyLine, the magically infused designer options too. I didn't know which you would like."

She just stares before slowly reaching out and stroking one. "Pretty." She seems enthralled, and it's odd but ridiculously hot.

"Oh, and there's this." I feel kind of dumb now, but I hold out her old, tattered duffle bag the ghosts helped me track down. I wince. It doesn't compare to designer clothes and lavish gifts, but when she sees it, tears fill her eyes, and it's all forgotten as she rushes to me and takes it before laying it down gently.

"Thank you, thank you, thank you," she yells, kissing my face before opening it softly. "This holds the last items I have of Simon and my mum, things I thought I'd never see again." She delicately unwraps some frames from clothes and bites her lip before moving around the room and setting them in places.

She's decorating and making it her home.

It has us all swelling with happiness and power.

When she returns to the bag, she freezes with her hand on something. "I had forgotten about this . . . Oh Nox, how did she know I would need it?" She pulls out a box and turns to us.

"Need what?" Nathair asks.

Swallowing, she flips the lid open to show us a mask that matches ours. We just blink. "Your mother?" I query.

"She was a seer. I found this in her rooms before I left. I called it to me," she admits softly.

"It's beautiful," Nathair says. "She knew you would need it. It means your destiny has long since been written, but that is a good thing."

She doesn't seem convinced. "You can always choose your own path," I tell her. "Even now."

That makes her smile, as if I said the right thing, and she covers the box before placing it on the table and backing away, clearly not ready to don it yet, even as images of her wearing that while she fucks me fill my head.

Giggling like she can hear me, she flops onto the bed, looking around. "You didn't have to do this. I don't need it."

"No, but you deserve it," Nathair replies without hesitation. "You deserve everything, my queen, and we will always give it to you."

The smile she aims at him melts my heart. This isn't about money or gifts; it's about the fact that we thought of her. It's because we went the extra mile to try and make her feel at home and give her things before she needs them. It's the thought, not the expense. He could have got her a flower and she would have loved it.

"Thank you," she says seriously. "I've never . . ." She shakes her head. "I never imagined, in my wildest fantasies, that my life could be like this. I had lots at my old court, and I never wanted for anything, but not like this. It was never a home, does that make sense?"

Nodding, Nathair drops to his knees before her, and I hold back my shock.

A blood king kneels for no one, especially Nathair, but here he is, kneeling before our queen.

"It does. This will always be your home, *draya*." He looks at the photos. "And your past is always welcome here. We are not trying to erase it, just give you a better future to make you happy."

"I am," she tells him. "I'm happy in a way I never thought I would be. Even when I realised I was finding my mate, it felt more like a pipe dream or a responsibility, something I should be excited over, but this?" She reaches out and strokes his face before looking at me with a grin. "This is real, and I cannot wait to spend every day together."

"Us too, Althea, us too," I promise.

Twenty Four

Althea

They leave me to look through my gifts as they head off to work. If I focus, I can feel them through our bonds, and if I want, I can find them. They are right, though. I'm tired. I pushed myself hard today, so it's nice just to relax. I can't resist looking through the clothes again and picking something out to change into. There's a wide selection and a lot of different styles, as if they all picked some things for me to wear to match them.

I find myself choosing some black trousers, which are similar to cargo pants but made from soft fabric that seems to tighten to my body, then a chainmail shirt. It's lightweight and has a white and silver glow—definitely fey magic. I slip the halter over my head. It ends at my navel with a cowled neckline and feels like butter as I move.

Grinning, I spin before stumbling as a stabbing pain makes me double over with a gasp. It takes a moment for the familiar pang to register, and my eyes widen as I rush to the toilet and pull down my underwear.

Oh shit. I stare down at my underwear in shock.

I haven't had a period since just after I changed. They aren't common. In fact, unless we choose to, we don't get them. When I was sick from drinking human blood, I never worried about it because my body was dying, but it seems my body is currently deciding for me.

Fuck.

The door slams open, and seven kings with weapons and bared fangs crowd around the threshold as I crouch above the toilet, my knickers down.

My mouth opens and closes before I squeak, "Period. I guess dying messed up my body."

They all relax, and Reve wiggles his eyebrows. "I'll be happy to help you clean up," he purrs, making me laugh. Period blood is a rarity, and if I were to let another drink it, it would give them an insane amount of power. However, it's an intimate act that's usually shared between mates. I've never done it myself, but at his comment, an idea comes to mind.

I'm just about to suggest we do just that when Azul freezes, and his eyes turn completely white before rolling back into his head.

"Shit." Lycus, who is the closest, catches him as if he's worried Azul might fall, and I drag my knickers up as I send my power through my body to stop the blood for now.

Suddenly, he's back, and his eyes are wide. "We have to go now!"

"What's wrong?" Nathair asks as the others prepare, their masks appearing at their sides and then on their faces.

"An attack, a huge one. So much death, so many bodies . . ." He shivers.

"I can feel it," Osis says sadly. "The souls are crying out. Azul is right."

"Then let's go," Nathair commands, and then they look at me. "Are you coming or staying, *draya*?" He leaves the decision up to me, but I'm a judge now, and it's time I act like it.

I straighten with a smile. "Coming."

I thought the mask would feel oppressive, but it actually feels warm, almost like a second skin that moulds to my face, and when I put it on, the others just stare before Conall barks, "We do not have time to show you how beautiful you look right now, but we will later."

He seems sad as he takes all of our hands, and then we fade into the shadows before reappearing outside of a four-story house. The lights are all off despite the fact that the moon is high in the sky, and when I sniff the air, the scent of blood hits me, as do waves of terror and death.

I shiver. "There was a lot of death here."

"I feel it too," Osis murmurs.

Lifting my hand, I blink when blood rises off the stone steps. "Vampyr blood," I confirm. "Young, almost . . . almost like a child's, as if they have not fully matured into the change yet. It feels wrong, different."

"That's because this is a place for those without families, those who have been orphaned and left without a court," Lycus explains sadly, nodding his head to a sign on the wall that proudly displays the words Halfway Home with a vampyr symbol.

He's right.

None of us move for a moment, knowing what we will find inside.

"It is our duty," Nathair reminds us and then strides to the house.

We follow him inside, but as soon as we step through the door, my eyes close in agony. I can sense so much death here, I almost choke on it, and the pain staggers me. I know they can feel it too, but it must be worse for Osis, who is hanging back, and Azul, who is doubled over, panting.

"Are you okay?" I whisper.

He nods and straightens. "The ghosts all came to me at once. I am okay, but they are all dead." There is no inflection in his voice, but I can feel the pure agony in his mind, so I take his shaking hand in mine.

"Spread out. Take a floor each, and check every single body," Nathair orders grimly.

They split up effortlessly, used to working together, and I hesitate before he pulls me with him. I hear the others heading upstairs, but we move down the darkened corridor on this level. Paintings and pictures hang at angles or have fallen completely. Glass crunches under our feet, and blood trails lead us into a front room where I turn away and breathe through the sickness that assaults me.

When I look back, tears fill my eyes.

Filling the room like broken, macabre offerings are at least twenty children, ranging in age from around two to fifteen. Their bodies are broken, and their open eyes are unseeing, but the terror that stains their skin and souls almost has me gagging.

There are so many bodies.

"There's so much blood."

"They couldn't feast anymore, but they kept killing because they enjoyed it," Nathair says angrily. "This was a senseless murder."

"Why?" I croak.

"Because some people are evil, *draya*, and it is our job to stop them. We have to check the bodies."

I nod and step into the room, and we check the bodies for signs of life, having to be sure. Tears drip steadily under my mask, and my hands shake and my stomach rolls, but I keep moving forward, trying not to look too closely at their faces, knowing they will haunt me.

When I crouch by a little girl who couldn't have been any older than five, I can't help but sob. Her afro is drenched with blood, her legs are broken at odd angles, one hand is missing, and there is a gaping hole where her throat was. "They were so young, so defenceless. They didn't stand a chance."

"No," Nathair replies as he looks around. "Whoever did this was a vampyr. They are the only people who know about these types of houses. They wanted death. They wanted a massacre."

"It's the same upstairs. The guardians are dead, and they were tortured. One was pinned to the ceiling and crucified. No one is alive," Reve says grimly.

"He . . . It was a he," Azul offers, teeth gritted. "That's what they are telling me. He smashed through the door just after the moon set and ripped through their masses. He hunted them for sport and fed."

Reve claps him on the shoulder, and Azul leans into him.

"We have to find who did this," I whisper, crouched between the bodies, their blood staining my palms and soul. "We have to."

"We will. We are going to track and hunt him tonight. This cannot wait for the usual judgement. Someone who was willing to do this and kill for pleasure needs to be stopped before they do it again. We need to find any scents or—" He keeps talking, but I stumble to my feet and climb over the bodies to something behind the door that calls to me.

I find a bloody handprint, but it's too big to be the child's. I close my eyes as I focus on it. "I have his blood. It's only a few drops, but it's his mixed with the kids'. I think I can use it."

"Then do it," Nathair orders.

Nodding, I call the blood to me once more, watching in my mind as it floats from the wall and ripples above my palm before soaking into it. Memories, thoughts, and emotions hit me. I know I scream as I fall, and I vaguely feel arms catch me, but I'm lost in the bloodlust and pleasure this killer gets from murder. I see snippets of kids running, screaming, begging, and crying as they try to hide. I watch him rip them to pieces and laugh as he does it.

Tears trail down my face for the senseless murders and the pure bliss he feels.

Arms wrap around me as I dive deeper, when all I want to do is pull away. I force myself to track him through the blood and back to the body. I suddenly find myself in his mind, and the pure evil that's inside him sticks to my thoughts like tar. Again, I force myself deeper to see where he is.

"Underground," I murmur. "There are bodies there, and people who are alive." I know I'm speaking out loud, but I feel disjointed, easily lost between body and mind. "It's wet. I can hear a train above. Wait, there's a sign."

I beg him to turn slowly so I can see it. The rest of the room is fuzzy until he looks at it. It's dark, dim, wet, and cold. Then he turns like he can feel me, and I can almost see the sign.

"Almost," I whisper.

"Well, hello," the voice purrs.

"Shit, he can see me," I yell.

"Pull back now!" Reve demands.

"Almost there," I protest, but just then, his thoughts turn on me, attacking me like daggers, and the tar traps me. I scream at the psychic assault as agony pierces through me.

"Pull out now!" Nathair roars.

"Got it." I yank myself back, crumbling into their arms before ripping off my mask so I can pant. My shaking hand lifts to feel blood dripping from my nose and eyes. His attack affected my body. "He could sense me. He attacked me. Could he have killed me?"

"Yes," Reve says grimly. "You leave yourself vulnerable when you transfer to another. Do not ever do that again, not with one that's so evil and strong."

"I know where he is," I tell them as Osis gently cleans my face with a cloth, and I lean back into who I realise is Zale, his warmth making me relax even as I tremble. "There was a sign, West Fourteen and Third. I think it was a sewer."

"Then that's where we go. Zale, take her home—"

"No." I sit up. "I'm fine, and I'm going with you."

"Not after that. He knows you now. The path works both ways," Nathair begins.

"I do not care. I'm going with you. I am either one of you or I'm not," I snap. "Which is it?"

Sighing, he responds, "One of us. Fine, but you do not touch his mind again, no matter what, okay?"

I nod, and Zale helps me stand. "You need to feed," he tells me, "to regain your strength if we are to face him."

"I don't want to weaken—"

Several arms are thrust towards me, making me grin, so I select one at random which turns out to be Reve's. When I bite into his flesh, he groans and falls to his knees. I watch him as I drink, and when his eyes lift, they glow with hunger and power.

Licking the wounds, I pull back. "Thank you."

He pants. "I just came so hard, bloody woman. It's very inappropriate to go into a killing dungeon with cum in my pants."

I smile, which I never thought I would expect, and then I look around, and it fades. "What about this?"

"We will anonymously alert the courts so they can collect their children. It is only right."

I nod again and follow them out, wanting to leave all the death behind. Anger consumes me for the one responsible. I saw into his head and found evil there. He's done it before, and he will keep doing it until someone stops him. He enjoyed it, and now he knows we are on to him.

It's going to be one hell of a fight, but I know with them at my side, he doesn't stand a chance.

He will rue the day he crossed the blood kings and queen.

We are above ground, standing at a crossroads.

"A church, really?" I groan. It's on the intersection, its doors open with candlelight glowing from within. Luckily, it should be empty this late at night. "A serial killer vampyr is hiding under a church?"

"Ironic," Reve mutters.

"Dramatic, more like," Lycus offers.

"Vamps always are," Conall mutters. "Just ask Nathair, with the whole silk robes get-up."

"I like comfort." He frowns, and I smile. Even in the darkest moments of our roles, they make me smile. "Plus, you weren't moaning when I gifted you a matching one for Samhain."

"Wait, you all have matching silk robes?"

Seven sets of wincing eyes meet my gaze, and I can't help but laugh, doubling over as I wheeze. "I'm just . . . imagining you all . . . sitting around in them."

"Easy access, love," Reve whispers. "If you're good, I'll show you."

I lean into the closest person, which happens to be Zale, as I continue to laugh. He catches me, his grin concealed under his mask.

"Okay, I'm okay," I tell him, even as I snigger.

"You sure?" Conall teases.

I nod, trying to catch my breath, the vision of them in robes replacing the ones the evil serial killer put in my head like rot. Maybe that's why they did it. It seems like something they would do.

"Okay, so we walk in there, climb underground, find the serial killer, and then what? Head back to court?" I ask.

"Usually, yes, but this time we'll kill him where he stands. He will not be given a trial. He has been judged," Nathair explains, his voice booming with destiny and power, and the others instantly straighten. "It is so."

"Okay then, let's kill this sick fuck," Reve says with a fist pump.

"No, it must be her." Nathair looks at me, but it's not his voice. "She must take first blood tonight."

"First blood?" I ask cautiously, knowing whoever is speaking isn't Nathair.

"Your first judgement. It is so." Nathair rolls his shoulders. "I guess you are doing the killing tonight. Are you ready?"

I bite my lip but nod, needing them to trust me to do this.

"Then let's begin," Azul states, and as one, we cross the road and head into the church.

Despite the myths, vampyrs do not burst into flames inside holy ground. In fact, we can even drink holy water and touch crosses. We are not evil, not like demons, but they are a whole other topic for a different day. We are entities of the darkness as we move through the pews like ghosts and turn to the door. They follow me, as if knowing I can feel the call of him on the air.

He has been marked, I realise, by me, and that's why I must kill him.

I selected and hunted him, and now I must pass judgement.

Twenty Five

Althea

We descend the staircase, heading into the abyss of the basement within the church. Our steps echo against the stone as we spiral downward. The passageway is cold and barely lit, but we don't need light to see.

We are the predators who hunt in the dark, after all.

The church was empty, so I easily guided us to the door that led us down.

After what feels like hundreds of steps, we reach a basement, ignoring the rooms down here and instead searching the floor for another door. We find a hatch at the back that's partially covered by a tarp. I move the covering away and rip the door open, recoiling at the stench of death and blood.

Looking up, my hood pulled up and mask in place, I say, "He's down there," and then I cross my arms and drop down.

Landing with a splash, I look up and spot the swatch of light before moving out of the way as the others leap down after me. I face forward, focused on the dark tunnels that make up the sewers under the church. Rats scurry past us, sensing the predators in their presence, and then there is nothing but shadows down here.

Conall will love it.

Once I know they are all behind me, I follow the killers blood, pointing to his location like an arrow. His blood feels wrong and out of place inside me, but I keep it there for now as we follow it, turning right then left. Finally, it starts to vibrate, and I know we are close.

I switch to speaking internally. He can sense our approach, but there is no reason to give ourselves away too easily.

Just down here, I inform them, sensing that he's close.

The tunnel widens, showing a gated door that stands partially open, as if to invite us in, and I can almost hear his mocking laughter which offers that very same thing.

I'm not afraid of it.

I have died, I have been shunned, and I have been judged.

He is nothing.

I step through the gate and stop hiding. He is waiting for us with his head tilted back. His clothes are tattered and covered in blood, and he has a shaved head with a wicked scar across his forehead. I also notice he has no eyebrows or hair anywhere that I can see. He's tall and lanky with protruding fangs and huge claws.

"I knew you would come," he sings.

His voice sounds wrong.

Pushing back our hoods in sync, we spread out, keeping our masks in place as we face him.

"You have been judged. We are here to deliver your sentence, slayer." The words tumble from my lips as if dragged from a deep well within me of the god's blood.

With my eyes on him, I expel his blood from me, feeling it drip to the floor.

"My sentence?" He cackles. "Oh no, I think I will be the one doing the judging around here. I felt you in my mind, and you were delicious, so ripe and powerful. I'm going to eat your heart," he roars as he flies at me. I push him away with Conall's wind, like a fly.

He slams into the wall, and I jerk my head at the humans tied to pipes along the wall. "Help them. He's mine," I tell them. I feel them step away, our bonds open and strong as their powers flow through me.

When he climbs to his feet with a maniacal laugh, I slam his blood from the floor back into him, but instead of healing, I send it to attack.

He yells and stumbles back, but when his head swings up, he only appears more dangerous as we begin to circle each other.

"Who are you?"

"We are the judges," I answer.

"Name," he hisses rabidly, spittle dripping down his face.

"What is yours?" I ask in response. He is clearly feral and belongs to no court.

"Sam, Sam the butcher man." He chuckles. "And I'm going to feast on you."

"Sam, do you have any final words?" I ask in a calm manner, pulling my power tight like a weapon, ready to release.

"I bet you'll taste as innocent as those kids did. I bet you'll scream just as prettily."

"Very well."

He's covered in blood, his victims' and his own, and I call to it now. His victims' blood turns on him, cutting into his skin and making him howl. Grinning sinisterly, I open the wounds wider, and my power courses through me as I cut open his body until he falls to his knees, ripping at his own skin with an animalistic roar.

I unleash the power gathered inside me, and it throws him back against the wall, pinning him in place as I let the shadows fall away from me. I release his body, watching as he falls to the ground and writhes. His eyes, nose, and ears leak blood, his body one giant wound that cannot heal.

Pulling off my mask, I glare down at him. "You are weak, you are nothing, and may your death be haunted by the souls of those you stole."

I lift my hand and curl it into a fist when he leaps at me, ripping all that power, all that blood, from him. He explodes, shattering like a vase, not a person. His blood spatters me and everything around us, and his beating heart rolls to my feet. With an angry grin, I stomp on it, ending him.

The judgement is complete.

As if guided by something beyond me, the power leaves me with a soft wave, and I turn to see the others watching me. "It's done, time to go home."

The humans were wiped and dropped at a hospital. Once we reach home, I instantly drop my clothes to the floor, and then Nathair guides me to a huge room. Gargoyles are positioned in each corner, and snakes are built into the stone above. Candles light the space, bathing the room in a warm glow.

The only feature in the room is a giant, stone square bath in the middle, which is sunken into the floor and filled with warm water.

He holds my hand and helps me down as I step in, and I sink until my head is covered, washing away the blood. When I emerge, they are surrounding the tub, their masks and cloaks gone.

"Your first judgement is complete. How do you feel?" Nathair asks softly as I float.

"Good, is that wrong?" I ask quietly. Something about this chamber feels important, and I don't want to disrupt that.

"No. After my first judgement, I felt invincible, good, like I was finally making a difference and helping people," he murmurs.

"After my first judgement, I cried happy tears," Azul admits.

"I thanked them for saving my soul," Conall says.

"I begged to do another, to make the evil inside pay," Lycus offers candidly.

"I enjoyed killing." Reve grins, but there's something serious in his tone.

"I guided the souls of their victims, and I felt . . . peace," Osis murmurs.

I look at them and can't help but smile. Each one of them has their own pasts, their own reasons for being given a second chance. I have been blaming myself for a long time, but maybe it's time for me to start forgiving because how can I fully move on with them and enjoy my second chance while I still hold onto the hurt and horror of my past?

I was a child who was so young and clueless, and I felt the world break me.

Now, I will be the one to heal it with their help.

"Are you coming in?" I ask them before I turn and dive underwater.

We have a lot to learn about one another, but while we were bonded during the judgement, I felt their souls. I saw them, and they were brilliant. We have the rest of our lives to learn each other's wants, hopes, desires, and pasts, but for now? It's enough to feel them so deeply interconnected with me.

I will no longer be alone in the darkness, and I will have others to rely on, and I know that with them, I will never want for anything. I need to show them that I am all in. It is time to accept who I am, new powers and strength included, and to be the queen my blood kings deserve.

Hands grip my legs and yank me back, pulling me through the water. I spin, only for lips to slam onto mine. Fingers thread into my hair, and our legs twine as they push us to the surface. We break through, and I open my eyes to see Zale. He grins at me as another body presses to my back—Nathair. I'd know him anywhere.

"Who needs to feed?" he calls.

"I do," Lycus rumbles, wading into the water with his hungry eyes on me.

"Then let's lay our queen back so you can feast between her thighs," Nathair murmurs in my ear.

I never thought I'd like being controlled so much, but the worship and hunger in their gazes is enough to make me wet and wanting. Desire pours through me, causing my fangs to ache. They can have every inch of me. I'm theirs as much as they are mine, and I want everything they do.

Their wishes push through my brain, and I see myself from their rose-tinted vision. I groan as Nathair lifts and carries me to a bench I didn't notice in the middle of the water, where he places me before he leans down and kisses me.

"Not rose-tinted," he murmurs as he pulls back. "It's the truth, but let us prove it." He steps back as Lycus grips my thighs and drags me down the bench so my feet dangle into the water. It laps at my sides as his hands trace up my thighs and he licks his lips.

"I wanted to eat this pretty cunt when I was shifted. I can't wait to feel you come apart on my face," he growls as I gasp.

Hands grip mine and drag them up. I lift my head to see Nathair holding one and Conall restraining the other.

Reve lounges on another bench, watching me hungrily, with a cheeky grin on his face. "She loves having her cunt eaten. She screams so prettily."

"Is that right?" Lycus asks me, even though he knows.

"Yes," I groan, arching my back, and Zale leans over and sucks one nipple into his mouth with a groan.

I search for Azul and find him a few feet away. I plead for him, and he comes over, dropping to his knees in the water next to me before placing his hand on my stomach.

Lycus buries his face between my thighs. The scrape of his beard makes me jerk my head around, and I meet his eyes as he grins against my pussy. His eyes close as he inhales. "Nox, you smell delicious. I cannot wait to be drenched in your cum. I want to smell it every day."

Fuck.

I moan as his tongue licks a path across my pussy as he watches me. He dips it inside of me and growls, gripping my thighs and yanking them up so they frame his face. He attacks my cunt like a starving man, destroying me with his tongue and flicking my clit before thrusting it into me over and over. I begin shaking, so close to coming it's insane.

"Release your blood," he growls, holding my thighs prisoner. "I want to eat this pretty pussy while you bleed. I want it to cover my entire face while you come for me."

My power does as he orders, and his moan is so dirty, I close my eyes, but I drag them open as the others groan. Lifting his face, he lets me see my blood dripping across his lips and beard, staining his skin as he grins.

"Fucking delicious," he snarls before burying his head back between my thighs.

I shatter with a scream when his fangs drag over my clit, my legs jerking and shaking, and then fangs sink into each wrist, only heightening my release while Lycus eats me.

I slump with a whimper.

"Again," he snarls against my pussy, nipping my clit.

"I can't!"

His fingers thrust into me, making me cry out and arch, pushing my nipple into Zale's mouth as he bites and sucks. Pleasure arcs straight to my clit, and then another mouth wraps around my other nipple.

Reve moves closer on my left, stroking his fingers over my jumping pulse in my throat, and it feels like he's stroking my clit as Lycus starts to thrust his huge fingers in and out, all while eating my pussy like it's his favourite dessert. He pulls his fingers out and offers them to me, so I curl up to lick them clean, tasting my own blood and cum.

He sucks on my clit as he thrusts his fingers back inside of me and curls them, hitting that spot that has me screaming into another release. Turning his head, he sinks his fangs into my thigh as Zale and Azul bite my breasts, and Reve sinks his fangs into my neck.

Each of them are fangs deep inside of me, and an explosion rocks through me.

My voice turns hoarse from screaming as I come over and over, the pleasure washing through us, solidifying our connection.

Finally, I slump and they pull back, all falling to their knees, blood drunk, as I lie here, coated in my blood and cum.

Lycus groans as he leans against me, lapping at his bite marks.

Blood coats my thighs, and he licks every single drop away.

"Nox," I whisper.

Nathair laughs as Reve kisses my aching nipple where his fangs pierced. "How does she taste?" Conall asks.

"Like nothing I've ever tasted before, like power and sin. She tastes so good, I could have come from licking her," Lycus growls, his tongue rolling out as if he can't help himself.

"Fuck, I want that. Be a good girl and sit on my face for me. Let me taste our queen's blood," Conall demands, lifting me and taking my place as he drops me onto his chest. Hands grab my hips and haul me up until I'm straddling his face, and then his tongue spears me, making my head fall back.

I ride his face as he grinds me into him, eating me greedily. I feel their eyes on me as hands stroke my body, worshipping me. Their power flows through me, and I feel their want and need.

"My queen," Azul groans, dragging his lips across my neck. "You are so beautiful. Look at how we serve you, how we worship you. You have seven kings at your disposal, begging for a taste. You have the serpent of age, the oldest of our kind. You have the master of shadows and darkness buried under you. You have the dream master, who is waiting his turn, and the black dog, who is baying to be inside you. The spider is drunk on your taste, and the underworld guardian is helpless. As for me, you have the ghost desperate for you. How could you ever see yourself as anything but magnificent? You are powerful and so beautiful, armies would die for you, gladly going into battle. This world doesn't stand a chance."

Oh gods.

I splinter apart, and they catch me. I fall back, and Conall growls, trying to drag me back to his mouth, but Azul lifts me, and Conall is dragged away. Reve is suddenly there, gripping my hips as he slams me down onto his cock.

My eyes actually roll back into my head as he uses Azul to hold me while he lifts and drops me on his cock. "Lay her back," he growls, and Azul leans us back so Reve can climb closer and throw my legs over his shoulders as he hammers into me.

"Shit, you should feel her." He groans, dropping his head to my chest. "She feels so good. She's gripping my cock so tight, I can barely move. God, I bet she would feel amazing with you in her ass, Azul."

Nox!

I grip Azul's head as I roll my hips and meet Reve's thrusts.

It's raw and hard fucking. Azul grips my bouncing breasts, tweaking my nipples, as Reve slams me down onto his cock, harder and harder.

"Oh gods, please," I beg. I can't help it. I can feel all of their pleasure, their desire, and it spills through me.

Azul's hand slides up, his thumb poised at my mouth, and I suck it greedily as Reve groans. He slaps my clit, making me jerk and writhe as an orgasm rips through me. Bearing down on him, I grind onto his cock until he can't take it.

His roar splits the air as he stills, pumping me full of his release, and then I'm pulled off him, panting and shaking, with his cum sliding down my thighs as I'm turned and pushed onto my hands and knees. Azul slams his cock into my mouth.

Whimpering, I grip the base of his length, sucking him hard and letting him thrust all the way down my throat. He holds himself there as a hand slaps my ass.

"Don't make him come just yet, greedy girl," Osis says. "That's it, nice and slow. Taste his big cock and make him work for his release in that hot little mouth."

Groaning around Azul's huge length, I roll my eyes up to see his head thrown back as he slides from my mouth and thrusts back in.

A hand slaps my dripping pussy. "That's a good girl. Now get my dick all wet for me. I'm going to take this pretty little ass while Zale gets your pussy." His hard length presses against my pussy, and I grind into it, clenching at the thought of all of them filling me. "Fuck, you love that idea, don't you? You love the idea of being stuffed with our cocks, every hole dripping with our cum, my greedy girl."

I nod, sucking harder and grinding back into Osis's cock as he rubs it along my pussy, bumping my clit. I come again, screaming around Azul's cock. Suddenly, Osis slams his cock into my unprepared ass, and I scream, turning my head so I don't bite Azul's cock, and it slips free. I try to escape, but hands grip my hips and haul me back, pulling deeper onto that hard cock. Pain and pleasure mixes, making me writhe and dance on it.

"Fuck, such a good girl. Your pretty ass is so tight, you are going to make me burst before I even get all the way in," he praises, sliding his fingers across my clit. "Brother, get in her cunt before I cream in her ass."

Whimpering, I hang my head as Zale slides beneath me, his lips sealing on my nipple before I feel his hard cock prodding at my pussy.

"That's it, beautiful, slide down his fat length. Take it all. She's greedy for it, brother. I can feel her little ass pulsating around me as you touch her."

I can't take it. I rock onto Zale, sliding him inside of me and groaning as he thrusts up, filling me. The feeling is so overwhelming that I scream as another release washes through me, making me jerk on them. They both groan, and then Azul's cock presses against my pouting, raw lips.

"Suck him down, Thea," Osis orders, spanking me hard. "Be a good girl and suck his cock so we all come in this hot little body at the same time, and then you're going to be the greedy little slut you are and ride my other brothers, aren't you?"

Nodding, I look up at Azul as he grips my hair and slides back into my mouth. They find a rhythm quickly, pushing and pulling, until I'm used between them. Their hard cocks claim every inch of me. Dirty words of praise are whispered to me, and their pleasure booms in my head, making me nothing more than an overstimulated hole needing to be filled.

I can't take it. I fuck them harder, sucking and pushing back while grinding down to hit my clit.

Osis groans. "Shit, she looks so pretty using us to make herself come."

"He's right," Nathair says. "I've never seen a better sight than you all stretched out, being used." He projects the sight from his view, and I moan loudly, gripping them all harder.

Azul snarls, "Her mouth feels too good. I'm going to come."

"Not yet, brother," Osis murmurs. "Make her work for your cum. Make your queen suck every drop from you."

Sucking harder, I reach out and cup his swinging balls as I clench around the other two. Their roars fill the air as they hammer into me, using me until Azul stills and yells his release as it spills down my throat. Zale groans, grinding me onto his cock and filling me with his cum. Osis pulls me back and forth on his cock before he groans, his head hitting my back as his cock jerks inside me, filling me with his release.

They fall away, leaving my body, yet I still need more. I slide into the water and head to the first man there, who happens to be Nathair. He catches me as I leap at him. My hand slides down and grips his cock. He grips my ass and guides me as I sink onto his length, my head falling back as he fills me.

A hand suddenly wraps around my throat, keeping my head tilted back as fangs pierce my neck, making me scream as I ride Nathair.

It's Lycus, I realise.

His huge cock prods my ass until Nathair lifts me so he can slam into me, taking my ass as he drinks my blood. Turning my head, I go to bite, but Conall catches my chin and slams his cock into my mouth. "Do not bite me, my queen. Actually, go ahead, I don't care. It won't stop me from coming down your throat."

I'm trapped again, in the best way. Lycus releases my neck before lifting me for Nathair and sliding me down their dicks as Conall hammers into my mouth. Nathair leans forward and bites my nipple. Blood gushes down my body as he bites across me, opening wounds and not feeding. The scent makes me buck, and then Lycus's fangs sink into me again as he pummels into my abused ass, slick from his brother's cum.

I can't breathe or move; all I can do is feel.

I come again, blacking out this time, but it doesn't last, and when I flutter my lashes open, I meet Nathair's bright eyes. He growls and presses his lips to my neck as Lycus roars, hammering into my ass and finding his release.

He slips away, and I suck harder at Conall until he groans and pumps his cum down my throat so deeply, I can't even taste it, and then he rips away as Nathair turns me. He pushes me against the side of the pool and fucks me hard and fast, his lips finding mine.

Come for me. Let me feel it across my cock. Let me see my queen shatter for me again, he tells me inside of my head, his silken words almost growled. His cock pounds into me, hitting those nerves that have me whimpering into his mouth. I wrap my legs around him and give as good as I get.

It's relentless and brutal, and with a yell, he tears his lips from mine, his hips stilling. Pleasure explodes through him, and he pumps it deep inside me.

His release sets me off, and I come again, unable to even make a noise as the waves of pleasure swallow me.

I hang limply in his grip, slick with blood and cum. I am exhausted but sated, and I look around, licking my abused lips.

The water is red with our blood, and I can't help but laugh as I lounge on top of my kings. Their fang marks cover my body, and mine cover theirs.

They are mine, and I am theirs.

This is my mating bond, not the false king who rejected me.

I was always destined to be theirs, and now I am.

Twenty Six

Althea

The days pass in a blur, and I train every day, all day with the guys. Usually, it's one-on-one, but sometimes I train with two or three at a time. I get stronger, faster, and more powerful, and the more I feed from them, the more our connection grows. Our bond is so solid now, I can hear their thoughts and desires at all times.

It's a real mating, and it's perfect.

At their urging, I make this my home, adding decorations here and there, and I also make sure to wear clothes each of them likes. I love seeing their eyes blow with lust before they bend me over the closest object and fuck me like there is no tomorrow. I heal faster now too, which I noticed after a particularly harsh rutting with Lycus.

We haven't hunted since the serial killer, though, and I think they are giving me time.

My robes and mask were cleaned and are hanging in my closet. I know they go out and track our next judgements, but they are allowing me to ease into this now, and now I'm bored and tired of being stuck in the court. Don't get me wrong, it's beautiful and I could spend a lifetime exploring all of the rooms, but I have a need to help, to do something.

I can no longer sit still, so after we eat, when Nathair usually divvies up duties, I lift my hand. "I want to hunt with you tonight."

He blinks. "Are you sure?"

"Yes." I try to contain my excitement, but I'm sure he can hear it in my voice or my thoughts.

"Then we will all go to show you the ropes."

There's a whoop, and I wink at Reve as he rushes to his feet.

"I'll go pick your outfit," he offers.

"No, I will!" Lycus roars, scrambling after him.

I hear Reve grunt, and then he comes flying back into the kitchen, sliding across the floor on his ass, but he jumps back to his feet and flies after Lycus as the rest of us just watch.

Nathair chuckles and glances at me. "Not worried? Reve will just dress you in straps, and who knows with Lycus."

I shrug as I sip my wine, curled in Osis's lap. "I like everything they pick anyway."

"You are too kind to us," he murmurs as the others clean up around us.

After I kiss Osis, I stand and then straddle my king's lap, sensing he needs it. He grins as he holds me, and I lean down and kiss him, making him groan. It can be hard juggling so many needs, but luckily, my connection to them allows me to sense when they need my attention, even if they won't ask for it.

"No, being kind would mean wearing nothing but your blood." I climb off his lap and wink. "But maybe another time." I sashay from the room, knowing they are all watching me hungrily.

There will be time to play later, though, because now, it's time to hunt.

Nathair was partially right. There are a lot of straps, but luckily, Lycus toned him down a bit. My breasts are barely covered and pushed together by black leather straps that crisscross down my stomach and up across my neck. A red snake crosses my belly, and I knew it would drive Nathair mad—they had to hold him back from fucking me when I showed them.

My legs are encased in red leather trousers, and the heels are wicked sharp and long, so I can use them as weapons as well. My hair is slicked back in a high ponytail, and my makeup is fabulous with red lips, thanks to Reve who had fun playing with it, and smoky eyes.

Conall called it so sexy, he bookmarked the image to fuck himself to later. Azul simply grinned, and Osis blushed prettily. It's safe to say they liked it, and even Zale practically breathed fire when I first appeared. Luckily, or unluckily, I managed to get out of the court mostly unmolested—Lycus had made me come on his fingers as he dressed me, but I don't tell them that.

Jealousy pounds through me, and I know they heard that. *Oops.*

Oops later, baby. You'll be coming all over my cock, not his, Zale promises, making me laugh as we walk up to the club.

I remember a night not too long ago when I came to a place like this. Thinking about it makes me smile because even then, I wasn't alone. They were with me—hunting me, but still with me. Hadn't I been thinking about how I wished I weren't so alone?

This time I'm not.

We don't wait in the line. We walk right up to the door and head in, ignoring the looks and whispers of the curious bystanders. To them, we are just faces in a crowd.

We stride past the coat check, through the double doors, and into the club that covers the entire underground of the block. Writhing bodies drunk on blood and nectar crowd the dance floors on different levels. Blood booths are along the back wall for feeding and fucking, and there is more than one orgy taking place. There's a circular bar running up and down all the floors, which is connected with vampyrs sliding down to grab bottles from below and then back up to serve.

The place pounds with bass, the music sexy and thumping in time with our hearts. When I used to come to places like this after I first changed, the power staggered me, but now it just makes me grin. I feel more than that when I'm sucking my kings' cocks.

Don't you forget it, Conall says.

I used to love these clubs. I visited them when I first changed because my court couldn't reach us here. We would drink and fuck our nights away, trying to forget our future and worries, I admit.

Reve chuckles in my head. *And now you hunt in them. If only they knew who stood in their midst.*

Nathair grins at us. *Split up, you know the drill. Thea, you go with Azul.*

I cock my head. I love playing with Azul, but I figured Nathair would want me close. For a moment, our bond closes, and a message just for me floats through my head.

He hates places like this. He used to be paraded and used. I normally wouldn't bring him, but he insisted, and I know with you at his side, he will be okay.

I nod and instantly take Azul's hand, pulling him after me as I move to the flat edge of the platform and leap to the one above. Why have stairs when we don't need them?

We wander around the second layer, watching people dance and fuck and feed, waiting for someone to misbehave. It's an arduous task, and I find myself swaying with the music.

"Do you want to dance?" Azul says out loud.

"No, it's okay." I grin, knowing he would probably hate that.

"I'm here by choice with the most beautiful woman in the world at my side. Now, would you like to dance?" he asks again, his scarred face hidden in the darkness. He notices the direction of my thoughts and smiles. "I chose whom to display myself for, and I always will for you."

Smiling like an idiot, I lead him to the edge of the dance floor so there aren't too many bodies pushing against him, and then I plaster myself to his chest to protect him while also feeling all those hard muscles against me. My arms circle around his neck as I wind and grind my hips. He groans and watches me move before dragging me closer and rolling his own.

I feel his hard cock as he sways and dances with me. Laughing, I turn and drop, dragging my ass up his body and making him moan. It's indecent, but I don't care. I love his reaction. He grips my hips to the point of pain and pulls me back as we dance to the music.

Nathair laughs. *Okay, kids, time to focus.*

Spinning, I lean up and kiss Azul, laughing as I pull back to see his expression, but then something catches my eye over his shoulder—a familiar head of hair and a grin I know better than my own. He's in a booth, holding a drink in his hand and surrounded by people.

Simon.

My whole world crashes down.

TWENTY SEVEN

ALTHEA

*F*UCK, NATHAIR SAYS. *COVER her. We can't be caught while hunting. There will be too many questions and too many people.*

I know we are supposed to work in the dark and no one is supposed to know, but for a moment, I ache to call out. They are right, though. It would cause a commotion. I have to let him go.

Conall wraps his shadows around me, concealing me, as Reve projects something else. All the while, I stand here with my heart thumping in pain and happiness at seeing him alive and well.

Come on, time to go.

Nodding, I let them lead me out the back door, where we break into the darkness. I'm about to speak when the door clangs open behind us.

"Althea!" a familiar voice yells.

I spin to see Simon looking around.

"No one can see through our gifts," Reve murmurs. "How strange."

"I—" Simon slumps. "I could have sworn I smelled her. Maybe I really am going crazy." He rubs at his face, and I notice how tired he truly looks, so I push their power from me. They allow me to, feeling my breaking heart. My brother is hurting, and I can't let him suffer.

"You're not crazy," I murmur.

His head snaps up, his eyes widening, and for a moment, he just stares at me, so I crack a grin.

"Is the bondage get-up confusing you? Do you really not recognize your best—" I grunt as he tackles me against the wall. Wrapping my arms around him, I bury my face in his neck, and he holds me tight as he cries.

"You're here; you're alive. I knew you were. Oh gods, Thea, I thought I felt you die. It felt like everything in me stopped," he sobs before pulling back and cupping my face. "You're . . . You're okay. How?"

"I—" I lick my lips and look back. I can see my guys, who are shielded.

It is your choice, Nathair promises. *We will support you no matter what. If I still had family left, I wouldn't be able to stop myself either.*

"It's a long story," I finish as he runs his eyes over me. I do the same to him, drinking him in greedily.

He seems shorter, but I realize he's hunched as if he's in pain. His eyes are sunken in, and he has a scar on his cheek that he didn't have before. For it to leave a scar, it must have been bad. I reach out, and he jerks back as I trace it, smiling guiltily.

"Simon, how did this happen?"

"A long story," he retorts and then seems to remember and steps away from me. "You left."

"I had to—"

"With nothing but a fucking note!" he yells. I feel the guys tense, but I hold them back. He has a right to be angry.

"To save you—"

"Did you not think that my life without you wouldn't be worth saving?" he roars and then deflates. "You were—are my family, Althea, all I had. My dreams, my future, were wrapped up in you, and you just disappeared. I didn't know if you were alive or dead. I couldn't function, couldn't think about what to do next when you weren't there. We had always done it together." His breath hiccups, and when his eyes meet mine, they are filled with so much agony, I stagger. "How could you leave me? Do you not think that I would have stood at your side? Did you not think that I would have fought every single one of them for you?"

"I didn't want that for you," I tell him. "Don't you see? I left to give you a chance. Simon, I started to die because I was rejected by my mate, and I didn't want you to watch that."

"So you thought me not knowing was better? I constantly wondered what happened to you!" he spits bitterly. "Althea, you broke my heart."

"I'm sorry," I whisper as I hurry closer, but he yanks his hands away, and I wrap my arms around my waist. "I couldn't bear to destroy your life, Simon. You're the only family I have, the person I love with every inch of my being. I was doomed to die, to be lost without that bond. I didn't want that for you. You can be angry at me, but you have to know I did it because I love you, and I felt like it was my only way out."

"I cannot forgive you," he snarls.

"Okay." I step back. I don't blame him. Despite my excuses or apologies, I hurt him, and he's allowed to be angry. I have no say in that, just like he had no say in me leaving. "I'm sorry, Simon. I hope you know that. I love you." I wrap the shadows around me, unable to take his hurt and anger anymore. I never wanted that.

He spins. "Althea, no!" he pleads. "Wait, I'm sorry, please! Please, don't leave me again!" He falls to his knees as he shatters. "Not again, please, please." His head bows.

Conall unwraps the shadows. *Go to him, I can feel his pain.*

We all can.

I drop to my knees before him and pull him into my arms. "I will never leave you. I'm always with you."

"Promise?" he whispers brokenly.

"I promise," I murmur as I hold him close, relishing the familiar comfort. "But I need to go. We can't be seen. It will raise too many questions—"

"No!" he exclaims. "I just found you. I'm not letting you go again."

"It's not forever." I cup his face, imploring him to trust me, though I don't deserve it. "I promise, it's just for now. Do you trust me?"

He hesitates, and that breaks my heart. "Yes," he finally says.

"Then tell no one. I will find you again," I vow, and then I press my lips to his forehead, and when his eyes close, I let them take me away.

I fall to my knees once we are in our court, and they huddle around me, holding me as I cry for everything that went wrong.

I cry for my best friend who has been hurting worse than I could have ever imagined, and I cry for the future we had planned. They hold me the entire time, offering me shelter and protection.

I cry myself to sleep, and when I wake up, I find myself in a huge, foreign, four-poster bed in a room with large windows that allow moonlight to shine across the black silken sheets. I turn my head and see arched ceilings and a balcony, all decorated in black and gold.

"My room was closest," Nathair says, burying his face in my neck. More arms tighten around me, and I raise my head to look around. Reve has his head on my boob, because of course. Conall has my feet on his chest, and he's snoring. Lycus has a hand on my leg, his body turned away from me. Azul is between my thighs with his head on my stomach, Zale is curled around my hip, and Osis is at my back. All of them hold me in some way.

"They didn't want to leave you when you were so upset, so they piled in here." Nathair sighs. "It's quite annoying."

I grin and snuggle down into their warmth. We have things to do, but for a moment, I just hold them and let them comfort me. I reach down and pet Azul's hair as I stare up at the ceiling.

"Stop thinking so much," Reve mutters. "I'm trying to sleep, and my pillow is very comfy." He squishes my boob and goes back to sleep.

Nathair chuckles. "You heard the man."

"I'm sorry," I whisper, and he stiffens. "I know I shouldn't have exposed myself to Simon. I couldn't help it—"

"I meant what I said. If it had been one of us and it was our family, we couldn't have resisted either. Our job is a lonely one, and I would never hurt you by keeping you from your brother," he whispers.

"Nope, or we'd kill him," Zale offers sleepily, propping his chin on my hip. "None of us blame you. We just hate that it hurt."

"It felt like my heart was breaking," Azul murmurs.

"Mine too, and I didn't know I had one," Lycus grumbles.

Conall stops snoring and groans. "Why are you talking? Why do you hate sleep?"

"Because I'm going to eat our girl's pussy," Osis jokes, and Conall sits up, his arms windmilling with a yelp as he falls from the bed.

Reve groans and buries his face between my boobs. "Go away."

I let them bicker around me, a smile curling my lips. "I forgot what he smelled like." They freeze. "I had forgotten."

"He loves you very much," Osis says carefully.

"Yep, but if he had insulted you one more time, I was ready to kill him," Azul remarks without reproach. "But he is okay. I have my ghosts on him, keeping watch. He's sad, but he's okay."

"You did that for me?"

Azul lifts his head, his eyes clashing with mine. "I would do anything for you," he replies without shame.

"We all would," Conall says as he climbs back on the bed and kicks Lycus so he moves over.

"Your heart seems fuller now, though, since you have seen him. We cannot bring him into this life, but there is no rule that says you cannot see him. After all, he found you, not the other way around," Nathair murmurs, his words slow, as if he's thinking it through as he speaks.

"Tricky little vampire," I purr as I slide my hand down his arm.

"Clever." He smirks.

Reve groans dramatically and lifts his head. "Why must we keep talking when I am in heaven with my head between a pair of magnificent breasts? Why do you hate happiness?"

Rolling my eyes, I grip his chin and pull him up, kissing him until he's dazed. "Do you accept my apology?"

"Huh?" he grunts, completely speechless for the first time ever, making me giggle.

"I'll go get some food started," Osis says, slipping from the bed and padding naked to the door.

Conall sighs, and he and Lycus roll from the bed. "We'll help."

Azul kisses my side, and then he and Zale slip from the bed as well. "We will carry on hunting. Are you coming, Reve?"

"But boobs," he whines.

I laugh as Zale comes back, grabs him, and hauls him up, leaving Nathair and me. I flip over until I can see him, and his hand slides down to grip my ass as he sits up in his bed, looking every inch the impressive king he is.

"I think they are giving us privacy." I smile conspiratorially.

"Oh, I think so too," he murmurs, his eyes hungry as he watches me. "I wonder whatever for."

I pretend to think, tapping my chin as I watch him. "Maybe to rest?"

"I've rested enough, as have you." He grabs me and hauls me up until I'm above him. "How about we do what they all wish they were?"

"And what is that, my king?" I purr as I lean down and lick his plump lower lip.

"Fucking you until neither of us can move," he rumbles beneath me, his hands roving possessively over my skin. "Marking up this delicious body of yours and tasting every single inch in the darkness where we belong." His fangs dig into my lip, making me groan as I sit up and straddle him. "So, my queen?" He arches a brow. "What do you think?"

"I think you're talking too much." I grab his hard cock and sink down onto his length. It's a tight squeeze. I'm wet, but he's huge, and I groan as I work myself down until I'm finally fully seated. He watches me with nothing but love and worship in his eyes, his inner monologue filling my head.

So goddamn beautiful.

Even the moon itself is jealous of my queen's beauty.

She's so tight, and she feels so good. Don't embarrass yourself.

Despite the fact that he's thousands of years old, I make Nathair lose control, and that makes me clench around him until he groans.

"Ride me, my queen, I'm yours."

I see the truth in his head. He loves his men, his brothers, and doesn't mind sharing, but he thinks having me all to himself is heaven. I make a note to try and divide my time better. It's hard since there are so many of them, and I enjoy them all equally as much, but his thoughts are valid.

I grip his hands and drag them to my breasts as I roll my hips and claim him. The moon bathes us both in its glory, just two beings of the night twined together through blood and fate.

I keep my eyes on him as I ride him, and he leaves his mind open so I can feel his worship and see his emotions.

So good. Nox, it was never like this before. How did I end up at a goddess's mercy? I never want to be anywhere else.

Rocking faster, I let my head fall back as I claw at his chest, making him groan and thrust up into me harder. We work together at a leisurely pace that drives me closer to the edge of release with each thrust.

"Feed, my king," I command, and he rises, the angle deepening, making me moan.

Gripping my hair, he drags my head back until my throat makes a long line, and then his fangs scrape along my skin. "When you come on my cock, I will. I want to taste the pleasure in your blood."

His other hand slides between us and dances across my clit as I speed up, bouncing on his cock. My sharp nails dig into his shoulders, clawing until blood wells and rolls down his back, making him groan against my skin. His fingers pinch my clit, and my release explodes through me, and only then does he strike. He slides his fangs into my throat and drinks down my cries, my pleasure, and my blood as I writhe on top of him. When he pulls back, I slump, but he rolls us, keeping us connected. Grabbing my hands, he stretches them above us and pins them to the bed before he begins to kiss me, letting me taste my blood. All the while, his hips move in slow, rolling thrusts as he fills my squeezing cunt.

"So beautiful." I heard the words in his head, but something about hearing him say them out loud has me crying out against his lips as I lift my legs and he drives into me, the force rocking the bed.

"Harder, please, Nathair!" I beg, my head tossed back.

Groaning, he slams into me, the force making the bed creak. "More," I demand.

He speeds up, and I hold on as he fucks me. Each thrust caresses those nerves that make me wild beneath him, and then I can't take it any longer. I reach up and sink my fangs into his throat, and with a roar, he hammers into me as I feed until we both still, our releases taking us once more just as there's another ominous creak and the bed breaks under us.

We end up in a tangle of limbs and sheets and look at each other wide-eyed before laughing. "This bed has survived centuries, yet one night with you, my queen, and it's destroyed. That's how powerful you are, and that's how crazed you make us," he croons as he kisses me, our bodies still intertwined. "I look forward to spending the rest of our lives breaking as many as we can."

"Me too," I promise with a soft smile as I turn my head and look at the moon.

I feel the power of it soak into my skin, along with his love, as he starts to roll his hips again, filling me softly and slowly with his huge length. His lips, filled with promises and love, drag along my neck as we make love in the aftermath.

This is what it feels like to be mated.

Twenty Eight

Zale

"I NEED TO GO see Simon."

I don't even act surprised because none of us are. After her and Nathair's epic lovemaking, which left us all hard and wanting, she came in and demolished the food we made.

"I won't tell him about all of this." She grins. "But I need to see him. He's hurting, and I'm worried his life is going the wrong way. I need him to be happy, and I can't be happy without him. I can live without him, knowing he's got a good future, but not like this."

"We would never expect you to," I tell her as I lay my hand over hers. "We can make it happen. If he doesn't come here, then it doesn't break the rules, right?" I look around, and they all nod in agreement. Even if it did, I think they would be willing to do that for her just to see her happy. Watching her sob after seeing him was enough to rip our cold hearts to shreds, and when it comes to our queen, there isn't much we aren't willing to do to see her happy.

The inner steel I saw in her when she walked into that circle like she owned it awoke something in me, and when she died, it hurt, so I cannot imagine the way Simon feels.

"Is there a place you used to go?" Azul asks softly.

"No—wait, yes. There's a human coffee shop we used to go to. There were never any other species in there because it reeked so badly of humans. It was our place, and we went there to get away from everything," she replies sadly.

"I will send a message to my ghosts for him," Azul says, and then he leaves for a moment before he returns. "I will let you know if he starts heading there."

"Thank you," she murmurs, looking around at us all. "Thank you so much. I know we need to work on sorting the courts, but—"

"Your happiness is important," Lycus interrupts.

"We have our race and the courts to save, but we cannot do that if we are broken ourselves," Osis reasons.

"Osis is right." Reve nods as he demolishes a sandwich. "We'll come with you and remain hidden, of course, so you're not alone."

"Thank you," she says with bright eyes, looking so sincere and beautiful for a moment, I just stare before I realise I have sopping wet hands, and then I hurry to finish cleaning up.

"In the meantime, we could—"

Azul interrupts, "He's on his way, quickly too."

Althea jumps to her feet nervously. "Then I guess we better go." She looks down at the silk robe she's wearing, and with a nervous laugh, she hurries to her room.

She's adorable when she's nervous. I dry up, and we all wait for her to come back. Instead of her usual clothes that display her incredible body, she's dressed modestly in some tight blue jeans, boots, and a hoodie. She looks cute as hell, but even baggy clothes cannot disguise her beauty.

"Okay, let's do this."

ALTHEA

We materialise just outside of the shop, and they follow me in. Luckily, Simon isn't here yet, so I pick a booth in the back room where it's quiet and there are shadows this late at night. Conall uses them to hide the others, and just knowing I'm not alone is enough. I order our favourite drinks and wait.

I don't know why I'm nervous, it's just Simon, but I am. As time passes, I focus completely on the clock, so when the chair in front of me scrapes back, I almost jump.

"Bit jumpy, eh, Thea?" he teases, and it almost makes me cry.

I nod, licking at my lips. "I got your favourite matcha latte."

"Is yours straight black?"

I nod, like a robot.

"I guess some things don't change." He grins, and then we just stare at each other.

"I'm so sorry—"

"I'm sorry I yelled—" We both start at the same time and then laugh, all nerves leaving as he reaches over and takes my hand.

I grip his like a lifeline. "I'm sorry I hurt you."

"I know. I'm sorry I yelled. I might not like it, but I know why you did it," he replies. "I liked the get-up though." He wiggles his brows. "Very Blade."

"Exactly what I said!" I gush, and he laughs. "I missed you," I murmur, and his gaze drops to the table. "Tell me everything. How have you been? Have you found the love of your life yet, the one to tame you?" I plead. I've missed him so much, and all I thought about when I was sick was that I hoped he was happy. I need to know that I didn't give him up for nothing.

"It's been . . . hard," he hedges.

"Please tell me, and don't sugar-coat it. We never did before." I squeeze his hand. Although I wish he had found happiness, I won't shy away from his pain.

"Well, after you left, I went a little . . . crazy. I searched for you, and when I couldn't find you, I blamed them, the court, and started getting into fights."

Oh, Simon was never good at fighting.

As if he can hear my thoughts, he cracks a smile. "It didn't go well. They punished me and gave me warnings, but what else could they do? Well, one night, I got drunk and I saw him . . ." He looks at me worriedly. "The man you were supposed to mate."

I flinch, and he stops, but I squeeze his hand.

"I lost it. He was sitting there without a care in the world, with girls draped all over him, and it wasn't fair. It wasn't fair that he had everything while you lost everything because of him. I just snapped. I managed to cut him up pretty good, but he's a king." His hand drifts self-consciously to his scar. "They burned this into me as a reminder to never attack him again. I think the only reason they didn't kill me was because they felt sorry for me."

"I like it. It makes you look distinguished," I say, sensing his insecurity, "but I wish you hadn't done that. It doesn't matter."

"It did to me. He hurt you, Thea. He hurt my best friend. He needed to pay for that. I'm so sorry, Thea. I wish I had done more when it happened. I wish I had done things differently."

"We cannot change the past," I tell him as I take a sip of my coffee. "But we have now, and I'm okay. Seriously, I'm better than okay. I'm good. I'm really good."

"You look it, but how?" he asks.

"Long story, but answer me first. Have you found anyone?" I wiggle my eyebrows. He blushes and looks away, and I almost clap giddily. "You did!"

"Er, it's not exactly normal, but yeah." He scrubs at his head. "I shouldn't mention it."

I laugh. "We've never been normal."

"He's not a vamp, Thea." He waits, expecting judgement.

"So fucking what? Are you happy?" I retort.

"So happy. I met him when I was in a really dark place, and he saved me, Thea. I tried to push him away, feeling guilty for being happy when you weren't there, but he stayed. He always stays, and he fights for me every day," he gushes, a warm gleam in his eyes.

"That's all that matters. I don't care if he's a bloody troll as long as he loves you like you deserve."

"Not a troll, but he is a wolf," he admits shyly.

"You dirty dog." I lean in. "Is it true about the whole mating thing? You know, the moon and the bites?"

"Oh Nox, yes, it's even better. His people didn't like me at first, but he didn't care. He just declared that I was his and said to hell with it. Now I spend more time with the pack than the court unless they call me back."

I can't help but press for details. "His dick—"

We are standing right here.

"So big," Simon replies.

Althea, Nathair admonishes with a sigh.

Don't worry, I'll be sure to tell him yours is bigger, I tease.

"And you, are you happy?" he asks, clearly noticing I'm not saying much about what happened to me.

"I am," I answer truthfully. I'm happier than I ever thought I could be. For so long, I had the prophecy hanging over me, the vision, and then the mating, but now I'm free. I don't tell him that, however, since it will only make him ask more questions.

Leaning back, he watches me as he sips his drink, eyeing me suspiciously. "Where have you been, Althea?" he demands, and I wince, knowing I'm in trouble since he's using my full name.

"I-I can't say," I answer lamely.

He thrusts his chair back. "Then we are done here. I won't put up with you lying to me. You disappeared for so long, and then you came back looking like this and with so much power, it almost hurts me to look at you, and you can't tell me? That's bullshit and you know it. We tell each other everything, so clearly, I don't know you anymore. You left my life once, fine, then I'll leave yours now."

"No, wait!" I scramble to my feet and chase him out onto the street. "Simon, please!" I follow him down an empty side street as he tries to get away from me, and Nathair suddenly appears before him, making him stumble back with a yell.

"She asked you to wait, Simon," he states calmly.

"Who the—what the fuck?" he shouts, looking from me to Nathair. "Who are you? How do you know my name?"

"Nath?" I murmur pleadingly.

He inclines his head. *I will not let you lose him. You cannot tell him everything, though, Althea, because I do not know what the gods will do.*

"Althea," Simon demands.

"He won't hurt you," I reply, leaning into the wall. "You might as well all come out."

One by one, the shadows disperse, revealing the guys, and Simon just gapes.

"Nice to meet you, man," Reve says, swinging his legs where he's perched on the ledge of the building.

Simon just blinks, so I move closer. "Simon, these are my . . . friends?" I hesitate.

"Mates," Nathair corrects silkily.

"Erm, yep, these are my mates," I finish, and he just gapes from me to them before closing his mouth. I'm stiff, waiting for the blow.

"I don't know where you went to get them, but take me with you," he whispers, making me laugh and relax.

"I can't tell you everything. I wish I could, but I just can't. I'm happy though. I wasn't for a long time. I was struggling, and I got blood poisoning. They saved me, though, and now I'm free of the rejected mate bond and the court."

"That's good." He nods, sneaking looks at the guys before leaning into me. "So, all of them?" He wiggles his eyebrows, and I nudge him with a laugh.

"Come on, let's walk and talk." We loop our arms together and head to the nearby park we used to visit. We find our bench and sit as my kings spread out around me, talking and laughing but keeping their eyes on us while giving us privacy.

"They are stunning, like, all of them. I'm very jealous. Tell me their dicks are tiny. Tell me they are quick shots."

"Nope, sorry." I chuckle. "They are incredible and all mine."

I hear them purr in my mind at my claim.

"So, you can't tell me?" he asks sadly.

"I'm bound not to," I admit, "but it's for a good reason."

"I know it is. You always had a destiny, Thea, and I'm glad you found it and your happiness. He never deserved you," he explains.

"I know. I wish I could tell you everything. I have so much . . . but I guess this will have to do for now."

"It's enough," he replies, "just knowing you're alive and happy."

I nod and watch as Conall pushes Reve into a pond, making me giggle. He comes out spluttering and pushes his hair back. It shouldn't be as sexy as it is, but when he winks and dives at Conall, desire flames inside me.

Simon groans. "I mean, that's just not fair, and you got seven."

"You have a wolf." I chuckle. "Simon, you said you were glad I left the courts. What did you mean by that?" It has been bothering me since he said it. After all, aren't I charged with cleaning them? I need to know what he meant. It seems important.

He laughs bitterly. "They have changed a lot. They are not good places anymore. It's as if they are just giving into their baser instincts. There's so much death and torture. Specter was almost shunned because of your rejection, and they spiralled. The king—the bastard who rejected you—lost a lot of followers, and he keeps others out of fear now. I just meant I'm glad you're not part of that anymore. They would have used you as a pawn, or worse."

I'm not a pawn, not anymore. I'm a queen, a judge, and it's my duty to stop it. I call for the others, and they come closer. "Tell me everything."

Simon throws us confused looks but starts to talk. We listen intently, and when he's done, we share a look.

"What?" he demands.

"Simon, I think we are going to need your help." I look at Nathair. "We need someone on the inside so we can judge them. I think . . . I think I was always supposed to see Simon again, and I think it's part of the puzzle." As if to confirm it, my powers pulse inside me. "It seems like the gods have been playing again, but this time, they decided to play with us."

Nathair hesitates but sighs. "We are making this up as we go along. Nox, what can it hurt? If they want us to do this duty their way, then they should have been more specific." He grins at me. "At least now you can tell him everything . . . or it might be easier to show him."

Twenty Nine

Conall

Simon screams as I release him from my shadows, stumbling on the stone floor of the judgement hall.

"I think he's going to be sick," I murmur, watching him.

"No, he's not." Althea chuckles. "Oh, wait."

Simon turns and pukes, and she winces as Reve slaps some money into my palm.

"You bet on that?" she mutters, and I give her my kindest grin. She hits my chest as she moves over to her friend. "You're okay, just breathe and let it pass."

He groans before he straightens. "I'm good. Nox, that was embarrassing."

"It's okay. The first time I did it, Reve nearly shat himself," I share, trying to get back in Althea's good graces.

"Dude!" Reve yells as Thea and Simon giggle.

"You did." I frown, confused about why he's mad at me now.

"And what did I say after?" Reve hisses.

"Not to tell—oh." I wince, rubbing at my head. "Sorry," I say, and when I glance around for help, everyone is laughing.

Reve huffs and looks at Thea. "In my defence, I would still be hot."

"You would," she tells him with a placating grin, and then she looks at me. "Any more embarrassing stories?"

"Well, there's the time Lycus—"

"Nope, you're done." Lycus pulls me into a headlock, and I lose myself in the fight. He flings me into the wall, and I grab him and throw him to the floor as we roll across it.

Zale and Azul sigh and wade in, yanking us apart.

"Boys!" Althea calls, clapping her hands, and we all stop and look at her. "No bloodshed in here, okay? Take it outside."

"Got it." Grabbing Lycus, I drag him outside with me, hearing her laugh trail after us.

ALTHEA

"Sorry." I grin at Simon. "Seven men can get a little . . ."

"Too many balls?" he offers.

"I was going to say testosterone, but yup, let's go to my room." I look at the others, and they nod.

"I'll make sure they don't hurt each other too badly," Azul says as he and Zale follow them.

"I'll make some food," Osis offers.

"You don't need to do that," I respond, and he grins.

"I like taking care of you."

"I'll be around if you need me, *draya*." Nathair sweeps me into a kiss and then leaves me with Simon, who is swooning. I smack him then drag him to my room. Once there, I flop onto the bed. He wanders around and snoops, not that I expected differently. When he reaches the pictures of us, he looks at me. "You kept them."

"Of course." I frown. "It was all I had left of you. I missed you every day. It didn't feel like home here without them."

He smiles sadly before coming to lie down next to me. We roll until we face each other, our hands automatically clasping, like we did when we were kids. "This place, these men . . . Tell me what's going on, babe, because I'm starting to think things like a cult, or maybe it's a prank TV show."

Laughing, I snuggle closer to him. "I don't even know where to start."

"At the very beginning, padawan," he teases.

"Okay, well, it all began when I started to kill humans—"

I tell him everything, fuck the gods. He listens the whole time, asking a few questions here and there, and when I'm done, I sit up and face him. He turns over, and I wince as I wait for his reaction. "Si?"

"I'm just taking it in. Please hold."

I nod, grabbing a pillow and tugging at the edges nervously, and then he sits up.

"So, all seven of them are kings and they are yours?"

"That's what you took from it?" I laugh, hitting him with the pillow as he grins.

"It's the important details . . . Do they all share well?" He wiggles his eyebrows, making me laugh harder, and then he pulls me closer. "It's a lot, Thea, but I understand now. I understand why you stayed away. I'm so sorry you went through all that alone. I can't even . . . The idea of you dying destroys me, so I'm so glad you're back and you found them, even if I think the gods have given you a shitty fucking deal. I mean, saving our race? Way to be cryptic and helpful. Couldn't they have been like, 'Here's a list of people to kill?' Oh no, it's just, 'You must save our people.' It's some chosen one bullshit. What is this, *Divergent*?"

We share a matching grin, and he pulls me closer.

"I'm glad you told me," he whispers, "and I'll help any way I can, even if you won't tell me about their penises and sharing."

The door opens just then, and Osis freezes on the threshold, his face flooding with heat. "Oh, he's a shy one," Simon whispers like he can't hear and sits up. "Come in, handsome. Is that pizza? Oh my god!"

Simon falls in love with Osis, and he slowly warms up to my best friend, getting less shy. In his usual Simon fashion, he charms Osis, and they become friends in seconds. I eat as Simon tries to learn everything about Osis within the span of a conversation, and eventually, Reve drifts in, as well as the others. They welcome Simon like he's one of them, uncaring about their differences. They banter with him like they do with each other, and I almost cry at the scene before me.

For so long, I thought I had to choose between these two lives, and now they are colliding, and I'm so happy to see them blending. I love Simon, he's my family, my brother, and I love my mates. Now, I get to keep all of them, and all my favourite people are in one spot.

"So then I punched him in the face for calling me a bloodsucker. He followed me and then kissed the living hell out of me," Simon says, "and, well, we were hooked after that. He said he knew the moment he saw me that I was the one, but I wasn't so convinced."

"What if you find a mate within the vampyrs?" Azul asks sadly.

"I won't. He's my mate. I know it," Simon replies, and for both him and his wolf's sake, I hope he's right because I've been on the other end of that scenario, and I couldn't imagine the agony they would all feel.

"So you're mated?" Simon asks and looks around. "You love my girl?"

"Simon," I hiss.

"With everything in us," Nathair answers, and the others agree, making me gape.

"See? Why were you worried?" He winks at me.

"I guess I wanted them to tell *me* they loved me first, not you, you know?" I glare, and he grins.

"She's always been like this." He huffs at them. "When we were kids, there was this boy, and he was obsessed with her. He would follow her around, and she just thought he was being nice and wanted to be friends. The poor boy did everything to prove how he felt, and she was confident they were just friends right up until he kissed her."

Lycus grins. "What did she do then?"

"She just stared at him dumbly then looked at me and told me I was right. They dated for a whole year after that. She's clueless of the effect she has on people, always has been."

"Have not," I mutter, crossing my arms defensively.

"We've not known you that long, love, and I can tell you that's true," Conall retorts.

"Do not team up against me," I warn.

"Or what?" Reve grins.

"Or you'll be sleeping in Lycus's arms," I counter as Lycus gapes at me.

"What did I do?"

"You started it," I point out, and he grins guiltily.

"You're beautiful," he purrs.

"Idiots. All of you," I mutter as Simon laughs.

"I'm glad you've met someone, or someones, who can keep up with you, Thea," he says with a soft grin, and it's clear what he thinks of them. He likes them all, and Simon's opinion matters to me a lot. He's the most important person in my life, and I'm sad I wasn't there to meet his mate with him.

His smile drops like he knows my thoughts. "You will meet him. I've told him everything about you, Thea. He told me that you must be very special for me to love you, and he cannot wait to try to impress you."

I roll my lip inwards to hold back my emotions. "Am I invited to your mating?"

"Only if you tell me about sharing."

I tackle him, and he laughs as I tickle him, and then I flop back.

"I missed you so much, Thea."

"I missed you too."

"I guess we better get started on saving our race then, eh? The quicker we do, the quicker we can all have one big, giant mating ceremony and get on with having lots of kinky sex." He rubs his hands together.

"I couldn't have said it better myself," Nathair says.

"I'm surrounded by morons," I mutter, even though I can't help but grin. "Okay, let's do this."

"Operation Vampyr Takedown, no, wait… Operation Day Walker?" Simon suggests.

"Day walker? As in *Blade*?" Reve asks. "He's badass!"

"You two are perfect for each other." Simon grins. "Okay, so which court do we start with?"

"Azul, what was yours?" I ask, and he stiffens, swinging his eyes to me. "I have a promise to keep, after all."

"Principes," he offers grudgingly.

"Then that's who we start with. Simon, what or who do you know there?" I question.

"I don't know much. They are sadistic bastards who usually keep to themselves." He bites his lip like he always does when he thinks. "But I might know someone there, a friend whom I met at a shady club when I was looking for you. He's not too bad, actually, for the right price."

"Contact him. Make it sly and say you just want to see the court."

He nods. "And I go in alone?"

"No, you won't make it out." Azul sits up. "Just get as much information as you can, and we will go in." He looks at me. "I will not put someone you love at risk, not in a place like that. If this vampyr is from that court, he's either someone's toy or he owns them. Find out which."

"He's right," I agree. "Okay, and then I guess there are the others."

"What about the one with your old rejected mate?" Zale suggests.

"We'll save that one for last," Nathair replies without checking with me. "We are going to put on a good show for him. He deserves it, deserves to worry and wait for the darkness to come for him. Let him suffer as much as she did."

"Wow, that was hot," Simon and I say at the same time and then descend into laughter. When we sober, I offer my agreement.

"Then let's get to it. It's time to save the world, boys and girls." I clap.

THIRTY
ALTHEA

I HUG SIMON AGAIN, and he buries his head in my neck. "Don't be a stranger, okay?" he mutters as he pulls away.

"I won't." I step back as Conall takes him home, and when he's gone, my shoulders sag. Turning to the others, I find them all watching me.

"He'll be okay, and he can come back anytime," Nathair promises.

"But the gods—"

"Will have to fight every single one of us to make us stop," he replies skilfully, and desire slams through me as I watch them. They are willing to fight the gods to ensure I can keep my best friend.

"Keep looking at us like that, and we will have an orgy right here." Zale laughs, making me grin. "Now, if we are going up against a court, we need to prepare."

I zone out as they divvy out roles. My eyes track Osis as he slips away, hunger roaring through me. I need to feed, and I want my tiger, so I follow him, leaving the others to plan. Leaning against the door, I watch as he lays out ingredients on the counter, ready to start cooking. I know he enjoys it, but I sometimes wonder if he does it because he feels like he has to.

"I'm hungry," I call out.

He jerks and spins around, his eyes widening at the sight of me. "Oh, well, I'm cooking now. Do you want something in particular?" he asks, and again, I get the feeling it's because he has to, not because he wants to.

Stepping into the room, I prowl towards him. He watches me come, his eyes darkening, yet he doesn't reach for me because he's not expecting anything. He is so used to being quiet and existing in the background despite the dominant streak in him.

"You," I say when I stop before him.

"Me?" His eyebrows rise.

"I need to feed," I explain when he just stares.

"I can get the others. Nathair—"

"No."

"Reve?" he questions, and I roll my eyes as I press against him. His chest rises and falls rapidly as he watches me, his expression hopeful yet resigned.

"Osis, I want to feed from you," I tell him softly, knowing he needs the words. Have I truly been overlooking him that much? It's hard to make sure I'm giving them equal attention with seven of them, but I need to do better. It's a fucking travesty that Osis thinks I don't want him. He was the first one I saw, the first one I met, and I have wanted him since that moment, so I intend to have him.

"It's okay, Althea. You don't have to feed from me out of pity—"

"You think it's out of pity?" I gawk at him. "You think I don't want you?"

"Please do not feel you have to just because you are with the others—"

Gripping his chin, I pull him closer so he can read the truth in my eyes. "I want you. I have wanted you since the first moment I laid eyes on you, and if I have to show you every second of every day, I will. It's been a hard transition, going from being alone to being with seven of you, but do not ever doubt how I feel. I ache for your blood, and I'm full of need when I look at you."

"Thea," he whispers, his fangs extending and digging into his lips, but I still sense his hesitation, as if he's worried I'm doing this out of duty or obligation. I cannot have that. My quirky blood king deserves better.

I grab his hand and guide it under my dress to my bare pussy, groaning as I part my legs. "Does that feel like I don't want you?"

He freezes, barely breathing as he stares at me. His hand clenches on my pussy as I whimper and grind into his touch. "You . . . You really do want me."

"Yes," I whisper, pressing closer. "I followed you, and the thought of feeding from you and fucking you made me so wet, you can feel it. I want you, Osis. Do you want me?"

"With every drop of blood inside me. I've never wanted someone so badly, but I never want you to feel like you have to have me. I would be happy being your friend and simply being near you."

"Well, I won't." I grin, leaning up and sliding my tongue along his fang. He moans, and the sound makes me clench around his fingers. "That's all for you, my blood king, so what do you plan to do about it?"

"Taste it." He drops to his knees, and I stumble, gripping his hair to hold myself steady as he throws my leg over his shoulder and buries his face in my pussy. My head drops back with a moan at the first touch of his tongue.

"Osis," I moan, shivering when he groans against my wet flesh.

"You taste even better than I could have imagined," he growls, dragging his fangs along my clit. "I want to choke on it. I want to be covered in it."

Oh Nox.

All of his hesitance is gone as he thrusts his tongue into me and starts to fuck me with it. The threat of his fangs only enhances my pleasure as I rock into his mouth. My hunger explodes, and he seals his mouth over my clit as he thrusts two fingers inside me, curling them to stroke along my walls until I come all over his face with a scream. My fangs are so sensitive that even feeling the air touch them makes me come again, drenching his face and tongue.

He continues to lick my cunt, tasting every drop of my release for him.

I pull him to his feet and slam my mouth onto his, tasting my own desire on his lips. I taste his surrender, need, and hope, and I let him taste that he belongs to me. Backing him into the counter, I drag my hand down his body, savouring the feel of his hard muscles and the warmth of his skin as he shivers for me. He's so responsive, it's addictive. I grip his hard cock, and he jerks and gasps my name. An idea comes to mind, and I know exactly how to show him how much I need him.

I drop to my knees before him, and his eyes widen. "No, Thea." He tries to pull me up, but I ignore him as I slide his trousers down, watching his cock bob free. He's huge, wider than I've ever seen before, and so hard the vein throbs and his tip leaks.

I fucked him when we were in a post-hunt faze, but they all blended into one. This, however, is just for us, and I savour it like it's the first time.

He's fucking beautiful, and I slide my hand down his length, watching it jerk and leak more precum. Grinning up at him, I circle the base of his cock and tighten my hold as I lean in and flick my tongue across the head.

He moans, and his hips jerk with his desire.

Giving a blowjob with fangs takes practice and trust, and there is nothing but trust and need in Osis's eyes as I lap at his cock.

I can't take him all the way back without slicing his cock, so I lick and suck on the head of his dick as he thrusts. His hands grip the counter as if to hold himself up, and the power I hold over this ancient king has me wiggling for relief as I taste his desire.

His musky taste drives me wild.

Licking down his length, I meet my fingers and squeeze before licking back up and sucking him as fast as I can without hurting him. I hollow my cheeks as his hips jerk and thrust wildly.

"Thea," he begs, my name a plea as I reach my other hand under him and grip his balls.

The moan he lets out almost makes me come, and I bob my head faster, sucking as I squeeze and working him until I feel him swell, knowing he's close.

"Thea," he pants in warning, but he didn't have to.

Just as he comes, I turn and sink my fangs into his thigh. He howls, his cock jerking and spilling all over me, and he comes as I drink from him. His body shakes and jerks with force as I drink. Leaning back, I lick at the blood and cum on my lips as he falls to his ass before me, panting heavily, his eyes wide and shocked.

I lick my fingers clean as I watch him. "Every time you doubt how much I want you, I want you to remember me on my knees, coming on the tiles from your taste." Climbing to my feet, I smile at him as I stroke his cock, feeling it harden again. "Understood?"

"Yes," he whimpers, closing his eyes.

"Good boy," I purr, and he jerks in my grip, letting me know he liked that.

"Do you need to feed?" I ask, hoping he does. I want to feel his fangs inside of me almost as badly as I want to feel his huge cock buried in me. Like he knows my thoughts, he opens his eyes and nods jerkily.

I step back until I reach the table, and then I hop up and spread my legs so he can see my glistening cunt. "Then what are you waiting for?" I tilt my head to offer him my neck.

He dives at me like a starving man, and I can't help but laugh as I wrap my legs and arms around him. My laughter ends in a moan when he nips at my neck, his cock dragging along my pussy.

Pulling back, he looks at me for consent.

"Oh god, Osis, please fuck me," I demand. Gripping his chin, I look into his eyes. "Fuck me with your huge cock and feed from me until I'm impaled on you right here."

He pulls his hips back and then slams into me, forcing me to stretch around him. The burn turns to pleasure as I fall back, gripping the table and knocking things off. I don't care. I wrap my legs around his waist as his fists meet the surface of the table next to me, and he flexes his hips, fucking me.

"Osis," I call, making him snarl and slam into me so hard, it pushes me across the table.

He rips off my dress, leaving me exposed below him. His gaze pins me in place, filled with possession and obsession, and his fangs are so long they have to hurt. "Oh Nox." I clench around his cock when he lifts my ass from the table to tilt me back, taking me deeper. "Harder," I demand.

Snarling, he does just that, the sound of our slapping bodies echoing around the court as pleasure explodes through me.

My hands connect with a bowl, and I lift it to see it's filled with strawberries. Grabbing one, I drag it across his lips, coating them in juice, and then I lift myself to kiss him. Gasping, he hammers into me harder, rocking the table from the force, and when I drop back with a moan, he grabs the bowl. He squeezes the berries and slathers them across my chest, and then his head lowers as he licks the fruit from my skin. His tongue dances across my breasts and flicks my nipples before he sucks them, making me clench around him. Groaning, he bites my breasts as he licks me clean, and then his lips glide up to my neck and without warning, he sinks his fangs into me.

I shatter around him, clawing at his shoulders and back as he continues to pummel into me, fucking me through my release and leaving me crazed below him.

Dragging my hands down his back, I grip his flexing ass and encourage him to move faster and harder as he feeds. "That's it, baby. Feed, take me," I rasp, tilting my head to give him better access.

His thrusts speed up, and I know he's close. I can't wait to feel him come inside of me, but I didn't expect his fingers to slide between our bodies and squeeze my clit as he pulls from my neck.

"What—" The question ends on a scream when he slams his fangs into my breast. The release takes me by surprise, ripping through me so forcefully, I arch off the table, and with a roar, he follows me, filling me with his cum as I milk his cock. He lifts his head, his lips dripping with blood, and it covers me as he buries himself as far as he can as he empties inside me.

When the pleasure suddenly abates, his head drops to my chest ,and I grip his once white hair, now tinted red, and stroke him as I try to breathe. My body is limp and drained in the best way.

A noise has me looking up, and I spy Reve at the head of the table with a bowl of something in his hands as he eats. "Don't mind me." He grins. "Just enjoying the show."

I can't help but giggle, and when Osis lifts his head, he smiles at the sound. He brushes my hair away from my face, and he gets this look in his eyes that sobers me instantly.

"I'm yours forever, my queen," he promises, and I kiss him, tasting the truth of the words.

Thirty One

Althea

"Don't—" Lycus groans, flopping back with a pained moan when I wrap the shadows around him once more, stroking them over his body until it arches into the air.

I'm practicing the powers that I borrow from them, and he happily volunteered to help, but little did he know, I planned to torture him all day, and I have. I heated his blood until he almost came, and then I created scenes of us fucking that left him on his knees, and now?

Now this . . .

"Fuck, don't make me come in my trousers again, baby, please."

I caress him with shadows until he's panting, his hips lifting as I hold him with them. I like to hear him beg, so I tighten the shadows around him, and he groans, thrashing in my grip.

"Thea!" he yells. "Gods, baby, please. Please, touch me. Taste me. Fuck me. Just take me, baby, please."

I hold him like that as I slide closer, grinning down at him. "Or what?"

His eyes narrow. He's been patient with me up until now, but I see the change come over him. His hands fist at his sides, and the shadows suddenly break. I scramble back to give him room as he shifts, my breath catching as he transforms into the spider once more, and when his eyes lock on me, I see his intent.

Shit.

I don't know why I run, since you shouldn't from predators, but I grin as I leap to my feet and race away. I hear his legs on the floor before I'm knocked to the ground and pinned. His heavy, furry body is above me. I drop my head, my clit pulsing in need as his legs part my own. It's wrong, so wrong. He's in his spider form, yet I can't stop myself from canting my hips as the sharp barbs on his legs cut my shorts and shirt away, leaving me naked below him.

"Lycus." I don't know whether my breathless plea is for him to stop or carry on. Either way, in this state, he ignores me. I teased him for hours, and now he's getting his own back. One of his sharp legs grazes down my back and across my ass before rubbing along my pussy. I groan and grind into it.

"Please," I beg, lifting my hips. I want him, even like this.

His leg moves away, and then I feel his silk starting to bind my body. It wraps around my arms and legs in a confusing pattern, moving so fast, it makes my head spin, and then I'm yanked into the air. I let out a scream as I'm hoisted up. My head jerks up to see the silk suspended from the ceiling, holding me aloft.

I'm suspended with my legs tied wide open for him, my hands bound at the base of my spine so my body is arched.

He tied me up so I'm spread for him. The silk swings slightly, and my thighs are slick from my own desire, but I don't see or hear him. I wiggle in the air, practically begging for him.

For anything.

I feel legs reach out from the darkness behind me, sliding along my back and my ass before stroking across my pussy. The possessive nature of the spider, mixed with the confusing touch, makes me groan as I sway in the bindings. His sharp, deadly leg rubs over my pussy and my clit, making me cry out, and I want to move, but I can't. I'm trapped. I know it, and he knows it. More legs grab me, holding me still for his assault.

His long leg slides back and forth across my clit until I scream, needing to come so badly, and when it thrusts inside of me, stretching me, I come.

It's so wrong and so right, and I clench around the spider's leg, coming so hard I almost black out. That leg stills inside me until my head sags, and then it slowly pulls out and pushes back in, stretching me around it. It shouldn't feel as good as it does, but the bumps and fur on the end of it drag along something inside me that has me gasping. It speeds up, fucking me so hard and fast, I swing in the bindings, my cum dripping down my legs and onto the floor, and then I come again, shattering around it. He pulls it from my clenching cunt and drags it along my pussy, collecting my cum before shoving it into my mouth. I have no choice but to choke on it and taste myself as my eyes widen, locked on the black leg protruding from my mouth.

Nox.

He pulls his appendage from my mouth, and his touch disappears. Anticipation races through me, leaving me on edge as I shiver and shake from the strength of my releases, and then very large human hands grip my hips.

"Lycus," I beg.

"You came so prettily. My beast is sated, and now I will be too." His hands slide across the bindings, and he fingers my clit, making me scream before his hands wander up to cup my breasts. He tweaks and twists my nipples until I'm whispering his name.

"Remember this next time you want to play, little one," he purrs in my ear, and the fact that I can't see him only heightens the pleasure racing through my body. "Now beg for me to fuck you. Beg me to take this pretty pussy like my spider did. Beg me to let you come again."

"Please, Lycus, oh gods, please," I beg shamelessly, arching into his hands as much as I can. I feel his hard, wet cock press against my ass and then my folds, coating his cock in my cream. "Please, please."

"Did you like it, my queen? Did you like my spider fucking you? Playing with your body like it plays with its prey?" he purrs in my ear.

"Yes," I admit without shame. "It felt so good inside me."

"Next time, I'm going to suspend you in a web and force you to ride it as you bleed for me." He groans. "And you will love it, won't you? I can feel your pretty pussy clenching at the thought."

"Yes." The idea of that shouldn't be as hot as it is, but I'm finding out a lot about myself, and nothing feels like a limit when it comes to these men. "Yes, please fuck me like that."

"Not right now, little one. First, I'm going to watch you break apart around my cock so many times, the others will come in here thinking I'm killing you. When you cannot take anymore, I will come inside of you and let them watch it drip from you." His hand slides up and grips my neck. "Are you going to squirt for your king?"

"Yes," I moan as his cock stops at my entrance. I try to move, to take him inside, but he holds me there, on the verge of ecstasy. "Please, Ly, please fuck me, my king!"

With a snarl, he slams into me. He's not gentle. Oh no, my king takes me hard and fast. One hand grips my hip, and the other squeezes my neck, cutting off my air. Spots dance in my vision, and yet I moan for more as his huge cock splits me open, and before I know it, I'm coming again.

He pulls out, and I whine, needing more, needing his promise. I feel the spider's leg again, and I scream as it slams into my pussy just like his cock did. There's a hiss, and I jerk when human hands grip my hips again.

"Lycus?" I pant as my head spins, still feeling that length inside my pulsing pussy.

"I broke my leg off inside of you so you can fuck it while I take this pretty ass. I want both of your greedy holes filled." I startle, worried about him, but he chuckles. "I regrow them. Now be a good girl and come around it for me."

His wet cock parts my ass, and he bends me forward in the bindings, exposing me, before his fingers slide easily into my ass. I clench and grind into the spider's leg, and I'm on the verge of coming again when he pulls from my ass. As I'm about to protest, his huge cock slides in.

The stretch is too much, and I feel too full, but then the pain turns to pleasure, and I cannot think. He starts to move with slow, measured, hard thrusts, and each time, the spider's leg impales me deeper, like a dildo, until I'm fucking both him and his monster.

His fangs grip my neck, just holding me as he fucks my ass, pumping his huge cock inside of me. The new angle presses my front against one of the silk bindings, and it drags along my clit. It's hard, but it feels so good, I couldn't stop him even if I wanted to, and when I come again, he doesn't stop. He punishes me, fucking me so hard and fast, I have to close my eyes.

"Again," he demands, and when he grabs the spider's leg and starts to fuck me with it in time with his cock, I come again just like he demanded.

I squirt around it, feeling it drip to the floor, and then I black out from the overload. When I come to, he's still fucking me, his hard thrusts making me sway and cry out, and then his fangs pierce my neck.

"Once more, queen," he snarls, sounding more like an animal than a man. "Once more, let me feel you come as I do."

"Lycus." His name is a mere whisper.

"Again," he snarls, slamming his fangs into me as he thrusts both his cock and the leg into my body. I come apart for him once more, and he roars as he stills in my ass, pumping me with his cum. I am completely and utterly destroyed.

He carefully pulls his cock from my ass and the leg from my pussy, and then turns me in the bindings until I see him. Lifting the leg, he licks it clean before he drops it. Lycus grips my chin and kisses me, and then he pulls back.

"Look at that, my queen. Look at the mess you made for me."

My eyes drop to the floor, and I see he's right. My blood and cum cover it. Cutting me down, he catches me and curls me into his chest.

"You did so good, Althea, so good," he purrs, kissing my head as I lie limply in his arms.

I hear footsteps and perk up, both of us sharing a look as the door opens, and then the very last person I was expecting to see steps into the room.

"So I have—I don't even want to know what was happening in here," Simon calls, covering his eyes, and I laugh.

Simon watches me as I sit. I had to clean up and find some clothes since Lycus destroyed mine.

The others chuckle, all knowing what went down, but I just smile, ignoring them. "Not that I'm not happy to see you, but you're back so soon," I tell Simon.

"I bet you were very happy." He grins, making me roll my eyes.

"How's the werewolf knotting?" I retort.

"Touché." He nods, conceding to me. "Okay, back to business." He points at Lycus, who just grins and grips the back of my neck possessively, not the least bit bothered about being caught during our sex games.

Simon points from his eyes to Lycus, making me laugh. "Simon?"

"Right, saving the world business." He claps. "So I may have asked around and got some information. It seems the court is holding an invite only party in two days' time. Some of the other courts are going, mainly those who enjoy, erm . . ."

"Pain," Azul says when Simon struggles.

Simon winces. "Yes."

"That is not uncommon. They have their predilections and come to court to indulge." Azul shrugs. "Getting onto that list would be hard, however, because they are regulars."

"Hard, not impossible," Simon offers. "It seems my friend was supposed to bring more people and welcome them to the fold. I told him I know someone who might be interested. Of course I gave them a fake name, but it should get you in. He wouldn't tell me much, just to be open-minded and that you are blood vowed never to discuss whatever happens there. I know it's not much—"

"It's more than enough," I assure him as I look around. "Time to get your fancy clothes out, boys, we are going to a party. It would be rude not to." I look at Azul. "Would you like to stay here?"

"No." He sits up straight under my careful gaze. "You will not go back in there without me. I can help you pick out the people and navigate the court politics. Without me, they will probably kill you."

"Are you sure?" Nathair asks, all of us knowing how much it will cost him to step back into the place that still haunts him.

"With my queen, I will do anything," Azul murmurs.

"Then we will go to the party," Nathair agrees, watching Azul carefully. "We will do our job. Simon, thank you. Please keep your ears open for anything else."

"Got it." He nods and winks at me. "So now back to what I walked into—"

"You really don't want to know." I grin. "It will scar you for life."

"Do not kink shame, Thea, how rude." He huffs. "I'll tell you about knotting."

"Deal, so—"

Lycus's hand covers my mouth, and I lick him, making him grin.

"Spoilsport," Simon mutters, and I wink at him. When Lycus pulls his hand away, I lean closer.

"I'll tell you later. Want to help me pick out a dress?"

"No, that's my job!" Reve yells, and then Zale hops up.

"No, you picked the last one!"

"No, he did!"

Nathair stands and looks us over. "I will pick the dress." No one argues with him, and Nathair nods at Simon. "You should get back before anyone notices your absence. You know how to get in contact with us, and remember,

Simon, you are always welcome here. Althea's family is our family. You have our protection now."

Simon sits up taller. "I will not fail you."

I guess I'm not the only one who feels Nathair's power. It's addictive.

"I know." He smiles softly at my brother and then looks at me. "It's time to talk you through what to expect, and we must commune with the gods and get their approval for this."

"I'm going. Gods? No, thank you, I want to fly far under their radar." Standing, Simon kisses me on the head on his way to Conall. "Stay safe, and Althea?"

"Yeah?" I call.

"Do not die on me again, okay?"

"Promise."

Thirty Two

Nathair

Contacting the gods is never fun. I have only done it once in my entire time as a blood king, and that was to save Azul as he descended into darkness. They are fickle creatures, they kill sometimes just for fun, and their reactions never make sense because they play the long game, not the short one.

It makes them unpredictable, and Simon is right. It's never good to be on their radar, but we must. This is too big to conduct alone, and we do not want to anger a god if they have taken special interest in a vampyr. We will ask for permission, even though I hate it.

We gather in the blood circle—what better place to call them—and we don our masks so as not to give too much away, including Althea. She seems nervous, but she shouldn't be. She has been kissed by a god, though we will try to keep that a secret as long as possible. They might take offense to that or worse, be intrigued by her.

"I will talk. Try not to draw attention to yourselves," I order them all.

"Remember, the gods do not care if we live or die. They play with lives like chess pieces."

"I got it." Althea nods and winks at me through the mask. "Show them how to play, my king."

Pulling the bowl closer, I rip open my wrist and bleed into it, and once it's full, I dip my finger in and paint the requisite symbols before I bow my head. "My gods, I call upon you to ask for your guidance. My gods, I beg for you to show yourselves. Alrehujo Kazarr Monserysl." I repeat it until the blood starts to glisten and then glow, turning gold before disappearing. I call to any and all, not just one, especially since I have no idea who will turn up at all. They all know of our roles, even though some hate it. We are above their wishes and whims for as long as we continue our jobs and don't annoy them.

We wait and wait some more, and when I feel a presence, I do not lift my head, knowing they could take offense to that. "Speak. Why have you called me, judge?"

Fuck.

I do not lift my head, nor do I move. That voice is familiar—the god of death.

He's a cruel bastard who takes great pleasure in pain and death, so for him to respond, he must be bored, but he is also the best one to ask. I need to be smart about this. "Judge, do I need to repeat myself?"

He is also one of the most powerful gods to ever exist. He bows to no other, and they all fear him. He is an outcast, even amongst them.

"We wish for your guidance," I tell him, trying to keep my tone respectful and calm. "We are determined to help our race."

He snorts. "Bloody vamps."

"To do so, we wish to hunt within the courts themselves and find the seeds of evil so we may extinguish them before they grow roots."

"Stop with the word games, king," he mocks. "I hate them."

Fuck, this is not going well. He's even more angry than usual, and I feel his power beating at us. We may be powerful together and separately, but nobody stands against a god, bar another god.

Althea!

I hear her thoughts before she lifts her head, and I turn to face her, trying to reach for her, but it's too late. "He is asking if you almighty gods would have an issue if we go into the courts and kill all the evil fuckers there," she snaps. "Is that clear enough for you now, god?"

"Careful how you speak to a god, child," he warns, his voice like death. "You are new . . . Oh, but I taste a touch of god magic on you." He steps closer, nothing but mist, and touches her. Any other would die, but she simply stands there and takes it. "Oh yes, a god indeed. Tell me, judge, what have you been up to?"

"Oh, you know, the usual," she jokes. "Tell me, god," she says mockingly like he did, and fear pounds through me. He could easily take her from us. I go to plead for her life when he laughs, startling us all.

"I like this one. She has fire." He steps back. "Kill whoever you want, I do not care. The more that die, the better for me, but be careful, judge, because not every god likes you and your kind, and they would not accept your attitude. You caught me in a good mood, so I shall let it pass. Now go, before I grow tired of you. Conduct your sacred tasks." He laughs once more. "And leave me to my dead."

"Is that all you have? Dead?"

"Althea," I hiss.

"Judge," he warns, his voice filled with power, yet she stands against it.

"I simply meant that it must be lonely, my god." There is respect in her tone at least.

The room is silent, and my cold, dead heart is beating in terror. "She does not know what she is saying—" I begin.

"Silence!" he roars at me, and I fly back through the air, hitting the wall.

"There is no need for a temper tantrum," she scolds. "I was simply asking."

"Why, judge? Are you volunteering to sate my boredom?" he asks, his voice careful. It's a word game.

I see the others closing ranks around her. They will stand with her against the god of death. I hurry back over, feeling the broken bones from his blow mending as I stumble to her side.

"No," she answers without fear in her tone. "I'm simply suggesting you should find someone who would."

"Interesting," he murmurs. "Even more interesting is the fact that these men are willing to stand against me for you."

"They are mine," she replies without reproach, "and I am theirs."

"Oh, how foolish love makes people." He chuckles. "Everyone dies in the end, little vampyr, and usually alone. At the end, all there is, is me. Remember that before you anger me again." I groan when he cups her cheek with his mist, and she cries out. I go to attack, but she holds up her hand. "I see your purpose, your power. Oh, you will be tasty when you come to me, but for now, I will leave you be." He steps back, and she sags. "Until next time, judges. I cannot wait for the souls you'll send me."

When his power is gone, I grab Althea and check her face. There's a handprint there that fades as I watch. "Althea," I snap, "he could have killed you."

"So?" She shrugs, pulling her mask up and grinning at me. "He didn't, and we have our permission." Leaning in, she kisses my masked lips. "I'm starving. Let's feed, shall we?"

THIRTY THREE

REVE

"NO." I VETO THE dress, and Althea strips out of the gaudy orange number. "It should be red."

"He's right." Conall nods, eating popcorn as we have a fashion show.

Azul nods seriously. "Then we could have matching red elements."

Nathair taps his chin. "Osis, Lycus, what do you think?"

"Huh?" They both jerk their gazes from Althea's ass, and Nathair sighs.

"If you cannot concentrate, you will leave," he warns them, making me grin wider.

"Concentrate? Have you seen her?" At Osis's response, we all turn to see Althea in nothing but a lacy thong and tall black heels. He's right, and we all stare, lost in the expanse of tanned skin, long limbs, and perfect ass and tits.

"No, behave," she tells us. "We need to be prepared. Red, Nathair?"

"Red," he murmurs then coughs. "Yes, red." He looks her over once more before turning to the dresses. "Be the death of me," he mutters, making her giggle.

He stares at the dresses for a long time, and Althea arches her brow. "Nath?"

"None of them are good enough for you." He huffs and steps back. "They do not do you justice. Nothing will ever be good enough to drape across your body."

Her eyes widen. He's completely oblivious to the effect his words have on her, and I hide my smile as she stares at him until he sighs.

"Maybe I could ask the fey—"

"Nathair, come here," she commands.

He frowns but heads over. She grabs him and kisses him. I watch, shifting my hard-on as he groans, and when she pulls back, he just blinks at her. "What was that?" he whispers, over his dress meltdown.

"Because you are incredible. Now, one of these dresses will be amazing, I promise, so find it for me."

Blinking, he turns to the dresses and just stares at them, not really seeing them.

"Dress, Nathair," I tease.

"Right, dress." He coughs, shooting me a thankful glance. After trying on five more, we finally find one we all agree on before picking out accessories. She eyes us hungrily, wearing nothing but the thong and heels as she scrapes her new accessories across her chest, leaving a cut. The sharp claws are made of fey silver and cover her nails. I can't wait to feel them in my chest as she rides me.

Azul is the closest, and she wraps her arm around his neck and tugs him to her. His mouth seals on the cut, making her groan as her head tilts back. She meets my gaze where I'm sitting forward in my chair. "Do you want to taste my blood?"

"Yes," I growl.

"Then crawl to me," she orders, her lips curved in a smirk. She knows the power she has over us. Naked and more beautiful than any queen before her, she stands tall and arches her eyebrow. "Well?"

When your queen orders you to crawl, you crawl. Slipping to my knees, I keep my eyes on her as I crawl towards her like she is my home, my everything, because she is.

I crawl towards my queen, stopping when I reach her leg then kissing up it until she lifts her heel and presses it to my chest, pushing me back.

"Kiss my shoes," she orders.

I lift her foot and trail my lips along the heel, watching lust bloom in her eyes. Her fangs lengthen, and as I sweep my tongue across her shoe, I feel her shiver. She might be in control, but she isn't immune to us. We are hers, but that makes her ours as well.

"Would you die for me, Reve?" she asks.

"Yes," I answer without pause.

"Would you kill for me?"

"Yes," I vow.

"Would you do anything I asked?"

"Always," I tell her with a kiss.

"Then rip open your throat and let me see you bleed so I can coat myself in it."

The image stuns me for a moment.

"When our queen gives an order, you do it," Nathair barks when I don't instantly obey.

"I plan to. Do you want me to do it with a blade, my queen, or someone else's teeth?"

She licks her lips, no doubt liking that idea. "Teeth. Lycus, rip him open for me."

Lycus hesitates but moves over. He doesn't usually use his fangs since he worries about our reactions. She chose him on purpose, and when his hand grips my hair and lifts me to my knees, I go willingly. I keep my eyes on her as I submit to him, knowing he's relieved when his teeth tear into my throat like a wild animal. I make no sound; I don't even move as he tears out my throat for her. I'd drain every inch of my blood for her to bathe in if she wanted to.

He lets me collapse forward, and I purposefully bleed all over her leg and thigh, rubbing against her. She drops to her knees and lifts my head.

Her claw-tipped nails drag along my chin, cutting me more as she leans down and licks it away before pressing her tongue to my throat, drinking and licking as it heals. When she moans, sitting back in disappointment, I drag her nails across it again, carving myself open once more for her. She covers the wound, drinking me down, even as I fall back from the bloodlust. She lifts her arm to my mouth, urging me to drink, and I slam my fangs into it as she feeds. When she lifts her head, her mouth, chin, neck, and chest are coated in my blood, and I spill in my pants at the sight.

"More," she demands, her eyes wild. "I need more."

I'm spent, though, and I'm so drained my cock can't even get hard again, so she turns and sinks her teeth into Lycus's thigh. He roars but holds her head as she feeds. When she sits back with a moan, her fangs are covered in blood, and her eyes glow with her power as they lock on Conall.

He pulls his shirt over his head and holds out his arms. "Come here, my queen, and feed," he purrs.

She hasn't been feeding enough, I project. If she's this hungry, then she needs to be feeding more. Fuck, we haven't been taking good enough care of her. She's almost feral with her hunger.

She probably didn't know, Nathair murmurs. *She is not used to the thirst. We will make sure from now on. Now feed because she might need you again.*

I nod, and Lycus offers me his arm. I feed greedily and lean back into him, watching as she slides across Conall's body and straddles him. Her hand reaches into his pants and pulls his cock free, and with a needy moan, she slams herself down on it.

Fuck.

My eyes are locked on her ass as she lifts, letting us see his huge cock spearing her, and then she drops back down. "Yes, my queen, take me, all of me, I'm yours." His head drops back, and he grips her hips, urging her to ride him as she slices into his chest with her claws and licks the wounds clean.

Snarling, he lifts and drops her faster, encouraging her to ride him, and then her fangs are in his chest, over his heart. He roars as he holds her tightly against him, coming inside of her as she wiggles on top of him, draining every drop of cum and blood. When he's spent and falls back with a dazed smile, Zale lifts her. She turns in his arms and sinks her fangs into his shoulder. He groans and stumbles, falling to the bed on top of her. Her hands grab at him, and he pins them above her as she snarls at him. He's a stronger man than I, and he resists her until she bites him again, and then he flips her, slams into her cunt, and takes her hard and fast.

We watch as she claws at the bed, coated in blood and staining the sheets as she pushes back, taking him, and then his arm comes around so she can bite him as he fucks her. Her teeth sink into him, and he roars, speeding up so quickly, we can barely see him. Flames blaze across his body and hers as he reaches down and rubs her clit until she mewls out a scream into his skin. He groans as she comes for him, dropping his head to her shoulder before finding his own release and slipping away.

Rolling to her back, she gets to her knees on the bed.

Cum drips down her thighs, blood covers her, and her hair is a mess, yet she's never looked so fucking perfect.

"Come, my queen." Osis holds out his arms. She prowls to him, and when she gets close, he grabs and spins her to avoid her teeth for now. Azul steps in front of her, sandwiching her between them.

Lifting her into the air, Osis holds her up as Azul buries his head between her thighs, eating her pussy and his brothers' cum as she writhes and shouts. She manages to twist her upper half, but Osis holds her back until she screams her release, and then he drops and turns her. Azul lifts her, and Osis slams her down on his cock as they hold her between them. Azul groans, rubbing against her ass, and when she reaches back and guides him inside her as well, I almost come again.

Watching them work her between them is a piece of art. She holds them tight, riding their cocks as blood coats their faces, but her hunger comes back, and when she sinks her fangs into Osis, he's done, coming inside of her with a roar as she feeds. He manages to stay upright and pass her to Azul, who spins her and bounces her on his cock while she grips his head, gently buries her fangs in his neck, and feeds as he finds his release.

When he is spent, Nathair catches her before she can fall and pushes her to her hands and knees. Lycus moves over and strokes her ass.

"Be a good girl and suck my cock without biting," Nathair says, "and I'll let you feed." Despite the fact that she's feral, he feeds her his cock, pushing into her snarling mouth with a moan.

Brave man.

Nathair uses her hair as a handle, working her mouth on him as Lycus drops to his knees and slides his cock into her pussy, working her between them.

Nathair drags her up and down his cock as he slams into her mouth, his head back as Lycus takes her pussy.

Their pleasure makes me grip my cock as I watch them.

"Good girl," he croons. "That's it, just like that, look how beautiful you are right now. You're taking us both so well, my queen. So good."

Lycus groans, powering into her harder and pushing her down onto Nathair's cock. He groans and stills as he empties into her mouth. When he falls back, she grips him, drags him close, and feeds from his thigh. His cock hardens once more, and he spills across her as Lycus hammers into her before roaring his own release and collapsing to the side. She turns and bites him again, but it's not long before he's done.

They litter the ground like broken dolls, every single one of them wearing smiles on their faces, and yet she whines, "I'm still hungry."

"Then come here, my love, and let me satisfy you," I call, knowing I can now that I've fed. Nathair was right, she probably didn't even know she needed to feed this badly, and now she's in a blood cycle. She will eventually be sated and pass out. I just hope I'm enough to accomplish that because the others are down for the count.

I manage to roll her and slip inside of her dripping cunt, groaning at the feel of her gripping me so tightly. I hold her neck to keep her from biting me as I rock my hips, taking her slowly.

"Reve!" she screams.

I grin and flick her clit, feeling her come for me, and I continue to power into her, knowing I need to exhaust her. I make her come twice more around my cock, fighting back my own release before I flip her and lift her to my mouth, eating her messy cunt until she comes again and again.

Finally, I slam into her and give her my wrist, chasing my own release as she sinks her fangs into me. I feel my life leaving me, and when my balls tighten, I pinch her clit until she screams and clenches around me as she comes, milking my release from me.

We both fall into a bloody, cum-covered mess.

Her eyes close, and her fangs retract. She's finally spent.

Thank fuck.

I slip into unconsciousness.

Thirty Four

Althea

I wake up sore, sticky, and confused. I remember last night like a haze. I had been so rough, so hungry. I can't ever remember being that hungry. I couldn't stop myself even if I tried. I fed and fucked them all, and I could still do it again, yet I feel sated and full, so I force my eyes open and turn to see them spread around me on the floor. They must have crawled closer. Reve is still half on me, snoring away. Lycus is facedown on the carpet, Nathair is curled against my side, and Conall is half on the sofa. Azul and Osis are near my feet, and Zale is by my head.

"Guys?" I croak, but they don't move. I sit up worriedly.

Oh fuck, did I drain them? Guilt gnaws at me. How could I do that? How could I be so careless? Tears fill my eyes until Nathair groggily lifts his head.

"We're not dead, my queen. It would take more than you fucking and feeding from us for that. We love your hunger, now rest."

"But I drained you all—"

"And we loved it." He pulls me closer. "I promise, *draya*, we loved it. We would gladly do it again. You clearly needed it, and now we need to rest and regroup, so close your eyes."

"I'm sorry," I whisper. "I should—"

"Do not feel guilty." He frowns at me. "This isn't like the old you." Obviously, he read my mind. "This was just your hunger, my queen, and we gladly fed it. Ask any one of them, and they will tell you it was the best night of their life."

"He's right," Conall murmurs. Clearly, our talking woke them.

"Anytime," Zale says. "In fact—"

"Behave, my cock is sleeping," Reve mutters.

I smile despite it all, thankful that they are all okay. I know they are my kind, my mates, but I need to be more careful. It seems the hunger snuck up on me, and I've heard of vampyrs killing their lovers when they are that deep in the thrall. I need to feed more often.

"There will be no complaints here. There is nothing more incredible than feeling your fangs in me," Azul tells me.

"I volunteer every time," Osis says, making me grin as I snuggle down between them.

"Okay. I'm still sorry. I will feed more often."

"Your new powers are riding you hard, and your body is growing to accommodate it, so it makes sense that you need more blood. I should have noticed. I failed you, my queen. I'm sorry," Nathair murmurs. "We won't fail you again. Now rest, and when we wake up again, we can bathe and relax."

Somehow, I manage to sleep more, and when I wake up, the others are all gone except for Azul. He's watching me, but his eyes are a million miles away.

He will need you tonight more than ever. This will be like stepping back into his own personal nightmare, Nathair whispers.

We will all work in tandem tonight to protect Azul. I hope, somehow, it will heal or help him, but I also worry that going back there will be too much for him, so I'll keep him close.

"Help me bathe?" I ask, and I watch him focus on me as a soft smile curls up his lips.

"Always, my queen." Standing, he offers me his hand, and I accept it gratefully, letting him tug me to his side as he leads me to the bathroom where the tub is already full, with rose petals covering the surface. We climb into the bath, and he slides me between his legs. The warmth of the water and the heat of his body make me sigh as I settle back into him.

For a while, we just lie here, holding each other without talking about what is to come tonight. Eventually, though, reality must come back, because with soft, shaking hands, he washes my body, and then I do the same to him. We have to wash my hair four times to get everything out, but once I dry off and wander back into the room with him, I feel better, and the others are waiting there, already dressed for the occasion.

They all wear matching suits, but with their own flair. Nathair wears a red silk shirt under a black jacket, which he left open all the way to his navel, his mark proudly on display. His trousers are tight and practically see-through, and his hair is a curtain over his shoulder. Reve has no shirt, just the unbuttoned jacket, but there's a red tie hanging from his leather trouser pocket. Conall has his usual boots on and a silk shirt, but no jacket. Zale wears his shirt fully buttoned, but the edges of his sleeves glow red with fire. Osis has fur on the trim of his suit, which frames his beautiful face, and Lycus has red ribbon tied back in his hair, and he's wearing the suit trousers but no shirt or jacket. As I watch, Azul slips away to get dressed, and I stand taller as they come over to dress me, their hands stroking my skin as they offer comfort.

I relax into them and close my eyes, hunger and desire warring through me, but this is about comfort and connection, nothing more. Once I open my eyes to look in the mirror, I gasp at the dress.

It's different than before.

It's a deep blood red with a V-neckline to show off my breasts, and the sleeves hang slightly off my shoulders. The cap sleeves are a silver circle of chain mail with spikes pointing into the air. The material pools behind me, a red fey silk that shifts like the movement of blood. Two slits lead up to my stomach, and when I move, I almost see everything. A small corset enhances my waist, and when blood touches it, it turns the material black. My hair is piled on top of my head in loose curls with some hanging down, and a choker necklace circles my neck to draw the eye to it.

I look beautiful and every inch their equal as they stand at my side, waiting for me to finish my perusal. "I love it," I murmur, and Nathair grins.

"They won't know where to look," he purrs.

"Good, it will be a distraction." I turn to them, grinning as I run my eyes over their bodies. "You all look incredible, and if I had the time, I would spend my evening showing you just how good you look."

"Later." Reve winks, making me grin, but it fades as Azul steps into the room.

He looks amazing. His hair is swept back to show off his incredibly handsome features and the scar on his face. His eyes pierce me as he steps closer, and seeing him in his suit makes me breathless. Pure black encases his incredible body, and the only colour on him is a hint of red in his pocket, showing just enough to mark him as one of us.

He looks good enough to eat, and he knows it. He grins, but it fades as he lifts his hands.

"What's this?" I ask as he gives me a black collar. It's gothic and beautiful with spikes around it, but it's still a collar with a black and gold chain dangling from it.

"For me. You will need a . . . need a slave if you are to get in, so I will be it." He swallows. "I know how to play the part. I am used to it, and walking in with me will annoy my old mistress and those who wanted me. It will intrigue them, and they will react."

"No," I snap. "Never. I will never use you like that."

"Please," he croaks. "It will keep me safe too. They cannot touch me unless they wish to anger you. I don't like the collar much either, but it will be chained to you, and I do like that. I can survive this with you at the other end, Althea, I promise. It will keep me linked to you, and it means I can hide behind you. I cannot be a judge tonight, because I do not feel it, but I can be this. Let me walk in on your chain. Please, mate, please."

I don't want to make this harder for him, and no matter how much I hate the idea, I can see the others agree with him. If it will keep him safe, then how could I deny him? They will have to go through me to get to him, and that means I can protect him further, even if I hate that it thrusts him into the spotlight before the very people who hurt, abused, and killed him.

My eyes close before I focus on his once more. "Are you sure?"

He kneels before me, presenting the collar. "I have never been surer of something, Althea, my queen, my mate. Please be my master."

Swallowing, I take the collar and eye it. It is beautiful, I will give him that, done in all black with spikes facing out as if to dare others to try and taste what is mine. The twisted metal heats in my hand and cracks open.

"It sees you. We linked it to your blood," Lycus explains.

I nod as I lean down and place it around Azul's neck, and once it's in place, it clicks shut. "Is that okay?" I ask.

His eyes close for a moment, and I read the panic on his face, so I kneel and cup his cheek. "Eyes on me," I whisper, but he's losing himself in the memories of the last time he wore a collar, and I refuse to let them have him.

He's mine.

"Eyes on me now," I snap. His eyes open and his memories screech to a halt as I send my mind into his and slam the door shut on them. "You are mine tonight, not theirs, and you will never be theirs again. You keep your eyes on me at all times, and only me. Only we exist, do you understand me?"

"Yes, my queen," he murmurs, shivering before he relaxes.

"Good." I hold him until he nods, fully relaxed, and then I stand, letting the silken chain slide through my hand. "Then let us go." I look at the others. "Let us go and destroy the court."

THIRTY FIVE

ALTHEA

We don our masks as we materialise just outside of the court. Black and gold filigree covers my eyes and the side of my face, inlaid with red jewels to match my dress and their suits. They wear half masks, which are black and beautiful. We stand in a line as I take in the court for the first time. It isn't what I was expecting. I know the party is invite only, but I was definitely expecting . . . more. The parties I saw and previously attended usually went to the extremes with entertainment, transforming the court into a musical environment.

This one is almost deadly silent, and that doesn't bode well.

The building itself is beautiful. Unlike the mansion of Court Specter and the sprawling, gothic estate of the Court of Nightmares, Principes Court is as modern as they come. Obviously, it's been updated recently. Done in all white, the square buildings are connected, without any windows to be seen, and beyond the white buildings is a dome of all glass. A blood-red moat surrounds the entire structure with a path allowing guests to cross.

"That is where the party will be," Azul murmurs, looking at the dome. "It is the throne room. Beware, there will be tricks and traps. They prey on weakness, and if you make one wrong move, they will pounce. They love to tear down and destroy others, so don't let them."

"And the king?" I question.

"He loves to collect pretty things. If you want this to work, then let him think he has collected you."

I nod and tug on his chain, wrapping it more securely around my wrist. "Let's get this over with. I cannot wait to feel their flesh under my fangs for what they have done."

I move confidently towards the court without an ounce of fear in me.

After all, what is there left to fear? We are the beings they should fear, and they invited us right to their door without even realising it. These nightmares are about to carve a bloody path through this gathering, and I cannot wait.

My blood kings, my mates, follow behind me, spreading out as I walk up the path to the open triple doors. I step inside and feel power wash over me.

If we were rejected, it would have killed us, Azul informs me, switching to internal communication so no one else can overhear what we are saying.

Lovely. Instead, it felt like a thousand ants ripping into my skin. I'm beginning to understand that pain is the currency here. The inside is just like the outside, screaming modern design, with black floors and walls and white ceilings. It shouldn't work, but it does. There are no paintings or decorative ornaments, just clean walls and floors with a red carpet leading farther into the court. No one greets us, and I don't even see anyone here.

Just as I think that, I step onto the carpet, and a man with black hair in a white suit and a white mask appears at the other end of the carpet. He waits for us, but I refuse to hurry, so I wander down the carpet like I have all the time in the world, and I can sense his irritation as I reach him. He holds a tray with wine glasses filled with champagne. I take one without a word and turn away, following the carpet. I feel his eyes on us, and I have no doubt his king is watching us through him.

We follow the carpet into the estate until we reach two closed doors with two men in matching white suits and masks standing there, their arms crossed at their stomachs. "Welcome," they say in unison, bowing their heads while opening the doors with a flourish.

How very dramatic.

Remember, they will watch our every move, so give them nothing, Nathair tells us.

With a blank face, a cruel smile, and the chain in my hand, I step into the madness beyond.

Unlike the rest of the court, this is exactly what I expected. Gone is the bland, modern expanse, and instead we are transported into a world of sex and blood. Music fills the air, sultry and sexy, coming from a live band in one corner. The singer is naked with fang marks covering her entire body, and I see a collar around her neck. I want to turn away, but I do not, feeling eyes on me from every corner of the room. There are shadowed parts of the venue for people to hide in, but most of the acts are on full display. Cages hang from the ceiling with people inside, crying as their blood drips into the laughing, open-mouthed creatures below.

The floor runs red with the blood spilled here.

In the middle of the space is a mound of pillows and blankets, which are covered with writhing bodies, all naked. The slaves and their masters are easily recognisable as they feed and fuck. There is one young man—so young he must not have even changed yet—with a collar around his throat as a woman in a red bra rides him. My stomach churns, and I fight my anger, keeping my power tightly locked away as I scan the room as if I'm bored.

Even so, I feel this place scar my soul, infesting me with a rot I will never get rid of just by simply being here.

There are stages spread throughout with torture acts transpiring on them. One has a stretching rack where a girl screams and begs, and on another is a man who's being crucified. A third has a man whose skin is being stripped from his back. The whole room is one big torture chamber, and the people here watch and laugh and take part with their pets, their slaves, sitting at their feet with chains and collars.

The fact that Azul was here makes me so angry, I want to kill them all with a flick of my fingers. Knowing he survived this time and time again only makes my estimation of my king go up. Anyone who could walk out of here alive and sane and still be as kind and as wonderful as Azul is a fucking saint. It reeks of pain, agony, and death, and blood saturates the air from every direction.

Watching over it all with a pleased smile is the king, who sits at the back upon a golden throne. An ornate crown is perched on his head, his chest is bare, and his legs are encased in red leather. Four women and five men writhe below him, tethered to the chains held leisurely in his hand. His irises are a piercing red, and his blond hair hangs to his shoulders. He would be handsome if it wasn't for the cruel look in his eyes.

There was never any way to escape in this court, and I do not know how the other courts didn't notice. He isn't even hiding it. He wears his need for pain proudly, yet I sense boredom about him, as if he's used to this and seeking excitement.

He is, always has been. He grew tired of his court and his usual playthings. Draw him to you, Azul murmurs. *Wander around the room and get angry for a reason. Let him feel your power, and he will come to you.*

Smiling in understanding, I tug him after me as I circle the room, ignoring the hungry and confused looks sent in my direction when I spot my opportunity. I hate this, but it's what I have to do. I stop suddenly to avoid a lumbering man on a chain belonging to a tiny woman, and Azul runs into my back. Snarling, I turn and lash out with my power.

"Watch it, pet," I snarl.

He winces and looks down, even as I brush his mind with love. My power rolls through the room, and all eyes turn to me. I feel jealousy, hunger, and want, and they suddenly crave a taste of it. I've made a spectacle of myself, but when the king stands and his eyes land on me, I know it's not the result I wanted.

He watches me for a moment, and then a woman in a white suit and mask appears at my side. "The king wishes for you to attend him." It's a polite request, but I sense the "or else" underneath. After all, you do not disobey a king in his castle.

The last one I was presented to rejected me. Back then, I was a scared, new vampyr, but now I stroll through the crowd, feeling my power wash over them. The Althea who died that night will never come back. This king does not scare me, nor will any other.

I'm a fucking queen, and before the night is through, they will understand what that means.

The king watches me approach, forgetting the people around him and at his feet, and once I reach him, I curtsy slightly, looking up at him through my lashes. A smile curves my painted lips as I purr, "My king, you asked for me?" I slide my power over him like a lover's caress, watching him shudder as hunger enters his gaze.

I feel the others tense with jealousy, but I ignore it for now. I need this to be good. I need him to believe I want him before I rip his court to pieces and feast on his soul.

"Who are you? We have never met before. I would know," he says, his voice thick with power as he tries to show off.

Interesting.

"I'm new to your . . . gatherings," I reply shyly, fluttering my lashes. "I was invited by a friend."

"I see, and what is your name?" he demands, stepping closer, dropping the chains in his hand to the floor. There's a gasp in the court.

"Althea, my king," I purr.

He holds out his hand, watching me. "Join me, Althea, and be my guest tonight."

I feel the tension as everyone waits for my decision. Clearly, this is unusual, and it just means that I get that much closer to what I want. "Of course, my king. I would be honoured." Laying my hand in his, I bite back my groan as his power instantly dives into me, searching for the source of my power and my secrets. He's trying to lay me bare, but I only let him see what I want.

He grunts in annoyance, but challenge sparks in his eyes.

He wishes to ruin me before the night is over, and I let him think I don't notice as I giggle and sit on the chair a servant scrambles to put next to his throne. He claps his hand on the throne, and the music starts again, the party in full swing as he turns to me. My men hesitate before fading into the background near me, while Azul slides to the other side of the chair and sits out of sight.

The king squeezes my hand in warning, but I pretend not to notice and instead keep the smile on my face as I watch him like this is the best thing ever.

"You have me at a disadvantage, Althea. You know me, and you know my court, but I know nothing of you. I cannot even sense anything. I am usually very good at reading people and learning their secrets." No doubt through pain and his power. "But you . . . you surprise me."

"A good thing, I hope?" I ask.

"An unexpected thing." It's clear it annoys him as much as it intrigues him. "Tell me one thing I should know about you."

I lean into him, but my eyes flick to where a female presses up against Lycus. His nostrils flare as he backs into the wall until he's plastered against it, his wide eyes showing his discomfort.

"One thing?" I purr, running a hand along the king's arm.

"Hmm," he responds.

"I don't like to share," I tell him seriously and then throw my power at the woman who is touching what's mine. She falls onto her back, screaming and writhing, and then I turn to the king with a smile. "Oops."

"Is that right?" He laughs, watching his own court member thrash in agony from an attack he doesn't seem to care about. "I will have to remember that. It is clear you like pain, though, or you would not be here. So tell me, Althea, what is your proclivity? To make it or to take it?"

Walk carefully, Azul whispers. *He is playing a game and moving you into position. I can tell.*

Azul is right. The king is waiting for me like a spider watching the prey in its web. "I'm more of a watcher." The smile he gives me tells me I've said what he hoped, and I want to take it back.

"Good, then you won't mind if we put on a show for you, will you?"

Fuck, I definitely said something wrong. "Of course not," I offer instead, even as I begin to worry. When Azul starts to scream in my head, I turn to see the issue.

Approaching the throne is a woman, one I have seen countless times in Azul's memories—his old master, the woman who tortured and abused him all of his life.

Her hair is a fake bottle red that flows down to her shoulders in fifties style waves. Her deep brown eyes are lined black and smoky, her skin is a pale white, and her lips are bright red. She's wearing black leather nipple covers with a black corset, a black mini skirt, fishnets, and knee-high boots, with a metal whip coiled at her hip. She's beautiful, but it's tarnished by the cruelty I know she is capable of. I hear Azul fracturing, and we instantly all rush into his mind to protect him.

"This is Cassandra, our show master," the king says. "Cassandra, this is Althea. Let's give her a good welcome, shall we?"

"Gladly," she purrs as she looks at Azul. "Welcome home, pet."

Fuck!

THIRTY SIX

ALTHEA

"OH, DO YOU KNOW our guest of honour's pet, Cassandra?" the king asks silkily, and I know he knows she does. It's all one big game, and they are waiting for my reaction, but I cannot give them one. Otherwise, I know they will turn on us. We have to play the game.

"Why yes, he used to be my pet. I did think he was dead though. I guess I was wrong. I am so happy about that. He was always my favourite. He screamed so prettily, but I'm assuming you know that," she addresses me, fluttering long, fake lashes as she steps towards him.

I sit back, crossing one leg over the other as I eye her. "He has never mentioned you." I grin, watching anger cross her face. "Maybe he was too busy serving me, but you are right about his screams. I do love them." I don't tell her it's the sounds he makes when I ride his cock, but I let it hang in the air.

Possessiveness rolls from her. She wants him, and she wants him badly. "My king, for my show, I ask for the right of tasting."

I stiffen, knowing whatever that is, it isn't good, and the cruel smile she gives me tells me exactly that.

"Would you consent, Althea?" the king asks me, squeezing my hand once more to draw my attention. The pain from his touch makes me refrain from voicing a rude retort.

"I'm afraid I don't know what that is," I reply carefully.

"Why, it just means what is yours is ours, for a taste of course," he replies.

"I see. As I said, I'm rather possessive and I do not like to share." I'm hoping that's enough, but I can see he doesn't like that.

"It is customary for a new guest to share her possessions." He won't let this go, and denying him will only play into his game, into their game. It would look like I'm refusing the king, and that would mean he has the right to kill us all. I hate it.

It will be okay. I know you will die for me, Azul murmurs, yet I still hesitate. *I can do this. I trust you to save me once more, my queen.*

I let the chain drop, and with a grin, she picks it up and yanks until he's on all fours. "Crawl. We are going to have some fun. Oh, how I've missed you."

Jealousy and anger surge through me, and I have to push them back because the king watches me closely, pleased he finally got a reaction. The bastard. I'm forced to watch as she drags him over to the middle of the room where people begin to clear an area. There's a table there, and she orders him to lie on it like a dog. He shoots me a pained, embarrassed look but climbs on and lies down. I sense the shaking in his bones as he prepares for pain, for humiliation, and his thoughts are slightly wild as they reach me.

Don't want her to see me like this.

Not again.

I turn to the others, pleading for them to help with my eyes. I could kill them all now, but I need proof of their crimes. I'm lost and scared. I cannot save Azul despite the power that resides inside me.

I am chained by our roles.

Trust us, Nathair offers. *Play along.*

Swallowing back my own need to scream, I turn and see the king watching me carefully, so I smile as I force myself to relax, even though all I want to do is rip them to shreds.

Cassandra circles the table as she grins at us. "I used to have such fun playing with him. He was so hard to break. I wonder if he will be the same this evening. Tonight, for you, my king and honoured guest," she says, "I will do just that. I will taste his blood and his body, and his screams will fill the room for you."

I have to watch as she climbs onto the table and runs her sharp blood-red nails across his chest, carving into it as he swallows back his howl of pain.

Please! I beg them mentally. I sit forward as if to watch, but it's really to stop myself from leaping from this chair and attacking them. Possessiveness and fury roars inside me until my powers growl, and I know the king senses it, his own lashing at me and trying to batter me down. While Azul is tortured, there is a war between the king and me that I have to focus on or I will die.

I have to trust the others. I feel Reve slip into his mind while the others step before him, shielding him. He takes the brunt of the torture while projecting happy images to Azul, taking him far away as she hurts him. When she doesn't get the reaction she wants, I sense her anger. He's smiling and distanced from what she is doing to him, but I am not.

I focus on the king, smiling at him as I let go of the last shred of control holding my power back, and I watch as he slumps in shock as it rips through him like his did to me earlier. I let him feel every drop of it and show him the truth of who I am.

"A queen," he rasps, blood dribbling from his mouth, ears, and eyes. Some start to notice their king, their concern filling the air. I'm tired of playing their games. I've seen enough. Their king is corrupt and willing to watch the torture of innocents. Not only that, he encourages it, and every single person here watched and helped, unwilling to stop it.

I judge and find them all guilty, and their souls will be mine.

"That I am, but I am so much more too." I smirk as I lean into him, feeling my men move closer. "I'm your worst nightmare. I'm here to judge you and your court, and you, my king," I purr. "You have been weighed and have been found wanting."

"What do you mean?" He watches me, fear entering his eyes as I continue to effortlessly thrash him with my power, and my kings reveal themselves at my side.

"I mean that your court and your sick, twisted games are going to end tonight. Ironic, isn't it, that the man you tried to ruin is now the one coming back to do just that? Now be a good boy and sit there silently." I pulse my power into him, sealing his mouth and binding him to his throne he loves so much.

He lived upon it, and now he will die upon it.

Standing, I notice Azul's torturer, Cassandra, has stopped and is looking from me to her king. I flick my fingers, and she flies through the air, away from my mate. "She is his. Everyone else is fair game," I tell them as I glance over at my men. "Consult with Azul, but I'm sure he will agree."

The matching grins on their faces are sinister and hungry.

They might be judges, but tonight we all feel the glee of killing the people responsible for Azul's pain. Maybe the god of death was right and I am dangerous, because there is nothing I wouldn't do for my judges, for my kings, including breaking my oath. It just so happens that tonight, my duty and my desires align.

"Change," I order as I stand taller, looking over the court that's finally realising something is truly wrong. They try to leave, but Conall slams the door shut, trapping them in with us. "Kill them all," I demand of my men, of my nightmares.

Screams ring out as Zale transforms into his black hound and leaps into their masses. Lycus scrambles up the wall, and people fall all over themselves to escape him. Osis prowls towards me, swiping at those who get in his way. Conall disappears into the shadows, while Nathair's snake strikes, swallowing a man whole. I grin and rip the mask from my face, and my own judge's mask appears in its place, conjured by my powers. I feel the king trying to fight my binds, but I send my power into him, subduing him as I step into the chaos.

Bodies and blood fly around me as I walk towards Azul, who sits up and rubs his head. His body is coated in blood, and when I reach him, I hold out my arm. "Drink, my king. Drink deeply and heal, and then revenge is yours."

He slams his fangs into my arm, making me moan as I hold him to me. I turn away and watch my men rip through the masses. Every now and then, I see them hesitate, and when Azul communicates, they knock that person out and lay them before the throne, while the others are killed instantly. Nathair strikes, pumping them with venom. Lycus's spider catches people in his web and then kills them with his own venom. Zale bounds through the crowd, setting those in his way on fire before ripping into their throats. Osis does the same, ripping them apart with his teeth and claws. Reve has people screaming before him as he laughs.

I'm drawn back when Azul licks my hand, and I press my head to his. "She is yours, as are any of the others. Go." I push him, and he walks through their masses as his armour and mask appear. Gone is the scared man Cassandra called her pet, and in his place is the warrior that was always there, waiting to be set free.

Conall clears a path for him with his powers as Cassandra tries to run away. Standing in the middle of the massacre, I watch the man I'm falling in love with take his revenge. I expect him to play with her, and to a certain extent he does. He follows her as she tries to escape, and when she finally gives up and turns to him with a wicked smile, he simply rips her heart out and sets it on fire, turning away as she crumbles.

She isn't worth it, he tells me. *It was all I dreamed of, but revenge is empty. She doesn't deserve any more of me. She's dead, and that's enough.*

I nod and turn back to see the crowd gathering before the throne until the screams finally stop. Bodies litter the ground, those who were judged and killed. The rest are awaiting their judgement. They are angry, scared, crying, or begging.

Some still try to fight as I walk around to the throne where their king awaits his own sentence. He's furious, but he's scared, too, as he tries to break free of my power.

The remaining crowd is on their knees, bleeding and wanting to beg for their lives as my men circle them like nightmares. Turning to the king, I sink my fangs into his neck to embarrass and ruin him, and when I step back, I grin at him with his blood on my lips, and then I turn to his people. "Tonight, you will face judgement for your crimes. Everyone here was invited because of their proclivities for violence and pain. You relished the torture of others, and you took pleasure from it."

"We did as we were told!" someone yells.

"Silence!" I roar. "That will be judged. You can't lie to us. We will discern the truth from your blood. If you are found innocent, you will be let go. Otherwise, you will die just like your king."

Turning to him, I smirk. "You are not worthy of your throne, the one you made out of death and pain, but tonight you will die on it." I focus on the bleeding wounds on his neck and send my power into them, watching as his life force pours from the punctures. He starts to die, and then I step closer. "Goodbye, false king. May you burn in your victims' blood for all time." I thrust my hand into his chest and send Zale's power down my arm, burning his heart and stepping back as his body turns to black ash on his throne.

Those who were chained are freed, and they stay at the back, watching. I nod at them, seeing them relax, and then I step towards the masses and hold out my hand. We do not have time to judge them one at a time, but they are all bleeding in some way or another, so I close my eyes and call it to me. It slams into me, filling me with their power and memories, and I stagger as I sort through it. I point wordlessly and blindly, feeling my men end the guilty ones, until only the innocent remain—those who were forced into it.

Only five people stand before us.

Two men and three women.

I jerk my head, and Reve leads them to the others at the back as my men transform and move to my side, their judge masks on their faces.

Turning to those I freed, I let my mask fade away. "We were all like you once—used, hurt, forgotten, and weak. No more. You are free. Spread the word of the judges, of the blood kings and queen who are coming for those within our race who wish to break our covenant. Their crimes will no longer be forgotten and dismissed. They will be punished. They will be judged." As they begin to ask questions, Conall wraps his shadows around us, and we disappear the way we came.

We take the souls of those we collected with us, their blood coating our bodies.

Principes Court is no more.

Thirty Seven

Azul

As soon as we reappear in the judgement room, they surround me. Althea rips off my mask and searches my face. I smile under her inspection, her worry for me palpable. The jealousy, possessiveness, and anger I could feel in her mind surged from her when they took me, and that's what got me through the walk to the table, and then Reve was there.

He transported my mind far, far away. We were back in bed, and she was smiling at me as she held me. I was safe and happy, and when he released me, I woke up to chaos. My body was in agony, but the wounds quickly healed with my queen's blood, chasing away the reins of my old mistress and court.

I finally got my revenge, something we are not supposed to do, but my mate gave me the chance to get vengeance for what they did to me. My brothers and my queen judged and killed the wicked before freeing the others. Now, no one else will ever have to live like me, but I can sense her thoughts now. She is worried we shouldn't have done what we did, that she pushed me too far, and that she should have known they would use me against her.

Cupping her hands, I lean in and kiss her softly, wanting to reassure her. I hate how upset she is. Doesn't she understand the gift she gave me tonight? "I'm okay," I promise. "Truly, look through all of me." I open my mind, needing her to feel my honesty. She slips inside and searches, and when she sags with relief, I know she sees the truth.

For the first time in a long time, I truly am okay. I'm finally free of the nightmares and restraints that place put on me. It's almost as if knowing they are no longer walking among us has lifted those last few chains that were holding me back.

I feel Nathair alongside her, worrying for me like he does everyone. Reve is surprisingly absent, and I see him stalking away.

Althea watches him go with a frown before smiling at me. "How do you feel now that they are gone?"

"Is it wrong to say that I feel good?" I respond.

Judges are supposed to let go of our pasts so we can protect our people and judge the evil without prejudice, but how can I when I still bear the scars of their torture and could see them doing it to people right before my eyes?

"No," Lycus responds, surprising us all. We know his history, but Althea doesn't, so she looks confused. "Vengeance feels good, especially when you know it will stop future evil. Do not second-guess yourself."

"Yes, yes, all this mortality is sickening," comes a mocking voice, and we all turn to see the god of death shielded by shadows. We should kneel and pay homage, but we did not call him, so we hesitate.

Althea doesn't, stepping forward. "We didn't call you."

"No, but I wanted to congratulate you on your successful hunt. I had so much fun with the souls you gave me." His voice is filled with laughter, and the power in it almost makes my ears bleed.

Althea feels it, but the god blood inside her must help her endure it. "Is that all you wanted?" she asks carefully, knowing better than to annoy a god. She might amuse him, but he could kill her with a single thought.

"It almost sounds like you are not pleased to see me," he responds suspiciously, and the lash of power he releases drops us to our knees—all but Althea who steadfastly remains on her feet.

"It was a simple question, and I meant no offence," she replies with a mocking curtsy.

I prepare to leap at her and shield her from the blow he will no doubt land, but instead, he laughs. "I think I like you, little vampyr. I find you amusing, an odd trait. Maybe I'll let you live. It seems you might be beneficial to me with all the souls you will send my way."

"Most gracious," she responds carefully.

"But I would be careful, Althea," he warns. "Not all are happy with you after tonight. I might even be concerned if I were you." He vanishes as quickly as he appeared.

"We need to find a way to block him from popping in like that," she mutters.

"A god will always find a way," I tell her, as unhappy as she is that he keeps appearing in our home.

"When a god offers a warning, you listen," Nathair murmurs with worry in his tone. "Something is coming. We need to prepare."

"But what?" she asks as we climb to our feet. "We were careful. No one knows who we are."

"Some do, and they hate us for simply existing, but they leave us alone. If someone were to seek answers for what happened tonight and learned the truth, well, the god of death is right. It might be more than we can handle," Nathair muses and looks around. "Rest, because I have a feeling we will need it." He turns and strolls from the room, his mind already a million miles away.

Althea shares a worried look with us, but I smile reassuringly. "Do not worry. Tonight was a good thing, my Thea," I assure her, and the smile she bestows upon me is worth all the torture and pain. "I have a feeling, however, that someone needs you more than I do tonight."

Worry clouds her eyes as they flick to the corridor Reve disappeared down. "Reve."

I nod, bending over and kissing her hand. "Go to him. He protected me tonight, and now he needs his queen to make it better."

With one more searching look, she ensures I'm okay before she nods and hesitantly follows the path he took.

All of us watch her go, entranced by our queen.

Thirty Eight

Althea

I search for Reve but cannot find him. Finally, I realise I'm using my eyes and not my link to him—the one that feels an awful lot like a mate bond. Focusing internally, I feel him blocking himself from me, from us all, as if he doesn't want us to worry.

But I do worry.

He shielded Azul from the worst of the torture tonight, but what was the cost of that? How did Reve pay, and why doesn't he want me to know? Feeling his brothers' concern, I block them too, needing it to just be us, and then I follow the bond deeper into the court, deeper than I have explored yet.

It's cold and dark, as if no light has even existed here in centuries. The doors are closed, locked, and forgotten, and there are sheets over the furniture. My footsteps are loud on the dark grey stone that seems to slope down, and when the hallway finally ends in a giant stone archway, I peek inside to find Reve.

These must be his rooms. Unlike the corridor behind me, this space is warm, and low light spills out from candles spread around the room on different surfaces and the flames burning in the fireplace. There's a sunken oval bed in the middle with silk sheets, and it's filled with blankets and pillows. A vinyl player sits on a fur rug before it, filled with records, and the low crooning of a rock song emanates from it. On the left is a small pool surrounded by rocks with steaming water.

The whole room is draped in silks and warmth, and it reminds me of a sanctuary. Is this where he comes when his dreams and abilities are too much?

I spot him lying amongst the pillows and silks, with one arm over his face. He's so lost in his own head, he doesn't even hear me at the doorway that shimmers with its own power. His trousers are half open, and everything else is discarded.

His corded muscles clench as he twists slightly, his tattoos moving with him as if they are alive. Reve is a masterpiece, but right now, his hair is a mess, as is his mind, and he needs help. As I step through the nearly invisible barrier, a small gasp leaves me. I expect him to sit up, but he just freezes. It felt like his power washed over me—his version of a door perhaps? It makes me wonder how powerful he truly is if he can have that here at all times.

"Go away, Nathair," he mutters.

"Now I'm worried. Don't get me wrong, it's a compliment since he's very beautiful, but he definitely has a bigger dick than I do," I say with a grin as I move over to the vinyl player and watch it turn before chancing a look over my shoulder.

He's sitting up now with his arms propped behind him, his chest tight with muscle and strain. Reve's eyes are wild, his hair is a mess, and he's still covered in blood from tonight's killings. He looks untamed and lost and oh so beautiful, it makes my heart ache.

"Althea, I'm fine," he mutters, and I raise my eyebrow as I turn to face him.

"If you say you are fine, then you are either a terrible liar or you expect me not to care." I move towards him, crawling onto the bed and kneeling before him.

He watches me carefully.

"Well, which is it?"

He lies down with a groan and stares up at the ceiling, so I crawl next to him, lie on my back, and stare at the ceiling too, which is when I realise he's effortlessly projecting a whole night sky across it with his mind.

He doesn't speak though, and I can feel his internal struggle, our bond holding us tightly together even when he tries to push me away.

"You took him away from the pain, but that meant you felt it, didn't it?" I ask Reve.

I feel him startle, and when I glance over at him, his eyes close for a moment. "How did you know?"

"Because I know you would risk everything for him and the others, so of course you would take it." I take his hand, but he tries to pull away, and for a moment, old doubts rear their ugly heads before he sighs and glances over at me with tears in his eyes. I see so much vulnerability and pain in his gaze, I forget my own worries for now.

"I couldn't let him go through that again, Thea," he whispers. "I gave him good thoughts, but someone had to experience it. I don't know how he survived so long there. I truly don't. It was such a short time, and I'm—" He shakes his head and looks away. "Weak, I'm weaker than him. I thought all these years, all this time, would make my mind and body stronger, and that I could handle anything, but I'm still the same, scared little boy I was in the past."

This is about more than tonight. This is about his past. I haven't asked the others, and I only know about Nathair's and Azul's pasts, but their deaths are their own unless they want to share it. I would never force them to tell me, knowing it's the hardest moment of their lives, but I can almost feel Reve's desire to talk about it.

"Have you ever talked about your past with the others?"

He laughs bitterly. "They saw it, so we didn't need to talk about it."

"Yes, you do," I murmur. "Just because they saw it doesn't mean you dealt with it. I'm here if you need to talk, Reve. The only way to let go of the painful memories is to give them life and let them go."

"I don't know if I can," he admits after a moment of silence. "I'm ashamed, and the idea of you knowing the worst parts of me—"

"But that's what this is, don't you see?" I lift up and meet his eyes. "For good or bad, this bond is forever, but friendship and love are about knowing the best and the worst bits about the other person and still loving them. It's about knowing everything about the other person, including their hopes, dreams, and fears. You have nothing to be ashamed of, baby," I promise as I lean down and kiss him. "There is nothing that could ever make me turn away from you, any of you. We have all done things we are ashamed of, and we are atoning for that by helping people, so no matter what you think about your past, it shaped you into the man you are now, and I like that man. A lot."

"Yeah?" he croaks as he watches me. "How much?"

I laugh, glad to see a hint of that teasing gleam back in his gaze. "Much more than I ever thought I could."

Swallowing, he searches my face. "I wasn't raised in a court," he tells me, and I lie back down with my head near his to make it easier for him, but I don't release his hand, and he holds mine tighter, as if it's a lifeline. "I wasn't raised with my own kind at all. I was adopted when I was one by a lovely couple who couldn't have kids. No one knew my real parents, so no one knew who—what I was."

I turn to him, my heart racing, and he chuckles bitterly. "They abandoned me to a human way of life, and it was a good life, don't get me wrong. I got to celebrate Christmas and birthdays, and I went to football practice on the weekend. They loved me so much, like I was their own, and for so long, I believed I was. I was happy, and I was human—albeit small, no matter how much I ate or worked out. It wasn't until my eighteenth . . ."

Oh Nox.

"I changed. I died. I was terrified and so scared because I didn't know what was happening. They had gone away for the weekend, and I was getting ready to go to a party. It was agony, and when it ended, I was so glad it was over and that my parents weren't there to witness it, but then I came back, and I wasn't me. I was so hungry, so fucking hungry, Thea."

Oh gods, I couldn't imagine going through the change alone, never mind not knowing it was coming. The elders guided me, the others too, and they fed us right away. If not . . . Oh Nox. If the thirst is not fed by powerful, ancient blood right after the change, it becomes uncontrollable and leaves the newly turned feral, unable to control themselves.

"I hoped they would never come home and just leave me like my real parents. I was a monster, and I couldn't control myself. I barely kept myself from leaving the house and fulfilling this evil thirst inside me, but I should have known better. They would never leave me, and they would never abandon me. They loved me, Althea." He looks at me, his blood-red tears dripping down his face. "And I killed them. I couldn't stop myself. I tried, gods, did I try, but I couldn't stop. I tore into them like a beast. They begged and pleaded. They didn't understand—how could they because I didn't—but I needed their blood. I still remember flashes of that, of my hands deep in my mother's chest as she stared up at me in horror, and my father's broken, drained body at her side, reaching for her even in death. I killed them, Thea. And it still wasn't enough. I was so hungry, and the taste of the blood only made it worse."

He starts to sob, so I wrap myself around him.

"I remember seeing the gift bag—they brought me a present from their trip—and it was splattered with their blood. I didn't care because I was just so hungry, and I licked it clean."

His body shakes with the force of his sobs as I hold him.

"It was like something broke inside me. I barely remember the days after, only flashes, as if this other creature had taken over me. I drained our neighbours, a lovely old couple who knitted me jumpers every Christmas. I killed someone who was on a morning run. I killed so many innocent people, all because of this thirst I couldn't control and because the people who were supposed to love me, supposed to guide me, gave me up and didn't care about the consequences. When the guys tracked me down and judged me, I was so relieved. I remember feeling peace for the first time since that night, but the memories were still there. The blood of all those innocents stained my soul, and that's why I came back, because I owe it to them all, not just my parents who did nothing but take in a child and love him." He lifts his head, his face streaked with blood-red tears. "They were good people."

"I'm so sorry, Reve. I'm so sorry for what you went through, but you know that wasn't your fault, right? You never should have been left alone to go through the change. You should have known what you were and what was coming, and you should have been guided and supported. You cannot help what you did. You didn't kill them for sport or fun; you had no choice. It wasn't a conscious decision. You loved them, and they knew that."

"Their last memory is of me killing them like I hated them," he sobs. "I loved them. I loved them so much, and they died thinking I hated them."

"They did not." I cup his face, forcing him to look at me. "They knew it wasn't you. They loved you, Reve, and they knew their son, and that was not him, not you. They died horribly, yes, but you suffered just as they did, and I guarantee they knew you loved them and would never want to hurt them. I'm so angry that you had to go through that. I'm so fucking angry, and I'm so sorry."

Nodding, he rubs his head against my chest, and I hold him there, stroking his back as he cries for the innocent boy who didn't stand a chance. Slowly, his tears stop and he calms. I hum to him, protecting him until he pulls away enough for us to curl together. The silence surrounding us is filled with broken hearts and pain. I need to replace it and remind him of the good, not just the bad.

"Tell me about them, about your parents, the good bits," I encourage him. He grins, and although it's shaky, it's there.

"Let me show you."

He still feels raw, but I think he will for a while. It's clear he never dealt with what he went through, and if I didn't love Reve before, I do now. I turn my head and gasp when a couple appears on the ceiling. It's like watching a film. I watch as he learns to ride a bike and breaks his arm. There is a memory of when he was sick and curled up under a blanket with them. There are Christmases, birthdays, and New Year's celebrations, and I fall in love with the couple who raised the man I love.

When it's over, I turn to him. "Thank you for showing me."

He nods. "What about your parents?"

"I never knew my dad," I admit. "My mother died when I was really young, so I barely remember her, only the prophecies she left behind. I had no family."

"You do now," he says seriously, and I smile.

"I know."

We go back to watching the stars, hand in hand, our legs entwined, when my own insecurities raise their ugly heads. He doesn't need this now, but I begged him to be honest with me, and I know he would want the same, so despite the fact that I hate having to admit this, I know I have to.

"Reve," I whisper softly. He's hurting, but I need him to know. "Please don't block me again."

"What?" He frowns, and I feel him looking at me, but I continue to stare at the ceiling, feeling raw and vulnerable.

"I didn't like the feeling of being blocked from our bond."

"Why—" He cuts off, and when he speaks again, he whispers, "Because your mate did that."

I nod, and then his hand touches my face and turns my head so I'm looking at him.

"I'm so sorry, Thea," he whispers, his eyes showing his concern. "I didn't think, and I never want you to feel rejected. I just didn't want you to have to feel all that."

"I know," I murmur, and I do, but it was hard to stop that momentary flare of panic when it felt like I was being rejected again.

"I will never do it again. I promise, Althea," he croons, pressing his forehead to mine. "I'm yours, all of me, even the ugly parts if you want them. I will never block myself from you again. I'm sorry I made you worry, even for a second, but you have to know we are not him, Althea. We will never reject you, never leave you."

"Because you don't have a choice," I retort, and I don't know where this is coming from, but I guess old insecurities are hard to get rid of.

"No, because we chose you, Althea. We choose you every single day. The judge's bond does not include feelings, which you know. It is just that, a bond you could have with any stranger. We chose to feel for you, we chose to love you, and we chose to make it a mate bond. You have to know that."

"Prove it," I demand, my breath hitching. "Prove you want me."

He rolls and pins me, pressing his lips onto mine.

I taste the truth on his lips.

Groaning, I lift my legs and wrap them around his waist, sliding my hands across his shoulders. I trace his tattoos as he moans and lifts his head, his eyes blown with desire as he watches me beneath him.

"If we ever got to choose our mates, Althea, I would choose you every time. I would be yours until the end." Leaning down, he swallows my response, kissing me again as his hands make quick work of the dress I'm wearing until I'm naked below him. He kisses down my chest, across my breasts and stomach, and down, ignoring my pulsing pussy. I rub my thighs together for friction and lift my hips to encourage him, but he slides down and undoes my heels, kissing along the arch of each foot before moving up my body to my lips. "Every time, Althea, we would choose you to be ours. Let me show you."

He lifts me and carries me into the pool, the warm water making me gasp as his fangs scrape across my throat. "Reve." His name is a plea as I grind against him, searching for relief. My hunger wars with my desire to feel him buried deep inside of me here, in his sanctuary, as our two, raw hearts align.

I would choose him too.

I would choose all of them.

In fact, I chose them to be my mates. I was destined for this great love, just like my mother said.

His hands drag along my skin, washing away the blood from tonight. He rinses away my doubts and our pain until we are clean and reborn together. Reve leans me back on a ledge before he drops to his knees in the water and suckles on one of my nipples. My head falls back to the edge of the tub, and my eyes close in ecstasy. I slide my fingers through his silken locks as his mouth teases my nipple into a hard point. Pleasure arcs through me like electricity, straight to my throbbing clit, and my whole body comes alive for him. He watches me as he turns his head and tortures my other breast, kissing and licking until I'm writhing under him and begging him to make me come.

His thoughts fill my head, and all the dirty praises I hear make me claw at him.

Nipping my breast, he slides his talented lips up my chest, across my throat, and to my ear. "You are so beautiful, my Althea, a fucking goddess. We might be nightmares, but you are a fucking dream, one I want to live in," he croons, his words nearly causing me to tear up as I grip him and flip us.

He laughs, holding me tight, as I straddle his lap and reach for his cock, stroking his length. His laughter cuts off with a groan.

Smirking, I press the tip of his cock to my pussy and lean in, watching him flex as he tries to tug me down. "Say you're mine," I murmur. "Tell me I'm yours."

"Yours, I'm yours." He groans, his eyes tight. "Now fuck me, mate."

Moaning, I slam myself down on him, taking every hard inch of his cock inside me. We both gasp at the feel of me stretching around him. Pleasure arches through the bond, filled with love, happiness, and friendship.

A true mating.

"Mine," I groan as I ride my mate while he watches me with adoration. The water slowly laps against us as I reach out and steady myself with my hands on the edge of the pool. His dark, hungry eyes watch my swaying body as he grips my hips and helps me.

"Yours," he replies without shame, his heart hammering in time with mine as our bodies move together. He tilts my hips so he hits my clit with every thrust, and my head falls back. "That's it, mate, ride me until you come. Let me feel it. Take what you need."

His words encourage me, and I speed up as he seals his lips around my nipple, winding me up until I'm moaning. I ride him faster and faster, churning the water around us. My pussy clenches around him, and the pleasure grows until it explodes through me and I scream his name.

He kisses me through it, and when I slump, he turns me and presses my back to the wall as he starts to move with slow, soft thrusts. My eyes open and lock on him.

"There she is," he murmurs. "Eyes on me, Thea."

Nodding, I wrap my arms around his neck and lift my hips to meet his soft thrusts. Something passes between us until we are both panting and searching each other's gazes. The bond is so strong, it almost fills the air around us until we struggle to breathe.

The fucking turns into something slower and sweeter.

It's not rushed, hungry, or desperate, but soft and true, the type that lasts forever.

Our lips meet in a perfect kiss, our souls locked together as our bodies move as one. The pleasure builds until we tumble down together, wrapped around each other.

When we finally break apart, both of us are panting, and the slow grin he gives me sends butterflies shooting through me.

"Understand now, Thea?"

I nod because I do.

It doesn't matter if I was supposed to be mated to that pathetic king, and it doesn't matter if this was only supposed to be a judge's bond. It's so much more. I'm theirs, and they are mine.

We are choosing each other, and that is worth fighting for, even in the darkest of times.

Thirty Nine

Althea

I fell asleep in Reve's bed last night, wrapped around him, but when I wake up, there are more bodies that must have come in during the night. Azul is curled around my feet, and Lycus is at my back, snoring away.

I relax and reach out to all of them, checking on each one. Osis is outside, padding around in tiger form, Nathair is in the library, Zale is with his wine, and Conall is with his tea. Closing my eyes, I let my mind wander as I absorb the silence and peace. I have nowhere to be and nothing to do for once, so I just let my thoughts drift, and they turn to my mother, wondering if she knew this was always coming.

She said I would die young, but I've done that, so it makes me wonder what else she knew.

Did she always know they would be my mates? It also makes me think about my father. Who was he? She never mentioned, and no one else knew. Was he her mate? Did he love her? Did he want me? Would he want me? Would he love me? Does he even know?

I suppose it doesn't matter, but a small part of me can't help but wonder why I never knew him—unless he was just a one-time thing. I guess I will never know.

"You are thinking awfully hard this early in the morning," Lycus grumbles in my ear, tugging me closer like a giant teddy bear. "Sleep, pretty girl."

"I would, but I seem to have become a vampyr blanket," I tease, making him huff. Reve moves closer, and I stroke my hand across his bare chest and the gravestones there. There are two above his heart, and now that I know what they mean, my heart breaks a little for my love.

"But you're so comfy," Lycus whines, tugging me closer. Reve whimpers and shuffles closer so he's pressed against me again, making me giggle.

Azul sighs, crawling up my body until he's propped on my hip, and then his gaze goes to Reve. I see his worry there, so I reach down and stroke his hair, watching his eyes close for a moment. "He will be okay," I assure him.

"Are you sure?" Azul whispers, his voice tight, no doubt worried he caused his brother pain.

"Yes, I am." My eyes go back to Reve. "He's stronger than any of us. He will be okay."

"Not physically. I am the strongest," Lycus mutters, flexing his arm, and I grab his bicep and grin at him. He wiggles his eyebrows as he shoots me a toothy grin, and even Azul chuckles.

Motherfucker. Lycus, you dick, why is your spider's silk all over the training room? Zale grouses, and I get a vision of him with his arms half held in the air, his body tangled in the silk harness we played in.

I descend into laughter, then the vision of what we did slips into Zale's mind, and he fake gags.

Oh my god, is this actual cum? Am I tangled in your cum web?

Reve flops onto his back, grinning with his eyes closed, his hair sweeping across his face. He cracks an eye open. *I didn't know you had it in you, baby. Good on you.*

Nathair, we need a new rule. If they have weird spider sex, they have to clean it up! Zale complains indignantly.

I get a mental eye roll from Nathair. *He's right, but Zale, please calm down. It isn't the first nor the last time you will be covered in someone else's cum.*

We all burst into laughter, even Osis and Conall who are deep in the court. It fills the air, and for a moment, I get a sliver of pure happiness from Nathair that his home is filled with love and joy once more before he shuts it down.

"I'm going to cover his room in a web," Lycus whispers to me.

"Oh, I want to help." Reve pops up, and Azul grins and nods.

As I watch, they all stumble from the bed and then the room so they can prank their brother. Honestly, I'm not even mad. I can't help smiling as I get up and slip on one of Reve's robes, which just so happens to be silk with his initials monogrammed on it—no doubt a present from Nathair—before I go to find the others.

I reach the kitchen, which is the hub for everything, but no one is here, so I pour myself a cup of coffee, slip on some oversized shoes, and then head outside where I have not explored much yet.

Beautiful flowers reach up towards the sky, and I spot roses, lilies, dahlias, irises, and so many more spread around the area. There's a fountain in the middle with a pentagon courtyard. It's stunning beneath the stars. To the right is a telescope positioned in a seating area with a fire pit and chairs surrounding it.

Wandering into a flower and wild plant garden, I find a huge oak tree with a swing hanging from it, and I can't resist. I kick off my shoes, feeling the grass and flowers under my feet as I wander over and sit, my coffee in hand as I start to swing. It's on a slight hill, and the rest of the court's land is spread before us.

I see a tennis court, a pool, and some outbuildings, and beyond those are woods. Beautiful trees stretch up into the midnight sky. Some people fear the dark, but I've always loved the stillness between dusk and dawn and all the endless possibilities. Maybe it's a vampyr thing, but I can't deny there is so much beauty in the dark.

There's just something about it, and I let my eyes close as I swing gently, embracing that feeling.

A soft sound has my eyes opening, and I grin as Osis pads towards me in tiger form, his paws carefully avoiding the flowers so he doesn't crush them. I forgot how huge he is. His head butts into my knees, making me grin even as he almost knocks me off. He's bigger than I, and his paws, which are larger than my head, end in sharp black claws. His fur is a pearly white with black stripes, and his bright eyes shine brighter than the stars above. When he nudges me with his wet pink nose, I giggle, causing his ears to fold back.

"Hey, beautiful," I murmur as I stroke his head, and for a moment, my gaze drifts around. "It's amazing out here, isn't it?"

He chuffs, and I take that as a yes as he curls up around my feet with his head on my lap. I pet him as I sip my coffee and take in the night with him at my side, protecting me. Once my coffee is gone, he pulls his head back and wanders behind the tree. I crane my neck when Osis appears on the other side, smiling softly at me. His hair is half held back, with pieces framing his stunning face. His bright eyes soften with emotion as he watches me. He's wearing a black coat with a white fur trim that reminds me of his tiger, and some leather trousers and boots.

He comes and sits next to me on the swing, pushing us gently. "I wasn't sure if you wanted to be left alone," he murmurs.

"Never," I reply, taking his hand and leaning my head on his shoulder as we swing gently.

I remember when Nathair warned me to be careful with Osis, mainly because he's so sweet and kind and wears his heart on his sleeve, but in this very moment, I am the one who's in danger—in danger of falling completely and head over heels in love with him so completely that I won't be able to be parted from him.

He just has a quiet strength and sweetness I didn't even know I was craving until he came into my life.

"Reve told you about his past, didn't he?" he asks suddenly, and I lift my head, trying to follow his thoughts.

"Yes?" I ask, frowning at his profile, and he nods before blowing out a breath.

"I never told you mine," he begins, and I reach up and turn his face so he's looking at me.

"You don't have to if you don't want to," I tell him softly and truthfully. I want to know everything about the men I'm falling in love with, but not at the expense of their own well-being. I do not want to reopen old wounds.

"How can you love me if you do not know me?" he whispers, searching my gaze. "I love you, Althea. I'm not afraid to say it. I love you, and I'm so grateful you became a judge and that we have this bond, but I want you to love me the same, and maybe, one day, you will, but you have to know who I am. You deserve to. We saw your pain and your past, so you should know ours the same way."

"Osis—"

He leans in and kisses me, silencing me. "I'm not as good with words as Nathair, nor as good with visions as Reve, but if you will allow me, I can show you my truth. I can show you what led me here."

I search his gaze and see his hope there, so I nod. Taking my hand once more, he cuts along both of our wrists with a sharpened nail before pressing them together—a blood exchange.

I close my eyes, and he does the same, our foreheads pressing together as we both delve into the bond. This time, though, I follow him through the open door in his mind, watching as he presents me with a flipbook of memories. With his hand still in mine, I dive in.

He's younger in the vision, and I cannot tell when it takes place, but he's barely past eleven or twelve and holding the hand of a beautiful woman who looks exactly like him.

My mother, he explains.

You look like her.

They have the same icy white hair and bright eyes. She's stunning, and as she smiles softly down at him, I can sense her love. *I grew up in a court like everyone else,* he tells me, flipping through the memories quickly and showing me moments of him growing up in a bright, loving court. *But my mother always said I was too trusting, too naïve. I thought it was a good thing, but I never played the catty games or spoke with a silver tongue like other members of court, and one day, just like she said it would, it ruined me.*

The flipping stops on the vision of another beautiful woman. This one has brown ringlet hair that hangs to her shoulders, bright amber eyes, and dainty fangs. She's in a blue corset dress and smiling at an older version of Osis. A teenager maybe?

Angelica, he says, *was my first love, or so I thought. I'd always known her. She was the most beautiful woman at court and so popular, I thought I never stood a chance, but one day, we actually ran into each other physically, and I helped her escape a creep at a ball. We absconded into the night, and the rest is history.*

He avoids showing me anything that might hurt me, my sweet Osis, and instead shares moments of them together, holding hands, going on dates, and exploring the world together.

We were together for just over a year, and I was madly in love. My mother never approved, she didn't trust her, but I was so deeply in love with Angelica, she could do no wrong in my eyes.

We fade back to the swing, and I see tears in his eyes.

"But that was before I knew the truth. You see, Angelica never loved me, and it was all a game. The creep was her partner, and what I thought was fate was just her scheme. She wanted me to love her, wanted me to be infatuated with her so I would do anything she wished. My mother was a powerful vampyr, and the king of our court had his eye on her. He loved her. He'd lost his mate a few years before, as had my mother, and they had grown close, but Angelica's mother was jealous. She wanted the king's attentions, and Angelica wanted the power and status that would come from being bonded to a king if her mother were to take the queen's place, so they hatched the plan together. The male was her true mate, and I ended up divulging secrets. Posing as the king, my mother's love, Angelica and her mother sent a message to my mother and lured her outside. They killed her, Althea."

Tears fill my eyes as I'm plunged back into memories.

I watch as Osis runs across frozen grass to a crumpled body in a long white gown coated in blood. He screams as he drops to his knees next to her, turning her over to see his mother's frozen face, her lips parted and blue from the cold.

"No!" he screams, his hands scrambling across her, but there is so much blood, and she has long since passed.

He's bowed over her, sobbing, when the king finds him. I see a tall, powerful man with a crown drop to his knees and shout in agony.

He loved her so much. They had been best friends since they were kids, and she was gone. He thought I did it. It looked that way, and I didn't even fight as they led me to the dungeons. I was shocked and in so much pain. They were going to kill me, and I thought it was best because of all the pain I was in, but then Angelica appeared in my cell to taunt me, to explain her plan and boast about how I had fallen right into her trap.

"I loved her, Althea," he continues out loud. "I thought she was there to save me until she ripped out my broken heart and shattered it to dust. My own naivety had gotten my mother killed, and something inside me broke. I remember descending into my own grief, my own madness, and one night, when the moon turned blood red, I changed into my tiger for the first time and broke out of the cell."

His eyes drip with tears.

"I'm ashamed, but I let the tiger take over and shield me. Fuelled by my anger and pain, he—we hunted them down. I ripped the woman I was in love with apart, along with her mother and mate. I bathed in their blood and screams for my mother's death. When I changed back, I was still covered in their blood, and I simply went to my mother's grave and waited. I wanted to die, wanted them to find me. I knew I had to pay for my crimes. Only,neither the king nor my people ever found me. Instead, Conall, Lycus, and Nathair did. They carried me back here, and under another blood-red moon, I died. I thought I could join my mother and beg for forgiveness, but the god told me she had already passed over. He offered me a choice to come back and stop what happened to me from happening to others to protect my mother's legacy. All I ever wanted was for my mother to be proud of me, so I agreed, and I came back."

"Do you regret it?" I ask.

"Coming back or killing them?" he murmurs, blinking as if emerging from his own grief again.

"Both."

"No to both. I killed them, Althea, and I can't take that back. No matter what they did, I took their lives away, but it also made me who I am today and brought me to you—a woman I truly love, one who deserves my heart completely."

"I don't know—"

"You do." He covers my lips. "I know you worry I'll fall too easily—my mother did too—but I vowed never to love anyone again, and then you came. With one smile, one look, and you stole my heart. I saw your past, your soul, Althea, and it was so beautiful, so pure and deserving. How could I not love you?"

"I don't ever want to hurt you like they did," I murmur as I stare into the face of one of the purest people I have ever met. "How could you still believe in love?"

"Just because one person used it against me doesn't mean it's not real, and it doesn't mean I shouldn't love anyone else. If we stopped believing just because of the people who hurt us, then the world would be a very dark place. I believe in hope and happiness, and I choose it every day. So, Althea, I love you. You have my heart, and I'm hoping and believing you will never shatter it like they did."

"Never," I vow as I stare into those eyes. "You have mine too, you know. That's the difference between her and me. She never deserved you, Osis, and I don't think anyone ever will, but I'll try." I kiss him. "Thank you for telling me your story."

Smiling against my lips, he brushes my tears away, and my breath catches as the moon bathes him like a lover. "Of course. Now how about I feed you?"

He gets up and takes my hand, leading me back inside. He wears a wide grin on his face that wasn't there before, and I look up at the moon and thank whoever is listening that they saved this man for me.

Forty

Althea

I'm lying across Osis's chest, with Conall holding my other hand as he reads a book. Nathair is opposite us with a huge tome, though his eyes keep darting to me every so often, and they soften as they trace my features. I feel Nathair's joy over Osis's happiness.

We are relaxing and enjoying our downtime when a bell chimes. It's loud and dramatic, making me sit up. Nathair frowns and shuts his book with an audible slam, and then he exchanges worried looks with the others.

"Stay with her," he demands and disappears in the blink of an eye.

The others hurry forward to surround me.

"What is it?" I demand.

"An outsider," Zale murmurs, sitting at my feet. "The bell chimes if something that isn't supposed to be here enters, like a warning system."

"We need to help—" I start, but then Nathair appears.

"Not a person, a letter." He holds up an ornate, golden envelope with unreadable black script on the front. When he flips it around, there is a bright red seal with a crown and a sabre.

Oh shit, even I recognise that.

We learned about it as kids.

It's a letter from a union, a meeting of the courts.

Sitting, Nathair carefully opens it with a nail and unfolds the thick, pure-white parchment, clears his throat, and starts to read it to us. The room seems to drop in temperature as we all wait with bated breath, a bad feeling flowing through our bonds.

TO THOSE WHO RECEIVE THIS LETTER, BE AWARE THAT YOUR PRESENCE HAS BEEN ACKNOWLEDGED. THE COURTS DEMAND A VIEWING, AS A COURT. EVEN WITHOUT CLAIMING THE TITLE OF ONE, YOU MUST UPHOLD THE LAW. WE EXPECT AN INVITATION BY THE BLOOD MOON OR ACTION WILL BE TAKEN.

THOSE WHO RULE AWAIT YOU.

"They didn't mention the killings," I murmur.

"They can't prove it was us, and to accuse without proof is death for them. No, they are playing games and trying to walk us into a trap so they can learn our secrets and wiggle into our masses."

"We cannot allow them in." I might be young, but even I know what the other courts are capable of. "What about our duty? What about remaining anonymous?"

"It seems that is out of the question," he responds.

The others nod their agreement, and my eyes narrow. "You don't seem upset."

"We knew this day would come eventually," Zale remarks. "We could only hide in the shadows for so long. Although we never wanted to join court life, it might be beneficial for us now, since they are our prey."

"He's right," Reve agrees, "and I do love a good party."

"We will be weak against an attack. There aren't enough of us," Azul mutters.

"Doesn't the law state that to be classed as a court, you must possess fourteen or more members? If not, won't they simply absorb our power and claim our court as a family unit?" Lycus muses.

"Correct," Nathair murmurs.

"So what do we do?" Osis asks, and we all look to Nathair for answers, but it is Conall who speaks.

"We call for more, of course." He shrugs.

"We cannot accept more into our midst," Nathair begins as he works through the logic when I clear my throat.

"The law, if I'm not wrong, states that to be a court, you must have fourteen or more creatures of the night, correct? It does not state what type of creature."

The grin he gives me is slow and filled with hunger. "You brilliant, clever girl," he purrs.

"Wait, what?" Osis asks, confused.

"We don't have to call other people, just other creatures of the night. After all, we are the Court of Nightmares, so we will give them that." I know my smirk is downright diabolical, but the idea of getting one over on the courts and seeing their faces as they walk into a gothic nightmare? Priceless.

Not to mention my rejected mate will be there.

"It's brilliant," Reve says as he leans over and makes gooey eyes at me.

"He's right. It is. You are incredible," Conall growls, making me shiver.

"Focus." I flash fang at them enticingly. "What do we do first though?" I query.

Nathair looks around before straightening, determination flashing over his face. "We throw a party and send them an invitation. If they want to see, then let them. We will play their game." Standing, Nathair moves to a desk in the far corner and sits heavily, stroking his fingers over the wood. "My mother carved this for me for the day when I would take the throne. I have never used it as a king, so I guess now is as good a time as any." He opens a drawer and takes out some matte black paper. Placing it carefully on the desk, he picks up a quill and infuses it with his power.

Some use blood, but that can always be tricky since it can be used against you in spells, so spelled ink is always best. Moving closer, I lean into his shoulder and watch as he begins to write, the ink coming out a metallic gold with a shimmer of red.

DEAREST SANGUI,

YOU ARE CORDIALLY INVITED TO ATTEND THE FIRST BALL OF THE YEAR AT COURT OF NIGHTMARES.

A COURT ONCE HELD IN GREAT ESTEEM, KNOWN FOR ITS GRANDEUR AND POWER. ALL MONSTERS, MURDERERS, AND VAMPYRS ALIKE ARE WELCOME AND ENCOURAGED TO DRESS TO KILL.

HELD THE NIGHT OF THE BLOOD MOON, JOIN US FROM SUNDOWN TO SUNUP FOR A NIGHT YOU WILL NEVER FORGET.

THE COURT OF NIGHTMARES

The others gather closer, peering at the message. "Well, what do you think?"

"Very nicely done, my king," I purr as I lean down and kiss his cheek. "And now, we have ten days to plan a ball."

"Then I guess it's time to split the tasks. We want to make an impression after all. I'm thinking of terrifying seduction. How about everyone else?" he asks, and laughter is his answer. "Then let's show them why they shouldn't mess with the Court of Nightmares."

"Are you sure?" Zale asks.

Zale and Lycus stand behind me, and the others are busy working on their assigned tasks to not only get the court ready, but also us for our audience. My role is to recruit the nightmares I mentioned. I was so sure about my idea, but now I don't know. What if they attack us? What if they turn on us?

After all, the monsters that roam this world and call the night their home are just that—animals and beasts.

They cannot be tamed, but we can create a bond with them, which is similar to that of a mate bond if they so wish. It, of course, involves the same thing everything in our world does—blood. I've never heard of anyone doing it and surviving before. When I was a child, someone tried to call a dragon and was burnt to a crisp for his trouble.

They prefer to be left alone, and they are not pets, but they are all often searching for a home with nowhere to fit in in this rapidly expanding world. That is what we are going to offer them—a home, a sanctuary, and protection. The land here is great, greater than I even knew after Nathair showed me the maps. There is a whole city's worth of land they can inhabit and make their own, and in return, they will help us keep our court.

"You do not have to," Lycus adds.

"No, I do. My mother and the god once said that the creatures of the dark are mine if I am brave enough to call them, so it's time I do that. Trust me." I drop both of their hands and step barefoot and naked onto the grass before the woods. My hair is loose, and the wind blows the strands across my back. Upon my head, I wear a crown Nathair gave to me.

I go to the beasts as a queen, naked as the day I was born, with nothing to offer but my title, my protection, and my blood. There will be no lies between us, just me in the moonlight as I call out into the darkness.

Picking up the ornamental sacrificial dagger that Lycus procured from the court's stash of spelled weapons, I start to speak. My voice is sure and steady as I say the words in our ancient language, almost seeing them float into the air and stretch out into the world.

It's a call, one that must be followed by a sacrifice.

"*Vejok reteh, olhah magicaiil, a furthol mehin.*" Roughly translated, I am asking for the nightmares to come forth and find their home. I continue to chant as I focus on their meaning, infusing them with power and intent, and with a gasp, they explode from me.

My eyes close and my head snaps back as my blood drips steadily to the grass and soaks into the ground and out. Spreading through the night, I follow the journey like a million different pieces. Pain racks my body from the force of it, and my power feeds the blood, making it stronger as I continue to chant.

As I touch on those beasts lingering in the dark, they lift their heads and gnash their teeth, feeling distrust and anger at being called by another. I try to send soothing thoughts and show them the truth, but I don't know if it works as I fly back into my body and stumble forward. My hands catch on the grass to stop myself from falling face-first to the ground. My power snaps back to me, making me groan.

The wounds on my inner arms aren't healing, thanks to the blade—they will only heal when the spell is complete.

I wait there, my sliced wrists dripping blood into the soil and grass. My mates stand behind me, and our court, our sanctuary, is lit up like a beacon as I wait for the beasts to answer our call. I pray to the gods that they won't kill me.

Nox, I hope I'm strong enough to save us.

My hope starts to dwindle as I think that they will ignore my call like so many others, when the trees begin to move before us. I call out to whatever moves within the forest, my voice soft and strong.

"We will not harm you. We present no danger to you." I bow my head in deference because these creatures have been alive long before any of us and will be alive long after us. They are ancient beings deserving of respect.

I hear someone gasp behind me, so I lift my head and look up through my lashes, a wondrous smile curling my lips when I spy the creature that steps free.

"You are beautiful," I tell them, and they are.

They are an utterly stunning, beautiful nightmare.

It is a hydra, a creature that has not been seen for millennia since it ate a few gods and was deemed evil. Those gods were trying to kill it, so it was self-defence.

Four heads, similar to a dragon's, wind around each other as its eyes blink at me—black, red, purple, and blue—stolen from the gods it killed. Its body is similar to a dragon's as well, covered in iridescent blue scales with spikes along its back and tail, which is long and thick, thicker than any of the trees behind it. Its six legs are coated in the same scales and end in three toes with long, black claws ready to slice its victims to pieces if it does not set them on fire or eat them first. It is one of the most feared monsters in history, and also the most elusive. So why is it here? Why is it close?

You, the growled voice says in my mind. *I felt your power the moment you came into this life. I felt your call even then, and I was curious. It awoke me like no other has.*

Then I'm truly lucky, I reply.

It rises higher to show its power.

I know the creature before me can enlarge to its full glory, which is bigger than any city or monster, with over nine heads, but it appears before me now in a smaller, no less threatening form, which gives me hope that it wants what I am offering.

It wants a place to belong.

What do you want, life stealer?

Life—oh, vampyr, got it. This time, I speak aloud so the others can hear me. "We wish to offer you a deal without chains, like so many before us. We also do not wish to kill you."

"That would be foolish," it says out loud, chuckling as smoke blows from one nose.

"It would," I agree with a smile. "To maintain our safety, our family, and love, we must become a true court, and to do that, our law states that we must be over a certain number. We trust none of our kind and want nothing to do with them, considering we have our own duties, after all. I have always been at one with the night and a god" —it hisses then, and I wince— "and my mother, a seer, told me I was one with the nightmares. She was right. I may never grow as large or as powerful as you, but my soul is like yours. So, I offer you a deal, hydra, one of sanctuary and peace, and in return, you can leave whenever you wish after the blood moon if you desire to, but you must be here for the viewing so we may keep our home. You will always have sanctuary here, a place we will protect for you."

It watches me, its heads twisting and untwisting as I wait. "Why? Why choose us monsters?" it demands.

"Because I am one," I answer truthfully. "Because I feel more at home with monsters than people."

"If this is a trick, blood drinker, I will use your bones for toothpicks."

"It is not." I lift my hand. "See the truth. All I offer is trust, peace, and a home."

I wait with bated breath, and it keeps its eyes on me before sliding closer and towering above me like the force it is. I hold my arm out, and one head bows over it. Softly, a rough tongue bigger than my whole body dips to taste my blood. I wait, knowing if I'm found lacking, this hydra will kill us all for treachery.

Its eyes narrow, and my heart stutters before it steps back and bows, shocking me to my core. This is a creature that has never bowed to another, even a god, and yet it bows to me.

"You are worthy. I see the truth in your heart, vampyr. Your soul is purer than I have ever felt, even with the blackness of a monster. I accept your deal, for I grow tired of this world, and I will find a home here for a time." With that, it turns and slips back into the trees. Now, with my blood in it, I can almost feel the hydra moving across the land with great speed before it finds a small lake with a private, shaded beach and slides into the water there, accepting our land and us.

I turn to my mates behind me, seeing their expressions of shock and relief, but then I feel the ground shake beneath me and know another approaches. It seems as if my blood, my power, is stronger than I realised, and I am calling all the greats from their slumber.

Let us hope I can survive it.

When the ground stops trembling, I glance at the woods as a delicate figure drops to the ground before me. I instantly freeze as some fear trickles into my veins when she pushes her hood back. Although this one almost looks human, she is anything but. She is a banshee or a hell screecher, as they call her in our lore. Born from the agonised souls of betrayed women throughout history, she has more raw power than even the fey, and nature does her bidding. They are known to be reckless, angry, and downright crazy sometimes. This one watches me carefully. Her big black eyes are locked on me, and she's beautiful bar the twisted sneer and sharp teeth she reveals. Her blonde hair blows in the wind, and her presence sings with power.

"You called, young one?" Her voice is beautiful, melodic, but I know all too well how easily that could change, so I choose my words carefully. Unlike the hydra who would kill me for lies, this one would kill me for fun. She seeks chaos and violence. I can taste it.

"We are seeking nightmares to join our court. In return, they will have sanctuary and a home here—no chains or restrictions," I offer slowly.

"You wish to bind me?" she screeches, and my eardrums pop and bleed.

I cannot hear until my rapid healing kicks in, and even though I can't see, since my eyes burst and bleed, I call out, "Never, we wish to bind no one. Simply an exchange."

"I will never share power. Do not call me again or it will be your death. Consider yourself lucky that I feel your purpose."

I feel her depart as my eyes slowly heal, and I blink, chasing the pain away as my shoulders slump.

"You will not win them all over. Beasts are meant to wander. This one was probably just too interested to pass up your call. A banshee would never fit here. They are meant to wander alone," Zale explains, and I nod, knowing he's right, but I hope more come and if they do, they will stay, because our lives depend on it.

As if drawn by my silent plea, more creatures slide from the woods.

I see a wendigo, with long, clawed arms and sharp teeth, but he has a stutter when he calls out. There is also a shapeshifter, who turns into a replica of me, which is freaky. A puk, which resembles a small man carrying a bow and arrow but with wicked fangs and the inclination for trouble, also steps forward. A mermaid emerges from the trees, his hair beautiful and alluring, although his skin is blue and his eyes are blood red. A pixie, who is a water spirit smaller than the palm of my hand but equally as bloodthirsty as us, is also with them. A chimera hides at the back, as if it's unsure.

All are creatures of nightmares, and all are equally as beautiful and dangerous.

I offer them the same as I have the others, and I let them choose.

Lifting my arms, I wait for them to decide with my expression soft and truthful, and they descend upon me like a pack, licking and tasting my blood. If I were lying, they would sense it and kill me in a heartbeat.

Slowly, they slip away to find their homes. They will come and go as they please, but it suits our purpose, and I will just be more careful about where I walk outside.

I almost feel Nathair's happiness that his once forgotten lands are filled with life once more, even if those lives thrive on death and blood like us.

I'm about to stand, thinking that is all, when an honest to Nox unicorn trots from the woods. Unicorns are not beautiful and sweet, like fairy tales describe them. No, their true form is a skeletal horse with a horn, fangs, and dancing eyes. Oh yes, they can appear beautiful, and even in this form, there is a certain macabre loveliness to them, but they will kill as quickly as they will change.

I call to it, and like the others, it drinks and disappears into the forest, its laughter trailing after it.

"Quite the menagerie we are making." Lycus grins, making me chuckle.

My blood still drips, however, which tells me there is more to come, so I wait, even as the moon moves across the sky. I will wait forever if I must.

A troll appears some hours later, but it leaves at the mention of the others. The solitary bastards hate other monsters, so I don't take it personally, even if I was jealous of his ridiculously long lashes. I continue to wait as my blood spills. Zale urges me to feed, but I know I cannot, not until this is done.

A cyclops appears and quickly accepts my offer. I sense her loneliness as she lumbers back into the woods to find her own place.

I still sense more, however, and I know there is something else we are waiting for, something watching from afar to see how I accept these deals, and only when it's satisfied does it appear.

A dragon, a true dragon, lands in a cloud of smoke before me.

It's stunning and deadly, with a spiked body covered in glimmering purple and black scales. Its eyes are a mixture of the two, and smoke rolls from its mouth and nose. It watches me carefully, its frame easily half the size of the hydra's true form.

"You do not have to repeat your offer, for I heard what you are proposing."

Dragons are known as hoarders who live and survive alone. There used to be many of them in the sky, or so the history says, but now they are almost dead thanks to their nature. Seeing one in the flesh is shocking, but not as much as its next words.

"I will tie myself to you and this land. I only ask for one thing."

"Ask it," I murmur.

"After, when I'm ready, you will call another for me."

I blink, and it huffs.

"Another of my kind. My love is beyond the grave, and I know you can reach her. If you will do this for me, then I will be yours. I will do anything you wish."

The agony in his words pierces my heart. "I don't know if I can," I admit honestly, not wanting to lie to him.

"You can. I can sense it. I only ask that you try," he replies.

"Then I will. I give you my solemn blood oath." Relief flows over him as he bows and tastes my blood, and when he straightens, he doesn't leave like the others. Instead, he waits.

"I have been waiting so long for someone like you to come along," he says.

"Like me?"

"The champion of the dark, of us nightmares who have been deemed too ugly and frightening to love. The god who spoke to me so many years ago was right. They said a warrior of the dark was coming, and she would be amazing." After this, he leaves me staring after him.

I am drained but elated.

I get to my feet and stumble.

Lycus and Zale help me up, holding both arms. My head is woozy, and I'm weak from blood loss and the power I exerted.

"Here."

They both thrust their bleeding wrists at me, and I drink quickly, sensing the spell is finished . . . for now at least.

I cannot call any more, since my power is drained, but I can always do it again.

Either way, we have more than enough to be classified as a court.

Now, it's time for them to settle in, and I hope we'll endure long enough to survive the next battle.

FORTY ONE

LYCUS

I CHECK ON ALTHEA to see her curled around Zale, both sleeping happily, and then I head back to Nathair for my next assignment. The man is walking around with a clipboard, ticking things off his list. I guess he hasn't thrown a ball in a very long time so it has to be perfect, but the sight of him wearing silk monogrammed pyjamas with his hair tied back in a bun and a serious scowl on his face as he glares down at the clipboard is just adorable.

If the other courts could see us now.

"I can hear you," he calls without looking up.

"I wasn't hiding," I reply as I push off from the wall.

"Why does it take so long for the fey to get back to you?" he mutters, scribbling something furiously on the list.

"So, I'm guessing planning is going well?" I grin, and he throws me a glare as I chuckle.

"I hate balls, but this needs to be perfect. Half the battle is expectation and aesthetic. If we make them see our show of force and power, they will believe it."

He sighs, dropping the clipboard to his side as he rubs his head.

"How is she?" he asks, even though he's gone to check on her every five minutes himself.

"She's fine, just resting. The spell took a lot out of her, but you should have seen her." I know my eyes become dreamy as I remember the sight of my mate on her knees with a crown on her head. She was so perfect and powerful, even as she kneeled. The nightmares came to her, but how could they not? Even I felt the call deep within, my spider wanting to respond and beg for her to take him. They must have felt the same way.

She's so powerful. Any other would have died from the power of that spell or the blood loss, but not her. Not our Althea.

Not our queen.

"I did." He grins. "It was hard not to watch. She's incredible, isn't she?"

"I think her power even rivals that of the gods," I comment without shame. "In my time, we would have worshipped her as one." Shaking my head, I can't help my toothy grin. "I would have gladly made sacrifices in her name and followed her anywhere. I still will."

"We all would." He grins, but then his smile fades. "Lycus, I've been meaning to talk to you about something." His voice is almost hesitant. "I guess I didn't realise until she came how . . . how starved you were because the others' fear stopped you from feeding. You have to know you are family, our brother, and we would die for you."

I shudder but force myself to respond. "I know you would willingly die for me, but that's not the same as being willing to feed me." That's the brutal truth, even if it hurts them. It's something I've had to live with, and I didn't realise how much it hurt until she came along.

"You're right. We should have done better. I guess fear is still a hard thing to overcome, even for us. We will do better." He moves closer, laying his hand on my shoulder. "We will, brother, and we all owe you an apology. We should have been there for you no matter what. I'm glad you had Zale and now have her, but know this—you are always welcome on my vein, brother. Even if you wish to kill me for it, I promise you here and now. I swear on my blood." The importance of the promise shakes me to my very soul. Nathair is proving his love for me. "As your leader, I will ensure it never happens again."

Nathair has always taken too much on himself, and he's so quick to blame himself for everything. Azul was hurt once in a judgment, and he locked himself away for weeks. He might have been appointed first, and we might follow him, but he has to know this isn't all on him.

"We do not follow you because you are perfect, Nathair. We follow you because you are strong and smart, and we trust you to not lead us wrong, but we all make mistakes. I'm okay. It happens. You do not have to be strong all the time." He blinks in shock as I cover his hand. "And now that we have her, I think you are starting to realise that. She's good for you. She's good for all of us."

"I know," he admits, his eyes filling with nothing but love. "This ball will be hard for her."

"It will."

We share a look, both thinking the same thing, when Reve chimes in as he wanders into the room. "Oh, I'm so down for that."

Me too, Azul adds.

Definitely, Osis and Conall say at the same time.

I'm with you, Zale adds, and the grin Nathair and I share is pure evil.

"Good, now back to our jobs." Nathair claps, his clipboard coming up once more. "I want to send word to Simon. It's important that he's here for her, even if he has to be with his court. We have the monsters, but I want someone on the border at all times in case there are any issues or any more turn up. Reve and Osis are on decorations, and Azul is sorting security with Conall in case anything goes wrong. I want you and Zale to switch between teams and keep her as well fed as possible. She's going to need to be strong for this."

"Got it, boss." I nod. "Don't forget to feed, okay? It's been a while since you did."

We don't need to as much as Althea, since our powers are settled and not starved like hers, nor are we using them as much, but we must keep strong for her and our duties. I can't remember the last time Nathair fed properly, and when he blinks, it's clear he cannot either.

"You are right. Can I feed from you?" he asks.

"You don't need to prove yourself, Nath." I sigh, and he frowns.

"I know, but I wish to feed from you, brother. Would you deny me?"

I still know he's doing this to prove a point, but I could never deny my brother, so I hold out my arm, trying my best to contain my powers and stop the venom from pumping through my veins. He's fed before, they all have to get used to the venom, so it shouldn't hurt him anymore, but still I brace for rejection.

Carefully, like he expects me to turn away, he takes my arm and lays a gentle kiss over my pulse. There is nothing sexual about it, it's a gesture of comfort, and then he slowly slides his fangs into my vein, carefully and softly, as if I'm breakable.

I shudder at the feeling. You never get used to it, and my cock hardens as he begins to feed. He keeps his eyes on me the entire time, showing me there is no fear there, only satisfaction and hunger, and when he pulls away, he licks the wounds clean and wipes his mouth before squeezing my hand. "Thank you, brother."

"Always." I mean it. I would do anything for my family.

It's the way I've always been, and it's what got me here, after all.

Lycus, she purrs in my head, and Nathair and I share a grin.

"Go, she needs you."

I nod and turn to hurry to her side.

"Oh, and Ly?"

I still, and I feel a wave of love and comfort wash over me. "We are lucky to have you, all of us. We might have forgotten it for a moment, but we truly are. We couldn't do this without you, warrior."

I swallow back the lump in my throat, tears forming in my eyes.

Warriors do not cry, after all, or so I was beaten to believe.

I incline my head sharply and follow the call of my love, sliding into bed next to her. Zale is gone, and she turns into my embrace, wrapping her body around me tightly like she feels how close I am to shattering. This wasn't for her. This was for me, I realise, and that's what makes the first tear fall as I pull her close so not an inch is between us. Her heat and gentleness calm the banging war drums inside my heart, softening my hard edges like flames over the swell of a sword.

"He fed—" I begin, not realising I'm trembling slightly.

"I know." She lifts her head and places a gentle kiss on my lips. "I know, my love. I feel it." Her hand covers my heart. "You do not have to tell me."

Shutting my eyes, I tug her even closer, burying my head in her hair and inhaling her scent until I feel more put together again. It's as if a wound is healing, one I did not even know was there, but she did.

She came into our lives, determined to heal and love us.

She was always supposed to be ours, and I will never let her go.

She's trapped in my webs now, and both me and my spider will protect her until our dying breath, but Osis was right in what he said. She should know all of us. We should lay ourselves bare to her. After all, we know her story, her crimes, and her past. She only knows what we tell her, but she deserves everything. I wish I could give her beauty, but what I can offer her is the edge of my blade until the very end.

My warrior's heart and my kingdom.

Without a word, I lift my head, slice into my wrist, and press it to her mouth. Her eyebrows rise in question, but she greedily licks away the blood, and through the connection, I drag her back to my past so she can know who she holds, loves so sweetly, and claims as her own.

I might never be the sophisticated king like her ex-mate, or a noble like Nathair, but I hope she chooses me anyway because I choose her.

I am not as good at this as the others, and the edges of my memories are sharp as if to inflict pain, but I show her everything. I show her why I was judged. I show her the truth of my heritage, my greatest sins, and my greatest humiliations and hope she still loves me.

I was a great warrior once, riding into battles on horseback. I won many battles and many wars, and I show her snippets of some, of coming home soaked in blood but always victorious for my king who was a friend.

She needs to understand how I was born and raised into battle. My mother was a battle-forged warrior who led our court, and during battle with the werewolves, I was born into blood and death. It was all I knew. Our fires bloomed bright and around them, we told stories of our victories.

I was so happy and sure on my path, until that all changed one night.

My boots are silenced by the mud sliding under my feet, my leather armour slick with it along with the blood from today's win. We captured and freed another village from the roaming ferals. The fires of our warriors light up the night sky at the perimeter, and our tents are set up for the night so we can rest, bathe, and eat before we start our ride to the next village to win yet another battle. We will not return to our king for over twelve moons, until we have freed the villages in our sector. We will return victorious. We always do.

"Captain," a warrior greets as he passes, thumping his chest. I repeat the action, which is a sign of respect.

The village is quiet now, the inhabitants safe and sound thanks to us. Their small huts and homes are built close together in a circle with the well and bonfire in the middle. I'm usually exhausted after a battle and planning the next one. My brother, Arthur, says I work too hard, but I want to prove myself to my king. He gave me this chance to lead after all. I cannot let him or my family down—even if it's just my brother now. He's here, and tonight, I find myself wanting to drink and reminisce rather than plan.

I just have to find him first. Usually, he gathers with the others at the fires, protecting the perimeter in case any others attack or sneak up on us, but tonight he wasn't there, so I am searching the village. I'm just about to give up when I hear a scream.

It cuts through the night, filled with agony and terror.

Yanking my blade free with a clank, I sprint towards the sound. Those fucking ferals must have snuck past our defences. I will have their heads for letting them through. I just hope the villagers are okay.

The scream continues, and I spin in a circle until I locate the house it comes from. Storming up the wooden steps, I kick in the wooden front door, ready to attack the ferals, only to freeze.

Horror, confusion, and pain flash through me.

"Brother," he calls, his face almost a replica of mine, just younger. He scrambles up, his battle trousers undone. A young girl lies facedown against the wood with a split lip and a black eye, and tears stream down her face as she watches me, but there isn't hope in those young eyes. There is nothing but resignation, an age-old knowledge of the women who have come before her.

She thinks I will rape her too.

Like my brother just was.

Turning my head, I purge my stomach of its contents.

"Brother," he calls again. "You can have her next if you want. I didn't know you were usually into the rewards, but feel free. She's the youngest and most attractive, my reward for so many kills—"

I slam him back to the wall, growling in his face, and he frowns, his expression clouding even as he struggles, but he should know better. After all, I raised him. I taught him everything he knows, so he cannot best me.

Warriors have integrity.

"Why?" I demand.

His features become stiff as he watches me. "It's our reward. We protected these peasants and saved them from certain death. It is the way."

"It is not our way!" I roar, slamming him back into the wall. "We do not take what is not ours."

"No? We take lands that are not ours. We also take their food and shelter," he argues. "What is one more thing? We deserve it. We live and die to protect them. They owe us this."

Sickness turns my stomach again as I stare into my brother's eyes, seeing nothing but his utter belief—belief that he is in the right and that I will side with him. That everyone else will too. What happened to the little boy who used to chase me around with the wooden practice sword, laughing as we danced? What happened to the little boy who used to clean the wounds of the little girl next door when she fell?

Is he truly gone?

When I search his face, I realise he is, and I never saw it happening.

I drop him as I step back. "How many?"

Standing, he rolls his shoulders back and smirks at me cockily. "Who knows? Every battle."

Oh god. My soul shrivels from knowing that he had raped and pillaged after every battle we had won, while I hid in my tent, so intent on our future victories that I was blinded by my own greed and need. We vowed to protect these people . . .

Instead, we have been destroying them. I'm almost sick again at the memory of me riding out of their villages after battle with my head held high and mighty. They had watched us with mistrust and pain, and I thought it was from their losses, but no. It's because of what was done to their people by the very warriors meant to save them.

"We took an oath," I croak. "How dare you?"

"Everyone does it, brother," he snaps. "Stop being so fucking good and just take what you want. It is our right as warriors!" he yells.

"No, it's not true." I stumble back, my eyes going to the young girl holding her ripped brown sack dress together. Her eyes are darting between us and the blood pooled under her and across her legs. The sight sears me to my very soul.

He stole her innocence, and with it, he sold his soul and lost his own.

Gripping my sword tighter, I look back at him. His hands are spread wide as he watches me, yet he doesn't seem scared, as if he knows I will always protect him like I have before. "Brother, go back to your tent and hide away like you always do. Let us true warriors rejoice and collect our rewards. Our king does not care."

"No, he cannot know," I snap. He cannot. I trust him, love him like a brother.

"Of course he knows." He laughs. "Are you really so naïve, brother? How do you think he controls so many warriors? He doesn't care what we do as long as we win. He's even partaken in the spoils before."

"No," I snap. "No, not my warriors, not my king."

My world falls apart around me. All the good I thought we were doing . . . all the battles I have almost died in to protect those at my side, my king, and my brother were all for naught.

"You are such a fool!" My brother laughs, and for the first time, I do not see the warrior or the little boy I raised. I see the evil for what it truly is. His fangs are covered in blood, and his eyes are as dark as his soul. "You think the world is all battles and fighting for good, and look where it got you. You are completely alone. Even your own men hide their truth from you. You know nothing. You are a fool, Lycus—"

His words cut off into a gargle as I slice his neck. My heart is saddened but hard as I watch my brother drop to his knees, disbelief and fear flashing in his gaze as he grips his wound.

"Ly—" He chokes on the word, reaching for me in his panic.

Once I would have done everything to save him, but now I step back and watch him choke to death on his own sins. When his eyes lose all signs of life and he falls back, I kneel beside him.

I will not offer him peace, not even in death. Not for his crimes.

The brother I loved died many years ago, and this monster deserves this.

Slicing off his warrior braids, I pocket them and leave his body there to rot, but before I leave the house, I turn back. "I am sorry," I tell her.

"Fuck you! Your apologies mean nothing. Your men came into my village and stole everything! We are ruined," she sobs.

"I will make this right," I promise. "No other will suffer."

I spare my queen the bleak details, showing her snippets of me moving through the camp like a lost soul and killing every warrior—those I fought alongside, those I called family and friends. I take every warrior braid before I leap back onto my horse and turn to our castle.

"Lycus." I feel her sorrow for me, but I am not done, not yet.

I skip the journey that should have taken a week but only took me two moons. My anger and fury guide me as I race through the night and arrive at the castle in the middle of a feast.

I storm in, coated in blood and death, with madness in my eyes.

He sits on his throne while our people yell, drink, and eat as music plays. When they see me, silence descends. The king sits forward. His brown hair features many braids, ones he does not deserve. His golden necklace and crown are stolen, just like the girl's innocence.

"Lycus, my captain, what is wrong? Where are the troops?" he booms, afraid that we lost, and I see his fear that there will be repercussions in his eyes.

"All of them are dead," I snarl.

Throwing the braids at my king's feet, I sneer at him. I don't kneel or offer respect or gifts. I see nothing but a stranger on a throne, one who does not deserve it.

"I killed every single one of them for their crimes—crimes you knew about, that you allowed to happen."

"What?" he exclaims, looking from the warrior braids to me. "Lycus, what have you done!"

"You knew!" I roar. "You knew what they were doing, and you let them. You have stained my soul. You have dishonoured our people."

"We can discuss this. You didn't need to know, my boy. It would have hurt you."

"And now it is too late. They paid for their crimes, and now, so shall you. How dare you sit on a throne and claim to protect the people of your lands, all the while letting them be killed and raped? How dare you call yourself king? You are a

coward! You will die a coward's death!" Without giving it a second thought, I leap at him and swing my sword, cutting off my king's head before my people.

I toss it down with the braids, and then I drop my sword, knowing my duty is done.

I blink my eyes open to see tears dripping down Althea's face as she watches me. "Oh, Lycus," she croaks. "You didn't know. It was not your fault. You made them pay."

"It did not negate the fact that I had allowed it to happen for years. I think part of me always knew, Althea, that what we were doing was wrong, but we didn't care. I found out later that the ferals were trying to protect their loved ones in the village from us. We were the invaders, the evil, and I paid the price for it. My own people tore me apart, had me drawn and quartered, and then I was selected for this. I came back to avenge those who couldn't. How could I rest when so many other souls couldn't because of what I allowed to happen? I had so much death and destruction to atone for."

"And you have," she replies, gripping my face. "You are a good person, Lycus. More than that, you are a better warrior. You were blinded by love and following the orders of a king you believed in, wanting to believe the best of your duty, your people, and your brother. You know better now. That is not who you are anymore, and I am honoured to be in the presence of a man who was willing to kill his own to right the wrongs and stop what was happening. You are a true warrior, Lycus."

With those words, my heart stops aching, and a bone deep pain I have carried for so many years eases.

"I do not deserve you, Althea, but I will earn you. I will fight the rest of my life to be the warrior you believe in. One day, I will deserve you," I promise.

"You already do." She smiles softly. "Now, my warrior, we have a ball to plan for, a battle if you will. Shall we?"

Forty Two

Althea

"My king," I purr, watching Conall swallow as I saunter towards him. The others are all busy with preparations, but I know they are taking turns looking in on me. "You are about to check on those I called. Can I come?"

"Always." He pulls me into his arms, lifting me until I wrap my legs around his waist. "Like I would deny you anything, Althea."

"Anything?" I tease, scraping my fangs along his neck and making him shudder against me. "So I could ask for a palace."

"Yours," he replies hoarsely.

"A stampede of servants."

"All yours." He tugs me closer.

Grinning, I slide my fangs back and forth across his pulse. "A zoo? An island? A country? The world?"

"Everything. I would give you everything. I would lay it all at your feet and hope that it was enough." His hands grip my ass, rubbing me up and down his huge, hard shaft. "The moment I met you, I knew I would give anything to you to see you smile. Those before us have failed you, failed our goddess, but we will not. My queen, every single one of us would die—no, we would live every day just to give you anything you could possibly need or want. You will want for nothing and never lift a finger. We will worship you until the very end."

My heart clenches, and my claws dig into his shoulders to hold this man to me. I am the one who is lucky, and I will spend every day earning the right to be at their side. Don't they see that? "All I want is you."

"I'm yours, heart, mind, and soul. Everything I am is yours. Drain me, use me, fuck me, or rip me apart, just never leave me."

Pulling back, I see the truth in his eyes. He would let me kill him, use him, and torture him, but I never want to hurt them. I wiggle, and he reluctantly drops me. I step back, gripping his hand with a smirk. For a moment, he looks forlorn because I've left his arms, but then I tug him after me. "Are you coming?"

"I will follow you anywhere." He hurries after me.

I feel his breath on my neck as I wind through the court and out into the courtyard. The sun shines down on me, warming my skin, and the sweet smell of the flowers on the wind makes me smile. When I open my eyes, Conall is before me, blocking out the sun.

"Althea," he murmurs.

I walk forward, and he walks backwards, so I manoeuvre him where I want him until his knees hit the wide bench made for star gazing. Placing my hands on his chest, I push him, and he drops back. He doesn't make a noise, just watches me with hungry, hopeful eyes as I straddle him, lifting the skirt of the long burnt-amber dress that gathers under my breasts and flows behind me. I press my bare pussy to his hard cock through his trousers, making him hiss.

For a moment, I slip into his head, seeing me as he does. My hair is unbound and blowing in the wind, vivid with the sun and shining like jewels, and my eyes are bright with hunger and power. I look like the goddess he told me I was, and I feel his devotion, his pure, raw need and love in that vision. I groan and slip back into my own head.

"Please tell me you're going to sit that pretty pussy on my aching dick, or even my tongue. Anything, Althea. Let me touch you, let me see you consumed with pleasure."

Fuck, his dirty words have me circling my hips and grinding against his hard cock until he groans. His head falls back, smacking into the stone, and his eyes close in agonised bliss.

"Please, my queen," he begs, his fangs elongated.

"Nox, I love seeing you beg," I tell him. My clit throbs with how weak and wild I make him. Lifting my hips, I yank his trousers down to his thighs, freeing his huge length. It springs free, red and throbbing, the veins stark with his need. His hips lift as the air touches it, as if even that is too much, so I wrap my hand around his length and stroke him. I watch the emotions play across his face, the pure lust and worship.

I need him so badly.

Lifting myself above him once more, I press him to my entrance and lower onto his length. Inch after inch of his huge cock sinks into me until I'm fully seated, and we both pant, on the verge of coming from that alone.

"Althea." The way he groans my name has me shifting, and we both gasp as he sinks even deeper. I'm so full it borders on painful, and I have to move, so I start to circle my hips. He bites his fist as he watches me with half-lidded eyes, and his fangs drip with his blood. The scent makes me speed up as I ride his cock.

Pleasure spirals through me, and his own desire races through our bond, overwhelming my senses.

His big hands come up, and with a growl, he rips the dress down, spilling my breasts free into the sunlight. Sitting up like a feral animal, he sucks and licks my nipples as I ride him.

I tangle my hands in his hair, holding him to me as I wind and grind, hitting my clit with each twist until I yank his head back.

"Lie back," I order, and he flops back, his lips pink and raw from my kisses and breasts.

I keep my hand on his hammering heart. "I'm going to come on this big dick, over and over, and you can't come until I say so."

"Mine," he snarls, watching me.

Smirking, I lift my dress and flash him. His eyes lock on where his huge cock plunges in and out of me, and he roars, his cock jerking inside me at the sight.

His head smacks into the stone, again and again, as he tries to fight his release. The sight of this huge warrior, my shadowed vampyr, bathed in sunlight and so wild from my touch and pussy that he's hurting himself to follow my orders, kills me and sends me over the edge.

Maybe I was testing him to see how far I could push him, but he will always do as I ask, even if it hurts him.

Leaning down, I sink my fangs into his chest, making him bellow. His cock jerks inside me. "Come for me, my king, and fill me with your need. Let them all see how wild your queen makes you."

That's all it takes, and he roars, lifting his hips so much that I almost fall. His cum splashes inside of me, and I come again, but he's not finished. He rips me off him and turns us so I'm bent over the bench, and then his cock slams back into me.

I scream. I can't help it.

The new angle causes his cock to slide along those nerves inside me. Pleasure slams through me until my eyes cross as he hammers into me. My breasts press against the cold stone, his movements causing my nipples to rub along the surface. His big hands hit my ass cheeks hard, and the pain mixes with pleasure as he snarls and fights my fluttering cunt. Our cum drips from me, making the slide of his huge cock easier.

Gripping the edge of the stone, I drop my head down, but his hand twines in my hair and yanks it up before his fangs sink into my neck. I howl as I come once more, screaming into the sunlight. I feel other eyes on me, watching me be pleasured by their brother. Their fellow king.

His arm comes around, and he presses his wrist to my mouth. I sink my fangs in, feeding as he feeds. Blood races through us like a circle, ramping our pleasure higher until we both come again, the blood and pleasure spiralling until he finally pulls his fangs out, breaking the circle, and we both slump.

I delicately pull my fangs out and lick the wound, feeling his cock twitch inside me.

"My queen," he murmurs, resting his head on my back as he kisses my skin with so much love that it makes my eyes close. "How did I ever get so lucky? I don't know, but I will get on my knees and thank the gods who brought you back to us."

"I only want you on your knees for me," I snarl, and he smiles against my skin.

"Then only you," he murmurs, sliding kisses along my back. "When I can move again without falling over and embarrassing myself, I will take you to check on the monsters."

Giggling, I lie in his arms as we both try to find the strength to move after that earth-shattering fuck. No matter my powers or strength, I'm weak in the aftermath of it.

He sighs, and I feel him shudder. "I forgot what the sunlight felt like."

"You don't come out in it?" I ask, confused.

"I do as often as I can, despite living in shadows. I guess since I lived exclusively in darkness before I was saved, I just appreciate it that much more."

Frowning, I manage to turn over, and he collapses next to me. I face him, watching his closed eyes as he tilts his face into the sun as if he's soaking it up. "Why did you live in darkness?" I ask, knowing he's opening up about his past. I won't pry if he doesn't want me to, but when his eyes open and lock on me, I know he's ready.

That he wants to.

"It was my job." Reaching for me, he tugs me close.

I throw my leg over his thigh and press my head to his to give him my warmth, my everything if he needs it. He smiles, and it's almost bitter. "I was my old court's enforcer. My king was a cruel leader. He banished us all into the dark to feed into the myth, so I only emerged at night, hunting and killing upon his orders. I was so feared, people would scramble out of my way, so eventually, I started to hide in the shadows. I got really good at it, and I guess that's why those are my powers." He lifts his hand, and I watch the darkness play there. "I guess it's my comfort, but you never look at me with fear or revulsion, and I won't change that, my queen."

"Never," I tell him. "It will only make you love me more."

"There was a girl . . ."

For a moment, jealousy clouds my vision before I blink it away. It's foolish because we all have our pasts. He is here now, with me, and he needs me to listen.

"She was a human in a nearby village, and we shouldn't have even crossed paths, but one night, when I was on my way back from hunting down an enemy, I heard her scream. She was being attacked by bandits. I saved her and took her home. Gods, Althea, she wasn't even scared of me. She was grateful. She made me feel like her hero. I-I thought I loved her, but I think it was just need—the need to be touched and trusted. I was so desperate for anything that I blinded myself to the truth. She was human, and I knew it was wrong, knew it wouldn't end well, but I craved the softness of her soul."

"Conall, you are allowed to have loved before me," I tell him, but he shakes his head.

"You don't understand. I know now that it wasn't love. It never felt even close to what I feel now with you—the obsession, need, and goddamn desperation I feel for you. My heart beats out of my chest just from one look at you. No, I never loved her, not really, and that makes it worse. I got her killed because I was fucking lonely. That's it."

"I don't understand," I whisper.

"She was my weakness, Althea, the only one I had. My king found out, and he wanted to rip that weakness from me. He ordered me to kill her, and I did. I ripped out her throat despite her pleas, and in the end, she saw me for what I truly was—a monster lurking in the dark. She welcomed me that night, eager to see me, and I saw excitement and happiness in her mortal eyes. She let me in, and I killed her on orders, Althea. How could I? How could I do that? The bitter truth is, I cannot even remember her face anymore or how I felt with her because you've wiped everything else away, and I'm so grateful. I did a horrible thing. I killed an innocent whose only crime was trusting and loving me. After I had, I realised orders meant nothing. How could I carry on doing this? I knew he would never let me go, but just as I was about to fall on my sword so it could never be used for evil again, they found me." I know he means the others. "They judged me, and I was so grateful."

"Conall," I rasp, seeing the raw agony in his eyes.

"I killed her, Althea. She didn't deserve that, and that's why I'm here, to atone for all the innocence I stole. I feel so fucking guilty because I know even if I was ordered to do so, I never could have done that to you. I love you too much, yet I didn't even blink when it came to her. I killed her so easily. She loved a lie. She loved a shadow, the mist of a man who lived in darkness, and you get all of me. I don't know if that's good or bad because I did horrible things on the king's orders, yet I would do worse for you, my queen. I know you would never use me that way, I know it soul deep, but it doesn't stop me from feeling like I'm betraying you by even mentioning her."

Blowing out a breath, I cup his face. I see his struggle in his gaze, the one he hides behind darkness. "You are not betraying me, and you have every right to be worried, but I promise, Conall, I would never order you to do anything you wouldn't choose to do. I would rather kill myself than compromise your soul and integrity. What that king did to you was cruel and evil, and it warped you. You cared for that girl, no matter what you say, but she was dead either way, Conall. We both know that. I cannot change your past, but I can live it with you every day. You choose your path now, and you choose to be good. You are a good man, Conall. The past is gone, and even the future is far off, so just live in the present with me, in the sunshine. If you do, I promise to protect you, my warrior, like no one did then. I will live in the sunlight with you just as much as I live in the shadows with you. It does not have to be one or the other."

Bloody tears fall from his eyes, and I lick them away. "I love you, Conall, for everything you are and have been. It's time to let go of what happened. It's time to forgive yourself. I know if she could see you now, she would." I send a promise on the air to that girl who loved this man, telling her that I will protect and love him the way she did so he will never be lonely again.

"What if I can't?" he asks. "What if holding onto it makes me a good judge?"

"What makes you a good judge is your ability to see the good in people, to protect people and your brothers. You do not need to be in pain to do this." Pressing my hand over his heart, I kiss him softly. "Let go, my love. We will be here to catch you."

He closes his eyes, shuddering as I surge inside and wrap him up in my protection. How dare that king try to corrupt such a soul and dampen his sunlight? The others surge in as well, feeling their brother's need, and we hold him as he lets go of his pain, his past, and when his eyes open, I see his ghosts are finally gone.

I kiss him softly. "I love you," I promise. "Within darkness or sunlight."

"I love you too," he whispers. "So damn much."

Forty Three

Conall

Her soft hand, so much smaller than mine, holds on tightly as she grins up at me. Her bare feet sink into the ground, and despite her height, she still only reaches my chest, yet she leads me, and I follow like a lovesick puppy.

I would follow her anywhere.

Those little hands hold my heart and soul, and where she goes, I go willingly. I didn't even know I needed to be saved until her. I didn't know I was still so troubled by my past until it poured out of me and into her listening heart. I practically begged her to judge me, but she never did, not once. She held me tightly, as if she would protect me from the sharp edges of my past.

For the first time ever, I don't want to fade into the waiting shadows. Instead, I want to walk in the sunlight with her.

A lot of the monsters will be sleeping during the day, but we make a meticulous circle to check the habitats they have chosen. There's some blood, so clearly some are clashing, but no bodies, which is good. She smiles the whole time, like she has a secret that I don't know about, and I'm obsessed with her.

I almost stumble and fall because I'm focused on her, but she keeps me upright with a giggle that echoes through the forest, lighting it up.

I refocus with a clearing of my throat. I notice the chimera slipping by and nod at him. I can sense some of the others close, probably the pixie and the shapeshifter, but it's more out of curiosity than anything, so we keep walking, until something skirts my senses.

"Althea." I tug her to a stop, frowning, but she squeezes my hand.

"It's okay. I feel it too. It's watching us and deciding." Turning, she walks backwards, leading me. "When they are ready, they will come out."

"The call?" I ask, and she nods.

"A shy one." She shrugs, and the trees break out into a clearing.

The huge cave I used to spend a lot of nights in is before us, glistening with jewels and gems. The waterfall next to it is throwing mist everywhere. It looks like something from another world, which is why I liked it so much, and I didn't even know she was leading me here.

She sits on the edge, dangling her feet into the water, so I sit behind her, wrapping my arms around her, and we just sit, soaking in the water, the beauty, and the peace, knowing what is to come will be madness.

My senses pick up whatever is watching us as it moves closer. She must too, but she simply sighs and leans back into me. When it doesn't speak or make a move, she grins. "You can come out. We will not hurt you."

We wait, and a silhouette appears on the other side of the water, keeping it between us.

"What are you?" my queen calls, and I focus on the figure, also unsure what kind of monster this woman is.

Her hair is a bright blue, like the ocean, and it falls to her knees. Her black eyes are huge, and her skin is so pale, it's almost luminous. She looks like a mix between a fey and a pixie. She's a beautiful creature for sure, but she's nothing compared to the queen in my arms.

"A mermaid and a siren," the melodic voice replies. "If I were to enter the water, you would see my true form. I journeyed far from the ocean. I felt your call and had to know. I have spent so much time alone in the water. My mate and family were killed by poachers a long time ago."

I sense her pain and Althea rubs her chest, feeling it too.

"I am sorry," Althea tells her, and I can tell she means it.

The woman sits, dangling her feet into the water like Althea, and a change slowly comes over her legs until they morph into a blue and green iridescent fin.

"Beautiful," Althea says with awe in her tone.

"As are you, night being," the woman replies. "I am known as Tide, or I was when I had anyone to call me."

"Althea," my girl responds. "I am so sorry about your family, Tide. You have been alone since?"

The mermaid inclines her head. "That is why I came. I am lonely."

"Well, you are free to stay. We have welcomed everyone here and always will. We have no ocean close by though." Althea frowns.

"I will miss the call of the sea, but there is water here. I feel it. If you will allow me to, I would like to remain here, in these woods. I will find the water and a place to live until the ocean calls me home to my family. It only holds pain, but these woods hold magic and purpose. I can feel it. Something big is coming, and I am where I am supposed to be."

"Good or bad?" Althea asks.

"I am unsure, but I know whatever it is, it will change everything. May I remain on your land?"

"For as long as you need, and you are welcome inside the court whenever you wish to be around people, Tide," Althea calls. "You do not need to be lonely, not here."

"Thank you." She stands, slipping out of the water, and her tail transforms back to legs. "You're very kind."

We both watch as she shakes off any remaining water and then starts to walk away.

Tide stops and turns back. "Althea, be prepared. I can feel plans on the air, evil plans. You are playing one game, and they are playing another. Remember that."

"What the fuck does that mean?" I mutter.

"It means that this ball is going to be one hell of a party." Althea laughs.

FORTY FOUR

ALTHEA

NATHAIR IS STRESSED, SO later that night, after he still doesn't appear and we have all eaten, I go and find him. He's sitting in the library, staring at his laptop with furrowed brows. Sighing, I shut it and throw it onto the other sofa then take its place on his knee. He grins as I kiss him softly. I rest my head against his chest, and he begins to stroke my hair with a sigh, his own head leaning back as he relaxes.

"You are stressed."

"There's so much to do," he murmurs. "I need this to be perfect."

"So share the duties, but for tonight, it's time to relax," I reply.

"What do you have in mind?" He grins, still petting my hair, and I sigh in pleasure. The others slowly filter in, and Azul lifts my feet, placing them in his lap, while Reve leans into my side and the others sprawl out around the room.

"Read to me?" I request. "Read us all a story?"

Osis grabs a book and hands it over before settling before the fire. Nathair opens it, holding it one-handed as he continues to stroke my hair, and then he starts to read. My eyes close as his deep, whiskey voice washes over me, making the words seductive and comforting all at once. The tension in his body slowly starts to seep out as the story continues, and the others add sound effects and voices, making us all crack up, even Nathair.

There's no rush, no need for anything, as we enjoy our time together. My eyes stay closed as I soak in their comfort, their nearness, and everything I had been missing. Like Tide, I had been lonely, but now, I never will be again. They make sure of that. Even now, there's the desire for their bodies and pleasure, but over it is the sense of comfort, like slipping into a warm, welcoming bed and snuggling in for a deep sleep or a good cup of tea on a rainy day.

That's what they are to me.

Comfort. Happiness. Love.

No matter what I thought my destiny was, it was never that man or my past. It was always here, with them. Their hearts beat for me, and mine beats for them. Despite what we face, our duties, and what our powers demand, right now, nothing else matters.

As the rain begins to hit the window and lightning cracks through the air, I smile as hands stroke my legs, head, and side. Nathair's voice fills my entire being until I drift off to sleep. When I wake up, the fire is still crackling and the rain is coming down hard, hitting the window in a relaxing lullaby. The lights have gone out, and the others are sprawled out, snoring with their arms thrown across each other. Nathair holds my head protectively, a blanket is thrown over my body, and Osis is asleep, holding my feet.

Reve's head presses into my side, Conall is stretched over the other sofa, and Zale and Lycus are curled up together near him. With the rain as a soundtrack, I watch them before slipping from their arms and padding to the closest door.

The scent of fresh rain hits me, making my eyes close in bliss. In the distance, I hear the roars of my monsters. Stepping out, I hold out my arms and let the rain soak me with a wide smile. Giggling, I spin in it, just living in the moment.

Something about it sets me free as I twirl and dance in the rain. It soaks every inch of me as I jump into puddles.

I feel him before I see him, but I still don't stop.

Arms wrap around me, and he spins me in the rain, dancing with me to the song in our hearts.

Opening my eyes, I blink away the rain drops. His hair is plastered against his head, and his brilliant eyes are bright with love as he stares down at me.

Nathair. His name is almost a sigh as he winds me across the courtyard, our feet barely touching the ground as he dips and spins me, grinning all the while as he watches me.

He pulls me back into his arms until we are just swaying, our heads bent together as we slow to a stop. With a growl, he slams his lips onto mine. Pressing up on my tiptoes, I grip his wet hair and yank him closer, bruising his lips with the force of my kiss. His hands slide down my back, gripping my ass through the wet material of my dress, and then he lifts me. I wrap my legs around his waist until I'm kissing down from the new height. The rain falls around us like a curtain, just us and the storm.

Our mouths don't break apart as he sways us again, dragging my pussy along his jeans and the hardness there. The friction makes me cry out until my head falls back. His lips slide down my throat, sucking and nipping. "You are so beautiful, *draya*," he purrs against my skin, sliding my dress up until he can grip my bare ass cheeks and squeeze them as he sucks on my neck. Pleasure blooms inside me, and my eyes close in bliss.

"Nathair, I need you," I beg.

"You have me forever," he promises against my skin, his fingers stroking across my pussy as he licks my throat.

"Show me," I demand, gazing at the thunderous sky. The clouds are drawing in, gathering across the moon, blocking out the shine of the stars, as the lightning arcs across the sky. "Show me how much you love me."

Knowing what I need, he rips my dress off, tossing it to the wind and leaving me bare. A shiver goes through me from my need.

The water washes away our fears, our worries, and when I lift my head and meet his eyes, I see vulnerability in his gaze. This great blood king, who is more powerful than any vampyr alive, watches me like he's worried I'll be taken away by the storm. His hands grip me tightly, holding me to him as he lifts me and slams me down on his cock.

My scream booms with the thunder as his huge length splinters me before I reform around him, connecting us both body and soul. Our eyes lock, and our souls are just as tightly wound as we are. Our breaths become the same, our hearts beat as one, and his pleasure is mine and mine is his.

I can feel him claiming me under the storm as the very elements themselves try to take me from him. I feel his hands slide across my wet body, marking every inch, yet it's his soul that has me crying out as he echoes the sound.

I see it all. I see his devotion, his love, his loyalty, and his family. I see him. I see every flawed inch of my king, and I see that it's all for me. Every action, every thought is now centred around me as if I'm the beating heart of his entire world.

It leaves me breathless, and a sense of power slams through me.

One of the oldest, most powerful vampyrs in the world would raze this entire species, this entire planet, simply to make me happy again. There is nothing he would not do for me, and it shouldn't be as heartwarming as it is, but it makes me move with him, claiming him like he claims me.

I open every inch of myself to him, and I let him see the depths of my love and just how much I crave him—the serpent whose bite saved me. He's the one I look to for help, for leadership. He's my rock, my safe space, and my love.

Snarling against my lips, I return from the bond, blinking as I stare into his red eyes. His lips swallow mine, and he grips my ass as he moves me faster, making me ride him. Each slide drags my clit across his body, hitting it until I'm reaching for my release.

This is just us—raw, together, powerful, and one.

Our bodies move faster and faster as our lips tangle. Pleasure flows through both of us, our blood heating us as the rain lashes us. Finally, it becomes too much, and my head falls back as he bottoms out in me, hitting my clit against him, and the pleasure explodes like the lightning in the sky.

As the storm intensifies and thunder crashes overhead, I scream his name into the madness.

Lighting up the sky with my love for him.

FORTY FIVE

ALTHEA

I WAKE UP SLOWLY, the familiar silken sheets of my bed making me sigh. There's a hard body at my back and hands wandering across my skin, making me moan as I bury my head into the warm muscle in front of me.

There's a soft chuckle as my thighs are tugged open. I don't even lift my head until a tongue laps at my cunt, making me jolt. Sleepily, I blink and lift my head, scanning the pale expanse of skin before me—Osis. He grins at me. "Morning, beautiful."

I turn my head to see Azul watching me hungrily, his hands cresting over my breasts until my nipples pebble under his rough, calloused hands and his fangs descend. Just then, another long lick drags along my pussy, making me jolt at the pleasure.

I peer down at Reve, who smirks up at me. "I wanted to taste the storm." He winks. "Since we were not invited to that party last night."

My head falls back, my hands fisting the muscles on either side of me. Osis groans as Azul grips me tighter.

Reve laps at my pussy as Azul leans down and captures one nipple, sucking and licking it. When Osis realises what he's doing, he copies him. They nibble on my stiff peaks, and pleasure rolls through me, arching down to my clit which Reve teases.

"What does she taste like?" Osis murmurs, lifting his head, his bright eyes meeting mine. His white hair is tied back, but pieces curl down and frame his sharp, beautiful face.

"Like goddamn heaven." Reve groans, thrusting his tongue inside me.

I throw my legs over his shoulders, watching as he grinds his cock into the bed as his big hands span my hips and drag me closer so every inch of my pussy is covering his face as he feasts.

His fingers drag along me, following the path of his tongue, and then they thrust inside me. His two, thick digits spear me, making me cry out as I arch my chest for them. Suddenly, they are gone, and I blink my eyes open. He lifts the glistening digits to Osis, who bends over and sucks them clean. "Fuck, you're right." He groans as Reve slides them back inside me, stretching my pussy.

"Shit, I want to taste," Azul mutters, and Osis grabs his head and pulls him closer. I can't help but moan as Osis kisses him above me, and when Azul pulls back, he's panting, his lips glistening with my cream and Osis's saliva.

"I love how you taste," he tells me as he lowers his head and licks my nipple again. "One day, we are going to get you pregnant, baby, and when you are breast feeding, I'm going to love these fucking tits and drink from them while I fuck you."

Fuck.

I almost come apart, heat racing through me, as Reve licks and sucks my clit and Osis tongues my nipple. Every inch of my body is being claimed and used to bring me pleasure.

His tongue drags over my ass, licking my forbidden hole. "I'm going to cover it in my blood to get my big dick in and fuck this."

Fuck. Fuck. I'm not going to last.

Like he feels it, he lifts his head, his face glistening with my cream as he watches me. "I want to feel you explode as I feed." He shares a look with the others, and with a chuckle, he returns to my pussy and resumes his attack.

A third finger joins the others, curling inside of me to hit those nerves that have me writhing and crying out their names. My hands come up to grip their hair—one brown, one white. Fisting it, I push them harder onto my breasts as Reve nips my clit. I'm so close, so fucking close, my pussy flutters, and then he turns his head, adds a forth finger, and they all lift their heads in unison.

"What—" I start, but it ends in a howl.

I scream as they strike at the same time.

Reve bites my thigh, and Osis and Azul sink their fangs into my breasts.

All three pairs of fangs slide deep as they begin to feed, and the sharp pain makes me come. My pussy clamps on Reve's big fingers as I writhe, gripping their hair to hold them to me. My blood drips across my chest and onto my stomach, down my legs and onto the bed.

Their hands begin to massage it into my skin, and I come again until I can't see. When I come to, they are lapping at their fang marks, and I'm coated in sweat. Groaning, I use my fists in their hair to drag Azul and Osis up. First, I kiss Azul, tasting my blood, and without opening my eyes, I turn to kiss Osis. Our tongues tangle until their faces push together and we are all kissing, and I clench around Reve's fingers again.

Laughing, he pulls them out. "Oh, she likes that. Keep her wet for me, boys," he says as he slides his fingers down and circles my ass. His other hand slips under and lifts me until his tongue follows his fingers' path, licking and touching until I'm panting into their mouths. They swallow my moans of pleasure.

"Reve," I whimper, and I'm suddenly flipped.

A hand comes down on my ass, and a knee presses my legs open wider as I hold myself up on my hands. "One of you gets her pussy, and the other gets her mouth. Isn't that right, pretty girl? You want all three of us pumping our queen full of our cum?"

"Fuck yes." I toss my hair over my shoulder and crawl towards Osis, who's the closest. His white hair is stained with my blood, and it's smeared across his lips and chest. His fist pumps his huge, hard cock, and I lean down and lap at the tip. His head falls back, and his strokes stop as he holds it for me. His abs roll with his breath as I lick and suck the tip of him, the salty taste making me moan and dip my mouth down lower. When I swallow him all the way to his fist, he slowly uncurls his hold, and then I slide down all the way until he's seated in the back of my throat. He groans loudly and rolls his hips, tangling his fingers in my hair.

"I guess you get her pretty pussy," Reve tells Azul, and my ass is lifted again. I feel a body under me, but I don't look, not even as lips wrap around my nipples. For a moment, I begin to pull back, panicking about Azul being on his back under me, knowing he doesn't like it.

How could I not enjoy this? His voice fills my head. *I enjoy having you above me, tasting your mates and claiming me. Nothing could be more perfect.*

I relax and pull my mouth up, watching Osis lift his head. His eyes are blown wide, and his lips are parted. "You better get inside of her quickly. I'm not going to last in this pouty little mouth, not with her looking at me like that and sucking me so good."

"You heard the man," Reve says, and their hands grip my hips and sides to lift me.

Azul's huge cock presses to my pussy, and they hesitate, but I don't. I drive myself down, impaling myself on him, making us both cry out. I lick and suck at Osis's length, needing to do something to distract myself from my pussy being stretched so deliciously that I wind and grind my hips, needing to move.

"Behave," Reve orders, slapping my ass. "Watching you wiggle like that will have me coming before I even get my big dick in this tight little ass."

"Then get the hell inside me," I demand. "That's an order from your queen." I'm still in charge, even though I'm impaled on one man's dick and sucking another's. I could tell them to stop touching me and they would. I could order them to lie down, their hard cocks begging for relief, and get myself off.

Gladly, Reve says in my head, his powers wrapping around me and showing me exactly just that.

When I come back, I'm gasping from his vision. His cock circles my asshole, playing with me, and when I glance back, I see his wrist bleeding. As I stare, he wraps his bloodied hand around his length and strokes, getting it wet, and I groan before sucking Osis's cock again. I'm about to shout at him, but he pushes me down and slams into me.

I come. I can't help it.

The blood and the feeling of every hole being filled sends me screaming over the edge, but they don't let me relax, no. They fuck me through it, taking control. Reve's fingers dig into my hips, drawing me back onto his cock, and then Azul's hands yank me down until I'm fucking him. All the while, Osis thrusts into my mouth, his hands turning into the claws of his tiger and tangling in my hair, directing my mouth as he slams into the back of my throat each time.

"Fuck, her mouth is insane," Osis growls, glaring down at me. "Why do you have to be so perfect?"

Whimpering, I suck his invading cock harder, clenching around Reve's and Azul's cocks.

"You should see my view," Reve taunts. "Her perky little ass is wrapped around my cock, and her pretty, dripping pussy is taking another. Shit, never mind visions, I'm going to have this in my memory forever."

Azul moans. "I never knew it could be like this." His mouth drags along my breasts. "So loving and just so much pleasure."

The pleasure builds within me again with every stroke of their hands and cocks, but it's more than that. Our bonds become solid, like a conductor, transferring our pleasure between us and doubling each time.

It circles around and around until we are all crying out and we explode as one.

Like a tornado tearing through us, power explodes outward. Shadows roll in and block our vision until it snaps and we all slump, limp in hazy pleasure.

Fuck.

I don't know who thinks it, but we all echo it before I start giggling, swallowing around the taste of Osis's cum. My pussy and ass are still impaled and dripping with our releases.

"Erm, if you are done in there, I came to see you. Surprise!" Simon shouts through the door. Slumping back, I start to laugh. "I don't want to be traumatised, so I'm going to the kitchen with Zale!"

They chuckle, and then I hear their footsteps disappear.

"I can't move yet," I murmur, snuggling deeper. "He can wait."

"Thank the gods," Azul mutters, making me laugh again as he holds me tighter.

After washing, since I was covered in blood and cum and Simon must have heard and smelled what we were doing, I leave my long hair to dry and slip on some comfy silk shorts and cami top, adding a cardigan I stole from Nathair and some slippers. The others left to wash at my order because they tried to seduce me back into bed and I nearly cracked. The sight of all three of them, their muscles dotted with sweat, was a temptation for sure.

But I miss my friend.

Skipping down the steps, I cock my head and listen, finally hearing voices coming from the kitchen, so I hurry there. I step inside to find Conall sharing some wine with Simon and a man I've never seen before, but one sniff tells me he's a werewolf—a powerful one at that. Very powerful. Simon's mate?

His eyes are bright blue and slightly almond shaped, framed by long, thick black lashes. A mane of shaggy brown hair in many shades hangs in waves to his shoulders, tucked behind one ear to display a tooth through his lobe. He's handsome, with a thick, square face and full lips surrounded by a beard. He's wearing a plain T-shirt—as is custom with wolves who run hot and rip a lot of clothes during their shift—which stretches across impressive muscles, and jeans that are tucked into work boots. He looks casual and stern, but when he glances at Simon, I see his eyes soften and his lips tilt up in a secret smile, and right then and there, I approve of him.

Anyone who looks at my best friend like he hung the moon is good enough for me. Not only that, but I look to Simon to see his reaction, and it tells me all I need to know. He loves him deeply and he's happy, unguarded, and confident.

Good.

"Hey," I call.

"Thea," Simon says, hurrying over and hugging me. "I want to know details later," he teases as he pulls back and looks over his shoulder, blushing slightly and seeming nervous. I realise he's worried about what I will think of the wolf. Didn't I think the same about my guys? My best friend is my most important person, and if he didn't like them, I don't know what I would have done. I squeeze his hand and move over.

"I'm Althea. You must be the wolf, Elias." I smile reassuringly, and he stands, clasping my hand and shaking. His grip is strong, but he's not testing me. It's just his true strength because he's not holding back. I like that.

I wink at Simon. "You are right. He's pretty."

The wolf actually blushes, and it's adorable. "It's nice to meet you," he offers gruffly. "Si talks about you continually." He holds out his arm, and Simon slips into his grasp, and I almost swoon. I do let out a little squeal of excitement before tamping it down.

"And you, I'm so glad you came with him." I sit, and Conall heads over, kissing me softly. I stare up at him dreamily as he cups my chin and deepens the kiss until a cough interrupts us. I pull away with an embarrassed smile at Simon, but Elias grins knowingly.

"Sorry," I say, but I'm not really. "Where is everyone?" I ask Conall.

He hesitates, and then his mind slides into mine. *Nathair is with Zale, distracting him, not that he knows it.*

I frown, and Conall smiles sadly but doesn't explain.

Reve, Osis, and Azul come in with Lycus behind them. "There's our troublemaker." Lycus grins and kisses me hard.

"Fucking hell, can you save the porn shit for when I'm not here?" Simon huffs, and I yank on Lycus's hair, keeping him there with a grunt as I wink at Simon.

"Sure. Elias, do you want me to tell you about the time Simon got into the Freshno wine—"

"Kiss away!" Simon screams, practically throwing himself at the wolf and covering his ears, making me laugh. Turning back to Lycus, I kiss his captive lips once more before releasing him.

"Now I definitely want to know." Elias smirks at Simon.

"Do not, or I will tell them about the time with the frisbee," Simon hisses at me, flashing fangs.

I narrow my eyes. "You wouldn't dare."

"Try me." He smirks.

"Children," Conall admonishes, but he's grinning.

We both turn to him, wearing matching expressions of ire for his involvement, and he holds up his hands and backs away. "I'm starting to learn not to get between you."

"Smart, that one." Simon laughs, and we share a grin.

"So, why are you here?" I ask, changing the topic. "Don't get me wrong, I'm happy to see you."

"Well, Nathair said you need us for something. He's going to discuss it with us, and then I thought we could have a movie night or something and just hang, you know? Sorry, that sounds lame."

Elias clutches his neck possessively, offering him comfort.

I reach over and hold his hand. "I would love that. A lot has been going on, and a night off sounds incredible. What do you guys think?"

"I get to pick the movie!" Reve calls, and they all frown.

"No, Simon does, he's the guest," I murmur and then share a look with him.

"*Blade*?" we both say at the same time, and this time they all groan, making us laugh.

Forty Six

Althea

Osis and Azul put together some nachos and snacks, and after we demolish them, Nathair appears. For a moment, he eyes the wolf and then he sits down heavily, scrubbing his face. "Sorry."

I look behind him and frown. "Where is Zale?"

He looks at me, and something flashes across his eyes. "He'll be by soon," is all he says, and then he smiles at Simon. "It's nice to see you again, Simon, and nice to meet you, Elias."

"Sure thing, vamp man." Simon fist-bumps him. "So what do you need?"

"We need you and Elias to attend the ball we are hosting." Simon cocks his head to the side, and Nathair smiles and dives into what's happening. When he's done, Simon sits back. "I know you are part of your old court, but I think we need all the help we can get and the bodies to go with it. I understand if you can't."

"If I were to stand with you, it would be treason, and it would be within my court's rights to kick me out or worse," Simon replies, but his tone is almost conversational. He sighs and looks at Elias, taking his hand. "But if they knew I was in love with a wolf, they would kill me anyway, so fuck it. Let's do it."

"Simon," I start, but he smiles at me.

"You are my family, Althea. I will do anything for you, and you know that. Without you, the court isn't my home. Where you go, I go. I will always stand with you." He takes my hand again, and I hold his.

"We won't let them hurt you," I promise.

He smirks. "I know."

Elias chimes in then, leaning closer. "Nor will my wolves. They have accepted Simon. I have faced many challenges, and so has he, and we have won. They are loyal to us now and understand our mating. If you will have more monsters of the night, then I will bring my pack, and we will create a truce between your court and them."

Nathair's eyes flare wide in surprise. "You would do that?"

"For my mate and my mate's family? Of course. I assume Simon will become part of your court?" he asks.

"If he wishes," Nathair replies without hesitation. "Or both your pack and our court. Even if he chooses not to, he always will have a place here."

Elias nods and smiles at him. "Then we are with you. The vamps have gotten away with their shit for too long—no offence, babe—so let's stick it to them. My wolves will love it."

"Nathair." Lycus winces. "What about—"

"I will talk to him."

I frown, looking between them. *I will tell you later, my love,* Nathair promises telepathically, so I let it go.

"Now that it's all decided, I heard we are having a movie night?" Nathair says, and I grin at him.

"Yep, we need popcorn, chocolate, crisps, wine, and lots and lots of blankets," I tell him.

"Blankets? I shall see what I can do, my queen," he purrs as he stands. "You heard our girl. Thea, baby, you go with them to the cinema room, and we will meet you there."

Nodding, I kiss his cheek on my way past and lead Simon and his mate to the cinema room. I slide into one of the black leather sofas on the back wall. There are three across it, then chairs and a giant pit of cushions that would hold an entire court. Taking up the wall across from me is a huge screen. Simon and Elias sit next to me, with Simon leaning into my side as he holds his mate's hand, and I can't help but smile. We both need this.

"I'm glad you are with us. I hate the distance," I whisper.

"Me too, me too." He lifts his head. "I'm so glad you let someone love you too. I finally see you as I always did. You are magnificent, and your mother would be so proud of the person you have become."

"You think?" I murmur.

"I know." He squeezes my hand. "I'm proud of you, Thea, and I'm with you. I like them too, you know. They are good for you. You need someone to challenge you while also worshipping you. I don't know how you deal with that many dicks—"

"Simon!" I laugh.

"I mean, like, how many holes could you fill—wait, never mind. I don't want to . . . Do you stack them on top of each other? Or do you put a name in a bowl—wait, no, don't tell me." He groans, and Elias laughs and leans around him to see me.

"Don't tell him. It will give him ideas, and he's already more demanding in bed than a wolf."

"Elias," Simon admonishes, smacking his chest.

"Get some, bestie." I nod proudly, and Simon covers his face.

"Oh gods, kill me now."

"Nah, you're too pretty." His mate winks, making me laugh. "Plus, you suck cock like a Hoover—"

"That's it!" He stands, and without looking at us, he flips over onto the seat before us. "I'm not looking at either of you."

Elias slides closer and lowers his head. "Tell me all his secrets from when he was a kid."

"Well, there was this time—"

Simon leans over and glares at me, flicking his fang. Laughing, I start to tell his stories when there's a pained moan.

I lift my head in panic, frowning when I find Zale at the door. His eyes are wide and terrified, and his mouth is parted in a painful grimace as he grips the doorframe. He's not staring at me, but at Elias next to me. The wolf freezes and lifts his nose to scent the room, seeming confused.

"What—" He turns to me to ask for clarification, but Zale snarls and launches himself at the wolf.

Elias holds up his hands and backs away from me. "I mean no harm to your queen," he says carefully. "Or anyone here."

"Zale?" I stand and move towards him. He shudders, closes his eyes, and quickly turns and leaves.

I start to go after him when Nathair steps inside, watching him go. "Leave him, he needs some space. He will come back when he's ready."

"I don't understand," I say, trying to dart around him.

Nathair catches me and effortlessly flings me into the pit of cushions. Lycus is there, and he pins me down with a grin, his big body holding me captive. Reve prowls in and sits next to Simon, who seems worried. Osis and Azul flip into the pit as well, surrounding me, but my heart aches because a piece of me is missing. I feel his agony and horror, and it calls to me.

I struggle, but Lycus bites my stomach, making me freeze. "He's serious, Thea. Leave him, he needs it. Even I wouldn't go after him right now. He will come back to you; he always will. Give him time and trust because he needs to push back some memories."

Frowning, I look at the door, and even when the movie starts, I can't focus or relax. I reach out for Zale, trying to find a way into his mind to tell him I'm here, but he's locked down tight, rejecting me, and it rips my heart open, leaving me gasping in the dark.

"Shh," Lycus murmurs, holding me tighter. "Do not take it personally."

"He pushed me away," I mutter, old insecurities rising to the surface.

"It's just while he deals with his memories, I assure you," Lycus offers, trying to comfort me, but it's no use. I bury my head in his wide chest, hiding my tears. I hate the sting of rejection, and I work through everything I could have done differently until Lycus finally snarls and rolls to his feet.

"Hold her," he tells the others, and then he, too, is gone.

I watch the door in confusion, and a moment later, Lycus strides in with Zale over his shoulder and tosses him into the pit with me, his arms folded and angry. "You fucking apologise to our queen right this second for making her feel like you rejected her. I don't give a shit what you're dealing with right now," he snarls before he softens. "We understand, brother, but she does not, and she's hurting. I cannot stand it."

"Me either," the others say.

Zale turns to me on his knees, looking wounded, and when he sees me, he cries out and crawls towards me. I freeze, not reaching for him because I don't want to be rejected again, fearing that more than anything.

He buries his head between my breasts, holding me tightly. "I'm so sorry, Thea." He tries to surge his mind into mine, but I back away. If he wants space, I will give it to him. "No, no, no, please, my queen, please, I'm sorry. Please don't pull away from me." He lifts his head, tears flowing from his eyes. "Do not cut me off. I'm so sorry. I didn't mean to, please, Thea." It's the broken, raw edge of his voice that causes me to soften, and I wrap my arms around him, feeling his mind slide through mine as he lets out a sob, pressing closer until nothing exists between us.

"Sorry, sorry," he repeats as I relax, realising this wasn't about me. I took it the wrong way, and now I've made it worse.

"Shh, it's okay," I promise, stroking his mind with mine, and then Lycus climbs into the pit, pressing against Zale's back.

"You're safe. You're okay. She's okay," Lycus tells him, and Zale slowly relaxes. I struggle to focus on the movie, and I feel Simon watching us, but I continue to hold Zale against me along with Lycus.

When the movie is over, Simon whispers to Nathair, who nods, and then Simon crouches near me at the edge of the pit. "We are going to leave." His eyes go to Zale. "We will be back tomorrow, okay?"

I nod, taking his hand, and he smiles and squeezes my fingers before leaving with his mate. When they are gone, Zale finally relaxes.

I open my mouth to ask, but Lycus shakes his head. I lie back, just holding Zale, and someone else puts another movie on. Slowly, lulled by the music on the film and their body heat, I begin to drift to sleep, surrounded by my family.

I wake with a start, a howl jerking me upright. I flip over, the pillows in the pit trapping me, and I fight against them before I finally manage to get to my knees to see Zale's arms pinned by a struggling Lycus, while Azul covers his legs with his whole body. Everyone else is awake and worried as Zale howls and screams and twists.

"Help him," Nathair demands, gritting his teeth as he looks at me.

"How?" I whisper, my hand covering my mouth.

"He needs to remember where he is. Touch him, Thea," he begs, so I crawl towards Zale, but I'm unable to touch him due to his struggles. I give up and just fling myself over his lap, straddling him. He bucks once, twice, before freezing and turning his head towards me, his eyes shut tight from memories or nightmares, I'm not sure.

"Zale?" I murmur, and his eyes snap open and lock on me. He completely softens, like a puppet whose strings have been cut.

"Althea?" he croaks, his voice hoarse from screaming.

"It's me. It's me," I murmur, leaning down to stroke his sweaty face. Lycus and Azul still don't release him, as if they are worried he will attack or change. I ignore them and focus on his terrified eyes. "It's me. You are okay."

With a cry, he jerks up and dislodges them, wrapping himself around me. I hold him tight, stroking his back, and the others slowly relax. I eye them, wanting to demand answers, but from the hard glints in their eyes, I know I won't get them. Whatever this is, it's Zale's story, so I simply hold him as he clutches me.

The others filter from the room, leaving just Zale and me. Pulling back, I cup his face, noticing his eyes are red and swollen and his lips are trembling. "Shh, baby, I'm here. What's wrong? Tell me. I can't fix it if I don't know," I tell him.

"You can't fix it. You can't fix me," he whispers.

"You are not broken," I snap.

"I am. I thought I was okay. I thought I could do it. He wasn't a threat, but then I saw him near you, and it—it just flung me back there. My panic at losing you brought me back, but then the nightmare came. I'm so weak. I'm so sorry, Thea." He tries to scramble away, but I hold him tighter.

"Zale, you are not broken. I don't understand. Why do you fear the wolf?" I question, needing to know. Simon is important to me, as is his mate, but I will not let this hurt my mate.

My Zale.

"I—" He hesitates. "I couldn't stand you thinking less of me."

"I never will," I tell him honestly, and he searches my gaze and nods before he swallows. His tongue darts out to lick at his fangs nervously.

"I was a nobody at my court, not like the others, but I had friends, and I was happy. I knew I would never rise in the ranks, and I didn't mind. It was a good life. One night, a group of friends and I, all freshly changed, went to a blood party." I know them well. I went to enough before my presentation. It's basically a big orgy of sex and blood drinking for those fresh and new—a safe space to explore. "On our way back, blood drunk and being stupid, we took a detour. It was a way we had never been before. We ended up getting lost, and before I knew it, we were surrounded."

His eyes become distant, but he leans into me.

"Wolves, werewolves, they were everywhere. Our court had never had issues with them before, but I knew our history, knew our two races hated each other and it wouldn't be good. I tried to look for a way out, a way to escape, while the others either tried to flee or fight. I could hear the screams of terror and pain from the ones who ran into the trees as the wolves tore into them. They wanted to kill us. They weren't defending their territory, weren't attacked or provoked. No, they played with us. They wanted our pain. They hated us. I saw it in their eyes, Althea, and I never knew why."

Oh god. I cover my mouth, and he carries on.

"I managed to scramble over this massive boulder and just started running. I could hear them chasing me. My friends had either left me or were dead, so I was the last. I couldn't save them. I couldn't. I just kept running. One managed to catch me near the water, and I killed it. I was hurt, but I had always been faster than anyone in our court, and I made it back. I told everyone what happened before passing out. When I woke up, I was in a locked room." He meets my eyes. "They blamed me for my friends' deaths and called me a coward for not saving them. I promise, Althea, I couldn't. It all happened so fast, and there were so many wolves, I nearly died myself, but my court did not care."

I don't even have time to tell him that I believe him because he laughs bitterly. "I was punished before them all and made into a laughingstock. No one trusted me, and I was shunned, so I left. I couldn't stand it anymore. I started to internalise their hatred and jokes and began to believe I was to blame. I wandered for so long, trying to deal with it. I learned how to brew tea and how to survive, but I was never the same. One night, I couldn't take it anymore. I went to hunt down some wolves. It didn't matter who they were or what they had done. Unluckily or not, I didn't get far. I was heading into pack lands, and you had to go through this gate of sorts. I didn't know then why it was avoided, but I do now. The stone gate was empty, but when I drew close, it began to swirl, and before I knew it, a huge shape leapt out. I was bitten and dragged through. When I woke up, I was in a cave. I realised it had been a portal, a prison of sorts for a mythical being—a black dog. I thought it meant to kill me, but then I looked into its eyes and I could see a different plan. It changed me, but I didn't know it then, didn't know it had bitten me while I slept and turned my blood. I escaped once more, thinking I was so smart, but in reality, it let me go. I ran to the nearest court for safety. They took me in, and I dropped into a deep fever. At some point during my slumber, I changed. I changed into a beast just like him. I barely remember the days after. The next thing I knew, I was human once more, covered in blood with the remains of one of the court's houses splattered around me. I killed them, ripped them to pieces. I was evil. I ran once more, seeking an end to this." He pauses and takes a deep breath.

"If I'd survived, I would have changed more people and, in turn, freed my creator who was a god, a cursed one. The others stopped me. They killed me, but when I came back, I still had the black dog inside of me. I could then control it, since it was part of me and not evil like I thought. It could be used for good and bad. I thought I was over it all, but seeing that wolf brought it all back. I'm still that scared little vamp running in the dark."

"No, not in the dark, not ever again. Zale, I cannot change what happened to you. It's terrifying, and what those wolves did . . ." I shake my head. "But you know, just like vamps, some are evil and untrustworthy. We cannot blame an entire species for what they have done," I say softly.

He jerks like I slapped him, but I see the truth in his eyes. He knows that.

"It is your past to overcome, but I will be right here with you, and I will never let anyone hurt you ever again. If you need to be free of wolves, I will make it so, and if you need to face it, I will be right there with you. You are so much stronger than you could ever realise. You survived so much and tamed the beast inside you. You took a curse and made it good again. You can do this too. I know it. You do not want to hate and judge an entire race over the actions of a few." I place my hand on his heart. "But we can take it one day at a time. I cannot thank you enough for telling me. I'm so sorry I didn't know and made it worse tonight."

"Never," he croaks. "None of us expected it to be that bad. I am so sorry."

"Do not apologise to me. We all have the things that haunt us, but that's what this is—a haunting. It cannot hurt us unless we let it."

"How can you still touch me knowing I'm a coward?" He frowns. "Knowing this creature, this thing I am, was once evil?"

Eyes narrowed, I lean in and bite his lip hard, seeing his beast peek out. "I do not fear your beast, and you should not either. You said you found peace, but I think part of you still worries about it around me. I don't want that. Let the beast out to play, Zale. It won't hurt me; neither of you will," I murmur, sliding my lips along his.

He suddenly rips himself away from me and rolls onto the edge of the pit.

Panting, he tilts his head like an animal. His eyes are alight with the flames of his beast, and the growls he lets out has me shivering as I lie back, waiting for my beast to devour me.

"I do not want to hurt you. I couldn't live with that. I would rip my own heart out."

"That is proof enough that you never will. It is time to take down that last barrier, Zale. It is time to move on." I hold out my arms, waiting for him.

"Althea," he growls in warning.

It's clear he's holding back, and I realise that every time we have been together, he has been doing just that. I hate it. I want all of him. Maybe I'm greedy or selfish, but I want every single inch of him.

Tilting my head with a smirk, I trail my fingers across my shirt to the hem and slowly tug it up and off, leaving me in nothing but a red lacy bra. My nipples harden, peeking through the snake winding through the flowers over the cups. His snarl grows louder as he rolls as if his beast is trying to get out.

"Zale." I pout, trailing my hand lower to the waistband of my skirt. I slide it down my thighs and throw it towards him. He grabs it with a clawed hand and presses it against his nose as he watches me lean back once more. Now, I'm wearing nothing but a matching thong and bra.

Spreading my thighs, I let him see my pussy, feeling my wetness coating the fabric of the thong.

I slide my hand around my throat and down my chest as I widen my legs. "I need you, Zale. You don't want to leave your queen unsatisfied, do you?" I purr, sliding my hand over my stomach and down to cup my pussy. I grind my hand into my wet flesh. My moan is real, the spark of pleasure causing me to wind my hips, and it's that noise that finally breaks through his control.

Thank the gods.

His head drops back, and he bays as his skin rolls. I watch in rapt fascination as my man transforms before me—not quite man, not quite beast.

He's the best of both.

His arms thicken, and black hair sprouts from his skin, covering them. His legs triple in size and bow in the middle, more hair sprouting and covering those limbs as well. His clothes tear away from his body as the muscles on his chest expand. His entire body is covered in short black hair.

He is at least four times Zale's usual size, with huge rippling muscles. His cock is sized proportionately to his new frame, hanging hard down to his knee. I drag my gaze up, licking my lips, and focus on the rest of him. Black-tipped claws drag along the floor, scoring it as he transforms.

His face thickens and turns square, the mane of hair on his head flowing down his back. His eyes turn pure red, and his ears become pointed.

His fangs are longer than his chin, and I shiver in need, wanting to feel them buried in my skin.

He is breathtaking, and my pussy clenches in anticipation of all that power being used against me.

His head falls back when the transformation finishes, and the howl he lets out is pure possession and need—a warning to others that he is about to claim what's his, and anyone who tries to get in his way will be killed.

I can't help but pinch my clit, needing to come from that sound alone. It settles into my skin, into my heart, making me breathless as I roll my hips faster. When his head lowers, his eyes lock on me, and I still.

He pounces, moving so fast I don't see him until he lands in the pit a few feet away from me, his claws ripping cushions away to get to me.

His hands capture my legs, and with a quick, easy movement, he yanks me towards him. The strength and power in his grip make me shiver, and I can taste his ancient blood pounding through him. I want to feel that on me, in me. His tongue lolls out, long and black with bumps all over it, and he runs it up my leg before stopping at my pussy. "Mine," he rumbles and rips my thong off, yanking my thighs so wide it almost hurts, and then his tongue is on me.

My eyes roll into the back of my head, my chest arching as those bumps slide over my clit, feeling too fucking good. Pleasure and heat build inside, making me as wild as he is. His tongue covers the length of my pussy, lapping at my folds before thrusting inside me. I cry out, grabbing the cushions on either side of me, and my own claws rip into them, fisting their innards as I roll my hips, riding my beast's face.

"Please!" I beg, needing only what he can give me.

My blood cries for it, for him, for the beast between my thighs. It's something I didn't even know I was missing, but my body knew what our bond did not. We needed this, and it's determined to lock us together forever.

His claws drag up my sides, and it's then I realise he has four fingers now and his hands are almost split in the middle. When they cover my breasts, I moan as those fingers deftly roll and tug on my nipples as his tongue fills me over and over, dragging me towards my release. It's an assault, a claiming, and I am helpless to do anything but ride it out. For all my power, I am nothing but this beast's mate, and I love being controlled and used for my pleasure.

"Mine," he growls inside me, the vibration lighting up my body.

I slash my claws across my chest. He snarls, and his mouth leaves my pussy, latching onto my blood. He drags his long tongue along the cuts, tearing them farther.

"Yes, yours." I groan and grip his head, but all too soon, the cuts heal, and he slides back down my body.

He presses two of his thick fingers inside me, wrapping his tongue around my clit. It sends me flying off the edge. I slash and claw, and he growls at me, encouraging me. I feel flesh under my fingers, and the scent of blood fills the air as I come. When I can finally see again, he's above me, his chest marred and bleeding, and he's looking at the claw marks proudly.

"Mine," I snarl back.

Flipping me over with a snarl, he drags my ass into the air and slams that huge cock into me. He tears me, but I quickly heal around him, the pain blending with pleasure as he begins to pound into me, rutting me like an animal.

"Mine," he snarls.

I feel my blood dripping down my thighs, and then his fangs drag down my back, marking me like I did him. My back bows inwards at the bliss, and I cry out and come around his cock, yet he still doesn't stop fucking me. His cock seems to swell and hit parts of me I didn't know could be touched. They hurt so good.

"Yours," I respond, screaming as his fangs drag back up, slicing me open. The feel of his black fur, which is surprisingly soft, against my legs and back makes my eyes close as I shake.

"Zale," I whine, bucking under him until his fangs grip the back of my neck like he's holding a naughty kitten. I freeze, unable to help it. The domination and pressure make me his all the way through as he speeds up, chasing his pleasure and need to fill his mate with his release.

"Mine, mine, mine," he chants, and his cock swells in me so big, so thick that it finally sends me over the edge again. I scream and claw at the pit as I come, squeezing that huge cock.

"Mine!" he roars, striking my neck at the same time his cock swells to an impossible size within me, dragging along my nerves until I'm coming again, writhing beneath him as he pins me, feeding from me and filling my cunt.

I slump, and he continues to feed, his cock jerking as he fills me. His huge length stops any of his release from escaping. The pleasure becomes too much, and the last thing I remember is him lapping at the wound from his fangs before everything goes black and I slide into a blissful slumber.

My body conquered.

Forty Seven

Althea

I wake to a hellhound curled around me, his flaming red eyes locked on me. It's pure beast, with no hint of Zale, and I smile, reaching out to pet his side as he rumbles with happiness. He's so warm, I'm practically sweating.

He's not an animal like a dog; he's more like a werewolf. His beast is a living, breathing, sentient side of him, and it's clear he's thankful for being let out. The fact that Zale relaxed enough to change in his sleep makes me smile. My body aches all over, especially my shoulder, and I know that bite will scar. Good, let it. I'll wear it proudly. My pussy throbs, and when I reach down, I feel his sticky release covering every inch of my cunt, thighs, and ass.

I meet his intelligent eyes.

"When you are like this, are you part of Zale or is he in the back?" I wonder out loud, petting his soft fur.

He looks like a mix between a Doberman and a three-headed hydra. He's huge, even bigger than I. Flames burn inside his bright red eyes, his snout is tipped with a black nose, and huge fangs protrude from his mouth, but I feel safe, as if he would kill anyone who got close.

I would. This is our nest. The growling voice drifts through my head, and my eyes pop wide open. *I can speak through our bond. Zale is here, but he is sleeping. We are the same person, but not, if that makes sense.*

"It does," I tell him out loud. "How long has it been since you have fully shifted?" I ask curiously.

A very long time. He snuggles closer. *He never trusted me after the attack. He would make the others chain me or watch. I was so young and hungry. I tried to tell him that I was not in control then, but it did not matter. When he was reborn, his sins forgotten, I hoped I would be too, but he did not forgive, nor did he forget. He hated me for it. I am his strength, if only he would see that. I would never let another hurt us again. I would protect our mate and family.*

"I'm sorry," I tell him, digging my hands into his fur. "I think he was just scared, and in all honesty, I understand that. Maybe after tonight, you will have a better relationship and he will trust you if you earn it."

I hope so. You changed everything, mate. We both sensed it the moment you were reborn, and we knew you were made for us. He tried to stop me from reaching out and laying my claim, but you welcomed us both last night, and he allowed me to take my mate with him.

"Because I'm made for both of you," I tell him. "Forgive him."

He is young, and I do forgive him. I love him. I am him, and he is me. One day, he will see the truth in my heart and actions, and it will all be thanks to you. He cocks his head to the side. *The others, his family, have been outside for a long time. I did not let them in while my mate was asleep, even if they are family. Would you like me to?*

"Is that okay?" I ask. I don't want him to think I'm wishing him away, but he's right. Now that I focus on it, I can feel the others behind the door. They are worried, not enough to bust in here, but they want to make sure we are okay.

Anything our mate wants, she gets.

"Guys, come in!" I call then roll onto my back, but I leave my hand on him to keep us connected. A moment later, they file in, their eyes running over me to check for injuries before flicking to Zale. I see shock in some of their eyes, but not with Lycus or Nathair, who seem pleased.

"Brother." Lycus nods, bowing his head in respect. "May I enter your nest to touch our mate?"

The beast slowly inclines his head, and slowly, so he doesn't trigger him, Lycus slides into the nest near my back, keeping me between us, then slides his hand over my side. "My love, are you okay?"

"Better than." I stretch out, completely naked, and his eyes heat despite the fact that I smell like Zale.

"My favourite scent is my mate covered in my brother's cum and her blood," he growls. He looks at Zale then. "I am glad he let you out."

As am I. He would like to wake now. He looks at me. *I hope to see you again, mate.*

"You will," I tell him, stroking his muzzle. "I know it. Trust in Zale, and he will trust in you."

Relief floods his eyes as if he knows I won't let Zale keep him hidden away now, and with a lick of my hand, he starts to transform. I pull back, watching in awe. His fur melts into his body, his legs straighten into human limbs, and his paws turn to hands. When his shift is complete, the beautiful man I have come to love lies before me, naked with my claw marks still across his chest in three very distinct lines. They are light pink as if they healed and scarred.

His eyes pop open, bright with flames, and lock on me. "Thea," he murmurs, "are you okay?"

"Perfect." I lean in and kiss him. "Thank you for trusting me and trusting yourself." I pull back and drag my fingers lightly across the scars. "I'm sorry about this. We can try and heal them if you wish—"

"No." He captures my hand and lifts it, pressing it to his steadily beating heart. "I wear my mate's marks proudly, and I always will. Scar every inch of me, my love," he says, and his hand cups the bite mark on my neck, and he winces.

"But this is brutal. Nathair, we can heal this, ye—"

I turn his face back to me. "I also wear my mate's marks proudly." I snuggle close and press my head to his chest. He sighs, and both he and Lycus hold me between them, their hands wandering over my curves.

Nathair crouches and smiles at me. "I knew you could do it, *draya*."

I wink, and he looks me over, dragging his tongue across his lips. I shiver and glance at Conall, who smirks at his side, while Osis and Azul watch me hungrily. Reve is leaning back, his hard cock tenting his jeans.

All eyes are on me.

"We should, erm—" Nathair grunts. "Fuck, I don't even know what I was going to say. It smells like sex, your pussy, and blood in here, Althea, and it's driving us all crazy."

The hands wandering across me become rougher and harder with intent. My pussy clenches. If I were human, I'd probably be dead because of Zale's cock last night, but I'm not human. I'm a vampyr, with gifts bestowed by the gods. My body is healed and fully prepped, wanting them.

My mates.

My judges.

I want all of them, knowing everything will change soon. After the ball, nothing will be the same, and right now, I have them. It's just us, and I want them. It's that simple. Their hard bodies vibrate with the need to fuck me, and mine lights up with my desire for my kings.

"Prove it," I say with a smirk, throwing a leg back over Lycus and grinding my ass into his huge hard cock. "Show your queen how badly you want her."

"Is that an order?" He smirks.

"Yes, my king, a plea, an order, whatever will get me what I want."

"Which is?" Conall asks casually.

"All of you, my men. My mates. Your blood, your bodies, your cocks. I want it all."

"So greedy," Lycus rumbles, licking my neck. I moan as he grinds into me.

"Greedy, greedy queen. You want to be fucked."

"Yes."

"You want all of our attention on you?" Reve asks, smirking.

"Yes," I whimper.

"You want every single cock in here? Every single hand and mouth?" Azul asks, cocking his head.

"You want to be claimed by all of your kings?" Osis finishes.

"To be marked?" Zale adds.

Their voices and dirty words have my chest heaving as I nod and close my eyes. "Yes, gods, yes."

"You're our god," Nathair says. "We worship at your altar, so let's show her, shall we?"

"I think she needs it," Lycus murmurs. "She's rubbing against me like a needy girl. If she doesn't behave, I'm going to fuck this tight little ass she's teasing me with before any of you even get naked."

Nathair stands, about to step into the pit, when he hesitates, his eyes going to Zale. "I know you have claimed this as your nest for mating, so I ask permission to enter."

The respect and loyalty in his tone startles Zale, and his eyes widen as he looks around, realising none of the others have or would step into this pit where he holds his mate without asking like Lycus did. His gaze softens as he licks his lips. "Of course. You are my brothers. You are always welcome."

"Thank you." Nathair inclines his head and steps into the pit. He's only wearing that fucking silk robe, but he undoes it, letting it fall open to show his muscular chest. I groan and grind harder into Lycus at the sight of my king.

Just like the first time I saw them, they still steal my breath and make me crazy with need.

"Who do you want first, my queen?" he purrs, but I can't think beyond my need and hunger. "Or would my queen like her kings to take charge? You enjoy it when we use you for our pleasure and take your body without asking. Do you want that, *draya*? Do you want us to fuck you however we want?"

I moan, unable to help it, and he chuckles. "I take that as a yes. You heard her." Nathair slides the silken robe from his shoulders, leaving him naked.

Reve, the show off, doesn't just strip. Instead, he switches the overhead lights off then turns on the sconces, throwing the room into an erotic red glow as sultry music flows through the room. He peels off his loose tank, tossing it away, then his jeans are next, his cock springing free as he circles it with his hand, his tattooed muscles flexing as he watches me. There's another noise, and I look over to see Azul deftly and quickly undressing until he, too, stands naked. I whine and roll my hips between Lycus and Zale.

Lycus nips my beating pulse. "Behave," he warns.

Osis pulls off the low shorts he was wearing, leaving him naked, his cock jerking as I run my needy eyes over him. He grinds his hips in time with the bass rolling through the room. The crooning voice makes me gasp, and my nipples pebble, dragging along Zale's chest as he moves closer.

Conall simply rips his shirt in two and kicks off his trousers, climbing into the pit before Zale covers my lips with his. He kisses me needily as I lie between them. A mouth meets my foot and slides up as my head is turned, my lips pulled from Zale's and pressed to Lycus's. He devours my mouth, his hard cock pressing to my ass. I don't even breathe as they caress and kiss me. I feel more bodies surround me, and then I'm sprawled out on the cushions like a feast. My eyes open as Lycus removes his lips, and I see them all kneeling around me, their eyes on fire.

My judges, my mates.

"We thought you might like this," Nathair says, and he waves his hand. The others do the same, and I gasp as their masks appear on their faces. Desire pulses through me.

I stare up at them like a sacrifice, recalling the very first time I met them.

"Are you going to bleed for us, little one?" one of them asks, his voice echoing with power just like when they judged me. Just like when they killed me.

"Yes," I groan.

I reach up to knead my breasts, but two of them grab my wrists and pin them down. A knife drags down my chest, making me cry out as black lightning trails through my veins.

"Are you willing to spill your secrets and have all of your truths revealed by blood?" another questions.

"Yes." I arch up, and the blade slices a long line down my front. Blood pools on my torso and then begins to drip down my sides.

"Are you ready to die for us, little queen?" another asks.

"Always," I respond without hesitation.

"Are you willing to give us everything?" another demands.

"Yes, I'm yours, every inch of me. Body, mind, and soul."

"I want your heart," another whispers seductively as hands massage my blood into my skin, the power making me whimper.

"It's yours," I reply.

Hands stroke my entire body, avoiding my breasts and pussy where I need them. I'm unable to tell who is who as numerous hands touch me, making me moan and arch up, begging for more. My eyes hazily scan the masks above me, the red lighting only making them more menacing and hot.

If I focus, I can tell them apart, knowing their bodies and masks, but I don't. I let them touch, taste, and fuck me without names. l give into the fantasy of the unknown. I give myself over to them fully.

A mouth covers my nipple, and then another does the same to the other side, sucking and biting in sync as hands shove my thighs open. Two different hands hold my ankles, keeping them parted and wide.

A mouth covers my pussy, and then another, and two tongues drag along my wetness, tasting me. I lift my head to watch the two masked men kneeling between my thighs, and I groan out loud.

The haze of pleasure only continues to increase under their sensual assault and possessive hands. I drown in it, drown in them.

"We accept our sacrifice," one murmurs against my skin. "Before the night is through, we will have claimed your blood, body, and heart."

"Please." A thumb fills my mouth, and I seal my lips around it and suck as someone groans.

I force my eyes open to focus on the masked men surrounding me, worshipping my body. Tongues drag across my pussy, and one dips inside me while another laps at my clit. I wind my hips, riding their faces. Another two work at my nipples, biting and sucking until my desire roars through me, desperate for an outlet.

Hands hold me down and open for them so I can't escape. I have no choice but to take what I'm given, and then the thumb is gone, and a cock replaces it, shoving into my mouth. I suck it down, taking my need out on it as someone moans, deep and long, the sound reverberating around the room.

The sensations overwhelm me, and the cock pulls from my mouth just as my body locks up and I scream, falling into their arms as I come. I squirt into their waiting mouths, shaking as they continue their assault.

They don't let me relax or give up their possession, determined to gain my surrender, but they should already know they have it and me.

Suddenly, I'm jerked up and flipped over onto my hands and knees. A hand grips my hair and yanks my head up, and I meet masked eyes as a cock slams into my mouth, forcing its way to the back of my throat. At the same time, hands drag my hips back and slam my pussy down onto a waiting cock.

I scream around the cock in my mouth.

The abrupt pain fades to pleasure as a mouth continues to attack my nipples. I feel something hard slip across my ass, and then the scent of blood fills the air, making me groan as it drips across me. Hands massage the blood into my ass and part my cheeks before sliding the blood-covered fingers into my ass.

"Fuck, look at that," someone growls.

"Shit, I have to be inside her," another responds. I don't bother distinguishing their voices. I let them weave the spell with their anonymity, and then another cock fills my ass as the one in my mouth begins to move. They work me between them on their cocks, claiming my body as blood is dripped across me and massaged in, making me cry out. Those hard lengths slam into me harder and faster until someone groans and the cock in my pussy jerks, filling me. It's quickly pulled out, and another fills me as the others rut me, hard and fast.

The mouth on my nipples moves, and I whine as my breasts are pushed together from below, and I feel a bloodied cock slide between them. My eyes are blind with pleasure as I'm forced to take them all. I suck the cock in my mouth harder, and a moment later, it slams down my throat, and with a groan, cum splashes in my mouth before they fall away. I reach out blindly, gripping someone's thigh, and then another cock fills my mouth.

"Swallow, baby." It's Reve.

I shiver at his rough treatment of my mouth as he forces it open wider. A hand lands on my ass. "Behave, *draya*." Nathair is in my ass, claiming me as he holds back his own release while the others use me.

My body is dragged back as I cry out. I scrape my fangs over Reve's cock, and he roars his release, forcing me to swallow it as he falls back and another cock takes his place. I don't protest. I swallow them too, desperate for it. I come with a cry, clenching around the cocks inside of me, but none of them stop.

Fangs slam into my side as someone cries out, and I feel their cum splash over my chest. Groaning, I drag my nipples against them as I suck and push back.

I need more. I need them all.

"Good girl, make them all come, make them all yours. They are so desperate for their mate," Nathair growls, grinding into my ass. "Look at you, all covered in our blood. You're so fucking perfect, taking every single judge, every single blood king, and making them yours. Our fucking goddess. Our queen."

"Please," I beg, not even knowing what I'm begging for anymore. The slick sounds of our bodies are too much, even over the music. Their hands, their mouths, their cocks . . . It's all too much, and I explode once more.

I scream, taking them with me.

They roar their releases as they pump my pussy, mouth, and ass with it, staining every inch of me. Our bonds are wide open, and I feel it all. It sends me over the edge once more, and I cry out, making them groan until the pleasure finally stops and I slump. Slowly, their softening cocks slip from my body, but hands pull me into their waiting arms, unbothered about the substances covering me.

"I love you," I tell them. "I love you so much."

"We love you too," Azul answers. "Forever, my queen."

"Our mate," they say as one.

Lifting my head, I watch their masks melt away. My men are strewn around, blood and sweat covering them. I smile, my eyes sliding shut.

They did just what they said.

They claimed me—mind, body, and heart.

I am all theirs.

Forever.

Forty Eight

Nathair

"Thank you again for coming." I am careful with my words around the fey, knowing they can easily use them against me. Names have power, and although they cannot lie, it doesn't stop them from weaving the truth. They are tricky creatures with a penchant for mischief, but they love working with vampyrs and our immortal pockets, and they are the best in the industry, and my queen only gets the best.

"Please set up here." I gesture to the room I brought them to. It's a sitting room with nothing of importance or value they could either steal or sell. "I will fetch our queen."

One giggles as she watches me. Her hair is bright bubblegum pink, and her eyes swirl with magic. She looks like a doll, and she's beautiful, just like all fey are, but I know that appearances are deceiving. She tries to place her hands on my chest, both to flirt and sense my powers, but I step back. "My mate does not like to share. I would not suggest touching anyone you see here unless you would like her nightmares to be unleashed upon you."

She tilts her head knowingly. Despite her innocent appearance, there is a cruel elemental being peering through her eyes. "Of course. We cannot wait to meet her."

I incline my head and look at Reve and Osis. They are the calmest of us all, and they are less likely to give anything away without meaning to. Lycus and Conall struggle with word games, and Zale hates anyone else's presence after mating. "Stay with them and help them if they need it. I will be back."

Do not let them touch you or come near you. Not only does touch give them an edge, but it would upset Althea, I add silently.

Like I would. I don't want their hands on me, only my girl's. Reve snorts.

Never, Osis replies.

With another nod, I leave Reve and Osis behind. Let the fey flirt and play, they will not get what they are after. Despite the fact that we are paying them, they can be easily bribed to tell our secrets, so we are being extra careful.

Decorations have started to arrive, and we have to sort through them and put them all up. There are also some deliveries to retrieve, wine to brew, and food to prepare. There is lots to do, yet when I follow my bond with Althea and find her in my bathroom, nothing else matters. I know she loves it in here. She calls it a gothic cave and says it feels safe and homey, but seeing her in my space makes me weak.

I still at the doorway, my heart lurching at the sight. She is lying in the huge stone tub set before the window looking out over our lands. Candles dot every inch of the room. Her beautiful, tanned leg is thrown over the edge of the tub, and her head is tilted back as she stares at the moon.

"Are you simply going to stare, Nathair?" she asks without looking, and I can't help but smile, feeling pride at how easily she recognises us.

I hurry inside and drop to my knees beside her, knowing if I get into that water filled with black flowers and her silken skin, I will spend hours inside of her, and I won't keep the fey here any longer than necessary. I did not want them here in the first place, but they insisted. She turns her head, her face so beautiful, my mouth goes dry.

"We need you," I say before coughing. "For the fitting."

She laughs, the sound making my soul fly higher. "I better dry off and dress then." She presses her hands to the side of the tub and stands.

I stare up at her in wonder as water flows down her curvy body, leaving me hard and wanting. She peers down at me knowingly. I hurry to my feet and grab a towel and hold out my hand, helping her out. Once she's standing outside of the tub, I wrap her in the towel and pull her closer, unable to resist feeling her heat and curves pressed against me. I grip her chin and pepper her lips with kisses.

"Anything I should know about the fey?" she murmurs. It all occurred so quickly that I haven't had time to teach her everything, and sometimes I forget how truly young my Thea is. She is intelligent and possesses strength beyond her years, but in the ways of our world, she is a child.

"Yes, be careful what you say. They will use your words against you. They want secrets. It's what they trade with. They cannot lie, but they will twist their words and omit the truth if it works for them. They are fickle, powerful creatures, but if you earn their friendship, they are loyal to a fault. They are also more powerful than many know. Most vampyrs simply use the fey, thinking they are lesser because they have fewer numbers and no solid power base like we do, but do not be fools like them. The fey are a very powerful and ancient race. Respect that, and they will respect you."

"Got it. You respect them, huh?" she asks, her head tilted back to meet my eyes.

"I do. Like us, they were abused and used throughout the years. Their powers were stolen or kept under control. They deserve their freedom." I grin. "Just not with my secrets. I got drunk with a fey once, and he found out I have silk robes. Now I'm a laughingstock at that bar."

She laughs again, and it makes me grin.

"Get dressed, my love, and I will escort you and warn them to behave." I step back.

"Who will make sure I behave?" she teases.

I look back to see her smirking, alight with her power. "No one makes you behave, my queen."

My girl dresses in a long, flowing, red-silk dress and matching panties, and it's driving me wild as I clasp her hand and lead her back to the fey. Her hair is dry and hanging around her shoulders. She has no makeup, no bra, shoes, or crown on, but one look at her, and you would know who and what she is.

Pure power.

She glows from within, practically radiating with power, so when I step into the room, it's no surprise when the fey turn and their mouths drop open. The woman with the pink-haired fey is the main designer, Tinie. Her hair is choppy on top—the only fey I have ever seen purposely massacre their famous locks. Her bright-purple eyes are tilted up, and she's tall and willowy like most fey, but she's almost serious.

Almost.

Another helper, whose name I don't know, is flitting around. This one has long bright-green hair with matching makeup, including her lips. She's the shortest and clearly the youngest. Tinie heads our way, looking at Althea and no one else.

"I heard rumours that there was a new queen, but they didn't tell me you were a goddess." Althea jerks, and Tinie smiles. "I will not ask, so you do not have to lie to me."

Althea smiles fully. "I love your hair."

Tinie winks. "A man once tried to use me for it, so I got rid of it."

"Good for you. A man once tried to break my heart, so I gave it to seven others instead." She and Tinie share a secret smile, and then Tinie turns to me.

"Your queen will be fine. You can leave. We will not play with her too much," she jokes.

I narrow my gaze. "I appreciate your talents and business, but if I find out—"

"Yes, yes, probably a very frightening threat. Shall we begin, Althea? We do not have a lot of time."

Grinning, Althea turns to me and kisses me fully. "I will be fine. Go, you have lots to do." She taps her head, letting me know I can check in on her at any time, and then follows Tinie and is instantly surrounded by the other fey, who pick up her hands or hair and ooh and aww.

I groan, rubbing at my face, positive this was a bad idea, but I have to trust her, and she can call out if she needs me. I jerk my head, and the others follow me out, leaving our Althea to deal with the tricky fey.

Gods help her, she will need it.

FORTY NINE

ALTHEA

"TINIE?" I QUESTION.

She turns towards me and smiles. Her expression seems softer and more welcoming. I've met fey before. They are beautiful, deadly creatures, but I respect them.

I do know a few rules about fey—never ask their age, and never make a deal—and now, with what Nathair told me, I struggle to form a sentence that will not offend them or get me into trouble. She notices and softens further.

"We mean you no harm, vampyr queen." It's a vow, a promise, and my shoulders slump as I relax. I offer her my own unguarded smile.

"Good, I'm tired of being stabbed in the back," I admit.

"I have a feeling that is true," she says as she looks at the others. "Fetch the garments. We have created a basic silhouette. It will be big and long, but we will shape it to your body and infuse it with our magic, then we can figure out the smaller details. Is that okay? We will have to touch you and get very close."

"It's okay with me if it is with you," I reply. I make sure to lock down as much of my mind as I can, as well as my power. I don't want to give anything away, but I also don't want to insult her.

She blinks as if she feels my intention, and a true smile blooms on her face. "Thank you. Many simply make us suffer through the touch with their thoughts and memories beating at us alongside their power. It is taxing to hold it back."

I blink, and the green-haired fey laughs. "She thinks we use touch to gather secrets."

"We do sometimes," Tinie admits without shame, "but not very often, and it truly can be exhausting."

"I am sorry. Please let me know if I can make this easier," I respond, frowning at her. I hate the pain I see in her eyes. Does it physically hurt them to work their magic while fighting off the intentions of the wearer? How draining for them. No wonder they are cautious.

"Do not fret, for we know some do not do it on purpose."

"Some do," Pinkie says. "They like to watch us struggle. They want us to know how powerful they are. It's almost like a challenge. We have been punished once or twice for accidentally seeing what we should not have, even though they were pushing it into our heads."

I feel my brows draw together, my fangs lengthening. "They are fucking idiots and do not deserve your work."

"I like her." Green-haired smiles. "I'm Sereith."

Pink-haired nods. "And I am Wista."

"It is nice to meet you," I tell them honestly. "I'm excited to work with you."

"As are we. It's not often we dress a queen. Nathair didn't tell us much, so what style do we want?" Tinie asks, eyeing my body.

"Sexy." I pause. "It needs to show how powerful we are, while also showing our wealth and how unbothered we are by their presence. We also need to be better dressed than any of them. This is the first time they will see us, so it needs to be a showstopper."

They all grin as they step before me. "I think we can handle that. Don't you, ladies?"

"Oh, definitely." Wista giggles, and Sereith winks at me as she eyes my figure.

"She's got the body for it."

"That she does." Tinie winks. "Okay, Althea, let's get to work."

I stand before them in nothing but a thong, but they never make me feel uncomfortable. In fact, they make me feel beautiful. They constantly compliment me, oohing and ahhing over my skin, my curves, and my hair. I smile bigger than I ever have, and they seem to relax and become more comfortable around me.

I feel Nathair and the others checking in mentally, but I shoo them away. I'm fine, and I want the dress to be a surprise.

"What's it like being fey?" I ask softly as they work around me. I can't see what they are doing, but I feel material being dropped, touched, and pulled as their magic flows across them. Every now and again, they step back and talk to one another before moving back to me.

Unlike some who would shoot out a response, Tinie seems to consider her words as she plays with the material at my side.

"In some ways, it's great. We have a lot of freedoms that other races do not. There are a lot of judgements and preconceptions about us, though, that make other races quick to judge us and believe we are untrustworthy. It can be lonely. There are not as many of us left as there used to be. Some of us reject the new world and have faded away into nature. A lot of our elders and most powerful fey did that, while some stay out of duty or fear," she answers. "Sometimes, I envy you vamps with your courts because you have friends, families and lovers so close for help, comfort, or protection."

"It can be lonely too," I admit, and she lifts her head, giving me her full attention as I speak. "I only had one person I would call a friend, and in the end, it didn't matter because when it came down to it, he couldn't protect me." I look away for a moment. "I won't lie. Since I have found this court and my men, I've never been happier, but before, even with the manor filled with people, I was often lonely and misunderstood. It was like they were waiting for me to make a mistake, and it was hard to even learn who I was."

"I guess we all have our burdens to bear." Tinie grasps my hand and squeezes. "I am glad you found your happiness here. They seem like good men. We should know. We feel intentions."

"They are," I reply without hesitation. "They may be some of the only good ones left in my race."

"Not just yours." She smiles, but there's pain behind it.

For the next few hours, I stand and let them work. They talk to me about everything and anything, including me, and I laugh as much as they do. Despite us being two very different species, it seems we all share the same love for classic action movies and hot guys, and it's nice to have some girl time.

A while later, with my back starting to ache, they step away and nod, and I know they are finished.

"It's perfect," Wista says.

"Stunning," Serian agrees.

"It's the best work we have ever done," Tinie concludes.

"Spell a mirror," she orders, and the others hurry to do just that as she approaches me, turning me to face the girls who are conjuring something. She moves around the back, fixing the skirt as excitement pours through me. I block the guys because I want them to be surprised.

"Althea?" Tinie questions from behind me. I turn and smile at her. "My true name is Lilia. Only my friends know it, and I offer it to you freely. Never has someone shown us such respect or kindness in such a short amount of time. What they say is true. If you earn our loyalty, we are yours, and you have earned mine. I will come if you call. You have a friend in me."

"I'd like that," I say truthfully.

"Good." She smiles, and then she turns me to face a mirror where Wista and Serian are waiting with excited expressions.

I get the first glimpse of their work.

"I look . . ." I stare at my reflection in awe.

The dress looks black at first, but as I move, it shimmers with red, like there are jewels inside the material. Its long sleeves show off my shapely arms and circle over my shoulders and down across my breasts. It's cut low, all the way to my stomach, with plenty of cleavage on display, but it holds up the girls and pushes them together so they look good. The dress dips in at my stomach, hugging my curves, and then it flares out at my wide hips, trailing behind me on the floor. My legs show through two slits up each side, all the way to my hips, and metal work crawls across the shoulders and top like armour.

"Powerful. Beautiful. Sexy. Desired. You look like a queen. Add a crown and some jewels, and you will be the best dressed vampyr ever."

I turn to her and take her hands. "I cannot thank you enough, friend. I mean it. I look how I feel, if that makes sense."

"It does. Our magic works with what we have, and it uses you as its conduit. This is who you are. We are simply showing the world."

Wista grins. "You will be the best dressed vamp ever."

"Thanks to you three." I look at them then. "I cannot begin to express how much this means. I know Nathair is paying you, but is there anything I can do?"

"Your friendship is enough," Tinie, Lilia, offers, and I hear the truth in her words. "I'm sure we will see each other again, but until then, Althea, wear the dress with pride, and remember its power comes from you, from within, so show them exactly who they are messing with."

My eyes widen, and she smiles. "We might not pry, but we know everything from other vamps. Many have hired us recently for new outfits for a ball being held . . . here. We did not come to spy, so do not worry. I came because I was intrigued. Any person who can cause that much of a stir within the other courts? Well, it had to be one hell of a person, and it is." The others nod. "Whatever is coming your way, remember that they are scared of you and this place. They won't show it, but we felt it. They fear what is in the air, what you represent. I wish I could help you more, but know this: the fey will always come to your call."

Fifty

Reve

It's the night before the ball, and everyone is off completing a million tasks with Nathair as the taskmaster to ensure it is all perfect, but I sneak away. I have a plan of my own in my head.

I find her outside with her monsters, and I still as I watch her. She sits cross-legged as she talks to a dragon, laughing at something he said. Over the last week, she has befriended many of them, and they grow bolder, coming into the court sometimes. We eagerly welcomed them, and Nathair loved having the place filled once more. He even started cleaning out the rest of the rooms in case any would like to stay—not to mention the room they have been fixing up for Simon now that Zale has agreed to be around the werewolf when he comes to see his mate.

She turns like she feels my gaze, and the smile she bestows upon me stops my heart for a moment. When she looks away, freeing me from her gaze, I rub at the aching organ. It was hers from the very start. She might have been the one whose heart was carved out, but that knife cut both ways, and if she wanted it, I would rip it from my chest and give it to her.

Standing elegantly, she bows to the dragon who, with another look at me, wanders back into the forest. Althea strides towards me on bare feet, her hair curling loosely around her shoulders. She's wearing nothing but one of Conall's long dress shirts, and I actually drop to my knees. She just makes me feel the need to worship her.

She's so fucking beautiful and perfect. I need to crawl to her and prove it. She cocks her head to the side when she stops before me. "Don't get me wrong, baby, I like seeing you on your knees, especially when you're eating my pussy" —she smirks as I stare up at her— "but are you okay?"

"I just forgot how to breathe for a moment," I murmur as I stare at her, my plan seeming stupid. Her hand comes down, and I take it, letting her pull me to my feet as I stare into those bright, knowing eyes. "I wanted to show you something and steal you away for a little bit."

The slow smile she gives me makes my cock jerk, and I swallow hard. "Lead the way," she says, and without waiting, I turn and sneak her through the court.

We have to pause when Zale and Osis come into view, carrying a massive stone archway. Nathair is behind them, barking orders. Covering her mouth, I pin Althea there as she giggles behind my hand. They all stop and cock their heads, knowing that sound, but when they don't see her, they move on.

I tug her after me. I want her alone, so I quickly lock us in my room and turn to her.

"Close your eyes and don't open them until I say so, baby." Without hesitation, she shuts them and stands in the middle of my room, waiting. Closing my own, I curate the idea in my head and then open them, my powers flowing out. She gasps when it touches her but continues to wait with her eyes shut.

I tweak it a little then step closer, turning her so her back is to me. My hands shake from the nerves I feel. I love Althea with everything in me, and I know she loves me too. The bond we share cannot be shattered or broken, but in some ways, we are still learning things about each other, and in others, we know everything down to our souls. Still, I want to make her happy, and sharing this with someone else is a big thing for me.

"Open," I croak.

I know the moment she does because she jerks against me. "Reve!" she exclaims, looking around at the world I have created for us. It's our own slice of paradise. Stars shine brightly above us, the full moon is close enough to touch, and the ground is grass.

"I often come here to find peace. I wanted to bring you here and show you a place nearly as beautiful as you. How could I ever create anything even halfway as beautiful as you?" I whisper to her as she turns to look at me. "But I tried to show you the beauty of this world and make it perfect for you. Tonight, there is only us and the stars. There are no judges, no roles, no gods, just us."

She cups my face and kisses me softly, making me melt against her. "It's perfect. You are perfect." She looks around, marvelling at what I have created. She reaches out as a lightning bug floats past, then she giggles as it lands on her palm. It takes to the air again, and she watches it go as I watch her.

I watch the woman I am completely in love with, and I feel the need to tell her and make her understand just how much. I might have been saved a long time ago, but my soul was never free until her. It's strange, since she's now the one who holds it captive.

"No matter how our lives may have gone, I always would have found you," I tell her honestly. "I wouldn't have been able to rest if I didn't. You were always mine. We were all just waiting right here for you. Our queen, our love. I cannot do anything but thank the man who turned you onto this course because you were never his, Althea. You were always ours. I would have stolen you from him had you mated him. I would have killed him where he stood for even thinking he had a claim on you, on what is mine."

Her eyes water as she looks at me, and I lean in and lick the red tears away, tasting her blood. "You were made for us, Althea, and we were made for you. No matter what happens after, we have this. We have our happiness, and we have tonight." I step back unwillingly, my hand sliding through hers. "What shall we do with it?"

"I can think of a few things," she murmurs, and as I watch, she pushes her borrowed shirt down, leaving her completely bare as it puddles at her feet. The world around her shakes for a moment, my concentration breaking at the sight, and she grins. "Keep this world up, my love." She strokes her fingers across my face. "I would have found you too. I was always missing something. It was you, all of you. Each of you hold a piece of my heart, and no one will take that from us. Let me show you how much I love you and the world you have created for us." She drops to her knees before me.

My eyes widen. "No, I didn't bring you here—"

She shushes me as she unzips my trousers and shoves them down. I step from them, and my shirt is removed next. I'm as naked as her as she sits back on her perky haunches, her tongue catching on her fang as she groans. The appreciation and hunger I see in her gaze causes me to shudder, and my cock jerks in anticipation of her touch.

"I love you, Reve." She says it like she knows I need to hear it, and maybe I do. Maybe I did all this because I needed her to myself so badly, but she sees it. Smiling at me, she grips my cock. My head falls back with a moan before I drag it upright to see her.

My goddess is on her knees before me, worshipping me.

Her lover.

The moon shines brightly behind her, the world vivid and beautiful for her. Her tongue swipes down my cock, and she keeps her eyes on me the entire time as she makes sure not one inch of my cock is left untouched. Pleasure slams through me, shaking the world around me. I lock my legs and try to stop myself from thrusting as she licks up my hard, veiny cock and seals her lips around my tip.

I can't stop my groan as my hips jerk. Smirking, she pulls back and drags her tongue through my slit, tasting me. The sight is so erotic, I nearly spill there and then.

She drags her tongue over my tip, lapping at me. "Althea," I beg, reaching down and grabbing her hair. "Please."

"I've got you," she murmurs. "I've always got you." She sucks my tip into her mouth and swallows me down, cautious of her fangs.

Pleasure courses through me.

I lose all sense of the world, becoming lost in the wet, hot cavern of her mouth that's wrapped so perfectly around my cock. The slight edge of danger and pain from her fangs as she drags them back and forth along my cock makes me desperate. I thrust into her mouth as my balls draw up and heat gathers in my spine.

Humming around my cock, she sucks me down so good it hurts. Her other hand cradles my balls, massaging them, and I don't stand a chance. My powers go haywire around us, the vision straining at the edges and contracting like a heartbeat. It goes completely insane all because of her, and she knows it. She sucks me deep and hard, holding me at the back of her throat before pulling up and doing it again.

"I'm going to come, baby," I warn, but she tightens her grip on my cock, meeting my eyes as she sucks me harder, intent on making me come, and she does. I shatter with a hoarse yell, my hips jerking as I pump my cum down her throat. The world I created explodes around us, my power slamming into us. I cry out again at the force, and she whimpers, licking and sucking down every drop of my cum. I shake, about to fall as she leans back and cleans every inch of my cock. Her lips are bruised and raw as she grins at me.

I fall to my knees before her, grabbing her head as I drag her to me. I kiss her hard, tasting my release, and she drops back. I climb over her, opening her legs with my own.

Lifting my head, I look around us. "If you give me a minute, I can recreate it," I tell her. My powers have never done that before. I could hold them during anything, including torture, but Thea?

Never.

I didn't stand a chance.

"I don't need it. I just need you like this," she murmurs, reaching up to pull me down for another kiss.

My hands slide over her skin, touching her as she caresses my shoulders before she drags her nails up and through my hair. I whimper into her mouth, and she swallows it, wrapping her legs around my waist and dragging her pussy along my cock.

She's so wet.

I jerk back and look down. "Baby, you're fucking dripping." I meet her gaze. "Is it from sucking me? Fuck, Althea."

"You taste so good," she purrs, thrusting her chest into the air, so I lower my head and take her offering, sucking her pretty little nipples until she clenches her legs around me. "You felt so good, I almost came just from sucking your cock."

"Show me," I demand breathlessly. "Come for me, come for your mate with his taste still in your mouth."

Groaning, she grinds her pussy against my cock, and I watch her face transform. Her lips part on a pant, her body begins to shake, and then with a gush of power and cream, she comes for me. I kiss her, swallowing her moan as I grip her pussy between us to feel her pulse for me.

When she slumps back, I lift her legs and wrap the shaking limbs around my neck, pressing to her pussy. When her eyes flutter open, I slide inside of her slowly, unable to wait anymore. I need to feel her cunt wrapped around me and to complete our bond. We both cry out, her tight cunt still pulsing and gripping me as I slide home, where I belong. My eyes almost cross at the feeling.

"Baby, you're going to make me come again." I fall down, pressing my forearm to the floor and hitting that spot inside her that has her jerking. Her nails dig into my shoulders and drag me closer. The bite of pain makes me groan once more, and then I start to move, slowly sliding out of her pussy and back in. She's so perfect, I can barely breathe through my need to hammer into her and stay there forever.

Her hands slide down my back and grip my ass, feeling it flex as I slowly make love to her on the stone floor. Our bodies move, and our bond snaps tightly together.

Our lips meet in a tangle of tongues as we slowly come together, soft and slow and loving. It's a perfect union, and our bodies wind and coil until neither of us can take it anymore. Locked together, minds, souls, and hearts, our bodies splinter.

My cum fills her as she squeezes me with her own release. Blood from our fangs fill each other's mouths, and I swallow that too. It fills my bleeding heart.

We become one, and we are so tightly connected, we could never be without the other.

When we finally come down from the high, I lie across her chest, unable to breathe or move. She pants below me, stroking my back as her pussy flutters around my rapidly hardening length.

I can't take it. Grunting, I lift up and grin down at her. "Better hold on, baby. You got soft, and now you get hard."

"I can't wait." She grins before lifting up and kissing me then gripping my hair and yanking my head back, exposing my neck. "Fuck me hard, mate, while I feed on what's mine. I'll leave a mark for them all to see tomorrow so they know exactly whom you belong to."

"Fuck yes, do that," I beg as I slide out and thrust back into her. She groans, her pussy clenching tightly around me, and I have to grit my teeth against the feeling and fight the need to flood her with my cum once more. She's just that fucking perfect and goddamn sexy.

Slamming into her, I anchor us with my hands to stop us from moving with the force. Her eyes close in bliss, and her nails slice my back, causing rivulets of blood to slide down it. The pain and pleasure makes me snarl and pummel into her. She cries out, tears forming in her eyes from the force.

I can't help but roar when she sits up and slams her fangs into my neck, ripping it open and feasting on my blood. It covers us, but I still don't stop. I take her hard and fast until she convulses below me and screams. I watch her face contort in ecstasy as her pussy clamps on my cock with her release.

And I still don't stop, wanting to imprint on her forever.

I wrap my arms around her and stand, bouncing her on my cock as she wails. I turn to the bed with a smirk, my own blood still dripping steadily from the wound in my neck.

Throwing her onto the edge of the bed, I pull out and flip her before slamming home. I catch her thighs and push her head down as I take her hard and fast, snarling as my blood drips across her back and perky ass. I watch my hard cock slam inside of her, and it makes me even more wild for her.

My mate, my queen.

I know I will never get enough of this. Every time I have her, my obsession gets worse. I will spend our long, immortal lives buried inside her tight little cunt, worshipping my mate.

Her claws shred my bedding as she pushes back to take me. I fist her hair, yanking it up as I drag my fangs along her neck. Her perky little ass slaps against me with every thrust. I can't take it. I need her blood, I need her cum, and I need it now.

Tilting her up, I hammer my cock into that spot inside of her that makes her scream. I control her with my hand in her hair, and when it becomes too much, I slam my fangs into her neck. The flavour of her blood explodes in my mouth and sends me over the edge.

Her own screams fill the air as I pump her full of my cum, and she covers my dick with hers.

It's never-ending as I feed, my cum splashing inside of her until she whimpers as another release rolls through her. I feel it in our bond, and when I can't take any more, I pull my fangs free.

She collapses forward, and I gently pull my cock from her clenching pussy. My cum spills from it, so I push my hand back into her cunt and keep it there as she whimpers.

Leaning down, I lap at the wound on her throat. Her eyes are closed, and she has a blissful smile on her lips. "I love you forever, Althea."

"I'll love you until the end, Reve," she whispers back, her voice hoarse from screaming for me. A smug smile curves my lips as I climb up onto the bed and pull her into my arms where she belongs.

We lie in a pool of our blood and cum, our limbs tangled and breathing heavy. We share a knowing, loving look, and I can't help but grin as I reach over and push a sweaty, bloody tendril of hair from her face. "They will find us soon. I'm so glad we got this time with just us."

"So am I," she murmurs. "Hold me until they find us." She snuggles into my arms, and I close my eyes, sending up thanks to my family and the gods for making this woman and bringing her to me.

For giving me my heart back.

FIFTY ONE

ALTHEA

"I HAVE A SURPRISE for you," I tell Simon, covering his eyes as I nudge him forward. He's moving in.

He'll split his time between here and his mate's pack, and although the court won't handle it well, I'll make sure they don't exact their revenge on him. Part of me is so thrilled to have my best friend here, even though part of me worries what it will do to Zale, but he promised he can handle it.

While the party preparations have been taking place, I've been busy in here, making Simon's rooms a home for him.

"You know I hate surprises," he grumbles. "Like that time you convinced me you threw me a party, but I ended up tied to a tree in a field, covered in glitter."

"Which is exactly how you would have ended up had we thrown a party." I giggle, feeling like a teenager again. There's something about being around Simon that makes me feel free, young, and happy without responsibilities or power. To him, I haven't changed and I'm still me, Althea.

The girl who used to wake him when she had nightmares about clowns.

I lead him farther into the wing that, before now, was locked and abandoned. Nathair's only stipulation was that he was placed far enough from our rooms so he couldn't hear us having "raunchy, wicked sex," which was a good point, so at the moment, Simon nearly has a full wing to himself.

I nudge the door open with my boot and lead him inside, only stopping once we are in the middle of the room. I quickly scan the space before relaxing my hands. "Welcome home, Simon," I murmur as I drop them from his eyes. "Feel free to change anything, but I wanted you to have a home here, a safe space," I babble. "It's all been cleaned, and I did some decorating. Nathair says he can update anything you want."

My heart thunders as I look around once more to see what he is seeing for the first time. The rooms here all have the same cosy gothic feeling I love, and I know Simon loves that too, so I only enhanced it. The black and gold chandelier was already here, so I left it. I placed a fur rug across the stone floor, and the four-poster bed now drips in red and black silk sheets and pillows, with a fur throw over it. To the left are matching black side tables with candles to throw off a cosy light. Above each nightstand is an ornate black mirror I found in the other rooms. To the left is a balcony that overlooks the grounds, with two chairs and a table out there for him and his mate. Through the archway to the left is a bathroom. It still needs a little updating, but the stone walls were perfect to hang plants and add lights. It has a huge bathtub, and I added a gold mirror. Through the second door is a sitting room and a dressing room. Both need to be updated, but for now, I managed to wrangle in a red Chesterfield sofa and matching chairs. Overall, there's plenty of room to expand and add his own touches. I focused mainly on the bedroom and placed pictures of us on side tables.

Above the fire is a painting of a wolf howling at the moon—I couldn't resist. Nervous energy fills me as I fidget and let him take in the room.

"Well?" I bite my lip, watching as he turns in place, looking around.

He turns back to me, his eyes filled with bloodied tears. "Thea," is all he says before he wraps me in his arms, enveloping me in his safe embrace. I bury my head in his neck, and we just hold each other for a bit before he pulls back, grinning at me. "You didn't have to do all this, but I love it."

"Really?" I almost slump in relief. "Like I said, we can change anything. Nathair has contacts everywhere. But I wanted you to have a place where you are always welcome." I bite my lip, and he frowns, tugging on my hand as he leads me to the bed. We sit side by side like we have so many times before.

"I didn't need all this. I love it, but I didn't need it to know I was welcome here, Thea." He watches me carefully. "What's going on?"

"What? Nothing." I jerk.

"Althea, I have known you since you learned how to walk and talk. Something is wrong. Tell me, let me help. I might not be designed by the gods to save our race, but I'm a good listener, and I will do anything to make you happy and keep you safe. Tell me," he implores, holding my hand tight.

I search his face, noticing he looks older.

Was it really that long ago when we sat like this in a different room and whispered our hopes and dreams to each other? Our world has changed so much, yet here he is, holding my hand, ready to help in any way he can.

I couldn't love him more.

I chose my family, I chose him, and I always will. No matter where our lives lead us, Simon will always be with me. Even when I died, he was there. He's right. I need to tell him. I didn't know my own worries until they start to spill from my lips.

"I just didn't want you to think I moved on without you and that there was no place for you in my life," I admit. "Or in yours for me. I know you're mated and will eventually move in with him and the wolves and probably won't spend as much time with me or here, but—"

"Thea, you will always be my family. Being mated will not change that. Nothing can ever stay the same because we grow and change, but this bond between us never will. It will always remain and just adapt to the new circumstances." He holds me closer. "We are family, aren't we?"

"Always," I reply without hesitation, my voice hoarse.

"No matter what, it's you and me, Thea. Even death couldn't break that, and nothing else will. Yes, our lives are changing, but that doesn't mean we won't be in each other's. It just means there is more to tell each other about. We're not kids anymore, Thea." I laugh then, and he grins, flashing his fangs. "As much as I wish I could go back to the days when we would burrow under the duvet and gossip about who we like, we have to grow up, and you, Thea? You have grown up into a magnificent person, into a leader, a queen, and I'm honoured to be part of that life. Do not worry about me being in your life, Thea, or the other way around. There is no life without you. We are family and always have been. Just like they were destined to be yours, I was destined to be your brother."

Tears spill down my cheeks, matching his own.

"I love you. You're right," I tell him. "There will always be a place in my life for you. I can't wait to be part of yours."

"Me too," he murmurs and brushes my tears away, making me grin. "Now, how about for old times' sake, we gossip? Tell me about your mates' cocks. I'm betting they are big, right?" He wiggles his eyebrows, making me tumble back with a giggle. "I knew it!" he shouts, bouncing around to lie next to me. "Who's the biggest?"

Me, obviously, Conall says in my head.

No, duh, I am, Reve adds.

Shut up, all of you. She is trying to have some time with her brother. Leave her alone, Lycus snaps, and then softly adds, *but I definitely have the biggest penis. You can tell him that, and that I keep you very, very satisfied.*

Laughing, I block them all out, and Simon watches me with a confused frown. "They are talking about cocks in my head," I share, and he grins.

"Feel free to invite them to come here and argue about that. We could even do a show and tell." He flutters his hand across his face dramatically. "They are all so hot, but you know I like the big brutes."

"I know. Remember that meathead you dated from Vermillion Court?"

Simon gags as I cackle and roll over.

"He was so dumb."

"He had a huge cock, Althea. I am only a man, after all, so I'm weak," he whines. "And what about the cocky little fuck you dated? What was his name? Chad?"

"Chief." I cough with a cringe. "If I gagged him, it was good. He was so pretty, Simon." I turn my head, and we both burst into laughter.

"You better be talking about me," Nathair says, and we lift our heads to see him in the doorway.

"Nope. One of Thea's exes. Jealous?" Simon grins.

"Very," he murmurs, looking at me possessively. "Do I need to track this . . . Chief down, *draya*?"

"Maybe. He sure was pretty," I tease.

Pushing from the door, Nathair prowls closer and doesn't stop until his fists press into the bedding next to my hips, and he leans over me. "Just remember I'm prettier, and I will also cut out the heart of anyone who so much as looks at you, my queen. Unless you want him dead, maybe forget about him, but just to make sure, you can ride my pretty face later until you do."

"Gods damn." Simon groans next to me. "I'm sorry, but that's so hot, I have a boner. I need to go find my mate and make him all growly and jealous." Simon slides from the bed. "No fucking on my sheets, you heathen!" he calls as he jogs out of the door, and Nathair and I share a knowing grin.

"I'll buy him new ones. Fuck, I'll buy him a whole new fucking bed since I'm going to break it," Nathair promises. "Now, what were you saying about this other man, Althea?"

"You." I grin. "And Chief, he had these lips—"

His mouth slams onto mine, and my giggle turns into a moan as he dominates my mouth. His tongue lashes mine, licking at my fangs before he pulls back, leaving me groaning beneath him.

"What were you saying?" he murmurs, his eyes bright with mirth.

"Erm, lips, he had good lips—"

My head is turned, so he sinks his fangs into my neck. A scream escapes my throat as he pulls back, dripping blood over me as it dribbles down his chin.

"And these hands—"

"Thea," he warns as he growls. "I might be the oldest one here, but when it comes to you, I am anything but calm. If you keep winding me up, you'll find out just what I'm capable of when I need to reclaim my bratty mate."

"Then show me." I smile as I stroke his shoulders and back. "As I was saying, his hands—"

I don't get to finish my sentence. I'm flipped, and my face is smashed into the bedding. My leggings are yanked down, my thong too, and then his hand comes down hard on my ass cheeks. I yell and try to move forward to escape another blow. His other arm locks around me, holding me there as his hand, with all his immortal strength, punishes me.

"What were you saying, my love?" he purrs, his voice hard and demanding.

My ass cheeks sting with the force of his hits, but the pain warms to pleasure as I push back, my pussy clenching in need.

"His hands—" I gasp, trying to remember what I was saying.

"Like these?" His hand comes down again and again, this time across my pussy. The sharp sting makes me scream and fall forward, but he yanks me back up. "Words, Althea," he orders. "Did his hands do this to you?" Once more, he spanks my pussy, and cream gushes from me as I rock back into his blows.

"Althea," he growls, waiting.

"Yes, no, I don't know," I rasp. "He had big hands—"

"As big as mine?" he snaps as he brings his big hand back down once more across my pussy. The sharp sting pushes me higher, and I find myself rocking back into the air, desperate for another slap. "Answer me, Althea," he demands, rubbing my raw clit. "Were his hands better than mine?"

"Yes!" I mutter, and it gets me what I want. His palm slams onto my pussy, hitting my clit so hard that I shatter. I scream my release into Simon's bedding as he rubs my clit until I'm whimpering and trying to escape. It's too much.

"Well, did he make you come from punishing you, *draya*? Did he make you so wet it coated your thighs? Did he make you come without even sliding into that wet heat and fingering you with his big hands?"

"No, no." I shake my head, unsure if I want more or less.

"I didn't think so. Now, what else was he good at? We will work through the list one at a time until he is completely forgotten. You mentioned his lips, correct?"

I whine. I can't help it.

"Words, Althea, or I will guess, and you will not like it. Lips, yes?"

"Yes," I whimper, clutching the bedding.

Humming, he slides down my body, his lips following the marks caused by his hands, and I whimper and push back. Gripping my hips, he yanks them higher before splaying my wet pussy open for him.

"So wet, *draya*. You are dripping for your mate. Did you drip for him?"

"No," I admit, and he rewards me by sealing his lips around my clit and sucking hard. My back bows as pleasure claws at me. Just when I'm about to come, he releases me, making me cry out. He presses kisses to my pussy.

"Did his lips bring you pleasure?" he murmurs against my skin as I rock back, needing to come so badly.

"Yes. Why don't you see if you can beat him?" I challenge.

Chuckling, he presses his fingers inside me. "I can feel you gripping me, *draya*. You are so close, yet you dare me?" His lips press to my clit once more. "Challenge accepted, mate."

With his fingers still inside me, he begins to suck on my clit. The scrape of his fangs against my sensitive flesh mixes with pleasure as I rock back and forth. The pleasure grows within me, becoming stronger and stronger until it's too much, and I come all over his mouth with a scream.

Pulling his lips from my clit, he laps at my pussy and cream before pulling his fingers free.

"What else, Althea?" he demands, sliding up my body. His big hand fists my hair and yanks it until my ass is pressed against his throbbing erection.

"His cock," I reply, needing his so badly, I'll play along. "His cock was so good—"

He surges inside of me, his massive cock splitting me open as I scream. All words are forgotten, and pleasure tumbles over me until I come all over my mate's cock, and yet he still doesn't let up. He pulls out and hammers back into me, punishing me and showing me who is here right now.

"Who's pretty now, Althea?" he questions with a growl, the sting in my hair making me groan as he uses it to pull and push me on his huge dick.

"You, you, you," I chant, unable to take this game anymore. "Please, Nathair, please."

He keeps up his pace, claiming my pussy. Each thrust slides along those nerves that have me crying and convulsing. It's too much, and it's not enough. I can't even think. I can't see or breathe past it. I need . . . I need . . .

"Whom do you belong to, Althea?"

"You!" I scream, and he chuckles against my skin, knowing exactly what he's doing. Two can play at that game though. Pushing back, I clench around his cock until he moans. The sound goes straight to my engorged clit.

"Althea," he warns.

I do it again, pushing back to take his big dick deeper, and with a snarl, he pushes my head down and fucks me for real, giving me exactly what I needed. Our bodies slap together as he tweaks my nipples harshly before sliding his hand lower through my messy cunt and pinching my clit.

It sends me over the edge once more, and I squeeze his cock hard, milking it as I thrash from the force of the pleasure. His mind crashes into mine.

Mine, mine, mine, mine.

With a roar, he stills, his cock jerking inside me as he fills me with his cum. He slides out to the tip then hammers back in, continuing to spill inside me until we both groan and another release takes me.

I slump forward, giving up.

I'm boneless, and I can't move.

"What was his name, Althea?" he purrs in my ear, wrapping me in his arms.

"I don't remember," I murmur, and I don't.

Only Nathair.

"Good girl," he praises. "Now feed, my mate. Claim me," he says as he offers me his wrist.

Whimpering, I sink my fangs into his flesh. With a roar, he pumps his cum inside of me once more. His blood and semen fill me at the same time, claiming me fully.

"Ashes to ashes, dust to dust, blood is thick between us," he whispers.

Fifty Two

Osis

"It's time to call your monsters, my queen, and warn them," I murmur as I watch Althea flit around. Nathair won't let her help much because he wants to surprise her as much as everyone else. Plus, she has done enough. She is so strong and powerful, but she does not have to do this all alone.

Pushing from the wall, I catch her in my arms as she passes and whirl her around.

"I need to help—"

"Nope." I lean down and distract her by kissing her, but it soon turns into me groaning and pushing her to the wall. Our tongues tangle, and her leg hitches up, wrapping around my hip as I rip up her shirt and cup her breast. I crave her and her curves, and desire hammers through me. We finally pull apart, panting. Her eyes are unfocused when they blink open, and I smirk triumphantly at the scent of her desire perfuming the hall.

"Really? Do you know how hard it is to climb around the ceiling with a hard-on?" Zale mutters, and we turn to see them all watching.

"Oops." She grins but winks at me. "Okay, let's go."

I let her lead me outside. The ball is tomorrow, and we need to warn the monsters about what is to come. Plus, it will allow Nathair to put on the finishing touches without her seeing.

As soon as we are outside, she kicks off her shoes and sinks her toes into the grass, tipping her head back. After connecting to the earth, she moves towards the forest and stands there. "They are watching," she murmurs. Some venture closer, and I nod to them in acknowledgment. They are still creatures of the night—nightmares, if you will—and she is the love of my life, so I am cautious, but there is nothing but wonder and respect in the air.

"The ball is tomorrow. You do not have to attend for long, simply seeing you will be enough. If it is too hard, we understand, but I will not allow any to hurt you," she calls. "This is your home, now and forever, so show them that. If you need us, the door is always open. We cannot help but thank you again."

They slink from the forest. Some simply incline their heads or bow, and some place gifts at her feet, gifts of the land including flowers, seeds, rocks, and jewels.

The dragon arrives, and he waits for all others to lumber away before he breaks from the trees and stops before Althea. "Are we allowed to kill anyone tomorrow?"

"Maybe." She grins. "I guess we will see."

"It's been too long since I've had a vampyr toothpick." He laughs, making me grin.

"I'm sure we will find you something to much on. Are you okay?"

"Better than okay. These lands are beautiful," he murmurs fondly. "I was cautious of you at first, but I have been watching you. Your heart is pure and true. I thank you for your hospitality."

"No, it's us who should thank you," she responds, her hair blowing in the breeze. "Besides, I feel a lot more protected with a forest of monsters between me and our enemies."

He bares his teeth in a wicked grin. "Would you like a flight?" the dragon offers and bends his wing.

With wide eyes, she nods and hurries over in excitement. "Do you mind if I change and follow?" I ask the dragon, and he watches me with wise eyes.

"Of course," he purrs, and I quickly change into my tiger and stretch out.

I watch my queen climb gracefully onto the dragon and settle amongst his spikes. She is so stunning, regal, and powerful. Anyone can see that, even this ancient dragon.

With a look at me that lets me know he won't allow anything to happen to my mate, he stands and leaps into the sky. I race below him as he swoops, staying beneath the clouds so I can see them as trees brush my sides as I keep my eye on them.

Exhilaration pulses through me as my muscles stretch. The feeling of being free fills me as her laughter is brought to me by the wind, and when I leap onto a rock and roar, I watch her. Her arms are spread wide as she laughs. My heart stills at her beauty, and then my little queen stands, climbing onto his back and flying herself.

My heart soars with her as she stands atop a great beast, flying through the air as power flows around her. Nature is welcoming her, and the dark itself cocoons her. She is not merely a creature of the night.

She is the night.

She is the warmth in the shadows.

She is the comfort in the blackness.

She is the bravery within the shield of night.

She is the love and mischief you find after dusk.

She is everything and so much more.

She is power.

She is the future, and as I watch the dragon swoop back to our court, carrying such a precious being, I know this was always where I was supposed to be. Not just to help the dead, but the living too.

To help her.

To love her.

And that is exactly what I will do for all the years to come.

Never before has being an immortal appealed to me so much, and I get her for many, many years to come.

ALTHEA

Sitting around the table, I listen to them laugh and joke, and I soak it in. I never had this, not even at my old court—a family, a purpose, and a table filled with people who love and support me. It's addictive, and I've never been happier, but the weight of tomorrow keeps my shoulders rounded with worry as I wonder if we will all make it through.

What if they hurt us?

What if they try to kill us?

I cannot lose one of them. Each judge holds part of my soul, and without them, I would be broken and lost. This is bigger than us, but it doesn't mean I'm not worried about what will happen and that this might be the last time we are like this.

"It won't," Azul says, always so in tune with my thoughts. The laughter dies out as they all turn to watch me carefully. "We are stronger than anyone else, and together, we are unstoppable, Althea. We are judges. We will not lose. Trust in that, in us. You will always have us. I promise you that."

"Do not make promises you cannot keep," I snap as I shove my chair back, hurrying around to him and lying in his lap. He holds me possessively, tugging me closer as I press my head to his chest. "What if we lose? What if I am not strong enough? I couldn't bear losing any of you."

"Then you will not," Nathair declares like it is so easy. "I vow it on the old gods and the new. You will never lose us. Not today, not tomorrow, and not a month from now. We will win tomorrow, but to do so we need your confidence, your power, and your trust in us."

"Being brave is not the absence of fear," Lycus murmurs, reaching for me. "It is how you use it, harness it, and control it. I was terrified every time I rode into battle, terrified of dying and losing my men, but I didn't let it stop me, and you will not let it stop you either."

"Think of all the people we will be helping. Think of everyone who's suffering right now and depending on us. Think of the lives we will save," Reve offers solemnly.

"That is what it means to be a judge," Zale states.

"To be us," Osis adds.

"Together, we can defeat anything," Conall says as he looks around. "They will not break this court. They will not take your family, Althea. We can promise that, as long as you promise to be right there with us."

Fear is an emotion, but courage? Courage is a decision—a decision not to let fear win. Despite being afraid, I will continue to move forward.

Taking a deep breath, I blow it out and smile at them, flashing fang. "You are right. Tomorrow, we will show them what being a court really means. We will bring the Court of Nightmares back into our world, and we will cleanse it of all those willing to be the end of our race like the gods wish. After, we get our happiness together. There is no other option." I look around, meeting each of their eyes. "Understood? Not one of us dies or gets hurt tomorrow. We will be in charge, and we do not play their games. No, they play ours."

"We will show them what nightmares are capable of." Nathair grins, and it's cruel and so sexy, I wiggle. His eyes burn like he knows my thoughts, so I quickly look away so I don't get distracted by sex, but my eyes land on Lycus, whose fangs have grown from the scent of my need in the air.

"We should feed," I say, "to make sure we are all at our strongest."

"Fuck yes. Get your pretty ass over here for me, baby," Reve purrs.

"Or you get your pretty ass here," I retort, running my nail down my neck. After all, what better way to confirm our bonding than to offer comfort by feeding and fucking?

Lycus moves, grabbing me and throwing me onto the table. He lays me out like a feast as I giggle, which soon turns into a scream as they sink their fangs into my body.

Fifty Three

Althea

I know I'm dreaming. I can tell because Reve has been teaching me his dream walking abilities. I might not be as good as him, but I can "wake" myself, as he calls it. There's a dreamy quality to the vision, and the edges are jagged if I touch them. I'm being shown what whoever has pulled me here wants.

It doesn't feel kind or even like destiny like the other times.

I went to sleep surrounded by my men, my skin coated in our blood and cum from our feeding frenzy, and then I suddenly found myself here.

We are standing in a busy street in the city, but it's empty now. There are dark skyscrapers on either side of us, and the moon hangs high above us.

There's a man before me, his wide shoulders and muscular back concealed by a black suit. An ornate crown sits atop his head. When his voice comes, it's dark and cruel, and there's a familiar note to it, but I can't place it.

"I wondered if it would work," he offers. "Using the blood."

I continue to stare, and he chuckles.

"There was blood left at the scene of the killings, so I followed it and tracked down those responsible. No one who was there would speak, not about what they saw, but I hoard information, like some of our own kind willing to decimate a full court. That piqued my interest." He turns, and for a moment, he freezes, his eyes widening. "Impossible, you should be dead."

"Not impossible, difficult," I retort, my own shock quickly turning into anger. "But breaking our bond didn't kill me."

Standing there, filled with righteous energy, is my old mate.

The king who rejected me.

He looks the exact same, yet he watches me like I am completely different. I know I look the same, but I carry myself differently now. Gone is the timid, scared, young vamp, and in her place is an experienced killer and seductress. For a moment, his eyes run hungrily down my body, and a spark of anger flares within me.

"So you are the one who is killing your own kind? You couldn't handle the rejection, so you're taking it out on everyone else?" he taunts.

"Not really." I smirk. "You didn't matter that much. I'm simply ridding our race of evil. It has nothing to do with you."

He wanders closer, reaching out as if to touch me, so I step back, knowing touch will give him power over me. He could even use it to find me. As it is, I'm blocking as much as I can so he cannot go any further, all the while kicking myself. Even a drop of blood can be used against me, I know that, and he's here, proving it.

The ball is tomorrow, yet he couldn't wait.

Why?

"Oh, I'm betting it does, mate."

"Do not call me that," I snarl, flashing my fangs. "I am not your mate. I never was."

"Oh, but you wished you were, didn't you? I saw the longing in your eyes even as I broke your little heart. Do you know how easy it was to forget you? Shall I show you?"

Before I can respond, the city around us begins to crumble, falling away to darkness before he snaps his fingers.

He transports me with him, and I realise he must be using fey magic if he possesses a sloppy version of Reve's gifts. It's not as clear, more jumbled and chaotic, but I soon find myself staring down at him. He's asleep, curled in crimson sheets splashed with blood, with women of all shapes and sizes sprawled around his naked form, bare themselves bar his fang marks.

"Jealous, little vamp?" he taunts.

I eye the scene almost clinically. "Not really." I smirk, and smoother than he manipulated the dreamscape, thanks to Reve's training, I change the image. I don't let my guys' faces show, but I display my very own bed where my bare body is pinned down by male arms and legs. Bite marks cover every inch of my skin, as does blood and cum.

He snarls, jealousy flaring in his eyes for a moment before he conceals it. "So you are a fang whore now? Makes sense. Pity."

"Tell yourself whatever makes you feel better." I mock bow. "Now, did you want something?"

"You will die for your killings," he spits. "We cannot allow it. The council has already decided."

"Unless they assassinate us, which not even they could do, they cannot prove it. Isn't that why you all called for this ball tomorrow. To try and trip us up?" I circle him like prey. "It won't happen. You will lose, and anyone who stands in our way will meet the same fate as those you are here to avenge." Stopping in front of him, I lift my hand. "Until tomorrow, false king." I snap my fingers and cut the connection.

When I wake, I sit up stiffly. Reve is already watching me. "I blocked him. He will not be able to access your mind again. I allowed it while you were talking." He seems reserved, so I untangle myself and crawl towards him where he sits on the chair, clambering into his lap. His hands don't tug me closer like normal, but he doesn't push me away either.

"I was careless. I let him get some of my blood somehow. They know who is behind this now—me," I mutter.

"It doesn't matter. They would have found out tomorrow anyway. Like you said, they cannot prove it, and they would have to in order to demand our deaths. Besides, we are not playing by their rules, remember?" he reasons, but he seems cold and withdrawn. Then I realise why. He was spying on us.

"Are you jealous?" I ask, tilting my head, the flames casting shadows over his face.

His teeth grind as he watches me. "You still want him." It's a statement phrased as a barb.

"Not even a single drop of me," I reply without hesitation, and I open my mind to him. "See? Watch the meeting from my perspective, not just from afar. Feel what I felt. I didn't want him, Reve. I feel sorry for him, and when I look at him, all I think about is how lucky I was to escape him and find you, my true mates—men I crave more than I crave air. Men I need more than I need blood. I never needed him like that. Only you," I murmur as I lean in and cover his lips, letting him taste the truth.

"I wanted to transform his mindscape into a hellhole and fill it with nightmares until he begged for mercy," he growls, gripping me. "He wanted you. I saw it. He cannot have you, Althea. You are mine, you are ours, and I will rip him apart piece by piece if he so much as touches you."

"You'd do that for me?" I murmur, rolling my hips against him. Both of us are still bare from our feeding, so I drag my pussy along his hardening cock. He slams me down onto his dick. My head wants to fall back, but he grips my hair and pulls it until I meet his gaze.

"I'd do anything for you. You think I wouldn't rip apart your foolish ex-mate? I'd tear out his heart for simply daring to try to claim yours. I've been damned once before and given a second chance, Althea, but I would be damned again for you. Always for you," he snarls against my lips as he roughly fucks me from below.

"Yes," I groan, my eyes sliding shut as pleasure storms through my blood, making me climb higher and higher. "I'm yours, yours."

His lips wrap around my bouncing breasts, sucking my nipples. He drags his fangs dangerously across my skin as he bounces me faster. His other hand slides between us, rubbing at my clit hard, as if to get me off quickly to prove to us both that I'm still his.

Pleasure roars through me as I ride him faster, and then we cry out as one, our minds joined as we come. His cum splashes inside me as he groans. Winding my hips through the aftermath, I lean down and kiss his head before slowing to a stop.

The flames lick at shadows on our bodies as he lifts his head and kisses me. "I love you."

"I love you too," I murmur.

Smacking my ass, he lifts me from his cock, making us both moan, and then he throws me towards the bed. "Now go and wake your other mates and let them fuck any memory of him away," he orders, his hand leisurely stroking his blood and cum stained cock as he watches me with half-mast eyes and bloodied fangs.

I freeze for a moment, drinking in the sight of him before I do as I'm told.

They are the only people whom I will ever let order me around.

Not because I can't refuse, but because I love to obey them.

Turning back to the others, I crawl up the bed to my closest mate. Zale has his arm thrown over his face, his cock semi-hard even in sleep, and when I draw closer, it hardens further as if sensing me. Smirking, I glance over my shoulder to see Reve gripping his own, his fangs digging into his bottom lip as he watches me.

"Go on, little mate," he orders.

I turn forward, wrapping my hand around Zale's cock and sucking the tip into my mouth. I want to see if I can finish him before he wakes. Groaning, he shifts and lifts his hips to slide his cock deeper into my mouth. I watch him carefully as he starts to pant as I suck him all the way back and then pull off, only to repeat it. His hand drops, and I freeze, but his eyes are still closed.

"Thea," he groans in his sleep, and I suck him harder, all the way back like he likes. I dig my nails into his thigh, and his eyes slam open, locking on me. His mouth parts, but whatever he was going to say dies as I hum around his cock. Moaning loudly, he fists the sheets, his hips quickly finding a rhythm until he's fucking my mouth, and with a muffled cry, his cock jerks, filling my mouth once more, and then his cum floods my throat. I swallow every drop before placing a gentle kiss on his tip then crawling to the next body with a wink.

He watches me, open-mouthed and panting. I don't know how the others are still asleep, but like Zale's dick, Conall's cock is hard even in his sleep. Crawling up his huge body, I straddle his hips as I reach down and grasp him, pressing the huge head of his cock to my pussy before sinking down on his length.

His eyes open, and he reaches out to grip my hips. To stop me maybe? When he sees it's me, he groans, and his huge cock jerks inside me.

"Thea—"

I cover his lips with a finger as I lift almost completely off him. "Shh, baby," I purr as I drop back down. The force makes my breasts bounce, and he groans, watching with half-lidded eyes. Grinning, I wind my hips, chasing my own release as his hips help me. I keep my eyes on him the entire time, wanting to see every inch of pleasure I'm wringing from him.

Reaching up, I grip my breasts, tweaking and thumbing my nipples as I clench around him.

"Thea." His cock jerks as I speed up.

Suddenly, there's a hand on my back and I'm pushed forward. Something warm spills across my ass, and then a huge cock pushes into me. The pressure between the two causes me to cry out, and I hear the others waking.

My eyes close in bliss as I realise Lycus is behind me, and he and Conall work me between them—one in, one out.

Their lips slide possessively over my skin until I can't take it. I scream my release, and Conall follows me with his own roar, spilling inside me.

Not a moment later, I'm lifted off him, and a hand wraps around my throat from behind—Lycus. He snarls in my ear and drags his fangs along my neck as he hammers into my ass.

"Mine," he growls.

"Yours," I promise, pushing back to meet his thrusts.

"Shit," someone whispers, but it fades into the bliss Lycus is igniting once more. Sliding his other hand down, he thumbs my clit.

"Come for me, mate, now," he demands, and his rough command sends me soaring once more. I scream his name as he pumps his cum in my ass and then falls back.

Whimpering, I drop to my hands and knees, finding Nathair watching me hungrily. "Come and sit on your king," he orders.

I feel their cum coating my thighs and ass as I struggle up his body, but once I'm within reach, he picks me up and slams me down onto his waiting cock. Both of us moan in bliss.

Arms wrap around me, and he tugs me down. My lips meet his as I feel another cock prod at my entrance. My eyes widen as I jerk.

"Relax, love," Osis says, his huge tip prodding my entrance alongside Nathair, who stills. He doesn't move, just glides his thumb over my asshole as Nathair kisses me until I relax, and then Osis slowly works his cock into my pussy alongside Nathair. The burn is so strong, I writhe.

"So fucking tight," he murmurs. "So good. Azul, come take her mouth, brother, and distract her."

Nathair turns my head and then Azul's cock is there, sliding into my open mouth as Osis pulls out and thrusts back in. The feel of their two cocks inside of me is both so good and so wrong.

They claim my body, one pushing in and out, which shoves Nathair deeper until his cock rubs on that spot inside me that has me seeing stars.

"I won't last," Nathair says. "Not like this."

"Me either," Osis growls. "Come on, brother, fill her with your cum. You know she loves that. I would love to feel your cum dripping around my cock."

I cry out around Azul's length at the image, and Nathair yells, hammering up into me as I clench around them. With a guttural snarl, Nathair's cock jerks inside of me, pumping his cum deep, all while Osis is there, stopping it from escaping.

Slumping forward, I release my mouth from Azul's cock, but hands drag me off Nathair.

Lying back, Osis directs me to his cock but quickly turns me until my pussy is pressed against his mouth. My hand jerks his cock as Azul slams into my mouth. Grinding back into Osis's tongue as it plunges inside of me, I moan around Azul as I stroke Osis hard and fast. His precum spills over my hand, making the glide slick.

Groaning loudly, Azul hammers into my mouth as Osis laps at my clit before thrusting his tongue back into me. I speed up sucking and stroking, chasing my own pleasure. Osis copies, lashing my clit as Azul's hips stutter.

I seal my lips around him and suck, and with a roar, Azul fills my mouth with his cum. Swallowing it down, I pull my mouth off him and seal it on Osis's cock, making him cry out. His tongue lashes me faster as I grind back into his face, sitting on it until my own release takes over and I cry out, coming over his tongue as he spills in my mouth.

Collapsing forward, I lie across them, my eyes finding Reve who grins.

"Good girl," he praises.

"Wake me like that any time." Zale laughs.

"Me too." Their voices mingle.

Giggling, I climb into their welcoming arms as Reve joins us, wrapping me up between them as my eyes shut.

Lying amongst my mates, I can't help but think about tomorrow and what is going to happen.

We are going to face my rejected king and our entire race.

And we are going to come out victorious, covered in their blood.

We have to.

I will ensure it.

FIFTY FOUR

ALTHEA

IT'S THE DAY OF the ball, and everyone is extremely busy. Nathair is barking orders like a madman, and I've been told I'm not allowed out of my rooms until they are ready to show me the transformation. Instead, I am supposed to relax, pamper myself, and get ready for tonight.

As soon as we woke up, Reve and I told them about my night visitor, and we all agreed there wasn't much we could do about it, but it didn't stop them from being angry and jealous, which they readily admit. The possessive sex we had after, however, was worth it.

I'm not afraid to show them who I am tonight. Judges are meant to remain anonymous and in the background, but everything is changing, and although I will don my mask, I will also show them my face to look into the eyes of the courts who rejected, alienated, and hurt me and my family.

But first, it's time to be pampered.

I shave and polish my entire body. I wash my hair and blow dry it before curling it and leaving it to hang freely. I want to look good tonight to match the fey's incredible dress and also because it's an opportunity to show my mates what I look like all dressed up. They want me even when I'm in their stolen shirts and covered in fluids, but I can't wait to see their reactions to the dress.

If they had been there at my first presentation, I wouldn't have run. I would have walked into their arms. I'm more excited to see their reactions than for the outcome of this evening.

There's a pulse inside of me as the god powers flow through my blood, reminding me of my purpose. We have to cleanse our race and satisfy the gods so that we are allowed to continue to live. There will be a lot of death for those attending, but they think they will have a good time drinking, feeding, and fucking.

Little do they know, they are walking into a trap they set themselves.

I paint my nails and leave them to dry as I lie back covered in lotions they left for me. I don't know what my guys are doing, but they aren't here, and I'm bored for the first time since I came back to life. I wonder what they are going to wear tonight. I can't wait to see them.

I drift to the box Nathair placed upon the fire just for something to do, the one I took from my mother's room. My mask was inside, but I find myself running my hands over the lid, craving a piece of her even though it's been years. Part of me feels connected to it as I trace the ornate designs before opening the lid. I find my mask nestled safely inside, cleaned and just as it first was. The silken purple cushion makes me smile. Under the lid has the same designs, and I trace my fingers over them, only to frown when my nail catches on a raised edge. Brows furrowed, I carefully lift my mask out and turn the box so I have better access to the lid. I find a seam and carefully pry it open, setting the false lid to the side. Crossing my legs, I catch the bundle that tumbles out and leave it in my lap as I put the box to the side.

On the top of the pile is a folded piece of parchment with my name scrawled across it. I hesitate over the letters, a pulse of love shooting through me from the intention behind it, and I know my mother left these to me. I carefully peel it open, and a small image drops into my hand. I can't help but stare at the ultrasound.

It's me, it has to be, and taped to the other side is a photograph of my mother smiling widely, her hand on her rounded belly. I look so much like her bar the colour of my hair and eyes. I have the same tall, curvy frame and wide, unchecked smile. She was so beautiful. I trace her face before tugging the photo closer. There's another hand on her belly, reaching forward from the frame. It's distinctly male. For a moment, my heart freezes. I've never given much consideration regarding my father's identity. He has never been in my life, and I was never told who he was, but surely that hand has to be his? If so, then why did she keep this? Why give it to me?

Why didn't my father want me?

My heart aches as I stare down at the image, at the hand pressing protectively to the belly I was in. The gesture is filled with love, yet he's never once appeared in my life. Shaking my head, I drop the photo to the bed and pick up the letter, needing answers. I don't have my mother's gift of sight, but maybe she left me something.

My dearest Althea,

My little girl, how I wish I could see you grow up. If you are reading this, it is because you have found your legacy, your destiny, and I am not there to guide you through it. Know I wish I could be, and that I love you more than anything else in this world. I knew the sacrifices I would make to carry you, and I made them gladly. Not because of who you will become, but because you are my daughter and I love you. You are a part of me, a part of my true love, and the very best of both of us. I wish I could see you, not in visions but before me. I wish I could stand by your side as you face what is to come. It will not be easy, and I'm sorry.

I'm sorry so much burden has fallen upon you. I'm sorry you will suffer such hardships. If I could take them from you, I would without complaint, but my destiny, like yours, was always written in the sands of time. There is so much I want to tell you, but know this.

We love you more than anything, and every decision we have made has been because of this. I hope, one day, your father can read this to you, but I have made him keep promises you will never understand—promises that will lead you to the road you must take. Just know he's there, he's always been there, and he loves you just as much as I do.

I hope you find as much happiness as I did, even as short-lived as I know it will be. I have not told him that, so please tell him I'm sorry. I knew if I did, it would kill him. He would fight the gods themselves to change fate, and that, my love, I cannot have. Not when you would face the consequences. I cannot see all, although I wish I could because then I could see if you find love. If you find the half of your soul. If you do, hold on to it tightly and never let go.

My daughter, my beautiful, perfect daughter, please do not be angry at the world. Please remember that despite the darkness and evil that lingers within our people, there is also beauty and goodness. Not all who are lost are not redeemable.

I will always be here with you, just look and you will find me.

The gods take, as they are selfish, fickle creatures, but they are not all powerful. They are immortal just like us. Do not ever forget that. Do not ever forget that they are no better than you. Whatever you do, whatever you decide, will be the right decision because it comes from your pure heart.

Until the day we meet again,

Your mother

My fingers linger over the tear stains, the words replaying in my head as I scan them. She loved my father, and he loved her. They were mated, yet no one knew. No one knows who he is. Just how many secrets was my mother keeping? How far ahead was she playing the game to keep me alive and safe and guide me to this moment? For a second, I'm angry at her and how easily she saw into her future, but her words are pure and true. She loved me more than anything, and everything she has done is for me.

I wish she could see me too, just like she wished.

I can see how much she loved me in every word. Would I be willing to give up everything for my child? The answer is yes, always yes, so I guess part of me can understand why she did it. I wish she could have seen me like this, happy with my mates, to know it was worth her sacrifices, but one day, we will meet again on the other side, and I will tell her.

I will tell her everything, and I know she will be waiting.

I find myself picking up the picture again, tracing my fingers over the hands covering the belly. She said my father loves me and that he's close. Who is he? And if he's close, then why didn't he show himself when I needed him the most? I guess those are questions that won't be answered right now. Folding up the letters and pictures, I carefully place them in the box, not hiding them this time, and put it back on the mantel.

I sit back down, tracing over the ornate mask, and for the first time, I notice the little details I missed before. There is a joined sun and a moon, a snake, a skull, a claw mark, a swirl, and a spider. Every single symbol reflects my mates. My mother might not have known what was waiting, but she knew this.

She knew the men who would love me, and I have to close my eyes to stop the tears from falling.

Is it foolish to mourn a woman I never knew?

I don't think I care. She was my mother, and she loved me.

That's enough for me.

The dress is in my room after I come back from eating, and I pick up the fluttering note carefully attached to it.

Knock them dead.

I can't help but laugh, knowing Lilia wrote it and she means it. The dress is even more stunning than the last time I saw it, and I realise she added jewels along the slits. There are boxes of jewellery waiting on the bed, and I carefully open them. Inside the first is an ornate choker, with black diamonds and red jewels embedded around the neck. There is a matching crown, seven rings—one for each mate, I realise—as well as a bracelet. There is also a stretchy black garter to go around my thigh, with a red jewel hanging down from chains. It's going to look incredible. I slip off my robe and start to get ready, unable to wait to show my men.

I have to shimmy into the dress. I don't bother with a bra or panties, knowing my new friend made it to be worn without. Luckily, there's no zip, and as soon as it touches my skin, it heats and moulds to my shape, hugging my every curve.

Adding the jewellery, I turn to the mirror and almost gasp. I look beautiful.

My hair ruins it, however, so I tug it up and turn my neck and realise it needs to be up. Quickly getting to work, I pin it into a messy updo. A few pieces tumble down to frame my face, but it leaves my long neck on display. After adding a bright-red lipstick and smoking out my eyes, I slip on the black, five-inch heels and step back. I check it all out together, and for a moment, I just stare at myself.

I can hardly believe I am the same girl as the last time I wore a dress like this.

Again, it's not in the beauty of the dress, though that helps, or the jewels. It's in the way I carry myself, embracing who and what I am. I glow with power and confidence. Smiling at myself, I wish my mother could see me now.

We are waiting, comes the call in my head.

My mother might not be able to see me, but my loves can. Taking my mask with me, I turn to the door and step out, seeing them gathered in the stone foyer below. I don't even take in the room, too lost in the sight of my beautiful mates lined up side by side. They are so stunning, it hurts, and I almost stumble.

Nathair is on the left, his crown firmly in place, wearing a black and grey doublet half undone to showcase his skin, with some leather pants and high boots. A fur trimmed cape hangs over one shoulder. Next to him is Conall in an open vest and matching doublet, only his sleeves have been cut off and each wrist has a bracelet on it, his neck too, and I realise it has my name stamped across the gold. Possessiveness roars through me as he winks. Beside him is Lycus, who's wearing a chain mail doublet with trousers and big boots. His hair is braided back with jewels sprinkled throughout. His beard is trimmed, his eyes are lined with kohl, his mark is on full display, and hanging from his hair are golden letters that spell out my name.

Reve is posed with one hip out. He has on an open shirt, showing off all his tattoos, and leather pants with slices on the side. Smirking at me, he runs his tongue across his teeth, dropping his eyes to my body as I take in my name written in gold across his stomach.

Azul is staring at me when I look at him. Wearing a matching doublet, buttoned all the way to the top, and leather pants tucked into boots, he could almost be overlooked if it wasn't for his stunning face and muscles. His hair is messy, like normal, and his lips look thicker than usual. His eyes are lined like Lycus's, and dangling from his neck is my name.

Osis is smiling when I glance at him. His doublet has fur trimming the edges, and a few buttons are undone. He has deep black trousers on with knee-high boots, and his hair is half held back, while the rest frames his face. On his wrist is a golden bracelet with my name on it.

Zale is last, but certainly not least. His doublet is folded back to his elbows, and his skin almost shimmers with flames. His hair is pushed back in a new style that makes his sharp cheekbones stand out, and across his forehead is my name on a simple golden band.

They are breathtaking, and they steal all of the beauty and light so I am unable to look away.

Each one of them has my name somewhere on their body except for Nathair, and like he senses my confusion, he smirks and moves his hair aside in a flourish to show me a golden half cuff around his neck, proudly stamped with my name. I can't help but grin. They also have matching golden pins attached to their lapels with an intertwined N and C.

I just stand there, wondering how on earth I deserve these men and how we are going to make it through this ball without me getting my mouth on their cocks.

It isn't going to happen.

FIFTY FIVE

AZUL

"WOW," SHE WHISPERS AS she stares at us, but we are the ones who are shocked.

Our mate is always beautiful, but right now?

I drop to my knees as she approaches, unable to stand in the face of such beauty. Even the gods themselves would weep in jealousy at the vision before us.

The dress is something dreams are made of. It enhances every curve on my beautiful mate. Cinched in at her waist, the fabric hugs her thick hips and showcases her long, toned legs as she walks towards us. Her breasts almost spill free, and her arms and neck are decorated in jewels. I ache to bury my fangs in her so I can taste that beauty and power.

She actually glows like a goddess who came down to walk amongst us lowly mortals. The others start to drop to their knees next to me as our beautiful queen strides towards us, completely unaware that she is destroying us with each step.

She stops before us, her head cocked. "Are you okay?" she asks and peers down at herself. "Is it not okay?" She suddenly frowns, and I hate it.

With a whine, I drop to my hands and knees and crawl towards her. "My goddess," I murmur, rolling my eyes up to hers to let her see my truth. "We are not worthy."

"Look at you, my queen," Nathair growls. "Okay? Okay? There's not even a word in our vocabulary to describe your beauty right now." When I glance back, he has his hand over his heart like it hurts, and I understand.

Lycus's heart is in his eyes as he watches her, swallowing hard. Conall's shadows writhe, reaching for her as he kneels there, awestruck. Reve bites his own lip.

"Althea," Reve purrs. "Come sit that stunning ass on my face. Please, baby."

"Politely destroy me." Osis grins, but he, too, is on his knees.

She giggles, and it steals the air from my lungs as I simply look at her. I feel like I am staring at a masterpiece. Art. That's what she is.

"You all look so good," she says, biting her lip, the musk of her desire scenting the air. I sneak closer and lick up the split in her dress. She gasps as I move higher, shifting to my knees and gripping those beautiful hips before tugging the dress up with my tongue. I slide my tongue along her inner thighs to taste her desire.

Her taste explodes in my mouth, making me growl until I'm suddenly shoved out of the way and Lycus is there, lifting her onto his mouth. She groans, tangling her fingers in his hair.

"Behave," Nathair commands, his voice stern. "We need to prepare."

Lycus reluctantly releases her, and Nathair strides over and, despite his own command, he slides his hand into her dress and cups her pussy as he licks her neck. "I'm betting I won't last even half an hour with you in this dress before I have you bent over and filled with my fangs and cock."

"Not before me." Reve smirks as he hurries over, pressing against her back. "In fact, I'll take that pretty mouth and let them all watch as I claim my queen."

"Maybe we should," Osis murmurs, and we turn to him. "I'm just saying, fucking and feeding at these types of parties is normal, so maybe we should put on a bit of a show and indulge."

"I like that idea." Althea grips Nathair's hair and tugs his head back, making him groan. My cock jerks at the sight as her fangs drag along his neck. "Until then, baby, behave." Stepping away from them with a knowing smile, she holds out her hand to me. "And show me my home and ball."

Fifty Six

Althea

I'm escorted out of the court and to the front entrance so I can experience the full impact—or so Azul tells me—and it makes my jaw drop.

The entire court has been transformed into something out of a fantasy. The entrance is a huge stone archway with the words, "Enter if you dare. Welcome to the Court of Nightmares," written in our language at the top of the arch. Smoke and shadows billow throughout it, concealing what lies beyond, and ivy and dark-purple flowers crawl up the stone. A blood-red carpet leads right to it, making the entryway look grand, and huge candles line the wall to light the way, dripping wax across the floor. I step through the arch and gasp at the touch of magic that kisses my skin, and when we step into the area where the ball will be held, I'm stunned.

It's been transformed into a gothic fantasy forest. Gauzy red material hangs from the ceiling, and thousands of candles glitter in the black chandeliers above us. More candles are spread across tables, alcoves, and the floor in various sizes, and the flames cast the space in an otherworldly glow. The steps on either side of the main floor are covered with the same carpet as the entrance outside, and smoke and shadows swirl around the room, concealing the floor. Black and red tables are placed on the left and filled with decadent food of all colours. Red Chesterfield sofas are pushed against walls, framed with giant wingback chairs, with pillows and blankets to provide areas to feed and fuck. Beyond, under the stairs, are seven matching thrones all done in black and red. One is slightly higher than the rest, and it's placed in the middle.

Stone and golden decorations are situated strategically around the room, as are details that reference being a creature of the night, like moons, suns, stars, and monsters.

The courtyard doors are open, offering a view of the world beyond, where a giant water fountain flows with blood. A woman—who I realise is a replica of me—stands in the middle with a sinister smile and monsters gathered at her feet. Blooming flowers surround the lawn, which is filled with sculptures, a maze, food, and so much more. It looks like something straight out of a novel, and it's filled with magic.

I see my monsters emerging from the forest and the land beyond to gather outside and wait for the ball to begin. Simon, his mate, and his pack are due to arrive any minute now, so I take the time to just stare in wonder.

The sun is up, however, brightly illuminating everything. Conall winks at me. "We can't be the Court of Nightmares without the moon and darkness, now can we?" Striding to the open door, he calls upon his powers. He's embraced the shadows and darkness of his powers since his rebirth, but now I watch as my wicked mate embraces his control over the sun, absorbing it into himself and prematurely filling the sky with the moon and stars. When the enigmatic light of the night hits the room, it gives everything a sultry, sexual ambiance.

Conall turns, lit up from within from the sun. "I called the moon for you, mate."

"Come here, my love," I murmur. He strides over, and I groan at the sight of the sun trapped within his skin, casting rainbows over his body. "You are my moon," I murmur lovingly.

"And you are my sun," he replies, leaning down to kiss me until someone clears their throat.

"If we let you carry on, you will have her bent over the table and filled with your cock and cum before the party even starts," Reve teases, and Nathair laughs. "At least save it for them."

"We should." I smirk as an idea comes to mind.

"I know that look," Conall whispers to me, a wicked grin forming on his lips. "I'm with you."

Simon and his mate turn up with some of his pack in tow. They are all in matching black suits, but each has put their own twist on it, and they look amazing. They spread out throughout the court with the monsters, and we leave Simon and his wolf on the door, along with Nathair, while I prepare my plan. Power and presence are everything to those attending tonight. They expect a show, and that's exactly what I will give them. I'm going to show them exactly who we are as soon as we arrive, causing them to feel unsure and off balance, which will leave us in charge.

After all, this is our court. We are the nightmares, and they are our prey.

It doesn't take long for them to begin to arrive, and Nathair's voice fills my head. *The first ones are arriving.*

Keep them there, then let them in together before you come and join us, I reply, lying down on a sofa. I throw one leg over the back, while the other foot remains on the floor so my legs are spread, the material bunching at my pussy. I run my eyes over my other mates, who have stopped everything they are doing to watch me.

"Want to put on a show?" I purr, and before I can even explain, Conall is on all fours between my thighs, watching me hungrily.

"Are you sure, mate?" he murmurs as I mentally show them exactly what I want.

"That's a way to make an entrance." Lycus snorts as he reaches down and rearranges his hard cock. "I'll want to kill them for getting to see you like that though."

Conall nods, Zale winks, and Reve laughs, as does Nathair in my head.

Let me know when you are ready, draya, he purrs.

"I'm sure." I lean back. "Don't you want to claim your queen in front of them?"

Six matching possessive growls fill the air, making me smirk.

"Now is your chance." I don't get to say another word before the material at my waist is bunched up and a mouth seals on my wet pussy. His head will block their view of me, but it's very obvious what he's doing.

My gasp fills the air as his tongue drags across me, the wet sound making him shudder. The others spread out around me, driving my pleasure higher until I almost forget the plan.

Almost.

Now, I tell Nathair.

I hear them before I see them, their footsteps and chatter as they express their awe of the court preceding them as Nathair and Simon escort them into the ballroom. I know the moment they first see us. Their voices rise, but I ignore them as Conall's talented tongue slides into me, making me cry out. I feel the growing crowd watching us, the main spectacle.

Nathair moves over and joins us, possessively sliding his hand across me.

I let my head loll to the side, gripping my mate with one hand while the other trails over my breasts and throat. I meet Conall's eyes and smile as he licks my pussy for them all to see. I moan, my chest arching, and then Nathair appears above me, so I grab him and drag him down for a kiss. He whimpers against my lips, and I turn his head and slam my fangs into his neck as Conall sinks his fangs into my thigh, making me cry out as an orgasm rolls through me. Other mouths press against my flesh—one in my arm, one on each leg, and another on my neck.

My blood covers me, staining my skin, and the other courts have no choice but to watch. We ignore them like they are nothing to us, and instead fuck and feed, forcing them to wait for us to greet them.

When I'm done feeding, I pull away, licking at my bloodied lips as tongues lap at puncture marks, and then I smile at the gathering, noticing the lust in their hooded eyes, along with anger and confusion, and flash my fangs. "Welcome to the Court of Nightmares."

Fifty Seven

Nathair

THE MUSIC BEGINS AFTER my mate speaks, and I smirk at their lustful and angry expressions. Sitting up, Althea kisses Conall and stands, her skirt falling into place as we all move to her side and take her hands.

"Please make yourself at home. Everything goes here. You won't be able to cross into private areas, which are blocked, and don't antagonise the monsters." On cue, the dragon roars, causing some of them to stumble back a few steps. "Bloodshed and pleasure is the name of the game here, as long as it is given freely. I know you all have questions, and they will be answered in time, but for now, indulge in your darkest desires."

Osis's ghosts float through the room, making the gathered courts spin in wide-eyed fear and curiosity. Conall fills the room with his dancing shadows, and Zale's flames lick at the wall.

I share a smirk with Lycus before we fade into the shadows and transform, and then the spider and the snake slither out of the darkness. I make a good show of it, lunging at them as they stumble back. I move over and coil around my mate. She pets me with a grin as everyone watches us, including Althea's rejected mate and the leader of her old court, who has a smaller, cruel-looking man at his side. Everyone else watches us but him. He observes her, and I decide to watch him closely. He doesn't seem threatening, but something about his expression confuses me.

Lycus strolls into view, and people scream as he gracefully climbs up and over the wall, dropping down above our queen who reaches up and pets him.

"Please, drink, dance, and mingle. My mates and I order it." With a swish of her skirts, she turns and walks towards the pillows at the back, where she reclines. We all join her, monsters and humans alike. The monsters she called gravitate towards her, the meaning clear—touch her and die.

The crowd surveys us before they slowly start to explore. They talk amongst themselves, becoming comfortable, but they continue to throw us unsure looks.

They ordered this ball, and I can see the council in the back. They wanted this, but they didn't get it on their terms, and that is clearly throwing them off.

It doesn't surprise me, however, when the first person to approach us is Althea's rejected mate.

I'm curled at her back as she uses me as a seat. I hiss at him as he gets closer, and he stops at the sound, standing far enough away so he can't touch her.

"Althea," he says, "how nice to see you again."

I can feel everyone watching. They are beginning to realise who our queen is, but she is so much more than his rejected mate.

"I wish I could say the same to you." She grins. "But please, enjoy yourself. My mates have outdone themselves on this ball." She dismisses him, looking at the next person to approach. It's Sinclair, the leader of her old court, with the man whom I'm unsure of standing at his side.

"Sinclair," she greets, hesitating before nodding at the man at his side. "Druig."

"We feared you had died, Althea," Sinclair says, frowning in concern, "when you disappeared so suddenly after your rejection. We would have taken care of you."

"Of course, I simply needed space. I wandered for a little while before I stumbled into this court and met the men meant to be my mates. I am sure you can understand that I felt compelled to stay and, well, time got away from me in regard to notifying you."

"Of course," he replies smoothly. "It will result in a fine for abandoning your court, but we can discuss that later. Mates, you said? Will this be a recognised bonding, or are we looking at a choosing?"

Oh, he's playing word games, and my mate doesn't like it. Her hand tightens on Azul, and I tighten around her. The man, Druig, hasn't taken his eyes off Althea, but he watches me worriedly.

"Later," is all she murmurs as if she is not worried, but I can feel her mind working through the arising problems. "We are glad you and the council could come."

"We are happy to have been invited. It seemed we would never get invited to the new mysterious court."

"Not new," she corrects. "This court has been around longer than yours, Sinclair."

"That is King Sinclair to you." It seems like an automatic correction, but my mate doesn't like it.

"Maybe while I was under your roof, but now I am a queen, and if I have to address you as a king, then you have to address me as a queen." When he grinds his teeth, she smiles. "I thought so. These men are the only ones I address as king now. Please, go enjoy the party. We will await the council's response." She turns to Zale and begins a conversation.

I see both Sinclair and her rejected mate bristle, but since they are unwilling to cause a scene and show they are bothered, they fade into the party, waiting for us to make a wrong move. They won't get an opportunity to use anything against us, however. We were forced into this ball, but we have our own plans, and they do not include theirs.

No doubt they will try to corner us at the end, so that's when we will make our move.

After all, we have orders from the gods, and we do not answer to these men, especially ones as corrupt as the people in this room.

Fifty Eight

Althea

I'd be lying if I said I wasn't nervous, especially about seeing Sinclair, my old king. He could demand my return, and although it won't happen, he's within his rights unless I pay a blood price for abandoning my court. I know he will command it so he can use my blood to gain access to my power and court. He never cared about me before, not after he realised I was nothing like my mother. He's not a bad man, or even a bad king. He's just power hungry and used to playing the game like the other council and court members, but they don't realise that will all end tonight.

We are not playing the game; we are destroying it.

That gives me the confidence to ignore the questioning stares and whispers as I focus on my mates.

I lounge with them and greet those who come up to us. They are too scared not to approach us, wanting to be in our good graces. Eventually, Nathair and Lycus change back, and I am swept onto the dance floor. Sultry music pumps through the speakers as Nathair twirls me. When he dips me, he trails his lips up my neck, over my pulse, and to my ear. "I could eat you alive, *draya*. You are so beautiful. You are the most beautiful and powerful woman in this room. They are jealous that I get to touch you," he purrs and spins me out, bringing me in so my back meets his chest. He holds my hips as he moves us, and my head falls back against him as I scan the crowd to see them watching us.

Envy.

Lust.

Hatred.

Spinning, I hook my leg over his hip as we dance and smile at him. "They want us both. We must make quite the beautiful pair."

"It's all you, my love, my incredible mate," he murmurs, kissing me softly before twirling me out. My hand catches in another, and I grin up at Reve. Without missing a step, he tugs me closer and starts to sway me to the music, moving completely differently than Nathair's formal but sexy dance.

His eyes drop to my dress. "I'm going to rip this off you later and watch you ride my cock while you are covered in their blood." Leaning in, he nips my neck. "I wonder if they know they are trapped and that the beautiful queen they are all entranced by will end them before the night is through." He spins me, and I land in a strong pair of arms.

Lycus is a big guy, but when he picks me up and moves us around the room, carrying me, he's smooth and elegant. It's a strange dance, but I laugh as he lifts me into the air and smiles up at me. "My perfect mate. I have searched for you for so long," he whispers as he brings me back down, sliding my body against his until I groan. His hands drop to my ass and yank me closer, then his mouth comes down on mine. "All mine," he purrs, and then another body meets my back.

It's tall and strong.

Conall.

He dips me before spinning me into his arms, holding me with one hand on my back and the other clasping mine as he twirls me around in a perfect ballroom dance. I realise he's showing me off as my dress flares out and we move faster, circling the others until he stills in the middle and slowly dips me down to the floor. When he tugs me up, his lips brush mine. "My moon," he says.

"My sun," I reply, gripping him, but I should have known better. It seems all my mates are intent on dancing with me.

Zale rips me away, his fire burning over my skin as he growls and grinds me into his thigh, which he pressed between my legs. "I haven't had you nearly enough tonight, mate." One eye flashes red with his beast, and I shiver in his hold. "I will rectify that later with our enemies' blood covering our bed." With a lingering kiss on my forehead, he drops me into another pair of arms.

I sense Osis behind me. He holds me with my back against his chest, his arms wrapped around me as we simply sway to the music. His lips brush against my pulse in a promise, and I shiver, closing my eyes as I move with him, losing myself in the fantasy. There is no one else, only us and the music as our bodies move in perfect sync.

He nips my neck as a reminder and then steps back. My eyes open, and then I see Azul. He stands with his hand out, bent over formally to ask me to dance. I can't help but smile widely, almost swooning at my scarred warrior. He is putting himself in the spotlight for me, his mask nowhere to be seen, yet when I place my hand in his, he straightens, looking serene and happy. He wears his scars proudly.

For you, my queen, he says mentally. "It's because you find me beautiful. I see it every time you look at me," he murmurs as we swirl around the room, completely out of sync with everyone else and the music, but somehow, it fits us perfectly.

"That's because you are," I murmur, holding him tighter.

"You make me beautiful, mate," he replies as we dance. "Everyone here wishes they were me, wishes they could have you. They either hate you or want to be you, they can't decide."

Leaning in with a grin, I lick his lips. "How does it feel to be with the most desired woman then?"

"Like I'm exactly where I should be, serving my queen." He steps back, kissing my hand with a bow, and I watch with confusion as he fades into the background. Simon steps into view, looking dazzling in his suit.

"Want to dance, pretty thang?" he teases.

I let him take my arm and dramatically spin me around the room before I take over and lead, making us both laugh. It's a tradition from every party we have ever been to. Laying my head on his shoulder, I let my laughter fade as I move in his arms, swaying to the music. I thought I would never have this again. I hold him tighter, and he lays a kiss on my head like he feels it. I meet his eyes, seeing the same emotion there.

"I won't lose you again, Thea," he promises. "Family."

"Family," I whisper, and then we continue to sway, dancing away the hours together while our mates watch us.

Just two best friends holding onto the past for a moment until the present can invade.

FIFTY NINE

CONALL

I WATCH MY MATE and her best friend. There is so much pain and love wrapped in their embrace, my heart aches for her, and I make a promise there and then that I will never let my mate suffer without him again. My gaze is drawn away when I spot a vampyr and his friends cornering one of our monsters. Snarling, I storm over, not wanting this to interrupt the special moment my mate is having.

"Leave her alone," I demand, realising it's the mermaid, Tide.

"We are just talking. She's of our courts, isn't she?" The man turns, and I narrow my eyes on him. There is more happening here than just our intentions, and I will not allow anything to harm the monsters, so I step between them.

"You aren't talking anymore, little boy," I snap, crossing my arms, my shadows curling around me. "She is under our protection . . . unless you would like me to make an example out of you."

He huffs and looks at his friends. "She isn't worth it." He turns away and strides off, his head held high like he won. Shaking my head at his foolishness, I drop my shadows and step away so I'm not crowding her. "I apologise for their behaviour."

"I am used to the foolishness of men," she murmurs, and then she looks at me and smiles. It's a beautiful smile, but it's not like the one my girl gives me that makes my whole world light up. "You truly love her."

I tilt my head in question, and she laughs.

"You touched me by mistake when you were trying to protect me. Any other would have fallen under my spell. Only those truly in love do not. I have only ever seen it once . . . twice now. You love her." Her eyes seek out Althea, and she smiles softly. "I understand why. She is one of a kind."

"She is, and I do." I nod, gazing at my mate. "She is my everything."

"Hold onto her tight," she murmurs. "Love can be so easily stolen away." There's pain in her eyes like she knows this firsthand, and she nods at me. "Thank you for stepping in. I did not think you would like their intestines scattered about." She slides away as I gape after her.

Note to self, don't get in the way of mermaids.

I feel my mate's gaze and turn to her. *Is everything okay?* she asks.

Everything is fine, my love. I promise.

OSIS

I circle the dance floor, keeping an eye on everything. I see my love moving towards the thrones to sit, with Lycus and Nathair keeping track of her and moving close. Simon returns to his mate, and I ensure they are okay before sliding around the edges once more, checking on the monsters and the party. There are already people feeding and fucking, and the council is watching everything. Everyone is waiting for something to happen, and their anticipation is in the air, growing tenser.

I feel eyes on me, but when I turn to look, I find nothing. Instead, I move towards Azul who is talking to one of his ghosts who chose to be seen, no doubt to lend his power. When I approach, the ghost moves away, listening to conversations for us.

"Any issues?" I ask him softly, not wanting to worry our mate.

"Just a few disrespectful drunk vamps. One is too drained to walk, another is debating whether or not to steal something from us, and the council is planning their attack. Nothing else," he mutters, clearly uncomfortable with having so many enemies near his mate and in his house, just like I am.

"One night, brother," I remind him, clasping his shoulder. "Then it will just be Althea and us forever."

He sighs, rubbing his face as a ghost flies over to us. With a grin, I leave him to it. I nod as Lycus moves past us with a young female vamp in his arms, a supervisor from her court scolding her for overfeeding as he leads them from the party. Zale and Conall are stuffing their faces and watching our mate carefully.

I keep circling, my tiger needing to stretch. I wander outside and check the grounds. People are gathered out here to watch the dragon blow flames. It's clear he hates this, but he's doing it for Althea, so I keep my eye on them too.

Suddenly, I sense a presence behind me and spin. A female grins at me, and she's standing far too close, so I step back quickly, not wanting her overly sweet scent to invade my nostrils. She flashes dainty fangs at me, which aren't like my mate's huge ones. Her eyes are a strange pink colour, contacts maybe, and her hair is blonde and short. I don't bother noticing anything else, only details to identify her in case of an attack.

"What's your name?" she asks.

"You can address me as king. This is my court." We haven't discussed if that's correct, since there is only ever one king or queen when ruling a court, but we are all equal here no matter how much the council will disagree with that, and something about this woman makes me uncomfortable, so I don't want her to have my name.

Plus, names have power, and only my mate gets to have it.

I turn away, but she keeps up, trying to touch me. I dodge her attempts and glare at her, making her laugh. "I'm Freda from Elemental Court." She flicks her hair like I should be impressed, but I simply carry on walking, heading back inside to be near my mate. It's been a long time since I was thrust into small talk and the spotlight.

I hate it.

"You are very handsome. I can taste your power too. If you wanted to slip away to feed—"

I turn, focusing all my power on her. "I feed from my mate, no other. The mere suggestion is an insult, and you know that. Do not let it happen again." With an outraged glare, I turn away from her, ready to be at my mate's side, when pain suddenly explodes in my neck.

SIXTY

ALTHEA

I SIT UPON MY throne, watching and waiting, when I feel it. There is a sense of wrongness as something messes with the bonds I share with my mates. A sharp stab of agony, followed by regret, floats to me, and I lift my head, searching for the source. When I find it, a wave of anguish tears through me, stronger than when my first mate rejected me. My breath stops, and everything fades but the scene before me.

A woman's fangs are in Osis's neck.

She is feeding from him, my mate, and tasting what is mine.

He rips away, panting, and covers his neck with his hand, but I can barely see through the anguished tears welling in my eyes. The mate bond drives my intense instincts, and I couldn't stop if I tried.

"Did you let another taste you?" I roar, jealousy coursing through me alongside pain and possessiveness. The music cuts out, and our guests turn to look at me and then follow my gaze. I feel my other mates, my kings, surging forward in my mind, but I zone them out and focus on Osis.

On my tiger.

His face is pale, and his eyes are shadowed with so much pain, it makes my heart ache.

"Did you?" I demand, my tone lethal.

I can barely breathe through my fury and pain.

The word *betrayed* chants in my brain once more.

Dropping to his knees, Osis begins to crawl to me on the red carpet, his eyes filled with apology and pain. I feel my power slam through the room, pushing everyone back. Osis lowers his head, gritting his teeth, and continues to crawl through the bombardment.

I hear Nathair calling for me in my head, but I ignore him. I ignore everything but the man on his knees as he stops before me, tears swimming in his gaze and trailing down his face. A knife appears in his hand, and I glance at it and then back to him.

"Answer me!" I order, the words filled with agony, and the others in the room cry out with my pain.

I have been betrayed once more by someone who was meant to love me.

"You betrayed me," I whisper, but I know he hears it. "Just like the mate before you."

He staggers like I have physically wounded him, his face twisting in pain.

"My queen," he rasps, and I feel his own pain, his own self-hatred racing through him as he lowers closer to the floor. "I am sorry I let her touch me. I'm sorry I couldn't stop her. She tasted my blood. I did not want her to, I do not want anyone to touch me except you, my mate, my queen, but it happened. I offer myself to you for punishment. I offer myself in apology. Every inch of me is yours. I will prove it."

My heart stutters in pain and possessiveness. I know he would never betray me, but it doesn't stop old wounds from reopening and the instinct of matehood.

He rips his shirt open, tosses it away, and presses the knife to his chest.

I gape as he plunges it into his sternum, sawing through his skin and bone. There are gasps and cries from the crowd, but I don't take my eyes from him.

My mate.

He tears a hole in his chest, the bloodied knife dropping to the floor, and shoves his hand into the wound with a cry. Blinking rapidly, I watch as he searches around in his own chest cavity and, with a scream, yanks his heart free.

The beating, bloody organ lies in his palm.

"This has always been yours. Take it, my queen, because without you, it would cease to beat anyway. Take my heart and know I love you," he begs, his body swaying from blood loss and the lack of his heart.

He's dying.

I get to my feet and walk towards him. He tilts his head back, and even in death, I feel his love, his obsession, and his awe for me.

"I love you, my queen. Take it and make it yours once more."

I drop to my knees before him, knowing every eye is on me.

Leaning down, I lick the beating organ, holding his gaze as he gasps and dies, and in the blood, I see the truth. I see the woman grabbing him from behind and sinking her fangs into his neck before he could react. She tried to lay claim and gain power in our court to be a spy. I feel his revulsion, his hatred, as he thrashed and tried to escape.

"I will die before I hurt you," he whispers.

Lifting my head, my lips stained with his blood, I meet his eyes as they lose their brightness.

My queen, please. I hear the others in my head, begging me to save him . . . to forgive him.

Osis's lips move as his life drains from him. "My fate is in your hands. I'm sorry, my love. Forgive me, in this life or the next."

I gently accept his heart, holding it in my hand, and he starts to sag. I catch him and press my lips to his as I plunge his heart back into his body. He screams against me, thrashing as I kiss him.

I taste death on his lips, his soul ready to depart. "You are mine. I command you to live and be tied to me forever. I do not want your heart unless it is in this body," I state loudly, letting everyone hear. "You are mine, Osis, and so is this heart. Now breathe," I demand. "Live."

He shudders, his eyes filling with life once more. "My queen," he murmurs. "I love you."

"I love you too," I reply against his lips, and then I sink my fangs into his neck, replacing the stain of the other's touch. Despite the blood loss, he tugs me closer with a moan.

"Yes, make me yours. Please, my queen," he begs, his back arching as I throw my pleasure at him, and with a scream, he comes before everyone at the ball. When I pull back, I kiss him softly, lowering him to the ground, and quickly slice my wrist then press it to his lips to let him feed. Lifting my head, I scan the room, noting the horror, desire, and longing on people's faces.

Come be with him, I demand of my other mates. They appear, and I pull my wrist back and stand, leaving Osis in their protection as I zero in on the woman who dared to touch my mate.

The crowd parts as I saunter through their masses, creating an open circle around the woman. She might have done it on orders, or she might just have taken an opportunity, greedy for power and advancement, but it does not matter. Her court and friends betray her, leaving her standing alone with my mate's blood on her lips. She looks frightened as she watches me move closer, but then she tilts her chin up in defiance.

She's beautiful, with short hair and a tall, willowy frame, but I will destroy her for daring to touch what is mine.

"He tasted good. I could feel how much he wanted it," she taunts.

Fool.

Smiling cruelly, I stop before her, noting her flinch at my expression as she struggles to meet my gaze and stay on her feet against my power, and that is without me even trying, so I let it free for once.

My power fills me, causing my skin to glow from within, and with a cry, she drops to her knees—as does every single person in this ball. I let it grow, and she screams.

"Please, I'm sorry!" she cries, cowering on all fours to avoid my wrath.

It will not work. She touched what is mine.

She tasted what is mine.

"Your apology means nothing here," I say, my booming voice filled with power and anger. "You touched what is mine. You dared to taste my mate. My mate!" I roar, and she screams, blood pouring from her eyes and ears. It calls to me, waiting for me to use it, but I don't. I don't waste my power on her yet.

Instead, I grip her chin and drag her to her feet. She struggles, but she's weak, so very weak.

"Mine," I hiss in her face. "And you will pay for it."

"Too late, his blood is inside me," she spits, blood dribbling over her lips.

"You are right," I muse, but then I smile and focus on her blood, and I let my powers run free, calling to what is mine—my mate's blood. She howls, and it shatters windows and mirrors as I rip each drop from her and call it to me. It floats across the distance between us and absorbs into my skin. I feel the horror and confusion of the crowd as they witness my power, which has not been seen in centuries. "But not anymore." Not a single trace remains in her. She has no power over him. I make sure of it.

I watch as she tries to crawl away. Laughing, I press my heel to her back, pinning her as I look around. "What is the penalty for those who drink from others without consent?" No one answers, and my grin widens. "It is an old law, so I will forgive your lack of knowledge. Nonetheless, your ignorance will not save her." Reaching down once more, I turn her head and grip her fangs, ripping them from her mouth.

The scream that leaves her shatters my eardrums, but they will heal quickly as I toss her to the floor once more where she howls and covers her mouth, knowing what that means.

"You will never touch what isn't yours again," I tell her.

I cursed her to a long, painful death without the ability to heal herself or taste another again.

Leaving her there, where she screams and burns from the inside, I curl my hand around her fangs and look at the shocked guests. "Let that be a warning to anyone who thinks they can lay claim in my court. These men are mine. Their hearts, souls, bodies, and blood are mine. If you so much as look at them wrong, I will rip you to pieces and bathe in your blood while I fuck them." I smile.

Striding back to Osis, I crouch before him and offer him her fangs. "My love, she will never touch you again."

He smiles then kisses me wildly. "I love you."

"Music!" Nathair calls, grinning at me as I grip Osis's head and jerk it back until he moans for me.

His mate.

Sixty One

Lycus

I watched my mate in awe as she defended my brother, taking the life of another in her jealousy and anger. Her power flooded the room, and I'm not ashamed to say it made me flood my trousers with seed.

I don't regret what she did, and neither does she as she kisses Osis proudly, claiming him, but we still draw closer. They have seen what she is capable of now, and they won't make the mistake of coming at her directly. I can almost see the treachery and plans forming behind their conniving façades.

They are all on alert, and the court members of the woman who dared to touch our queen's man, our brother, are dragged away like naughty children. The others close ranks and wait, and so do we. They have no leg to stand on. That woman attacked unprovoked and drank without consent, so it was within Althea's right as his mate to defend him and seek retribution. That doesn't mean they will take it easily though. They came here to find proof of our so-called crimes and to take us down so they could implement their power in our court. They will use everything to their advantage.

Worried about what is happening, I shift quickly, and with a nod to Nathair, I take to the ceiling, hanging out of sight where they can't catch me in the darkness while I listen.

If anyone tries to attack my queen, they will perish from my venom.

I build an intricate web as I wait, spinning my silk and throwing it from the rafters. It won't cover the whole corner of the room, but I need to do something, and spelling my mate's name in silk is a good waste of time. Once it's done, and I hang from the edge, I can't help but seek her approval. Like she senses me, she gets to her knees on the pillows and searches for me. As always, she sees through the darkness and straight to me, her eyes lighting up when she sees her name. Love pumps down our bond.

I'm about to swing down to see her when a flash of something catches my many eyes, and a warning vibration lifts the hair on my legs.

I spot a vampyr trying to sneak around my mate and brothers as something silver gleams in his hands. She hasn't seen him yet, so I slam my warning into their heads, but I'm also already moving. Swinging across the ceiling, I land right behind him just as he lunges at my mate. One pincer clamps onto his arm, and the other pierces his shoulder as I lift him into the air. His screams fill the room as his blood runs down my legs. The blade he was going to sink into my mate's heart tumbles to the floor.

She was his sister, I tell the others down the bond, sensing his intentions and emotions through the blood soaking my hair. *He was going to kill Althea for it.*

Nathair stands slowly, glaring at him. "Which court claims him?" he calls out.

There is no response, so Nathair smirks. "No one? Your court does not wish to claim the brother of the dying female who also broke our rules this evening. You foolish male, now you will die too." He looks at Althea, who simply nods from her nest of pillows. For a moment, I hesitate, but then I see her bloodlust and excitement as she watches me.

She wants to watch me kill him.

She wants to watch her mate protect her.

She's such a vicious little thing.

I lift him higher so his screams echo around the room, a hissing warning escaping my spider at his audacity.

My mate.

Mine!

I smell her desire in the air, and it only spurs me on, my animal side taking over as I strike. Swiftly and steadily, I sink my huge fangs into the man's chest. His howls of agony only make me hold him tighter as I rise into the air, suspending us both as I pump my venom into him. My fangs pierce through him, sliding out the other side of his body, and then I finally release him, catching him in my silk. I keep him suspended as I watch and wait. A crowd gathers, both horrified and curious as he starts to scream and thrash in the silk, scratching out his own eyes as they melt and burn. His tongue liquifies also, and blood pours from every orifice. His skin begins to blister and bubble until it bursts open and peels away, leaving a muscle-covered skeleton before that melts as well. I leave him there and lower myself to the ground. The crowd surges away from me in horror, their hands covering their mouths.

I turn to my mate, but there is nothing but love in her gaze as she raises her hand for me. I hurry over to accept it, needing her. She tilts her head, and I hesitate when I reach her, but she urges me on by sliding her hand up my body to cup my jaw and draw me closer to feed.

My prize for protecting my family.

With the same fangs I just used to viciously kill the man, I bite my mate. She welcomes me with a moan, her head falling back as her arm wraps around me to bring me down. I'm careful, since my fangs are so big in this form, but she encourages me to sink them deeper, her eyes closed in bliss.

Our little monster fucker.

Our nightmare lover.

AZUL

I watch my brother's back as he feeds. The horror and revulsion on everyone's faces makes me smirk. Our mate moans loudly, and when Lycus releases her, he lays her down softly and steps before her in spider form, then he raises his legs and hisses. The size of a truck, he's a threatening sight, and it's clear what he is saying—do not try to harm his mate.

With one last hiss, the spider melts away and Lycus takes his place, panting and covered in blood. He drops to his knees next to his mate and cuddles into her side, licking at the wound on her neck. With a lazy smile, she strokes his head. My eyes go back to the man he killed.

I've only ever seen him use his venom once, but it's still a terrifying sight.

The man melted and bled from the inside out. Now, the ghoulish remnants remain strung up there as a warning, providing a nightmarish sight, which is perfect for us. Zale snuggles closer to Lycus, supporting him after what he did. The rest of us are spread out, watching our guests as they recover.

"How many more will be killed tonight? Is that why we were brought here?" a man calls.

I seek him out, and my hand moves to my sword, but my mate's voice stops me.

"You demanded to see us and our home, so that is what you are doing. You would try to stop my mates from killing those intent on killing me? I don't think so. Just because you hide your kills behind closed doors does not make you any better than us. You might be glossy and perfect on the outside, but on the inside, you are all just nightmares like us."

"We are not monsters, not like you," someone else retorts.

"Oh, darling, we are all monsters." She laughs, the sound throaty and beautiful, making my cock jerk. "Some just hide it better. You forget that I was born into your courts, and I saw the truth behind the curtain . . . the perfect façade you present to one another." She holds her hands out, and Nathair and Reve help her to her feet. Keeping their hands in hers, she walks forward and tilts her head, eyeing the crowd.

"Would you like me to start naming the sins of the courts? How about the harvest festival two years ago, where four women were killed for having sex with another court? Or when Specter held a party that turned into a bloodbath after a challenge was issued and denied. I can keep going. Those are only some of the very public slayings and embarrassments you have suffered, but it does not even begin to touch on what you hide behind closed doors."

"And Principes?" someone demands. Ah, here we go. "They were slaughtered not a week ago. Many believe it was you."

She smiles, not denying it. "If they were killed, or slaughtered as you say, then why do I see some of their court here?" She begins to pace before them. "Maybe it was simply those in the court who had broken our laws who perished?" she taunts. They won't outright accuse her, not after seeing what we are capable of, so they are fishing, and she's playing them perfectly, turning them on each other.

"And who are you to carry out our laws?" The man speaking is a council member and King of the Elemental Court. He doesn't seem angry. Instead, he almost appears curious. "That is the council's job."

Turning away, she starts to walk towards her throne, but she glances over her shoulder with a sardonic grin. "Then maybe the council should do a better job."

I can't help but chuckle, my eyes tracking my mate as I protect her back.

Better job indeed.

Sixty Two

Althea

The council is going to make their move soon. I can sense it. They are growing restless.

Now? I ask the others through our bond. Nervous energy fills me, not that I let it show. I know what we'll do here tonight will change everything, but it's something that needs to happen. Just because it's our norm doesn't mean it's right. Our race needs to be shown that we cannot carry on like this.

That is our job as judges, and tonight is our wicked show.

No better time, Nathair responds, so they stride over to the thrones. I follow them, but this time I do not sit. I remain standing, and when my mates spread out, standing before their own thrones, I smile at the gathered crowd. I ignore their whispers and palpable fear. Maybe they sense their own deaths.

Maybe they simply don't like this place.

Either way, it won't save them.

Nothing will.

"A little while ago, you asked who we are to carry out our laws. Would you like to see?" I call, my voice echoing around the room.

Our guests gather closer as Simon and his mate close the doors to keep them inside. Our monsters fade into the shadows with a cackle, knowing what is coming. Without waiting for a response, I wave my hand over my face, my sardonic grin the last thing they see. My mates do the same, conjuring their masks which are an extension of our power. I don't openly do this a lot, as it costs power, but it's worth it for the loud gasps as my seven kings and I stand before our thrones, our masks glaring at them. Our powers flow freely through the room. Shadows gather together and reach out their hands, the cold air of death making our guests shiver, and nightmares come to life, writhing through the room as they search for prey.

For sinners.

"We are the blood kings and queen. We are the law. We are the creatures who go bump in the dark. We are the watchers of crimes. We are the scales of justice. We are the hands of the gods. We are the sinners reborn. We are the judges," I boom, and the pillows on the floor catch alight, burning away to expose the judgement blood circle we had hidden underneath. Laughter peels from my lips at the fear now consuming each soul here. They might not know what we are, but they sense the touch of fate and death deep down, and it echoes around the room as my kings join in.

"What is the meaning of this?" my ex-mate, the Vermillion king, demands, still confused and trying to appear in control.

"Oh, you are pretty but quite dumb, aren't you?" I smirk behind the mask. "The council isn't doing their job properly. Our race is saturated with those willing to murder, steal, rape, and take what isn't theirs. Those in positions of power grow richer and more powerful, while those who are considered lesser struggle just to survive. The gods have grown angry at our wasteful use of our gifts and our spoiled attitudes, so they picked us. We are vampyrs chosen throughout the centuries who have been wronged by our race and given a second chance—a second chance to stop this from happening anymore. Over the years, the judges have silently watched and punished those who were deserving, but time is up. We have observed and waited for too long. Nothing is changing. One death makes a ripple, but many make a wave. You have forgotten what we are—who we are. You have forgotten our laws, and the judges have been ordered by the gods to cleanse the race or we will all be killed." For a moment, there's no movement, and then someone starts to laugh.

Others awkwardly join in.

"Funny, really funny." The Vermillion king chortles, turning to get the crowd to join him. "They are trying to justify their murder of our people! Ours! They are killers, nothing more, and the council will always protect our people."

I see some hesitate and head for the doors, clearly wanting out. I simply snap my fingers, and every single door and window within this room slams shut and locks, and they will not move until I release the blood binding I put on them earlier.

"The council has done nothing. It has grown weak. There is no escape, not now. Everyone here, every member of every court, will be judged. The wicked will be punished, and the innocent will be free to live a better life and create a better future for our people. You can laugh all you want, but it will not change the outcome. The powerful have preyed upon the weak for too long, but no more." I nod at my men.

It does not matter if they believe us. We are doing our duty because they failed, and it is time to begin. Unlike the others, we need no fanfare. This is real, this is life and death, and it will be conducted with dignity and the appropriate respect.

My mates fade into Conall's shadows and appear in the crowd beyond. There are some screams and shouts as people try to fight their way out. Simon and his mate come to stand behind me, and my monsters gather at the entrances and exits to scare those wanting to run. I do not enjoy this—okay, well, a part of me does, but a part of me is also sad that it has come to this. There will be so much death, so much waste—no, we will not enjoy taking all these lives, but we will do it. I made a promise and took an oath. The mark on my chest burns with purpose and power, ready to carry out our sacred duties. More guests turn to me and begin to beg, but I simply wait until my mates bring forth seven people—a mix of men and women. My mates push them to their knees before me, placing a hand on their shoulders to stop them from moving.

"You are to be judged. Do you wish to confess any sins beforehand?" My voice carries through the room, guided by a power much bigger than any of us. Sometimes death is necessary, and sometimes you simply cannot have hope. Sometimes bringing upon an ending is needed for a brighter beginning.

"Fuck you!"

"Let us go!"

"Council, save us!"

"My king!"

"They cannot save you now," Osis says so calmly that they begin to struggle more.

I nod, and Conall lifts his man with one hand and drops him into the circle before producing a knife and cutting his throat, spilling blood into the waiting bowl. I've never done a full judgement before, but I know how it goes. However, I didn't expect the bone-deep power that flows through me. Beginning with Nathair and his tie to the blood circle, it flows through us from the bond, showing us this man's life and powers. He sees it too; I know that from my own judgement. Tears fall from his eyes, and for a moment, I soften towards him before I receive some of his more recent memories.

He was a good man once, an enforcer, but now?

Now, he uses his position for personal gain. I watch as men and women are forced to serve and feed him for protection.

"You are found guilty."

Conall quickly and humanely rips out the man's heart and tosses it aside. His body is lifted from the circle and placed to the side, his blood covering the floor as the crowd screams.

The dragon roars at those trying to fight their way out, and the council gathers together, glancing around and ready to go to war.

It will not help them.

I turn my attention back to the waiting vampyrs.

We judge them one by one, and I speak the words out loud. Groups have formed, led by the council, who are ready to attack us, but I simply use my power to push them all to their knees, even those struggling to ram the door with a bench. My monsters flood the areas they left, blocking their escape even more with cruel laughs.

There is no escape.

Tonight, the Court of Nightmares will either be their tomb or their salvation.

Another seven are pushed before me. "Innocent," I murmur as I look at a sobbing man. He lifts his tear-stained face as my mates help him from the circle and over to the side where a few more wait, shocked and pale from facing their own mortality.

They are even thankful.

"We are not cruel," I call out to the rest. "We are simply doing what must be done."

This is taking too long, Nathair murmurs. *Eventually, someone will break through and get one of us.* He hates to admit it, but it's true.

We don't like to prolong this process, but this is too much, not to mention all it would take is one of my mates dropping their guard for a second for the council to pounce. I see it in their eyes. They still think they are in control.

"Maybe . . ." I show them, and they all turn to me.

"You think you can?" Nathair asks.

I nod, my mark pulsing with comfort. Stepping down from the throne, I face the partygoers once more. "You will be released once you are judged, but do not fear, for we hold no prejudice, and the blood never lies."

"You are crazy!" Someone tries to throw themselves at me, but Zale catches him by his throat and tosses him to his knees for the next judgement.

It's now or never.

I am part god, after all, and I'm beginning to realise this is why. Maybe this was always my destiny. Maybe this was always what my mother foresaw. I'm a sinner, a killer, a reaper, a queen, a god, a judge, and a saviour. I am everything. I am good and bad. I am one of them and above them. There is no stopping this now. Either the guilty will pass on tonight or all will, including the innocent. They each made decisions in their lives, and now it is time to face the consequences.

Stepping back, I hold my arms out and close my eyes, reaching for that glowing part of me. It feels like sinking into a hug with a loved one, lazy Sundays in your pyjamas with the fire going, or the sound of rain hitting your window at night.

I fade into it, and it flows through me and out, combining with my rose and thorns until they both rush through my veins. Comfort and pain. Give and take. Power and pleasure.

When my eyes open, tendrils flow from me and move through the room, glowing gold like that spark within me. I feel it transform me into something much more, and I see some of them drop to their knees in awe, others in fear. I wait as the tendrils touch every person in the room. The gold glow fills them with the possibility of what we could be, while my vines slither across them, and when I command it, they cut into their skin.

Power slides up those tendrils and back into me until I am full and overflowing. My vines tighten, and petals begin to fall as candles flare and grow brighter. True vines grow from the cement floor and shoot up across the walls before hanging down.

More blood, more power, and their thoughts fill me, causing me to stagger.

Give them to us, draya. *We are here, so use us.*

My queen, give to your mates. We are one, share it. This is not just your burden. We are a family. We are one.

Let us help.

We are here.

Their voices flood my brain, pushing back the pain from taking in so many stimuli.

Yes, yes, that's right. I channel it through me and to my mates. I become the funnel to the judges, the bridge between god and vampyr. One by one, each person is judged without being in the blood circle with us touching them.

I stand where I am, only I am not standing anymore. I am hovering in the air above them, lit from within. I glow like the flames surrounding me. My eyes are bright, illuminated orbs, and my hair floats with my power. I hear my god speaking through me to them, coming to collect their debts, their sins, and their souls to cleanse his race. They hear it too.

My men weave through the crowd, and justice is quickly served. Lives are swiftly taken and spared until all that's left are the innocent and those who can change—the ones my god believes are worthy of a second chance. After all, we were given a choice, so they should be as well.

Sinclair is amongst them, as is my rejected mate. Despite my feelings towards him, he is not a terrible leader, and his court needs him. In the memories I saw, he was kind and good towards them, although aloof. The years got to him. I almost feel sorry for him because he's been alone for so long, but he made his choice, and now I have made mine—to save the man who rejected me, disgraced me, and doomed me.

Slowly, the power recedes, flowing back into me. The light reabsorbs into my body, and my feet softly touch the ground as I blink and bring the ballroom into view. Over half of the guests who joined us this evening are still on their knees before us. Most are from the younger generation—unfortunately, time and immortality has a way of corrupting—but there are three council members left to guide them: Sinclair, my ex, and the older man who spoke to me from Elemental Court.

Balthasar, my powers whisper to me.

"You have been judged. You are free to go." I open the doors then without even looking. "But remember, we will be here at all times, waiting and watching. We will not let the actions of a few doom our race. We will rebuild now and become better. We follow the laws, we support the youth, and we create a better future. We must."

I turn away, heavy with exhaustion and the weight of the memories and lives we took. I know Azul and Osis feel them and are waiting to fulfil their duties, while Zale and the others start to carry the bodies to a pile to be burned.

I'm so focused on the next step, I do not notice the movement until there's a noise behind me.

"Do not touch my daughter!" Druig commands, and my head snaps around to see a blade coming for my unprotected back, and then he's there.

Druig, his own enforcer, picks Sinclair up, preventing him from attacking me, and throws him into the crowd.

Druig is . . . my father?

"Father?" I exclaim out loud.

Sixty Three

Reve

I TURN, FEELING SHOCK ripple through our bond. The man is the one Nathair had been unsure of, since he had been watching Althea intently. Is this why, or is this a trick? But no, we read his bonds. How did he hide that from us? Or did we not look hard enough? I filter through all the memories that flowed through us during the judgement and find one where he stands with a female holding a baby and send it down the bond to Althea. She staggers, looking from him to me.

"You are sure?" she asks.

"I can check," I reply.

"Althea—" He reaches for her, but she steps back, and his hand drops. He schools his expression quickly, but I saw the flash of pain on his face.

"Daughter? Impossible," Sinclair spits as he stands, furious his own enforcer thwarted his attack.

"No, not impossible." He sighs, rubbing at his head. "I did not want to do it this way." He looks at Althea. "Please understand, I had no choice but to keep this a secret. I promised your mother so you wouldn't be dragged into politics alongside me. I took the enforcer position to protect you and your mother, and when she—when she died, I stayed to protect you. I know you don't believe me, I know it's not good enough, but it's the truth. You are my daughter, Althea. I loved your mother. She was my mate."

He inhales a deep breath. "I have been so lost without her all these years. You are all that's kept me going. Tonight felt like a second chance. You are so beautiful, my daughter, so beautiful and powerful just like she said. Look at what you have become." His eyes are filled with tears, and he looks at me helplessly. "Do whichever test you are talking about." He kneels before our queen openly and honestly, reaching for her with hope.

She hesitates then nods at me, staring at him in shock and horror. Simon comes to her side, taking her hand, and she holds it tightly. Druig, her father, smiles at that. "Simon," he murmurs. "Glad to see I could help."

"Help?" Althea looks at Simon.

"He helped me get away. I didn't understand why..." Simon glances between them. "You do have his anger," he jokes, and Althea chokes out a laugh.

"Are you sure?" I ask her as I step up to the man who could be my beloved's father.

She nods, and I feel the bonds gathering in our head to protect her, but we cannot protect her from this betrayal.

Hasn't my mate gone through enough?

Gripping the man's head, I close my eyes and delve into his memories, sharing them through our bond as I see them. He lets me in, lets me see everything. I feel his devotion and love for his mate, along with his grief and agony over losing her. There is a memory of him holding her dying body as he bellows his agony to the world. Her hand comes up softly and covers his heart.

"Keep my promise, my love. I will wait for you on the other side." Then she, too, is gone, fading in his arms, and he is lost in the darkness. The only light is her, the baby with my mate's eyes. He watches over her from infancy to childhood. When she skins her knee, he is there. When she cries, he protects her without her even knowing.

Next, I see her as she is now, hurrying towards a door, and he watches her, knowing he will have to say goodbye. He wishes he could tell her the truth and take the pain away, but he can't, and he knows he has to let her go or lose her like her mother.

The door shuts behind her, and he sinks to his knees, clutching his broken heart. His whole reason for living is gone, but he gets up and carries on to protect her from afar as much as he can. I pull free, and the utter love in his memories, the parental protectiveness, brings tears to my eyes. When I look at Althea, she is on her knees, staring at the space between them, tears flowing down her cheeks.

"Althea," he croaks. "I deserve your hatred. I deserve for you to turn me away. I left you alone. No matter how close I was, you were alone, and I am so sorry. I couldn't bear to lose you." He licks his lips. "I will face you, daughter, for judgement once more."

"You already have," I inform him in a whisper.

"Not on these crimes. Judge me, Althea, for the crimes I committed against you."

"Stop it," she whispers. "Stop it." She shakes her head, stumbling to her feet and backing away. After everything she has faced, this is her breaking point—a father who always loved her but left her alone, even when she needed him the most.

My brothers step before her, blocking her from his view. "Now is not the time," Nathair snaps, crossing his arms. Zale is growling, as is Osis. I drop my hand from Druig and join them. Even though I can feel his pain and how badly he loves her and wants to make amends, I will always choose her.

I would rip myself open to have that chance with my parents once more, but this is her choice. A lot has happened today, and she needs time. I tell him as much as he looks at me. I nod, and he looks away, seeming to slump with pain.

"What do we do with him?" I ask the others, eyeing Sinclair, the king of her old court. "He attempted to kill a judge for doing her job." I want to rip him to pieces for even daring to touch my mate. Had it not been for her father, she might have been hurt or worse. We didn't expect it, and we should have.

We failed her, but we will never fail her again.

"Death," Lycus snarls.

"Wait!" he calls, getting to his feet, glaring from Druig to us.

"No," Althea murmurs and then pushes between us. "No more death. There has been enough. He was spared for a reason, and no matter our own anger at him, we cannot take a life that does not deserve it. He was judged and left alive for a reason. They need him."

"He tried to kill you even after being given a second chance. That isn't right," I snap.

"He made his choice, as did we. We cannot take his life this night."

"You might not be able to, but I can." We all turn to see her father behind Sinclair. With a snarl, he slams his fist into the king's chest and rips out his heart. We all gape in shock as the wide-eyed king falls, his heart clutched in Althea's father's hand. "He tried to kill my daughter. That's reason enough for me."

"He was judged," she whispers.

"He was not a good man, Althea, nor was he a terrible one. He could have become a good king if he wished to be, but his action this night only proved he didn't. Instead of choosing life and healing like everyone else here, he chose the old ways of death and murder to get what he wanted. He got what he deserved, and now it is not on your conscience as a judge. I will always protect my little girl, even if you do not wish me to."

They stare at each other, the king's heart still in his hand.

He committed treason against his court to protect his daughter. They have every right to come for him, despite the fact that the king tried to kill someone.

However, it seems like they, too, have had enough death. Balthasar, the older man on the council, steps forward. "I declare you innocent of all wrongdoing. It was clear he meant harm to her, and he has paid the price. There will be no more death tonight." He looks at our queen. "I cannot condone what has happened here this evening, but I understand why it has come to this. Our race thought they were above the law, and I sadly did nothing to try and change it, even if I hated it. I will now, and you are right. We need to be better. For now, we go home and mourn." He looks around. "The council will rebuild. Go back to your courts."

"But who will lead us now?" someone from Sinclair's court asks.

"He will," Balthasar states, pointing at Althea's father. "As enforcer, he was next in line. He will lead until another is officially voted in. As for the other courts without a leader, do the same. Whoever is next in line will lead until another is chosen. The council will support you in every way, but for now, we need to heal our wounds and figure out what is next." He turns to us. "We will be in touch, if that is allowed?"

"Yes," Althea answers without pause. "The judges have long been separated from our world, but we must be part of it. We will do anything we can to help."

"I guess the name of this place is accurate—Court of Nightmares. I know I will definitely be having some, but maybe we need some nightmares. Scare those who think they are untouchable to keep them in line." He smiles as he says it and nods at Althea. "We will be in touch, my queen. Thank you for an . . . interesting party."

We watch as those who remain of our race gather. There is no longer a divide between them as, young and old, they walk out the doors they entered so confidently at the beginning of the night. They have been humbled, stripped of their anonymity for their crimes.

They have been seen.

They have been judged.

They have been cleansed.

ALTHEA

Nathair sends everyone out to inspect each inch of the court. We cannot sense anyone nearby, but that doesn't matter because we can't be too safe. Our monsters fade back into the forest without a word, probably sensing how tired I am. Everything led to tonight, and now that it is done, I'm weary.

Once the guys return, they start the process of putting the bodies into a pile to burn, which is the only way to ensure their true death so Osis can guide them across the veil. I go to help, and Conall frowns at me.

"We just have to burn the bodies. You can go, Althea. You don't need to—"

"No, I am a judge. That means I'm a part of everything. I don't get to dip out of the ugly side of things simply because you love me. I am your equal." I bend down and drag a body over the pile, still wearing my fancy dress. When I turn to grab another, my power quivers in warning.

God power.

"Something is coming," I murmur just as the god of death himself emerges into view in the middle of the room, wearing a wicked grin on his lips.

"Bravo, little godling. I couldn't have done better myself—well, I could have, but still." He wanders around, looking at the bodies and blood, and stops before the man still hanging in Lycus's silk. "This one is interesting. It reminds me of my time in France."

"What are you doing here?" I ask as kindly as I can, but I am tired of people, being covered in blood, and having to monitor my words and actions. I just want to curl up with my men and let them hold me until the sun rises once more, reminding me of the beauty of the world.

"Death called to me," he answers, and he seems to be in a good mood because he didn't take offence to my question. He watches me carefully. "I will anticipate the souls who will pass over to me, but I have a feeling we will be seeing each other again." His head tilts, a frown curling his lips. "How interesting, a visitor." He vanishes, leaving me even more confused.

I glance back to see the others are equally as confused as I am, but we all get to work. It might not be the best part of the job, but it is still ours to do. We must honour the dead so they can cross. They have paid with their lives, and it is now our duty to ensure their safe passage. Their souls are free of the infernal pressures of life, and more importantly, they are clean once more.

Once they are piled up, we stand around the bodies in a circle, holding hands as we wish their souls the best. Zale sets them alight, and we watch them burn, ridding the world of the darkness, at least for one night. As they become embers and ash, I turn to Osis and Azul.

Their eyes are closed, and they glow brightly. I know they are helping the souls cross. We wait and protect them as they do their duty. After what feels like hours, they sag and open their eyes, clearly as exhausted as the rest of us.

"It is done."

I look around and smile. "This is going to be a bastard to clean up." Unable to resist, I drop their hands and start to race for the door. "Last one out is the cleaner!" I call, and their laughter is stolen away by our court as they chase after me.

Their laughter lightens my soul, removing some of the heavy price we paid tonight.

I reach my rooms first and quickly collapse, in my dress and jewels, on the bed. They arrive and climb in next to me, holding me to this world when it feels like I could float away.

As my eyes close, I realise our future together is always going to be like this—beautiful, tragic, and filled with both death and purpose, but also laughter and love.

It's in those stolen moments of love and laughter that we'll find the strength to go on, to fight the darkness when it becomes too much.

The world is a hard place to live in, but along the way, you might just find someone, or several people, to travel the path with you, lightening your load and making it worthwhile.

The climb is always the hardest, but the view from the top of the mountain is so worth it.

Sixty Four

Althea

I know I am asleep, but I can feel my loves' warmth surrounding me. Their hands anchor my body to our world and their hearts, but in slumber, I drift. I am not afraid, and unlike my visitor the night before, this one is filled with warmth and love.

Before she appears, I know who it will be—my mother.

I have so much to say, to ask, but as I stare at her hopeful eyes, everything fades and I run into her arms. They circle around me, warm and filled with love. "I am so proud of you, Thea, so very proud. You are an incredible woman."

Tears form in my eyes, even in here. It's all I've ever wished to hear from her. I miss a woman I never got to know, but in my dreams, I get my mother, even if it's just for a little while, and it's enough. It has to be because some part of me knows this will be the last time. The dead cannot wait around forever. She has to move on. She has to find peace, and my selfish need to keep her here cannot continue.

I hold her tighter for a moment before stepping back, our hands still clasped between us. We look so alike, like mirror images, but one is an older woman who never got the life she deserved and one is a younger woman who fights so no other ever has to make the same sacrifice. We are two women who are the backbone of our species, giving everything to save it.

The only difference is that I get to keep my life, my legacy, while hers lies within mine.

That will never disappear, even if this dream will.

"This is goodbye, isn't it?" I ask her softly.

She nods, tears falling from her eyes. "I have been given extra time no other has ever been granted, but it is my time. Daughter, I will always be here with you, and I will await you on the other side. I will meet you there, just not too soon, okay? I want you to live a long, happy life. Not because you are my daughter, but because you deserve it. Althea, you deserve to be happy and to live a long, safe life."

Swallowing against my tears, I bob my head and grip her tighter. "I met my father," I tell her, unsure how much longer I have with her.

She flinches. "Is he okay?" It's a simple question, yet I know everything he said was true. He was her mate, and she loves him deeply, which means he loves her too. If my loves asked me for a promise, wouldn't I keep it?

"He misses you fiercely and is trying to reach out to me," I admit.

She searches my gaze. "It is your choice." How does she know what I want to ask before I do? "I asked him to keep a very selfish promise to protect you. I cannot imagine what that has done to you both, but I would do it again. Sacrifices must be made, and he made his. All I can tell you, Althea, is that your father loved you from the moment I told him you were coming. He was excited for us to have a life as a family, but he never got that. I stole that from him, from both of you. I will not ask you to forgive him for the choices he has made after, but simply to remember that he loves you, Althea, with everything in him. If he didn't, he would be here with me."

"I know." I felt it in his memories, but it doesn't mean I can forget the lies, the deceit, or the fact that he could have been in my life, helping me all along.

Then again, she's right. Would that have changed the future? Would I have ended up here? I don't know, and I don't think any of us have the answers.

"I don't have much time," she says, looking around.

Clouds hover around us in the blue sky, as if we are floating above the world. I don't know if it was my choice or hers, but I do know it's beautiful.

"I love you, Althea. I need you to remember that. Whatever is to come, remember that. Remember that I love you. Remember that I made this choice, not you, so do not feel guilty. It is time for you to stand on your own now, but if you ever need me, I will always be deep in your soul."

"I know," I murmur. I want to tell her I don't want her to go, but that's selfish. Why should I get more time with my loved one when no one else does? I want to beg the gods to give her back to me and tell them I'll do anything, but again, that's selfish. She is right. These are our paths. Mine takes me away from her, but it will always lead me back in the end.

When the sun sets, she will be waiting.

"I love you," I tell her, squeezing her hands tighter. "Thank you for being my mother. Wait for me."

Her hands start to fade, and I step back as she smiles at me.

"You and your father," she promises, placing her hand over her heart. "Forever, Althea."

Our god appears at her side, and with a smile, he takes my mother's hand. "I will look after her for you, Althea, if you look after my children for me." I know he means our race.

"I will," I vow.

"Goodbye, Althea," he murmurs, and hand in hand, they walk towards the clouds. She only looks back once, wearing an expression so filled with love, it staggers me, and when I awake, my heart still bears the strength of her love.

I have to keep her wish and live a long, happy life to make everything she gave up worthwhile . . . and maybe I can forgive the man who is my blood.

"Althea?" Azul rumbles worriedly, his voice thick with sleep. "Are you okay?"

"Yes." I turn my head and meet his sleepy eyes. "Yes, I am. I will be." I take his hand and close my eyes once more, trusting in this brilliant, flawed world.

Sixty Five

Osis

My mate is still sleeping, her back pressed to my front. My head is buried in her neck, and I inhale her scent to calm my heart. My soul is locked with hers, just as my arms are draped around her body, holding her close. My cock hardens, but I ignore it, just enjoying the moment between wakefulness and sleep where I am at peace.

There are no duties, jobs, regrets, or memories.

I am just in love and happy with my mate asleep in my arms, my brothers wrapped around her. A family. A home. A future.

She buries her head deeper into the pillow with a sigh. Her dress is ruched around her, and dried blood flakes on her skin. I should wake her to bathe her so she is more comfortable, but I don't want to disturb this moment. Besides, none of us care about a little blood.

"What time is it?" she murmurs, inadvertently rubbing her perfect ass against my cock. Groaning, I try to shift my hips back, but Lycus snores and turns, throwing his arm and leg over Althea and me, making me grin.

"Early. Go back to sleep, mate," I murmur into her neck, feeling her shiver. The beautiful scent of her desire slowly drifts through the air, and when she moves again, it's with purpose. "Althea," I growl in warning. Unable to resist, I grind my hips into her ass, and we both moan at the friction.

I drag my fangs along her nape, making her moan loudly, and I stiffen, not wanting to wake the others when they need their sleep, but her moans are just too good, so I do it again.

"Either fuck or shut up, I'm trying to sleep," Reve mutters, waving his arm in the air before it flops down across Zale, and then he starts snoring. Althea and I freeze before she giggles softly. The sound sets my heart alight like nothing else. It's the sound of happiness, of my present and my future, and I crave it.

Osis, she says down our bond, her tone resonating with a need so deep, I could never deny her, not that I want to. I always want my mate. Even covered in blood and stained with the souls of our enemies. Even with death in her veins and a god in her heart. Nothing could ever turn me away from my mate, but her need undoes me, because she needs me just as desperately.

Turning her slowly, I cup her chin and lift her head so I can kiss her lips. It's a slow kiss, not urgent like usual. Grabbing her hands that try to explore, I slow them down. "We have all the time in the world, love."

Tasting her love, I deepen the kiss, our bodies melding together as one. She whimpers into my mouth, and I look through my brother's eyes to see Azul sliding his lips along her neck.

He freezes. *Is this okay?* he asks me, seeing if I want privacy.

Always, brother, I reply. *She is ours, all of ours, and she needs us all.*

That wakes the others up. The whimper of our mate is loud in the dark, and once sleepy vampyrs turn feral and possessive as they slide up the bed to worship their mate.

She nips my lip, and it makes me feel like a god.

Like I'm on top of the world.

I am untouchable as long as she moans my name like that. Her legs part as a mouth slides up her thigh to her pussy. Another mouth tugs down her dress to suck her nipple. Hands grip and caress every inch of her as the scent of her desire makes us grow bolder, stronger, and harder.

I swallow her moan as other hands join mine, caressing our mate. Slowly rolling her onto her back, I spread her out for them. I hear them moving, and when I lift my head, the bedding is ripped away before the others crawl back on, their fangs glinting with promise.

Gripping her chin, I turn her eyes back to me. "You're going to take every one of your mates, my queen. You're going to feed and fuck us all. We survived the night, and now we are going to show you how the rest of our lives will be. Understood?"

"Yes." She arches up, reaching out.

"How do you want us?" I ask, tightening my grip until she cries out. "Althea," I press.

"I want someone in my ass and someone in my mouth. I want someone in my pussy. I want Zale in my cunt while Lycus fucks his ass."

There's a groan, and I narrow my eyes. "What else?"

"I want to be covered in blood and cum. I want every single one of you," she replies, not the least bit bothered. "Please, Osis, I want you all."

"Then you'll have us," I tell her and look at the others, our bonds open so we can communicate silently. With a smirk, I lie down next to her and pat my lap. "Come claim your first mate."

She rolls onto me, crawling up my body to kiss me, my already hard cock jerking at the feel of her. She gasps, and I know Azul has ripped open a wrist and is rubbing the blood across her perfect ass. Pulling away, I flip her and slide her now blood-covered ass across my hardness. "Take every inch of me, my love," I purr in her ear. Helping her rise until my cock notches at her ass, I slide inside of her, slick with her blood and my need.

I work every inch deep until she lies flat across me, groaning and twitching. Closing my eyes, I grip her to keep her still and to stop myself from coming too soon. I want my mate to feel filled and satisfied before then. Opening my eyes, I nod at Zale who slides across her front. His tongue laps greedily at her cunt, making her cry out as her ass clenches around me.

"Fuck," I grunt, fighting my own need as she grips my cock like a vice. I can hear the wet sound of his tongue as he eats her, and within minutes, she's screaming her release. Gritting my teeth as she pulses around my cock, I watch Zale slide up her body. He kisses her softly, making her taste her own need, before I feel his cock pushing into her, stretching her pussy alongside me. She's so fucking tight, it almost hurts, and when he's fully seated, all three of us moan and twitch at the feel.

"I need to move," I finally say, lifting her slightly then pushing in and out. Zale copies the movement, finding a rhythm as Lycus climbs behind Zale.

He grips Zale's hair, who groans and closes his eyes. "Are you sure, mate?" Lycus murmurs.

"Yes, fuck him!" Althea cries. "Fuck me through him."

Lycus climbs behind Zale, lifts his wrist to his mouth, tears it open, and then smears the blood across his cock before sliding it into Zale. I feel pleasure reverberate down the bond, followed by love, and then Lycus starts to move. He fucks Zale's ass, which in turn fucks Althea down onto me. Gritting my teeth, I fight my own need, dragging my fangs along every inch of her I can reach as she cries out, reaching for her other mates.

Lycus snarls, his fangs large and proud as he speeds up, pushing her harder and faster onto my cock. "Fuck, this is too good," he growls, slapping harder against Zale's ass. Zale cries out before wrapping his lips around Althea's nipple and sucking as she moans.

She clamps around us, and her release triggers Zale's, who mewls loudly. He bites into her breast and feeds. I fight back my own orgasm, which is clawing at my balls and spine. Lycus bends down over Zale and buries his fangs in his neck, spraying Althea with blood as he feeds before both of them fall back, spent and overfed.

Panting, I scrape my fangs across her neck as she whimpers. Azul moves between her thighs and lifts her legs, sliding into her pussy. He takes her just like she wants, and she claws at his chest, cutting into it. Blood slicks us both as he fucks her hard and fast. I need to move, though, so I turn us all until we are on our sides again, and we fuck her between us—one in, one out. Azul fucks her messy pussy, while I take her tight little asshole.

My fangs slide across her neck before I sink them in deep. She screams as she comes again. This time I can't fight it. It sends me over the edge, and I roar against her neck as I spill inside her, pushing my cock in harder to stuff her with it.

Sliding from her ass to make room for her other mates, I collapse back onto the bed and watch as she rolls to her knees, pinning Azul and riding him. She strikes, and he screams, his cock pumping her full of his release as she feeds from his chest. When he's spent and unable to move, she turns and spots the others waiting.

I crawl over to Azul and lie back amongst the pillows, satisfied and lustful as I watch my mate crawl to Reve, who is the closest. He welcomes her with open arms, their lips meeting messily as their hands slide across each other before she kneels and wraps her lips around his cock.

Her pretty ass, dripping with my cum, is high in the air. Conall snaps, and tendrils of shadows wrap around her as he moves behind her. "Mine," he growls, and with a grunt, he fills her tight pussy.

I arch my neck to see. Reve's head falls back as his cock thrusts in and out of her pouty mouth, uncaring of her fangs. Her nails rip into his thighs, and his blood pours down onto the bed.

Her pussy is stretched by Conall's huge cock as his shadows tweak and play with her nipples until she moans. Her pleasure slams through us all as she comes for them so beautifully, and I spill once more. My hand grips my cock as I watch my mate take my brothers and drink her fill. Her head turns, and she sinks her fangs into Reve's thigh, drinking as he comes with a roar.

Conall follows soon after, filling her pussy with his cum as his shadows sneak into her ass and play with her until she rips her mouth away from Reve as she screams once more.

Only Nathair is left.

Our oldest brother.

Unlike every time in the past, he doesn't wait for her to come to him. Instead, he covers the distance between them and goes to her. He lays her down like a feast and slides into her pussy, connecting the circle of mates forever.

His eyes rise to us, and we quickly move closer, stroking her body. Lips meet hers, and our mouths cover every inch of her skin we can get our hands on. She cries out, gripping at us as Nathair slowly makes love to her, rolling his hips and making her moan. He keeps the pace slow and steady until neither of them can take it, and with a snarl, he speeds up.

He fucks his mate while she's surrounded by the rest of her mates.

Our names are on her lips as she begs for more. My fangs slide deeply once again, and the others do the same. It sets her off once more, and Nathair roars his own release before moving back and slamming his fangs into her pubic mound.

All of us drink from our mate while a soft smile covers her lips and her eyes shut in bliss.

The pleasure, love, and happiness she feels fills our bond, and our own love for her is pressed towards her.

Pulling my fangs free, I lick at the wound before collapsing. I am spent and so full, I almost overflow with power. The others lie down around her, stroking her as Nathair kisses her pussy, leaving her satisfied and covered in blood and cum just like she wanted.

"Good morning to you too," she says, making us crack up.

Just like always.

Gods, please let the rest of our lives be like this.

Sixty Six

Althea

Breakfast, or more like brunch, is spread across the table. Perched on Conall's lap, wearing one of their oversized shirts, I sit back, unable to eat another bite. Once he's sure I'm satisfied, he demolishes what I left on my plate, making me grin as I lean into him. I woke up the very best way today, with my mates making me see heaven, and now I'm feeling lazy. I know we have a lot to do, but for now, we just soak up the peace.

Sunlight filters into the kitchen, heating my skin thanks to my sun master—he says it's just for me. I can hear our monsters out on our grounds, and my whole family is here, even Simon and his mate, who are chatting with Zale.

Everyone is here . . . except for the last member of my family.

My mother's words come back to me. Can I forgive him? Is there anything to forgive? He was just keeping his promise to his dying mate to protect their child, even if it meant staying away to keep her safe. Wouldn't I do the same? I don't know, but I understand that he did what he thought he had to. He has regrets, and I'm beginning to realise I never really knew him.

But I want to.

I want to know the man my mother loved. I want to know the man who loves me enough to kill his king.

"I want to meet my father," I say, and silence descends as all eyes turn to me. I blush slightly. "Sorry, I was just thinking, and it came out."

"Are you sure?" Simon asks. He, more than anyone, knows my father, or knows of him. There is no judgement in his tone, only curiosity.

"Yes, my mother left me a letter. She made him promise to protect me even if it meant leaving me. I'm not saying he made the right choices, but everyone here has made the wrong one before, and we were all given a second chance. I think he should be too. If there is a member of my family out there ready to love me, then I would be foolish not to accept. I'm not saying it doesn't hurt, but I think I need to do this."

A hand covers mine. "Then we will do it with you." Reve didn't push me, even though he saw deeper into the man's mind. "I think he truly loves you, but it is your choice. You do not have to accept him simply because he is your father. If you want to, make him work for the honour. Blood doesn't mean anything without love. Remember that. But I would give anything to hold my family once more, and I don't want you to have any regrets."

"I know." I squeeze his hand. "Can we bring him here? To meet?" I gnaw on my lip.

"I will go now," Conall murmurs, kissing my neck.

"Wait, no, let me get dressed first. I don't really want to meet him with cum on my thighs while I'm wearing my mate's shirt." I blush, even though he definitely saw a lot worse last night.

Simon winces. "Too much information, babe."

Grinning, I stand. "Give me ten and then bring him . . . if he wants to come."

"He will," Nathair tells me. "And we will not let him hurt you, father or not, Althea. Your heart is ours to protect."

I kiss him softly then hurry from the room. Nerves and excitement fill me. I don't know if I'm making the right decision, but I don't think I'll truly know that unless I try.

What I said is true. I was given a second chance, so why shouldn't he be given one as well?

I wash and dress quickly in some flared pants and a comfy crop top, needing the comfort for what is about to happen. I leave my hair down and don't bother adding makeup. This isn't a formal visit. This is my father, a man I have known from afar all my life without even realising it. He always scared me, but maybe I never looked close enough because as soon as I step into the room, I see beyond his scary demeanour to the worry and hope below.

He stands quickly, shoving his chair back with a screech. We stand apart, staring at each other. My men are here as well, but I won't ask them to leave. I need them to get through this, plus they deserve to hear this. I need their opinion and comfort, and I readily reach for it as I move to the table and sit between Nathair and Lycus. They take my hands under the table as my father sits down opposite me, an untouched cup of tea sitting before him.

He looks the same as he always did, wearing a black jacket, pants, and top to blend in. There are lines around his eyes now—from worry or stress, I'm not sure—and his gaze is filled with too many emotions. How didn't I ever see that?

Was I not looking? Or was I blinded by my own?

Looking at him is like looking into the past, but I can see why my mother loved him. He is strong, sure, powerful, and a handsome man, but she fell for the soul I see in his eyes. He is a man willing to sacrifice everything for the ones he loves, and he's willing to risk his life to protect a daughter who never knew him.

"Hi, Althea," he says nervously, glancing around. "I have to say I'm surprised—happy but surprised," he rushes out, rubbing at his head. "I'm messing this up. I'm sorry. Would you like me to talk or listen?" he asks, and that, right there, is what gets me to relax. He is nervous like me, but he isn't arguing his case without listening to me. He wants to know.

That's when I realise he just wants to be in my life if I will let him.

"Talk for now if that's okay? I'm sure I'll have some questions, but I'd like to know what happened in your words without everyone else in the courts here," I reply softly.

"Okay." He takes a deep breath. "Firstly, I need you to know I understand you are probably angry and confused, and I am accepting of your feelings. You have every right to be upset and not to want me in your life, and if that's your wish, then I will leave you alone. I will always hope, but I will not pressure you."

"Okay." I nod.

"Okay," he murmurs. "I loved your mother, had for years, but I kept my distance. I was a new enforcer trainee, and she was the seer superstar, but our paths just kept crossing, and eventually she realised she loved me too. It was like that last barrier came down, and she revealed what I had known all along—she was my mate, and I was hers. We had a great year together. We kept it a secret, neither of us wanting to ruin what we had with the court. We planned to announce it when we found out she was pregnant, but everything changed. One night, she woke in tears, and when I tried to comfort her, she told me she couldn't bear to lose us both. I had no idea what she meant. She grew more distant, more worried. I knew her powers were taking their toll, but I had no idea just how bad it was until a week before your birth. She told me everything, and she had made her decision. She asked me, a man who loved her and you, to abandon her, let her die, and leave you."

I can hear the agony in his voice.

"I have spent my entire life fighting and protecting, yet she asked me to do nothing to protect the two people I loved more than this world. I left that night, needing space, and when I came back the next day, she was in labour. The stress, I think, brought you earlier than we expected. I was there the entire time, holding her hand and telling her that I loved her and we would figure this out. When your mother made up her mind, though, there was no changing it."

"Sounds like someone I know," Simon says, making us all smile.

"Yes, you remind me so much of her. She didn't make it, but before she died, she made me promise to protect you and keep you from this life until it was your choice. How could I deny her? I was going to lose her. A part of me thought that by promising, I could save her. It sent me into a spiral, and I almost took my knife and carved out my heart, but then I heard you cry. It was like waking from a dream. I held you in my arms, and you wrapped your whole hand around my thumb, and I knew I had to do everything to keep you safe. I loved you so much. You were mine, you were hers, and your mother was never wrong about her visions, so I told no one you are my daughter. I let them raise you. I watched every moment, you have to know that," he implores, reaching across the table. "I couldn't resist, even though I knew I shouldn't. I watched every day of your life, wishing I could be a part of it. It killed me day after day as you grew up and looked at me like I was a stranger, one you feared. It broke my heart, but I didn't care, because at least I got to be close. You grew into such an amazing woman, and your mother would be so proud of you. I know I am. You remind me of her," he croaks, tears falling down his face.

"I look at you, and I see her, the very best of us both. I'm so sorry, Althea. I could spend years showing you that I was in the background of your life, when you cut your hair, when you broke your arm . . . but I need you to know how sorry I am even though I would do it all over again. I would suffer every day again to get you here, where you were always supposed to be. You can turn me away, I deserve it, but please know I will always love you. I will always be there if you need me, and if you will—" He takes out a photo and places it on the table next to his other hand. It's of me as a baby in his arms, and he's looking down at me like I'm his entire world.

It's worn and crumpled from being held over and over again. The love pouring off of it is real, as is the look in his eyes. He expects me to turn him away and not forgive him for making an impossible choice for trying to keep his daughter safe, even if it killed him.

Now, faced with the truth, how could I ever turn him away? We won't be close, and it will take time, but that's what life is—second chances, healing, and love. It's about learning who you are and who you want to be. It's about figuring out who is important and who is worth fighting for.

This man is.

He's worth it.

"We are about second chances here," I tell him as I breach the gap and cover his hand with mine. "I'd say you deserve one too."

The sob that rips from his chest makes my own ache. "Thank you," he croaks, gripping my hand tightly. "I will take any part of you that I can get for however long you want me."

Smiling, I hold his hand back. "I know. How about we start with getting to know each other?"

Wiping his face, he grins. "I would like that."

"So would I," I murmur, staring at the face of the father I always wanted but didn't know I had.

Forgiveness doesn't negate the hurt, but it gives you a chance to move on. It also isn't easy, or everyone would do it, but it's a beautiful thing.

As is the love blooming between a father and his daughter.

My father booms out a laugh, clapping Lycus on his shoulder, and I can't help but smile. I was worried about how he would react. It's clear he's spent years loving and protecting me, and although I'm new to this relationship, he isn't, and his daughter is in love with seven very powerful, dark, wicked men. He accepted them easily with just one sentence.

"She loves you, and that is enough for me. You are good men or she wouldn't."

I could see it meant a lot to them. They were worried his reaction would hurt me or get between us.

"She was always like that." He grins over at me, his eyes sparkling. No wonder my mother fell in love with this man. He exudes life and love.

"True. You didn't see the time she tried to sneak out the window when you locked her in her room for misbehaving." Simon laughs, munching on pizza. "She fell down the drainpipe and had to limp through the back door covered in mud and leaves."

"She did not." He grins, looking at me like I'm the best thing in the world. "You disobeyed me?"

I shrug and smile. "Always."

"That's my girl." He winks and then leans back in his chair. "Simon, it's nice to see that you are happy and you found a nice boy to settle down with."

"Erm, you're not upset that he's a wolf?"

I'm quickly starting to realise my father has adopted Simon. Maybe he always did since no one ever really fucked with him. Now that I think about it, they probably didn't dare to, and it only makes me care for the man more.

"Why would I be? He makes you happy." That's as simple as it is for this man. "Now, do I get a tour of this place?" He looks at me. "If that's okay?"

"Of course." I stand and wave my mates away as they get to their feet. "I'll check on the monsters at the same time."

"Sounds good, *draya*." Nathair quickly kisses me. "We will get started on cleaning up."

"No, take me with you!" Reve calls dramatically, and Conall just rolls his eyes and lifts him, carrying him from the room. Simon smiles and bids my dad goodbye before following after them.

"I like them," he comments. "They make you smile."

"They do," I reply as I walk from the kitchen, and he follows me outside. "They are good men."

"I can see that. I like them." He shoves his hands into his trouser pockets as he walks next to me, looking around. "And this is one hell of a court. I'm not sure how we didn't know about it."

"They are good at keeping secrets." I shrug. "And it was forgotten over time."

He chuckles. "That is true. I don't think they will forget last night."

I hesitate slightly. "Probably not. Do you think I'm evil?"

"Never, Althea." He pauses. "You did what you had to, what the gods ordered you to. Plus, our race needed it. You saved us, so do not ever see it any other way." We start to walk again, this time in a comfortable silence that I hesitate to fill.

I lead him through the gardens, smiling when I see a pixie moving through the trees.

I look at him. "I spoke to Mum, you know?" He turns to me, gaping, so I stop walking to face him. "It was in a dream, but it was her. Twice."

"Is she . . ." He hesitates, barely breathing.

"She's okay. She's passed on now. I told her it was okay. She actually told me to give you a chance. I would have anyway, but she listened and helped me through my reservations. She also left me a letter that I will let you read it. She loved you very much."

"I loved her and always will," he whispers. "I wish I could have seen her just once more. I hold onto her in my dreams every night, hoping to see her face and embrace her once more."

"She's waiting for us on the other side," I admit.

"When it's my time and you no longer need me, I'll join her." He smiles, but it's a sad smile, and I realise I can give him exactly what he wants.

"Do you trust me?" I ask. I don't know why I phrase it like that, but I don't take it back.

"Always." He holds out his hands to let me do whatever I wish, so I take them and close my eyes.

I bring up the dream with Reve's powers and show him. I hear his gasp and feel his agony and love at the sight of her. "My love," he whispers, and when she speaks, he smiles, and when it fades, he stares at me in awe.

"Thank you," he whispers. "Whenever you need to see her, you can always look into my memories," he tells me. "They are yours. All of them."

"Thank you," I say, because I would love to see my mum through his eyes and learn about her life before me.

We start to walk again, feeling peaceful and serene.

"This place has something about it, something so . . ."

"Otherworldly?" I finish. "Like nothing can touch you here?"

"Yes." He nods. "Maybe it's the love I feel filling every inch of the place. I like it."

"Maybe . . . Maybe you could visit?" I offer.

"There is nothing I would like more," he replies honestly. "I . . . Uh, the court voted me to be the next king. It's not something big, but they want to crown me. Would you come? I understand if—" He starts to ramble.

"No one deserves it more. You have spent your entire life protecting our court, so of course they would vote for you to be their king, and I would love to attend," I say, taking his hand. "I will be your biggest supporter there, and it just might heal the bonds between our courts . . . and us."

I'm proud of him, I realise, and I'm glad he's getting his own life—this time with me in it.

"Good." He grins, taking my hand as we walk. "I'll look for you in the crowd."

"And I you."

Hand in hand, we learn to trust and love again. We start to learn about the other person for who they are. It's not just a simple blood bond, but a chosen one.

Sixty Seven

Althea

Once my father is gone, called away by his new duty, I find myself wandering around the court, looking at it from his perspective. He's right. It's different from when I first walked in here. It's not the court, but the feeling in it.

Life, I realise. It's filled with life and love.

Previously closed rooms are open again, and the sounds of laughter and friendship fill the court. I smile, realising we might just be healing too. We had a second chance, but it truly feels as if we are taking it now and not holding back. My mates are not punishing themselves anymore either.

I'm just about to go in search of my men when I feel something in the air, just like when I felt the god of death coming. They sense it through my bonds and come running, joining me in the room before our thrones just as the air splits and eight beings step out.

There used to be more, but one died for me. I drop to my knees, the others following my action. I might be dumb enough to sass the god of death, but I will not profusely annoy the gods of our world.

I bow my head, knowing it is rude to meet their gazes, not to mention their immense power would likely burn out my eyes—I already feel like I'm being flayed alive with all of them together.

They have come to see us, and for a reason.

"So these are the ones chosen to save the vampyrs?" a feminine voice remarks. None of us answer, unsure what to say. "I must say, I'm impressed."

I almost jerk from that.

"They did good," someone else comments.

"There was a lot of bloodshed," another says.

"Sometimes death is the only way to move forward because it brings rebirth," another muses.

"Indeed," the woman agrees. "You can relax. We are not here to hurt you. We are here in peace. You have saved your race. He said you would, but we did not believe him. He believed it so much he willingly gave up his life."

She means our god.

"Yes," she answers my internal thoughts, making me wince. "We will not interfere unless we need to. We like to remain impartial and in the background. We are keeping you in your roles to stop this from happening again. Protect your race, make sure they follow the laws, and keep them humble and good. Otherwise, we will be back. Know that we will be watching, but try to have some fun, won't you?"

Then, just as quickly as they appeared, they are gone. Gods are very busy after all.

I lift my head to see a ripple in the air, like a shuddering rainbow.

"Well, it appears that we have a job for life," Reve jokes. "I wonder if we get holidays or overtime."

I look at them and grin. "I'm guessing so, but let's not push it just yet."

"We did it," Nathair murmurs. "Thanks to you. This means we should celebrate. Our race is safe for another day, so back to our lives we go."

"Yes, let's celebrate." I nod, looking at the ripple again. A scream of horror echoes from the rift and fills my ears. I shudder at the pain and turn away, knowing better than to interfere with the gods' business. They might have spared us, but they could just as easily wipe us out.

We are the link between them and our race.

I wonder if there are others out there in other races doing the same.

I guess time will tell, but it's time to move on and live our lives.

To be the judges we promised.

To look to the future together.

As one.

Once, not so long ago, I knelt on this floor and accepted death with open arms. Now, I beg for a life filled with hope and not dread.

Life is funny that way.

Sometimes the ones who are broken, the ones who are about to give up, are the ones who have the most potential, if only they are given the opportunity.

Broken is beautiful.

Real.

Just like we are, working in the shadows.

Nightmares.

Sixty Eight

Althea

Everything is quiet after the gods leave. My men are busy putting the court back to rights, so I find myself outside with my monsters once more. They gather like they know I am coming, and I sit cross-legged on the grass before them.

The hydra, dragon, shapeshifter, puk, pixie, chimera, unicorn and so many more are all here. Even Tide lingers to listen to what I have to say.

They are a menagerie of unique and beautiful deadly creatures, one that aided us.

"You have fulfilled your duty to me. If you wish to leave, you are always welcome to." I smile. "But truly, I like having you all here. Our lands feel . . . full, but if you do leave, you are always welcome here. There will always be a place for you."

"I have other things to attend to. I know I asked you to call upon another for me, and I will keep you to that promise. Just not today. I am needed elsewhere." The dragon stretches then lowers his head in respect. "I, however, will accept that. I will be back, little queen. I have found friendship and a home here. Until we meet again." He takes to the sky, and some of the others melt away without a word, but others linger. One or two give me the same sort of response as the dragon, and when they leave, the hydra, puk, pixie, unicorn, and Tide remain.

"We would like to stay," Tide says, speaking for them all. "The dragon is right. We have found friendship here, safety, and a place to belong. That is rare to find."

"You are always welcome here. If you need us, we are at your disposal. I like having you guys here." I smile at them. After all, I know how it feels to be a monster nobody wants and to need a home. "I'll talk to Nathair about adding some structures and homes. Is there anything you need in particular?"

"Well . . ." The mermaid looks to the others and then seems to speak for them once more. "We could use some supplies."

I tilt my head, calling on Nathair, knowing he will make a mental list and have it done before the end of the day. "Go ahead, name everything and anything. This is your home, and what's ours is yours."

I sit and convey what they need to Nathair, and when they are done, I send him a mental kiss. *You are the best, my king.*

Anything for you, he purrs. *When you're done,* draya, *come and find me. I hunger for you.*

I shiver and clench my thighs together. *Yes, my king.*

That's my girl, he purrs, and I focus back on the monsters before me.

"He will sort it out. If you ever need anything else, you can come and get us. You are always welcome inside, but I think you prefer it out here, right?" I ask, hoping I haven't offended them by leaving them out here.

"We do," she responds. "We enjoy the freedom. I never understood your race's obsession with walls and living like bees." She grins as I laugh.

"I suppose we do." I stand, dusting off my ass. "But the offer still stands. Just maybe knock first."

That makes a few of them chuckle. "Trust me, we hear you even out here, so we will knock."

I blush at that but wave as they disappear back into the forest. Knowing they are here makes my heart feel so full, I can't stop my smile as I turn to go and find my king, hungering for him just like he does for me.

I use the bond to track him, tilting my head when smoke fills it. *Are you hiding from me, my king?* I purr.

If you want me, my queen, then hunt me. Find me. No cheating. He blocks off the bond with a husky chuckle. My fangs throb, and my pussy is slick with my own desire. I'm filled with a visceral need to hunt my mate like prey, and it's so strong I almost bend in two. After all, we are predators, and he just volunteered to be my prey.

Smirking, I close my eyes and focus. I rely on our bond a lot. It's just there between us, always telling me where they are and what they are doing. Of course they can block it if they want, but they never do, and it just flows through us, making us one person.

Without it, I feel like I've lost a sense, but it heightens my other senses.

I tilt my head, listening carefully. He led me here on purpose, which means he knows I can track him from here. His scent is everywhere, older and newer, and I focus on one of the newer ones, following it down the corridor. It stops suddenly at the corner, and my eyes lock on the fresh, bloody handprint on the stone.

Unable to help myself, I lean in and lick his blood, nearly coming from the strength and power within it. Moaning, I turn to flatten my back against the wall, my fangs so long they touch my chin as power and need blasts through me.

"Nathair," I call tauntingly, my voice sounding more primal than I'm used to. "I'm coming for you, my king, and when I find you, I am going to slam my fangs into that pretty neck while I ride your cock." I push off the wall and start to walk again, following the small droplets of blood. I smell them before I see them and can hear his soft chuckle somewhere in front of me. "I'll fuck you and ride you until you beg me to stop."

"Never." His whisper makes me shiver.

"Come and play with me," I sing.

"Find me, *draya*, I'm waiting."

I close my eyes and focus on his voice as I walk until it gets stronger.

"Find me before I make myself come to the thought of you draining me dry of my cum and blood."

"Don't you dare," I snap. "That cum is for me. You do not get to fuck your hand. You only get to come when I'm riding your cock and my fangs are inside you."

"Possessive," he purrs. "Better hurry then."

"If you come before I do, I'm going to chain you to the bed and make you watch as I drain every single one of my mates and take every one of their cocks, and only then, when I'm covered in their blood and releases, will I take you, and I still won't let you come until you beg me."

"Promises. We should do that anyway."

His voice is stronger, closer, and I realise where he is leading me—the pool. It's the first place we came together.

I speed up, blurring as I race to him. I refuse to let him come. I want it pumping inside of me. There is no better feeling than being filled with his release at the same time I drink his blood.

At the door, I rip off my dress and prowl in wearing nothing more than a lacy thong and snake bra I thought he might like. I planned to surprise him later, but now works. The water ripples slightly, and there is a bloody handprint on the side where he climbed in. Smirking, I start to circle the pool.

"My king," I sing. "Come out and play with me."

He's still hiding, so I decide to flip the game and slide my hand down my body to cup my pussy. "I guess I could always play with myself, but I'm so very hungry, my snake."

"Don't you dare," he snarls, thrashing, and the water shows his location.

Smirking, I release my hand and stalk the other way, my footsteps silent.

"I'm so wet, Nath. I need you so badly," I purr, throwing my voice as I circle the pool.

"You better not touch what is mine, *draya*," he snaps.

God, I love it when they are angry. Wild, angry fucking is the best. I reach down and tweak my nipple, moaning, and it echoes around the room, followed by his growl. When I round the corner, I see him, his eyes narrowed in anger as he glares in the direction where I was on the other side of the pool. He leans back into the side, naked and so beautiful it sends an ache spiralling through me. I need him too badly to wait.

Silently, I move over until I stand behind him.

"*Draya*," he calls with annoyance in his tone.

"Right here," I whisper. I grip his neck and rip his head back as I smirk down at him. "Got you."

His body is arched from my touch, and his thick thighs are spread where he's seated at the edge. I stare into his eyes, alight with need and hunger, before dropping my gaze down his body to his long fangs and then his throbbing, veiny cock held tightly in his grip.

"What are you going to do with me now, my queen," he purrs, tilting his head as he runs his hand up and down his cock.

Dragging him from the water with one arm, I slam my fangs into his neck. His back bows with a roar, and my hand slides down and around his body to grip his shaft. I stroke it, then I grip his tip and clench until he shouts. Pulling my fangs free, I tilt his head farther back. "You do not get to come for teasing me, not until I have at least three orgasms. Understood, mate?"

"*Draya*," he whines. "Please, I need you too badly."

Having this insanely strong man held in my grip, drenched in blood, begging for me to make him come, is a turn-on.

"What do you want, my king?" I murmur, licking at the blood dripping down his neck.

"You, gods, any way I can get you. Ride my face, ride my cock, I'll take anything, *draya*, please," he says, his body arching as I sink my fangs into him once more simply to watch him struggle. "My queen, please, please, your king needs you."

It undoes me, so I let him go. He slides into the water and whirls with a snarl. Smirking, I step back out of his reach, his dark eyes watching as I reach down and unclip my bra. I let it all drop to the floor, and then I bend and turn, showing him my ass as I slide my thong off. Once naked, I step into the water. He waits, sinking deeper, ready to pounce.

"Be good and I'll let you come," I murmur, approaching like he's a wild animal. I gasp when the water laps at my nipples as I sink deeper, and he snarls.

When I get close enough, he launches out of the water like a beast. I was waiting for this, however, so my hand snaps out and hits his chest. He flies backward, smashing against the statue behind him, and then I'm on him with my hand on his throat to pin him as he bites at the air. He's a beast, his snake coming forth in human form.

"Bad boy," I purr. "I won't let you come now. I'll use you."

"Yes," he demands, his cock jerking in the water.

Using the ledge, I slide my pussy along his length as he snarls and groans in my grip, fighting to get inside me. When he stills, I slam myself down, impaling myself on his length. Our moans mingle as I shudder, and he slams in and out of me with a snarl until I take over and begin to ride him. I take what I want, tilting myself until, with each thrust, I hit my clit. He speeds up, matching my movements. I don't let him sink his wickedly long fangs into me, knowing it would end it. I want to hold on, loving being in control of such an ancient, immortal being, but I know if he wanted, he could stop this at any point. He loves that I'm finding pleasure in using him, and he helps me along.

His huge cock hits that spot inside of me that has my head falling back as I cry out. Lifting, I narrow my gaze. "I'm going to feed you my nipples, my king, but if you bite me, I will be very angry, and I won't let you touch me again. Understood?" He stills, waiting. "Open your mouth," I demand. He does, his forked tongue flicking out. Moaning, I lift until I can offer him my breast, and his tongue darts out, lapping at my peak as I grind my pussy into him.

I explode with a scream, coming on his cock.

His teeth scrape me, but he doesn't bite. Instead, he continues his assault, switching breasts and working my nipple hard and fast, driving me into another screaming release. He licks and sucks me until I'm shuddering and slowly grinding my hips, barely able to hold myself up.

His cock swells inside of me, ready to fill me with his cum.

I still, knowing he's on the verge of erupting, and he slams his head back into the statue, the scent of his blood reaching me. "Althea," he hisses.

Lifting his head with a snarl, I get into his face, clenching my cunt around him as he growls. "Beg," I demand. "Beg me to let you come, mate, to let you fill me with your release."

"Please," he hisses. "I was a good boy, please, mate. Please, my love, make me come. Make me come like no one else ever could. I'm yours. You have my complete surrender. You have an ancient blood king pinned and desperate to come. Just one word from you would set him over the edge. Please, *draya*, my love. I need you too badly."

Not wanting to ride him anymore since he begged so sweetly, I lean in and offer him my neck, dragging his head closer. "Come, my king, come for me as you feed."

With a roar, he drives his massive fangs into my neck as he slams his cock into me so deeply it hurts. Pain and pleasure merge, and as he grips me tighter, hammering into me, I find my release once more. Snarling into my neck, he slams into me before roaring as he pumps me with his cum. My blood drips down from his lips as he throws his head back.

He's such a beautiful sight, and he's all mine.

"So I just add this?" I ask nervously, holding the drops carefully. I don't want to mess this up. Conall has been brewing this batch for a long time, and I would hate to ruin it, but I love helping him. He was so excited when I asked if I could help him tonight. The passionate way he spoke about his hobby turned me on, but I remain focused on getting this right and making him proud.

"Yes, just one drop with the dropper, Thea," he replies, and when I still hesitate, he shoots me a grin, steps behind me, and wraps his arms around me. He holds the dropper, and together, we add it to the vat. "Good girl," he murmurs into my ear, making me shiver.

The bastard chuckles and steps back, knowing exactly what he is doing.

Grumbling, I stir it like he taught me, watching as he chops up herbs. His bare back muscles clench with the movement, his hair hanging in braids over one shoulder. His trousers are low and tight on his taut ass. I almost drool at the sight of him. I'm a lucky girl, a very lucky girl. As he turns, giving me a good view of his arms as he chops the herbs, I watch the play of his muscles, and when he glances back, I'm just staring at him with the spoon held in my hand.

He gives me the same grin he gave me when he first saw me as he points at the brew. "Stir, Thea," he commands, but there's a silky quality to his voice. "And when this one is done brewing, I'll bend you over this table and you can show me all those dirty thoughts."

I can't help but grin at that. "All of them? We will be here for a while, mate," I tease.

"We've got time." He winks. "Now be a good girl for me and stir."

You bet your ass I turn around and stir like my life depends on it. I hear him laughing, but I simply grin and focus on stirring, and when it's left to cool down and the herbs are added, I step closer, running my hand down his chest. "I was a good girl, such a good girl. Do I get my reward now?"

Gripping my hips, he lifts me effortlessly and places me on his work bench.

"Of course, mate. I'm a man of my word." Sliding my skirt up to expose my bare pussy, he groans and drops to his knees before me, inhaling my scent as I spread my legs.

"No matter what flavour I make, I can never match the incredible smell and taste of your pretty pussy. I know because I've tried over and over."

My head falls back as his talented tongue runs over my folds, tasting every inch like he's savouring notes of tea or wine.

"Never be as perfect as you," he mumbles, circling my pussy with his tongue before pushing inside. Gripping his head, I lean back, grinding against his mouth. Watching him work for hours made me dripping wet, and I'm so close to coming already, it's almost embarrassing, but my mate loves it, cleaning up my cream before teasing my clit. He takes his time, pleasuring me like he approaches everything else—methodically.

"Conall," I beg.

His tongue speeds up as his shadows crawl along his arms, and just like the other night, one of the tendrils slips inside my pussy, wiggling. It feels so good as it stretches me and pushes against those nerves inside me. A smaller one joins it, sliding into my ass and claiming both holes as he sucks on my clit.

I scream as I come on his tongue and table.

Sliding up my body, he grips my chin and kisses me hard, forcing me to taste my cum as his tendrils slowly pull from my body. "See?" he says when he leans back. "In fact, stay there and keep that pretty pussy wet for me. I can keep tasting it as I try to replicate it."

And so I do. I play with my pussy as he works. Every now and again, he drops to his knees to taste me, only to end up making me come and squirt all over his table as if he can't resist, and then he goes back to trying to make a tea that tastes like my pussy for my mates.

Hours later, he seems happy, while I'm shaking and unable to move after having so many orgasms, I can't even count them. I jump down but almost fall to the floor on noodle legs.

He catches me and frowns at his work bench. "We have to clean our workspace when we are done, mate." Gripping my hair, he pushes me down. "Clean it."

Groaning, I lick up the stains of my cum for him. Lifting me, he leans down and does the same, and then he turns and kisses me roughly. "See? All better."

"I'm dead. I can't walk," I whine, and he hoists me into his arms.

"Then I'll carry you everywhere." He winks down at me. "Now let's feed you."

"Yes please, then nap."

"So demanding, little queen." He laughs, the sound echoing around our home.

SIXTY NINE

AZUL

"AGAIN," I CALL, WATCHING her form. She's holding the wooden sword I carved for her, and she channels my memories as she slices the blade through the air above her head and turns, bringing it down and ending in a crouch. "Good, you are getting really good."

"Then can I finally use a real sword?" She huffs as she straightens.

After she found me working out and practicing a few days ago, she demanded to join me, so we have been practicing a few hours a day. The first time ended with her on her knees, sucking my cock, because she said I looked too hot not to. I try to keep my distance now since we end up naked and buried in each other whenever we are close, which I love, but she wants to learn, and I will teach her. I will make her the best swordswoman there is.

"Soon," I murmur, wondering when the blade I ordered for her will be ready.

"How did you learn?" she asks, leaning on the wooden sword as she watches me.

"There was a man in my court who was a warrior of old. He taught me when I was allowed. When I came here, I practiced with Lycus and read books to be the best I could be," I answer without hesitation. "Again."

Grumbling, she does as she's told, and we run through every drill before I grab my wooden sword and spin it around my hand as I step closer.

Her mouth parts, so I slam my sword against hers before I end up bending her over rather than practicing. That can come after. "Focus," I demand.

"I'm trying, but it's so hard," she whines. "You are so hot."

"Later, I'll show you what else is hard." I smirk and clash our swords again. "Now focus."

Rolling her neck, she concentrates, and we spar across the grass. I take it easy, but she soon keeps up, and we spar for real. She picks up on my moves and uses them against me until we are both panting and staring at each other. Our swords fall, and we meet in the middle, our lips slamming together as we pant, but a clap makes us break apart to find Reve watching us.

"Looking good!" he calls. "Come here, brother."

I shoot Althea a fiery look but head over as she picks up our swords and follows.

"I thought you'd want this," Reve says and hands over the sealed parcel. "It was delivered an hour ago."

Grinning, I take it. "Thanks, brother."

"What is it?" my nosy mate asks, peering over my shoulder. I head over to the bench and lay it out as she follows.

"It is for you. Open it," I tell her.

She squeals, and I make a note to give her a present every day. She peels back the packaging and stares down in shock. I eye it carefully, making sure it's perfect. It is. The edge is sharp, and it's smaller than my longsword, so it's better suited for her smaller grip. I'll need to check the balance, but I trust the blacksmith who made this, since he's the best in the world. My oath to her is written down the centre of the blade.

Forever my heart.

She strokes it, and when she lifts her head, there are tears in her eyes. "It's perfect." She tackles me to the grass, and I can't help but laugh as she rains kisses down along my face. "I love it. I love you." She deepens the kiss, and I roll us, wedging my hips between her perfect thighs. I need her so badly. I can't wait anymore.

I keep my lips on hers, tasting her pleasure as I tug down her trousers. The tight pants make her ass look incredible. Her pussy is bare, as always, and wet and welcoming as I slide my fingers through her folds, feeling her need for me.

"I can't wait," she says. "Please don't tease me, my love."

"Never," I reply, kissing her again as I yank on the laces of my breaches, free my hard cock, and drag it along her pussy to get it nice and wet for her. I'm big, and even though she's needy, I never want to hurt her. Slowing the kiss, I press inside of my mate. Unlike our usual fucking, I move slowly and softly, rolling my hips as I claim her. Her tight, wet pussy fits me like a glove as I make love to her under the sun, showing her how much I love her.

She moans my name, and I swallow it, reaching under her to lift her ass and tilt her so my cock hits that spot that has her raking her nails down my back. I groan into her lips as we become one.

Pleasure rolls through us and grows, like the waves of the ocean, as we move together. The swells wash over us as I fill her with my length until, as one, we explode with a cry.

Panting, I press my forehead to hers, feeling her cunt fluttering around me as I come back to my body. My beautiful, strong mate lies relaxed and happy below me, her eyes open as she grins softly and cups my cheeks.

"My warrior," she murmurs.

"My queen," I reply as I slowly pull my length from her.

Reaching for her sword, I drag it along the mess on her pussy, christening it with our love.

Laying it down alongside mine, I roll to my side and pull her to me, closing my eyes in peace. My soul is alight with happiness. She took all the shadows and pain and made them hers.

Every inch of me.

She saved me, and now I will spend my life loving her like she deserves.

I smile up at the sun in gratitude.

I am so happy, it shouldn't be possible.

With my brothers and my love.

With my nightmares.

Seventy

Althea

"We are hunting tonight?" I ask with excitement. Despite my bluff at the party, I haven't been part of a true judgement from start to finish yet, and I'm eager. I just came back from dinner with Lilia, who I have become really good friends with. "Really?" I peer around as they rip into a feast.

"Yep. We still have to do our jobs despite the Blood Ball." Reve laughs, the name our community coined earning our mirth.

"There are those who didn't attend, and we still have to ensure everyone behaves, since people don't always change. Until they do, we are needed." Nathair shrugs. "What better time to strike than now? It will serve as a reminder, as well as be your first official hunt and judgement."

"Maybe I can steal you for a few hours before tonight?" Lycus murmurs.

I share a look with the others, judging their reactions. It's hard to balance my time between them, especially since I know they all need alone time with me, and I would hate to make anyone jealous or feel left out.

You are overthinking it. Surprisingly, it's Osis's voice in my head. His tone is stern but with a hint of amusement. "She has time." He nods at Lycus, who grins so widely, all feelings of guilt and worry evaporate.

He stands abruptly and grabs my hand. "Then let's go before they change their minds and try to kidnap you."

Laughing, I shove another slice of prawn toast in my mouth, waving at the guys as Lycus drags me outside and towards the forest. Swallowing around the thick slice, I wipe my mouth with my other hand and hurry to keep up.

"Where are we going? Into the woods to have weird, kinky sex? Because I have to tell you, we could have that inside, babe," I tease.

"We'll do that later." He winks as we step into the forest. The sun dims under the canopy of trees, throwing the forest into an ethereal light. Moss, swathes of lush, green grass, and fallen leaves decorate the ground. The trees here are old. I can feel it in my bones. The rest of the modern world falls away the deeper we trek into the trees, and I can understand why a lot of our monsters chose to stay.

Nathair and the others are busy working on the list of things they need, and although I sense some of the monsters are awake and about, they give us privacy, which I appreciate since whatever Lycus wants to do will probably end up with me facedown and ass up, just the way I like it.

Flowers of all colours grow around us, and foliage climbs towards the sun. It's beautiful and so peaceful. The birds sing their songs, the grass and bushes rustle with smaller prey animals, and the insects buzz with life. I find myself taking deep breaths of clean air, filling my lungs as we come to an old tree that looks like the rest.

"Stay here for a moment," he murmurs. I watch as he seems to disappear into the trees, but instead of feeling worried or scared, I tip my head back and close my eyes. All my worries fade to just feeling the world around me.

The wind tousles my hair, the sweet scent of the breeze fills my lungs, and the leaves brush my arms as I turn in place. When I hear a thud, my eyes snap open, and I find Lycus crouched before me. I tip my head back and raise my eyebrows. Did he just jump from the tree?

"Trust me, my love?" he asks, holding his hand out to me.

"Always," I reply as I lay my fingers in his. Tugging me closer, he slips his hands under my ass and lifts. I expect him to turn to the tree, which he does, but he presses me there and brushes his lips over mine.

"Then let's have some fun, my queen," he purrs and steps back. As soon as he does, his transformation comes across him, and his spider stands before me. I grin at him as he turns and lowers his body.

"You want me to climb on?" I ask.

Yes, Althea, trust me.

Shrugging, I use one of his bent back legs as a foothold. The hair there tickles my legs as I grip his back and heave myself up, swinging my leg over. He's so massive that it almost hurts my hips to straddle him, but I wrap my legs and arms around him as much as I can, and then without warning, he turns to the tree and leaps. My squeal fills the air as his legs connect with the tree, and then we scale it swiftly. My hair blows back as I peer down at the rapidly disappearing forest floor. Once we're high enough, we break through the canopy of the trees, and he stills on a branch so I can take in the brilliant sun glistening over the forest.

I spot the court in the distance, the building looking like an old gothic castle from here. Other than that, there isn't much around us. I guess I never really considered where we were before.

We live outside of the city, far enough away from the other courts to never be found if we didn't want to be. Before, there were many courts, and they were spread around the outskirts in remote places like this. Now, courts mainly gather within large areas like cities to remain part of this world. Safety in numbers and all that, he explains.

"I knew there were other courts. I just never really knew what happened to them." Our history is scarce this way, and I've never interacted with anyone outside of our city, who is the main branch of our race in this country.

There are a few more up north, but they tend to govern themselves and stay out of politics. There are others on different continents, and we have often wondered if they have their own judges or if, one day, we will be called in to help there too. As for what happened, time did. People died or were killed or simply moved on. Family lines died out or were mixed, and the smaller ones simply disappeared, along with their history. Nathair can tell you more if you wish. This area is all I have ever known, to be honest. Down here, we have the highest connection of power and courts, so I guess they just like to keep close.

"I guess." I lean into him, watching the play of the sun over the trees. "I can see why. It's so pretty here."

Some say it's where all power and magic are born, and that there is a singular place that draws and releases it all, which is why so many races gather here. I don't know if that's true, but I like the idea that we are all the same, gathering around a fire for warmth.

"I like that idea," I murmur, laying my head on him. We stay here for a while, just soaking in the beauty around us before we decide to move on. One of his legs wraps around me, holding me tight.

Hold on. He chuckles in my head, and before I can brace, he leaps.

I scream as we leap from tree to tree. He swings us between them, moving us quickly through the forest until it's almost a blur. My screams turn into laughter as I close my eyes and take in the feel of his strong body moving beneath me. We begin to slow, and when I open my eyes again, we are climbing up a huge, old oak tree. He pauses on one of the branches and lets me slide down. My legs wobble, and he catches me, pressing me back to the trunk.

Wait here, okay? Those many eyes blink at me. It's his voice in my head, but it's his spider that's watching me, and I startle when I realise how deeply they seem to be blending now. *For you,* they both tell me. He turns, and when he reaches the edge of the branch, he swings down. Gasping, I hurry to the edge, teetering as the branch thins, but he swings back up. We are in a slight outcropping of trees that seem to grow in a circle, and he swings between them, threading silk around them in the beginning of a web.

Knowing he's safe, I hurry back before he chastises me for moving. After all, we are very high up. I might survive a fall and heal easily, but it doesn't mean they would be happy about me hurting myself recklessly.

They are possessive like that.

He turns to check on me. *Are you checking out my ass?* he asks.

I laugh, my back to the tree trunk as I watch him swing between the trees, spinning his web. The silken strands catch the light and glow with power and beauty, and when it's done, he holds out his hand to me.

Without hesitation, I push off the trunk, race along the thin tree branch, and leap into the air. I close my eyes with a wide grin. It's like flying, and for a moment, I'm suspended in the air before I start to fall, only for the web to close around me, where I bounce safely as I giggle.

I roll towards the middle as the strands move with Lycus's big body as he heads my way.

His spider easily navigates the silken threads, moving in a smooth manner somewhere between a crawl and jumps until he stands above me. My arms and legs are spread as I bounce slightly, like that time Simon and I crashed a trampoline party I think was for kids.

"Did you build this for me?" I grin. "You've captured me in your web. Now what do you plan to do with me?"

Many, many things, little queen. After all, no one can hear you scream out here. His legs pin my arms and legs down, and then more silk binds me, spread eagle, feet above the ground in the middle of nowhere.

Just me and my monster.

"Then make me scream, mate. Let's test the sturdiness of your web and see if it breaks as easily as you will when you're inside me." I smirk, testing the bindings on my ankles and hands to find I can't really move them. He watches me struggle, which only pushes my shorts higher and pulls my top down until my breasts nearly spill free.

His eyes dart back to mine, and one of his legs slowly lifts, giving me time to protest, but I don't. He drags the sharp tip down my shirt, freeing my breasts. My nipples tighten in the cool air, and my eyes slide shut on a moan as my pussy clenches, remembering how one of those legs felt inside me. I fucking loved it, and when he drags that sharp tip across one of my nipples, I cry out. I meet his gaze, and he teases a nipple into a stiff peak. I struggle to close my legs to find friction, but I'm denied by his silk. Chuckling in my head, he watches me pant and struggle as he switches to my other breast, teasing that nipple into a taut peak before sliding his sharp leg down, over my stomach, to my shorts.

He eyes them, unsure how to remove them until, with a hiss, he simply cuts them away. They drift down to the ground below in tattered pieces, my bare pussy on display for the whole forest, making me shiver. With his eyes still locked on me, he drags his leg over my wet pussy, sliding it through the mess I'm making as my hole clenches. Pleasure spirals through me from how wrong this is, yet I want more.

His leg slides back up, circling my clit. I lift my hips, trying to get off. I need to come so badly, but he simply pulls his leg away and lifts it to my mouth. *Taste how much you need me, even in this form, my queen,* he tells me as he shoves it into my mouth.

I lick the tip, the hair making me shiver at the foreign feeling. Another leg slides across my pussy, teasing my clit before pressing into me. It fills me so deeply, my eyes cross, and I choke on the leg in my mouth. He slowly pulls it out of my lips, and in time with the one sliding inside my channel, he thrusts back in. He mimics fucking my mouth as he fucks my pussy with his leg, my cream covering it. I'm so wet, the slick sound of his movements fills the air.

Fuck, you should feel how tight you are gripping me, even like this, your monstrous spider. You're going to come for me like this, aren't you? Caught in the monster's web and spread wide, covering my silk in your need. If anyone walked in now and saw this, they would be horrified. They would think I'd taken you against your will, but you love it. Don't you, my little queen? You love being fucked by your monsters.

I whimper around his leg, nodding my head as I take him farther into my throat as the leg inside of me goes deeper than ever before and slants so the length of it rubs along my pussy, catching my clit with each brutal thrust.

I'm drowning in pleasure, trapped in it just like I am ensnared in his web.

You're so close. I can see it, can feel it. Your pretty little pussy is trying to milk my cum from me. Show me how much you want it. Show me how much you want me to fuck you like this in my web. Come for me, my queen. His words send me over the edge, and my pussy clenches around his leg, drenching him in my cum.

I scream with my release, and when my eyes open, human Lycus is above me. He spins us in the web so he's beneath me, with me straddling him, and then he slams me down onto his huge, hard cock, impaling me as I howl.

"Ride me, my queen, right here, above the trees, as close to being gods we can get. Ride your king for all the monsters to see and hear," he roars, grabbing my hips and helping me ride him. I lean onto my knees and hands, still restrained, as I roll and lift my hips. My head falls back, my hair flowing in the wind. I know he's right and the monsters are watching, but I don't care. I let them.

He's my monster too, and I want every inch of him. I want his cum buried so deep inside me it splatters through his web to the ground. I want everyone to hear him come for his queen.

"That's it, my queen, take me. I'm yours. Every single inch of me was created for your pleasure, from my big thighs to my huge cock, to bring you to the edge over and over. This mouth was made to lick that pretty cunt, and my hair was made for you to hold onto. So use it, use me, my queen. Fuck, look at you. I bet the gods watch you, wanting you, but they can't have you. You are ours. You are mine," he snarls as his head rolls back with a groan, his neck straining. I speed up, chasing my release but also wanting to feel his.

It grows between us. I feel it in our bond as our pleasure spirals higher.

Tightening my pussy around him, I watch him cry out and feel his heart hammering, pushing blood around for me, so I slide my fangs along his chest, cutting it open to see it drip with blood. The taste of it makes me move faster.

He fucks me, his eyes dark as they lock on me with a snarl, and when he sits up and sinks his fangs into my neck, I come with a howl.

He roars against my neck as he slams me down as hard as he can, buried to the hilt and pumping me with his scalding cum as I shake and writhe against him. When the pleasure ebbs, I slump onto him, letting him stroke my back in comfort as he licks his marks clean, and then we relax, lying on his web.

"I will write your name across a thousand forests. Everywhere I go, I will leave a web of my queen's name so they know how much she holds my heart and soul, and how she tamed the nightmares and made them her own."

Seventy One

Nathair

My mate and brother come back covered in dirt, webs, and leaves, their hands gripped together as they giggle, and I can't wipe the smile off my face. When was the last time I saw my brother so happy, so free, and embracing his other side? The answer is never, and to see my mate so pleased and happy brings me nothing but joy, even though it was not me who caused it.

"Time to get ready," I call when they get nearer.

"Of course, let me wash first." She leans up, pecks Lycus on the lips, and slides over to me, kissing me as well without shame or reservation. "You make me happy," she murmurs as she goes, and I can't help but grin, loving how deeply she is ingrained within my brain.

My thoughts are all for her anyway.

"You too, brother."

He nods, grinning as he heads past me. "Oh, and grab Reve, will you? He and Osis were being weird. I overheard thoughts of a dungeon. I don't need to know, just make sure they are ready."

I hear his laughter as he heads into the court, and for a moment, my eyes close as I focus on the energy here. Where there was once nothing but pain, death, and ghosts, now there is such love, life, and vigour, even in my forests.

This was always how this court was supposed to be, and it's all thanks to her, my queen.

Before I died, I always thought I was the most important and powerful creature, and that my stolen throne was proof. I never wanted to share power, but I was foolish because by sharing power, we are stronger and happier. I don't want the throne now, only her.

I would gladly kneel at her feet while she ruled, and that's when I realise why I was given this second chance. They saw something in me I didn't even see in myself, something she always sees—the ability to give what is necessary to help her lead our people.

I was born to love her, I just got lost for a while, but I've found my way now.

I know not every member of our species attended our ball, so that's why we are out here, not to mention I'm old enough to know that some people just don't change. Some do, we are prime examples of that, and I'm all about giving second chances, but I also won't be naïve enough not to check up on them.

We teleport to one of the most popular clubs our species visits. Dominos is for the vampyr population, and although other species do visit, mainly fey and wolves, the majority is made up of bloodsuckers. We ignore the line stretching around the corner. Usually, we would travel straight inside and hide in plain sight, but this was Althea's idea, and I see why as those in line turn to us.

Fear and awe show in their expressions. It's not just what we are wearing or the power flowing from us; it's the reputation we have created. Our entire race knows us and what we do. We no longer hide in the shadows. No, we hide in plain sight, and tonight, we let them know that we are hunting.

Althea stands at my side in a floor-length leather coat. Underneath, she wears a black corset, her judge mark proudly on display. Her matching leather pants are tucked into red, knee-high heeled boots. She looks sexy as hell, with her long hair curled back, her lips red and pouty, and her eyes glowing with power. She isn't wearing a crown, but with just one look at her, you would know she is a queen. Reve is dressed in matching hunting gear. My own leather trousers are laced at the top, showing off my happy trail, which she touches possessively. I have on an open silk shirt and nothing else.

Azul is wearing his gold and black armour, with pops of red to match his girl. Conall is only dressed in leather pants and matching red boots. Osis has on a floor-length fur coat with black fatigues underneath. Reve is wearing tight black jeans with platform boots and a tank that's partially ripped, her red lipstick kiss marks proudly displayed on his cheek.

Zale's bright eyes are covered by shades, and he's in black jeans and a shirt. He almost blends in, but flames roll over his skin.

Lycus wears his usual hunting gear, but he wears a necklace with a spider entwined with a female body, her body. They walk behind us, and we look imposing. I almost smirk when some patrons run from the line. I ignore their whispers and grin.

Power is being seen, she tells me. *We aren't hiding anymore, so let's remind them of that.*

Clever little queen.

She winks, and the door opens for us, the guard almost pissing his pants as she brushes past him.

As soon as we step inside, the sultry rock music slides through our bodies and heightens our bloodlust. It's dark in here to offer courage. There are curtained areas to feed and fuck, but most do it on the chairs, tables, and sofas. We aren't here to police consensual feeding or sex. We are here for those who break the rules. We ignore the bar and instead, we walk straight through the masses. It takes a minute for them to realise who's here, and then some bolt just like the others outside. Some narrow their eyes as if wanting to test themselves against us, and I dare them to try with a smirk. I'd love to see my girl hand them their asses.

They don't, though, because nobody here is that foolish. Instead, a man appears before us. "Queen and, erm, kings."

"You can call us judges," Althea offers, staring at him.

"Of course, judges. I am Mirton, assistant to Ethic, who runs this establishment. He warned us you may be visiting in the future and to escort you to a table that we have set aside for you. Your drinks are free too." He peers up at us. "We simply ask that any . . . business you have isn't conducted on these grounds."

"We will hunt here." Althea sniffs. "But we will not kill here. You can tell your boss that."

"Thank you." He slumps in relief before guiding us to the VIP section and gesturing to a huge booth with the best views of the club. "His personal booth," he rushes out. "Ethic wants it known that he wants no trouble. He follows all laws here, and any who do not are yours." He backs away, watching us carefully.

"I think Ethic is scared." I grin as I lean back, running my eyes over the club. Everyone is watching us in one way or another, all but one. There is a woman at the bar pounding down shots. Her bright pink hair clashes against everyone around her, and for a moment, I eye her. Something about her causes me to hesitate, and Althea tilts her head.

"I've seen her before." Suddenly, her eyes turn white, and then she nods. "Sorry, I was talking to a ghost. He says she isn't trouble, but something tells me she is about to be in a lot of it." She grins at us. "I guess I can talk to your ghosts, Azul."

Azul beams proudly at her, and as we sit back, focusing on the club, they focus on speaking to any ghosts that hang around.

"Another?" Zale asks, scanning the area while ignoring the drinks that were dropped off. They could be poisoned for all we know. I observe as Althea watches the pink-haired girl storm from the bar with a weird smile on her lips before she winks at me and focuses back on our hunt.

A man appears at our table. He's a big bastard, and old judging by the power flowing off him. He might as well have his cock out for a measuring contest with the way he's throwing his power around. I cover my smile with my hand and lean back as Althea runs her eyes over him, finding him lacking as she peers at him. "Can we help you?" she asks.

His muscles bulge as he presses his fists onto the table and tries to get in her face, but he simply can't because her power pushes him back. "I heard what you did."

"And?" she replies. "Congratulations?"

"You have no right. I don't know who you think you are, bitch."

A growl goes up at our table, but she holds up her hand with a sardonic smile and stops us.

"We won't stand for it. We will kill every last one of you."

"I would really like to see you try." She stands, causing him to stumble back, and holds her arms wide as the music cuts off. "Come on then, kill me, or are you all talk?"

He snarls and lunges for her. I tense, even though I know she can handle it. She laughs and then disappears, using Conall's magic to appear behind him. She taps him on the shoulder, and he whirls.

"Boo!" She laughs in his face as he falls to the floor, and then she presses her heel against his throat and pins him there as he snarls and struggles.

"Pro tip, don't pick a fight with the baddest bitch around." Leaning down, she applies pressure. "And that isn't you, not anymore. Try to hurt one of mine, and I will rip you to pieces and wear your ribcage as a corset. Do you understand me?"

He nods, eyeing her in fear as he realises just what she is capable of.

"Good boy, now run along before I decide tonight is the night to spill your blood and see if you are a sinner."

She lets him up, and he scrambles away, rushing to the door.

"Anyone else want to try their best? We are right here, so go ahead," she calls to the rest of the club, and when no one moves, she drops her smile. "I didn't think so, but let me make this very clear."

Her words are soft but deadly.

"Anyone who tries to hurt my family will face me, and I'm not the nice one. They are. We might be envoys of the gods, but make no mistake, I will kill every last person who lays a hand on them. Gods or no gods, nothing would save you." She glows with her powers as she speaks. "You want to challenge a judge? Go ahead, but once they beat you, I will rip you apart while you beg for death. I'm friends with ghosts, I've been to the other side, and I've met the god of death, so let me tell you, they'll let me keep you here as long as I want. Tell that to your friends." She turns back to our table. "Pick the judgement. I'm craving death and blood, and I'm going to claim my kings again in the aftermath."

"I have one," Osis murmurs, and Azul nods. "Con and I will grab him and meet you back at the court."

"I think we've tempted fate enough tonight." I wink as I stand.

"I'll take them all on if I have to," she snarls.

I grip her throat and pull her closer. "And win, my queen, but the idea is to save the race, not kill them, even if they are idiots."

Snarling, she struggles in my grip. I'd feel the same if someone just threatened her, so I tighten my hold, watching her eyes blow wide. "Later, my love, you can take it out on us, but for now, we have a job to do, so be a good girl and take us home." I trust in that, trust in her powers, and with a nod, she fades us from the club and back to the thrones in our court.

Our masks appear, the candles around the room flare to life, and the blood circle lights up. Conall and Osis appear, thrusting a man wearing shackles into the circle before appearing in front of their thrones.

"No, no, no, no," the man chants, searching for a way out, but there isn't one.

There is no escape from us.

We are the candle in the dark, the air in their lungs, and the blood in their veins. We are invincible, and they are our prey.

"You know who we are. You were selected because of your sins," Althea begins. "You have been trading in ancient vampyr blood, and it is being used to create disgusting and immoral things."

"No, please! He died tonight anyway. The old bastard couldn't take it. He died."

"Yet you still did it," I reply, and then I appear before him and slash his throat. His blood spills into the bowl. We all hiss with the magnitude of his crimes, seeing his life flash through our minds. He wasn't at the ball, since he's a rogue, which means we missed some sinners.

He's right, though, the vampyr died due to their treatment and passed willingly to the other side, and this man is responsible for his death and the illegal trade of his blood.

"You are guilty," we announce together.

"You are guilty. Your crimes are numerous. You have been sentenced."

"May the gods forgive you." Lycus steps forward and rips out his heart. We watch as he falls, his life extinguishing from his eyes. Unlike the man he killed, this was a mercy.

"Burn the body," I order as I look to Althea and her to me. "Then we need to show our queen how brilliant she did tonight, and how much her protection means, don't we?"

"You better," she orders, her coat falling to the floor as she wanders past the body and turns to us in the middle of the room. "Well, what are you waiting for?"

You, always you, draya.

Seventy Two

Zale

"Mate, where are you?" I call with a smirk. It's been a busy few days. I've been helping the monsters with their new buildings and the list they gave Nathair, so I haven't had much time with my mate, and I miss her. My beast demands to be close to his mate, as do I. I know she's around here somewhere. Earlier, I got snippets of her with her new fey friend and Simon when they were up to no good.

I want her now, though, and she's going to be all mine.

"I have something to show you," I shout as I tilt my head, listening for signs of her location. "Althea, if I have to hunt you down, it's going to bring out my beast, and he is going to want to claim you exactly where you are."

She shoots me an image of her cooking with Simon. "Oh, he won't care," I tell her. "He'll bend you over right there, so come to me," I croon.

In my mind, I feel her making excuses to Simon, and then she appears before me. "You wanted me, mate?"

"I missed you." It's the truth.

She moves into my arms, kissing me deeply. "I missed you too." I sense the truth in her words. "How about we sneak off for some alone time?"

She's over my shoulder before she can squeal.

I hurry through the court before anyone can interrupt us and try to steal her attention. My hand lands on her ass in a resounding smack of promise. "Mine," I snarl, speeding up, burning alive from the inside out with need and desperation.

I push the door to my room open and then slam it shut behind us, engaging the lock. I don't set her down until we are within the nest I built earlier, driven by need. Her back hits the many blankets and pillows where my bed once was, the piece of furniture now pushed to the side to create a barrier between us and the door. I didn't even know why I woke up and did it, only that I had to, but watching her lean back in the nest makes a growl leave my throat.

"Mine," I snarl, coming down on top of her and wedging my hips between her thighs. Her arms wrap around my neck, tugging me down farther as her shapely legs wrap around my hips, bringing me in tighter.

"Yours," she replies, kissing me softly. "Is this all for me?"

I jerk a nod, unable to do much else, a constant growl erupting from my lips. My animal side is driving me.

"It's amazing, so warm and comfy and perfect for you to claim me in, mate," she purrs, knowing exactly what I need and giving it to me, my perfect mate. "Claim me, Zale. Bite me, fuck me, and stain every inch of my skin with your cum until you are more settled. You know I will love every minute of it."

"Mine." I slam my lips onto hers.

Mine, mine, mine.

Must claim, mark, and let them all know.

"Yes," she whimpers as I move down and rip her flimsy dress off, leaving her naked beneath me. I'm too impatient and rough, but she loves it as I flip her, drag her plump ass into the air, and push her head down so her pretty pink slit is exposed, and then I go wild.

I howl as my beast fights to come out. We shift back and forth, but I still don't stop myself. I drive into my mate, slamming into her wet pussy as she screams and pushes back, begging for more.

I pound into her like an animal, rutting her, my body still changing behind her.

She grips our nest and takes me deeper. Her big breasts drag along the blankets, and her cream coats my cock, dripping down to scent my nest as I howl once more.

My claws pierce the skin on her hips as I hammer into her, and flames lick over our bodies. "Mine!" I roar, slamming my fangs into her shoulder, claiming her as she screams her release for her mate.

I still don't stop, driven by the animalistic need to claim.

To fuck.

I pin her with my fangs and cock and rut my mate. My cock swells, knotting inside her, until I come with a howl, spilling inside her as she screams for me again, clenching around my knot as one release flows into another.

I lose time, but when I come to, she is covered in cum and blood and happily stroking my chest.

My perfect mate.

Both my animal and human sides are satisfied, and I tug her closer. "I love you, mate."

"I love you too," she whispers. "All of you."

Seventy Three

Osis

"We have all been invited to the coronation." Althea grins as she flips into her bed, where we are all gathered, waiting for her after another successful night of hunting and judgement. She needed to bathe after and kicked us all out, saying it would take all night if we joined her since we like to make her scream for us. She's not wrong, but she's wrong if she thinks it will stop us now.

She narrows her eyes on me and sniffs. "Behave."

I smirk as I crawl towards her, knowing she loves watching my body move. I roll her onto her back, pinning her there. "Why?" I murmur, dragging my nose down her throat, inhaling the scent of my mate as my tiger roars and my inner peace shatters with the need to taste her. "You like it when I order you around, don't you, mate? If I ordered you to get on your knees and suck my cock with your pretty lips, you would soak it up, wouldn't you?" I demand.

She shivers under me, and I feel the others slipping away. I thank them mentally. I haven't had a lot of alone time with her recently, and they see that.

She groans. "Yes."

"Good girl, now spread those pretty thighs for me," I order as I lean back.

Eyes hazy, she spreads her creamy thighs, showing me her pretty pink pussy. It's already slick for me, and pride roars through me, as does need. My tiger scratches to get out and eat her.

"You already want me, mate?"

"Always," she says, gripping her thighs.

"Show me, touch yourself. Make yourself come while you watch your mate," I demand. Her fangs dig into her lower lip, and her big breasts flush with need as her nipples pebble. Those elegant fingers part her slick folds for me, and as I watch, she slips her fingers inside her tight, wet heat with a moan.

"Do you feel good, my love?" I ask, slowly standing and removing my clothes as I watch her fuck herself. Her fingers drip with her need, and she brings them up to circle her engorged clit.

"Yes, wet, so wet for you, mate." She pants, watching me as I stroke my cock, imagining it's her tight, wet heat. Moaning, she presses her fingers back inside her pussy.

"Keep those thighs spread, but play with those pretty nipples for me."

One hand slides up, and she grips her breast before tweaking and playing with her little tight nipple until she cries out, taking her fingers deeper and faster.

"You're so close, mate. I can see it. Come for me. Come for your mate."

With a scream, she clenches around her fingers, her pretty pussy gushing with her release.

Never before has there been a better sight.

"Good girl," I coo as I climb between her thighs. "Now, suck your fingers clean for me and taste how hard you came for your mate."

Shakily, she pulls them free and sucks them, her eyes on me once more. "Please, Osis," she mumbles around her fingers.

"Please what?" I demand, gripping her neck.

"Please fuck me, mate me," she purrs, popping her fingers free.

"Feed my cock into your pussy," I snap, on the edge of losing control. "Take every inch without my help."

Reaching down, she grips my length, presses it to her entrance, and lifts her hips to impale herself. I don't move; I don't help. I grit my teeth as I sink deeper into her wet heat, moaning when she struggles to get me all in.

"All of me," I snap.

Whimpering, she works herself harder, rubbing her clit until I finally settle all the way inside her.

"Good girl." Holding her neck, I start to move, and she cries out as I take her hard and fast, pounding into her.

Turning my head, I bite my arm, watching the blood trickle down it and onto her neck and chest, splashing her heaving tits. The sight is so erotic, I almost spill.

She clenches around me, crying out as I tighten my grip and hammer into her, claiming my mate.

Her body moves from the force of my thrusts. "Come for me, mate, and milk me of my release," I order.

With a cry, she does just that, clenching so tightly around me, I have no choice but to pump my cum deep inside of her. Falling forward, I catch her lips as we come together, and then I fall to the side, my cock still in her fluttering channel as she sighs happily. "I love you."

"I love you so much," she replies as I slowly untangle us, feeling the others nearby.

She might be mine for a spell, but she is ours all the time, and they file back in, climbing in to cuddle our queen. Balance is something I value more than anything, and they offer us that.

She also offers that to us with open arms.

"Osis?"

I hear her call my name and make my way through the foliage without hesitation. It's not like her to seek me out without checking my mind first, and I worry something is wrong. I prowl into the clearing, scanning the area before locking on her. I scent blood but find she's simply smiling at me.

What is wrong? I ask, ready to defend my mate, my tail thrashing as I pad over in tiger form.

"Nothing, I simply wanted to see you and spend some time with you and your tiger. Is that okay?"

More than, I answer, and an idea comes to mind. *You rode Lycus, correct?*

She starts to grin, and I chuff. *Dirty girl, I meant in his spider form, on his back.*

She giggles but nods.

Climb on. I turn and lower myself. She carefully swings her leg over me, and when her fingers grip the fur on my neck, I lift and start to walk into the forest. I move slowly at first, letting her get used to my gait, and when she's confident in her seat, I start to speed up. She laughs, the sound encouraging me to leap over fallen trees and logs and sprint. I would never let my mate fall, and she knows it. My tail lashes behind us as I race faster and leap higher as she holds on and cries out for more.

We explore the forest for hours at a slower pace, and I show her my favourite spots. We check on our monsters, and then once we're back at court, I help her down. Before I can transform, she leans in and kisses my forehead between my eyes.

"Thank you, mate, for showing me so much beauty and peace, and for letting me feel it through you."

Transforming back, I cup her cheeks and kiss her deeper until she sways into me. "Always, I will always be your balance, mate. Now, let's go find my brothers and have that family night you wanted. Simon and his mate picked the film this time, didn't they?"

Hand in hand, we head back to court. "Yup, a horror."

I groan, and she laughs. "Are you excited about the coronation tomorrow?" I ask carefully.

"Yes and no. It's still odd to know my father, but I need to be there, you know? I just worry about how everyone will react," she says.

"We will not let them affect you or his day," I promise, raising our joined hands and kissing her fingers as I hear Simon's laughter. "Now, forget your worries for tonight."

"Yeah, babe, it's zombie night!" Reve calls, and I roll my eyes.

"If you're lucky, I'll eat you just like they would," I murmur, making her laugh, and I know I've done the right thing. I will spend my life trying to put that light in her eyes and a smile on her face.

Seventy Four

Althea

I know the dress is important, since it's our first appearance as kings and queen in a social setting. We were all personally invited by my father, and I admit I want to go to see him and my old court, which means dressing the part for the coronation. Luckily, I have a new fey bestie who seems to appear whenever she feels like it, and the night before, she did just that. I explained my situation, and she disappeared with a mischievous smile.

It's now the morning of, and I'm beginning to panic, searching through the dresses that Nathair and the others bought for me, but nothing feels right.

"I don't even know why I'm so worried." I huff, turning away from the dresses in a panic. Simon is sprawled across my bed, watching me anxiously. "It's just a coronation, right?" Turning away before he can answer, I slide more dresses off hangers and toss them to Simon to hold so I can try them on. "She said she would help, though, and she wouldn't lie to me. She agreed it was important that I make a good impression on the council and the others, so where is she? Where is she?"

"Okay, breathe," Simon says, dropping all the dresses. "She will be here, and panicking isn't helping anything."

My mates are huddled on the sofa, wide-eyed as they watch us, and Simon throws them a glare. "Pussies, at least help me calm her down."

"Nope." Reve holds up his hands. "That's your territory. We called you in here for this exact reason."

I whirl on them with a glare, fangs flashing. Lycus hides his grin, and I narrow my eyes further. "You think this is funny?"

"Draya, you will look incredible and beautiful in any dress," Nathair says diplomatically, which is the same shit they have been saying all morning before they called Simon in for backup.

"Shut up," I snap and then soften. "Thank you, my love, but shut up."

"Erm, want me to kill someone for you?" Azul asks, looking genuinely confused as he rubs the back of his head.

How can I be angry in the face of that? "No, but thank you." I sigh, turning to the dresses. "I can just pick one from here. I don't even know why I'm so stressed."

Simon takes my hands and turns me to sit on the bed. "Because this is the first time you are not only attending an event as a queen, and as a mated queen, but in honour of the father you just found out about. It is normal to be stressed." He tosses my mates a glare. "And we can sit and talk through it if you'd like."

"Yes." Nathair nods. "Let's go through every reason you are stressed, and we can counteract them."

"Or you could just wear the dress I spent all fucking night making and had to bribe a troll to get awake juice for. Shut your pretty mouth and kick ass." A familiar female voice chuckles, and we all turn to see Lilia sitting on top of my dressing table, swinging her legs back and forth. I didn't feel her pop in.

"We really need to figure out how to stop that," Conall mutters.

"You're just jealous that I don't need shadows to do it," she mocks him. Another thing I love about my new friend is that she gives my mates shit, and despite the fact that they are incredibly handsome and powerful, she treats them all like annoying little brothers and prefers my presence without them. "Your fey godmother is here, so do not fret." She hops down, and I spot a bag draped over her shoulder, almost weighing her down.

"You came," I murmur.

Her eyes widen. "Of course I did. We are friends, and that's what friends do. Friends would not let their friends walk into a very important coronation looking like ass."

"She wouldn't look like . . . ass," Nathair protests. "She always looks beautiful."

"Aww, that's sweet, now shut up and get out," Lilia says, making me grin.

"Yup, I'll take that as my opportunity to escape." Reve leaps up, winks at me, and saunters out. The others check on me mentally before following, leaving me with Simon and Lilia.

"Right, let's get to work." She claps. "Simon, get me some snacks. I'll need them."

"Your friend was right. The dress is perfect," Simon says as we wait for the others to arrive so we can get going.

"Isn't it?" I grin down at the dress, feeling so much better. Something about her work always makes me feel more powerful and beautiful, even though she's told me a hundred times that it's not magic, and she just enhances what I already have.

The bodice is made up of iridescent grey feathers, which cup my breasts and push them up. Beneath my breasts, the fabric clings to my curves, cinching in my waist, and then floats out and down. The dress itself would be simple without the feather work and the colours. The material is an iridescent grey with streaks of gold and ruby throughout. The train gathers at the hips, almost like wings, and spreads out so when I twirl or walk, it flares out. We styled my hair in an elaborate updo, with my crown firmly in place and matching feathers threaded through my locks.

I feel beautiful. I feel like a queen and like I belong, which I know I do.

Stepping back into a court I never thought I would see again meant that I had to do it the right way, and I had to be different than the girl who ran away that night. I had to be me, and I feel like myself in this, which is very different than that scared, young woman I was before.

Simon is in a black suit with a matching golden tie to make sure we all look like we are part of the same court, openly showing his alliance. I told him he didn't have to, or he didn't have to come, but he wanted to support me and my father. I appreciate that more than he will ever know. When my guys appear, they are all wearing gold accents to match my dress and our court. For Lycus, it's a golden necklace hanging proudly between his huge pecs, framed by his suit jacket.

For Reve, it's a sheer golden shirt made from the same material as my dress, which he tucked into his trousers. Nathair has a similar shirt on, with his usual leather pants, and a feather wrapped around his hair to hold it back. Osis's fur trim is golden today, and his hair is loose, though feathers are woven throughout, and I almost drool.

Azul has a golden sheen to his armour and a golden sword. Zale stands at his side in a golden suit jacket, which he looks incredible in. Conall is the last to appear, tugging at a long golden coat, but he stops when he sees me.

"*Draya*," Nathair murmurs. "You look incredible, but more importantly, you look like you feel it."

"I do." I grin. "I'm sorry about earlier."

"Don't be." Reve shrugs. "It was funny watching them sweat. Wait until you get PMS."

That makes them groan, and Conall reaches out, offering me his hand. "Shall we, my queen?"

"Let's." I nod, and one by one, Conall wraps us in his shadows.

We appear before my old court. The iron gates are open, and a red carpet leads right up to the door where members of the courts mill about. Members from other courts arrive by car, along with the council, and I know it's going to be a huge crowd. For a moment, I linger and look at the place I grew up in, remembering the happiness and loneliness I felt here.

"Do you ever miss it?" I ask Simon.

"Sometimes, but mainly I just feel nostalgia for what we felt here, you know?"

I nod because I feel it too, the sense of safety I felt within these walls. How wrong we were, but it all worked out in the end. I keep Simon's hand in mine as we walk proudly up to the door. "I'm annoyed the council wouldn't let you bring Elias."

"Me too," he replies. "He would have looked great in a tux, but this is for vampyrs. Maybe one day, that will change and he can be at my side, but for now, we don't need to be seen together at these functions to know we are forever. He understands that."

"I should have made a fuss and demanded he be invited," I mutter.

"You couldn't. He's not technically a part of your court, and if we claimed he was, then he would lose his title as alpha and his pack would be taken. I hate politics," he mutters as we head through the doors.

"Me too. Me fucking too," I respond before every eye in the room turns to us.

The reception area is filled with people mingling and mixing. Keeping my face calm, I step into the crowd. They part for us, watching us carefully, as I wander through their masses to the ballroom where the coronation will take place.

I remind myself that I was invited, that I belong, but I still linger on the outskirts, surrounded by my men. When the gong sounds and Druig appears on stage alongside the council, gazes finally turn from me, and I relax.

My eyes sweep across the council before landing on my father. He searches the crowd, his face drawn and worried, but when he finds me, he brightens, and a smile curves his lips. I smile back, and he grins wider before focusing on what is being said. I glance around the court without eyes watching me. It hasn't changed much. I don't know why I feel like it should have, maybe because so much else has changed, but it looks the exact same as it always did.

Simon nudges me, and I bring my attention back to the stage where my father is kneeling, ready to be proclaimed king—a title he deserves. After all, he has protected this court since before I was even born. He knows the people and the laws, and he is a better king than anyone else will be, or maybe I'm jaded. It does mean there will be political dealings between our courts, but I have hope that won't ruin whatever relationship is building between us. We won't allow it to. He spent the past twenty or so years waiting, caught between the past and the present, so it's time he pulls back the curtain and lives his own life. He's finding his own purpose and happiness until the day he goes home to his love, my mother.

"Upon completion of your vows, you will ascend to the throne of Specter Court. You will provide for your people. Your blood will run throughout your people, offering nourishment, strength, power, and prosperity. Your throne will be where all enemies are felled and where comfort and protection are offered. Here, before our people, you will become the next leader."

My father bows his head, and I wince when the blade slices across his throat. I only saw a coronation once when I was younger. It is not often a king abdicates or is taken from the throne, and it's usually due to a challenge or death, which for immortals doesn't happen with natural causes.

My father's blood splashes onto the base of his throne, linking him to it, the court, and its people. Later, he will accept blood vows from all within the court, tasting drops of their blood to link them to him, but for now, this is symbolic. He doesn't make a noise, and I watch as the wound heals without a trace, his blood dripping along the ornate throne as he stands with a crown atop his head—a simple black coronet from his predecessor. In his black formal wear, he almost looks plain, but it's his eyes, his strength and determination, that make him stand out.

This is a man who will do anything for his duty, his people, and his daughter.

"As the kings and council of our people, we welcome Druig, son of Wraith, ruler of Specter Court into our midst. Long may he reign!" Balthazar calls out, and the words are echoed by everyone in attendance.

"Long may he reign," I respond, bowing my head in respect to my father. My father turns to me like he hears my voice, even in the throng, and lays his hand over his heart. It's a proclamation, a promise.

Music starts, and the crowd rejoices, celebrating the new king. The party spreads throughout the court, but I drift to the stairs.

I'll be back, I tell my men, and they don't argue, clearly feeling where I am going.

To her.

To my mother.

I walk up the stairs and to the room opposite where I spent my whole life. The door unlocks as I approach, and I slip inside, shutting it carefully behind me and looking around. Nothing has changed. It's still a mausoleum to a beloved dead woman. Sighing, I wander around, looking at the memories my mom loved so much she decorated her space with them before I sit on the bed, picking up a framed photo from the side table. It's covered in dust now, but I wipe it clean, seeing her smiling face reflected back at me. She's surrounded by friends, but I focus on her, tracing my fingers over her features.

It doesn't bring pain this time—well, not complete pain—but a softness for a woman I wish I had known better. Now, though, there is a man downstairs, a father, who is trying to get to know me, and I owe it to him to try.

It is time for me to let go and move on, like I have with every other aspect of my life.

Despite the party being in full swing, I sense him lingering at the door.

"You can come in, but you really should be celebrating and playing the game of courts and kings," I murmur, looking up to see my father.

He winces and comes in, sitting next to me. "A game I never wanted to play, but one I will now to keep you safe."

"You need to stop doing everything for me," I tell him, but I know it's useless. I would do anything for Simon or my men, so I understand. "You need to live for yourself."

"Maybe I am," he admits, nudging my shoulder. "Why are you hiding up here?"

"I needed to see this place again and say goodbye. I think it might be time to let go, don't you?" I murmur, looking around at the dust-covered room trapped in time, forgotten like she is. "She would hate everything being kept like this, as a memorial, dusty and forgotten, unused and unloved. This space should be filled with hope." I peer up at him then to see him watching me carefully. Reaching out to take his hand, I smile as I look around the room.

"Maybe it's time to breathe life back into it by opening the doors and filling it with love." I look up at him, meaning more than the room. "Don't you?"

"Yes." He nods, looking around and squeezing my hand. "I think she would like that."

"I do too." I hand him the picture I hold. "Moving on doesn't mean we forget or that we even let go. It simply means we learn to live with it and find happiness despite it. She is still with us, within our hearts and souls, but it's okay to be happy without her," I say, knowing he needs to hear it. "It's okay to live without her. She would want it, and I want it too. I want you to be happy, and I want you to be you, not a shell of yourself, as if you are somehow grieving her more by depriving yourself of happiness and the beauty life has to offer. She doesn't need that. She doesn't need our tears. She needs a beautiful life to watch. Give her that, and when the time comes, she will be waiting for you."

His jaw ticks as he looks down at the picture and then at my hand. "What if I don't know how to live without her?"

"Then we'll figure it out together. You're not alone now, and you never will be again."

Our smiles, although slightly sad, are filled with hope as we look around the room and say our final goodbyes. The next time I come here, I know it will be filled with someone else's life, someone else's happiness and family, and I like that.

It's good.

It's healing.

Giggling, I let Simon spin me around the dance floor, uncaring who is watching. I don't even focus on protecting us, knowing my father and mates are here and doing just that. There's a gasp and some laughter, and when I glance over, I see Lycus spinning Zale around the room. I fall into Simon as I laugh. Winking at me, Nathair takes to the floor, bowing to Reve, and then they start to spin around. Conall grabs Osis and spins him, and then Azul steps up to me. Simon winks and steps away, and I'm spun around between my mates, my laughter filling the room.

When I was here, I was always so lonely, even surrounded by people, but now I've never been happier.

All thanks to them.

After a few dances, my father steps up and takes Azul's place, and we slow down, just soaking in each other's warmth. I find myself snaking my arms tighter around him, and he wraps his around me until we are just standing still, embracing. I rest my head on his chest. There are no more lies or secrets between us, just a father and a daughter as they should be.

We stay like that for so long, the crowd parts around us, and eventually, we have to break apart, smiling at each other. Someone clears their throat, and I turn to see Balthasar. "Before you leave, the council would like to speak to you."

He bows. "If that's acceptable, my queen?"

I nod and search for my mates, but I should have known better. They arrive at my side and as one, we follow him to a private library off the ballroom. The door closes, and I move to a large chair and sit, crossing one leg over the other. My men spread out around me, a clear reminder and a threat. My father sits near me, showing his loyalty.

It's another game, but this time, they seem tired as they take their seats.

Maybe this game of courts and kings is coming to an end and the queens are taking over.

Maybe it's time for it.

"We simply wanted to keep open communication between us," Balthasar begins. He seems to do the speaking for all of them, but that's fine with me. He doesn't bullshit, and I like that. "We don't want any issues."

"Neither do we," I reply. "We were simply chosen for this job, as were you."

He nods. "I understand that. A lot has happened, and there were so many deaths, but although I hate how it happened, we can all agree it was necessary." They share a look and focus back on me. "We just wanted you to know that we will support the judges. You were right. It's time for a fresh start. The council and judges will work together to keep our people safe, but also to uphold our laws."

"I stand with them," the last king, my ex-mate, adds, looking at me shyly. "I have been a fool. I am sorry, Althea."

I accept his apology because without his rejection, I never would have found my home. We all make mistakes, and I refuse to hold a grudge over a man who never could have loved me the way I was supposed to be loved.

"I agree." I nod at the last member of the council, my rejector. "I hold no hard feelings. I do not need to. All we ever wanted was peace." I look at my men. "Peace and happiness we were never given in our other lives. Respect that, and we will respect you. We don't want games, just happiness." Maybe that's naïve, but it's the truth.

"Then that's what we shall work towards." Balthasar holds out his hand, breaking all tradition. Smiling, I reach out and clasp his hand, breaking traditions right alongside him.

"To happiness," I murmur.

He nods. "To the future."

That's what it comes to—a new future where no one will suffer like we have and, hopefully, one day, the judges won't be needed.

Until then, we are here, hunting in the darkness and stealing sinners' souls while loving each other with all of our beings.

Forever.

EPILOGUE

ALTHEA

GRIPPING MY WINE GLASS harder, I lean into the doorframe, wearing a soft smile on my face as I take in the scene. Laughter splits the air, as does a pillow as it sails across the room and hits Reve in the face. Simon laughs and stumbles back into his mate's arms as his shot makes contact.

Reve grunts and tosses one back, grinning himself. Nathair simply shakes his head, picking up a book and sitting down amongst the chaos, waiting for me. Lycus is speaking with Conall, heads bent together as they gesture passionately. Zale, Osis, and Azul are shutting the curtains, lighting the fire, and passing out blankets, pillows, snacks, wine, and tea. My long, gauzy black gown billows in the slight wind as I watch my family interact, soaking in the happiness.

There are no judgements or time for bad memories or unhappiness here.

This is us, our court, our happiness. In the distance, my monsters howl in delight, making my grin widen. As always, Nathair notices me first, lifting his head. He smiles, his face filled with love as he holds his hand out to me.

Come to us, draya.

Always, I reply inside his head, and I step into the library.

I was brought to this room on my very first night here, but the empty feeling of this place is gone, and now it's filled with family and people. Every part of our court now teems with life. Some call us nightmares, but we don't care. We are happy, and that's all that matters.

The gods may demand more one day, but that doesn't matter because we will be ready.

Our race is saved, for now, and we are doing our job.

Best of all, I got my best friend back and I fell in love with seven incredible men. I found my mates, my destiny, and they welcomed me with open arms.

They tug me down between them as they settle around me. Hands dance possessively over my skin, chasing away any chill or worry for the future.

Always, Azul says as he presses his head into my side. Reve lies across one of my legs, sliding his hand up my thigh, but I smack it away. Conall is under my middle, Lycus holds one foot, and Zale purrs with his head on my leg. They hold me tight so nothing could ever hurt me.

Not ever again.

Our love story started with a heart, and it ends with one.

"Okay, today's book is . . ." Nathair starts to read, and I meet Simon's eyes where he's cuddled with his mate. Our court is small, but I don't care. I have everyone I need right here, and somewhere out in the dark, my father is finding his own life.

They are all I will ever need.

I went from an orphan girl to a queen, and although my life wasn't easy, nothing worth having ever is.

This is not the end because there are so many evils in our world, so many races to be saved, and the gods are fickle creatures, but I can withstand it all with them.

My men.

My blood kings.

My judges.

My mates.

For now and forever.

Immortales corda ut.

About the Author

K.A. Knight is an USA Today bestselling indie author trying to get all of the stories and characters out of her head, writing the monsters that you love to hate. She loves reading and devours every book she can get her hands on, and she also has a worrying caffeine addiction.

She leads her double life in a sleepy English town, where she spends her days writing like a crazy person.

Read more at K.A. Knight's website or join her Facebook Reader Group.
Sign up for exclusive content and the newsletter at http://eepurl.com/drLLoj

WWW.KATIEKNIGHTAUTHOR.COM

Also by K.A. Knight

THEIR CHAMPION SERIES

The Wasteland

The Summit

The Cities

The Nations

Boxset

The Forgotten

The Lost

The Damned

Boxset

DAWNBREAKER SERIES

Voyage to Ayama

Dreaming of Ayama

THE LOST COVEN SERIES

Aurora's Coven

Aurora's Betrayal

HER MONSTERS SERIES

Rage

Hate

THE FALLEN GODS SERIES

Pretty Painful

Pretty Bloody

Pretty Stormy

Pretty Wild

Pretty Hot

Pretty Faces

Pretty Spelled

PRETTY LIARS SERIES

Unstoppable

Unbreakable (Coming soon!)

COURTS AND KINGS (STANDALONES)

Court of Nightmares

Court of Death (Coming soon!)

FORBIDDEN READS (STANDALONES)

Daddy's Angel

Stepbrothers' Darling

THE FORGOTTEN CITY SERIES

Monstrous Lies

Monstrous Truths

Monstrous Ends

STANDALONES

Scarlett Limerence

Nadia's Salvation

The Standby

Den of Vipers

Divers' Heart

Crown of Stars

AUDIOBOOKS

The Wasteland

The Summit

Rage

Hate

Den of Vipers (From Podium Audio)

Gangsters and Guns (From Podium Audio)

Daddy's Angel (From Podium Audio)

Stepbrother's Darling (From Podium Audio)

Blade of Iris (From Podium Audio)

Deadly Affair (From Podium Audio)

CO-AUTHOR PROJECTS – Erin O'Kane

HER FREAKS SERIES

Circus Save Me

Taming The Ringmaster

Walking The Tightrope

STANDALONES

Dark Temptations Volume One

(contains One Night Only and Circus Saves Christmas)

The Hero Complex

THE WILD BOYS SERIES

The Wild Interview

The Wild Tour

The Wild Finale

Boxset

CO-AUTHOR PROJECTS – Loxley Savage

THE FORSAKEN SERIES

Capturing Carmen

Stealing Shiloh

Harbouring Harlow

STANDALONES

Gangsters and Guns

CO-WRITE – Ivy Fox

Deadly Affair

Deadly Match

Deadly Encounter

CO-WRITE – Kendra Moreno

Shipwreck Souls (Kendra Moreno & Poppy Woods)

The Horror Emporium (Kendra Moreno & Poppy Woods)

Stolen Trophy

Fractured Shadows

Burn Me